VICTORIAN SECRETS
AN ANTHOLOGY OF VICTORIAN EROTICA

Edited by Davina Charleston

MICHAEL O'MARA BOOKS LIMITED

First published in Great Britain by
Michael O'Mara Books Limited
9 Lion Yard, Tremadoc Road
London SW4 7NQ

Victorian Secrets copyright 1996 by
Michael O'Mara Books Limited

A CIP catalogue record for this book is available from the British Library

ISBN 1–85479–797–2

Typeset by Keystroke, Jacaranda Lodge, Wolverhampton
Printed and bound in England by Clays Ltd, Bungay, Suffolk

CONTENTS

Extract from

THE SIMPLE TALE OF SUSAN AKED*

I HAD INTENDED to have made my dear readers acquainted with, at all events, the outlines of these exciting stories, but, alas! I have not the time. I must hurry on, and describe how I put in practice all that Lucia had taught me, and how I surrendered my maidenhead, and learnt the rapture which man, and man alone, can give to woman.

We paid our intended visit to old Penwick, and persuaded him to let me go to London sooner than he had at first thought possible, on the promise that, if I should be required at Worcester, I could return without fail or delay. Lucia also ordered some dresses for me.

She got me what she called 'decent' drawers, chemises, and stays, and in a very few days we were ready, and started for London.

It was early in August. Few people were travelling to London, that is in the first-class compartments, so that we had our carriage almost entirely to ourselves the whole way.

Lucia, expectant of the delight she most prized on earth, was bursting with joy, and radiant with pleasure. We were to have only a 'family' party. Allan MacAllan was to be Lucia's man; Sir James Winslow, Gladys's; Robert Dane, Annette's; and Charlie Althair mine. Not for one moment did Lucia leave me to my thoughts; she

* First published in Brussels in 1891.

either by design, or because she really was so excited herself, kept chatting, chatting, chatting to me, and always on the subject of the pleasure, so that, what with her words, and the vivid caresses she continually gave me, I was in a state bordering almost on mania when we at length reached London. Had Charlie met us on the platform he might have taken me into the ladies' waiting room, and had me there and then, and I should have offered not the slightest resistance. Lucia had continued to make me so lewdly randy – there is no other word to express my sensations. My heart and my cunt were on fire, and my blood ran like a torrent of fire through my throbbing veins.

A very handsome carriage and pair driven by a coachman in a splendid livery, and with a footman also, met us at Euston. Lucia spoke kindly and gently to both of the men, who touched their hats, and seemed glad to see her again. I looked keenly at them to see whether anything in their deportment showed that want of respect which, I had been taught to believe, marked the knowledge by men of their mistresses not being all they should be. But I saw nothing but the most well-bred respect, mingled with that affection which all good and well-trained servants show towards employers whom they love. In the state I was in, I could almost have given myself then and there to the footman, for he was a really handsome, well-made young man, and quite fit, as far as personal qualifications were concerned, to lie between a lady's thighs. I don't see why a lady may not desire a handsome servant man, just as gentlemen most certainly desire handsome servant women, so that I do not feel at all ashamed of telling my dear readers of what my feelings were on this occasion.

We drove rapidly though street after street. In spite of my throbbing cunt, and my beating heart, I could not but observe all that I saw, and the huge London, of which I was then seeing but a small portion, struck me with amazement. But the noise prevented much conversation and Lucia made me recline backwards, whilst the only way I knew of how intense her feelings were, was from the repeated hard squeezes she gave my hands.

At length we reached Park Lane, and drew up in front of what, from the outside, seemed so modest looking a house that I was rather disappointed. I had expected to see a more palatial looking building, after all Lucia's descriptions, but I forgot that she had described no more than the inside of the house to me.

A fine well-preserved elderly woman opened the door for us, and once we were inside, Lucia kissed her affectionately and introduced me to her. The old lady shook my hand and said I was a fine, pretty creature.

'Who's at home, Sarah?' asked Lucia.

'Miss Gladys is upstairs miss, and Mr Charlie Althair.'

My face, I know, became crimson on hearing that name. Then *he, he* who was to – to – oh! my goodness! *he* was already here!

Yes, indeed. At that moment I saw a lady coming down the stairs followed by a gentleman. The lady I guessed to be Gladys, and the gentleman I recognised to be my cousin Charlie, though it was years since I had last seen him, and he was only a boy then and I a little girl. But what a difference there was in him to what I recollected! There was a tall, broadshouldered, strong-looking man, young indeed in face, but a perfect man in form and figure, instead of the slip of a handsome boy as I remembered my cousin Charlie. Now he had a fine moustache, and the firm-looking jaws of a man. I think the thing that perhaps struck me most was the appearance of power in him. He looked as if he could pick me up, and put me on his shoulder, and jump with ease over a fivebarred gate, and I felt my heart jump with admiration, and I was glad that such a splendid man as he was going to have me. I did not feel a bit shy. Lucia had wound me up to such a pitch that I was shivering with desire, and all the day since we commenced our journey I had had the most extra-ordinary sensation in the lower part of my body in the 'organs of Love,' first as though millions and millions of ants were creeping and crawling in and out of my cunt, and all over my motte and groins, whilst by breasts seemed to be swollen and itching to be handled and pressed.

Gladys, for it was she, glided – you could not say walked, for her movement was more like that of a stately vessel wafted by a light breeze over smooth water – to Lucia, and the two women embraced one another with hearty hugs and kisses, pressing their breasts together, first on one side, and then on the other. They only said a few words to one another. It was 'Well! Gladys!' 'Well! Lucia!'

Then they separated, and Lucia flew open-armed to Charlie, and oh! how they kissed and caressed one another! I felt a great pang of jealousy as I saw Lucia's hand fly to the top of Charlie's thighs, move about rapidly as if trying to find something, and at last get it, not at all where I expected she would have found it, but half-way up to his waist-coat! I felt as jealous as could be of the hot kisses I saw Charlie giving her, and of the joy I knew she must experience feeling his hand stroking her, as it did, between her thighs.

But Gladys, who perhaps noticed the shade on my face, came to me smiling, and gave me oh! such a sweet kiss. What a mouth she had! what lips. It was a kiss which, woman as Gladys was, provoked desire even in me, who was, like her, all but a woman, for before midnight I expected I should be like her no longer a virgin! I returned her embrace with fire. My kiss seemed to electrify Gladys, whose thighs locked with mine, and whose hand sought for and pressed my bubbies, and she flushed as she said 'Ah! Susan, I see you are just what Lucia said you were! We shall be great friends, darling, I am sure. And how nicely you are made. You have quite a fine bosom, and I dare say,' she added with a meaning smile, 'you are as well made *here*' (she let her hand fall as low as possible and press against my motte), 'and I hope you have brought us an ornament which will be as much admired for its beauty and delightfulness as I am certain your face and figure will be!' And she kissed me again and again, looked into my eyes with hers, and oh! what eyes she had! They seemed to warm into my very marrow, and to dart torrents of desire and all-voluptuous longings!

Our embraces, caresses, kisses, made me for the moment half forget Charlie and Lucia, for I am a creature of impulse, and if my senses are powerfully affected, as they were at the moment by the sensation of Gladys's electrifying and really delicious charms, I cannot help yielding up to them. What a blessing this is for me! Dear reader, all men are the same to me! Yet that one who holds me in his arms is, for the while, the perfection of mankind! I forget all the others whilst I enjoy his vigour, his manhood, and the rapturous pleasure his exquisite prick gives me.

But if I forgot, or half forgot, Charlie, Lucia did not forget me.

'There!' she said; 'that's kissing and stroking enough! you two naughty girls! Gladys! Here is Charlie burning to know how his lovely cousin is made! and I am sure Susan would like to make his acquaintance, and that of holy Saint John Thomas, too!'

Gladys laughed, and I felt myself growing red – not with shame, but with the immense pleasure I knew was before me. As

I quitted the arms of the voluptuous girl, who had been adding fuel to the fire that devoured me, Charlie took me into his.

'How you have grown, Susan!' he said, as he kissed me, keeping his hot lips on my mouth, and passing his still hotter tongue along my lips from corner to corner.

'And so have you, Charlie dear,' I answered, as soon as I had the use of my lips to speak.

Charlie held me at arm's length, whilst he looked at me with eager eyes. His two hands held me under the armpits, and whilst he gazed at me as though he had that one chance of doing so and never would again see me and wished to remember me, he gently and gradually brought his hands towards one another in front, and then pressed them on my swelling breasts.

'What good bubbies!' he cried, and then he suddenly turned me round, so that I had my back to him, and pulling my head back against his shoulder, he again snatched the most voluptuous kisses from my mouth and felt first one and then the other of my breasts. Goodness! how different did his strong hand feel to Lucia's or that of Gladys! Surely some strange influence – perhaps the male influence – passed from his palm into my bubbies, and thence down to my burning cunnie!

I know it was quite different to being handled by Lucia, though, oh! what pleasure she used to give me when she squeezed my bosom with her soft hands!

'Come!' cried Lucia, who had been with Gladys watching all this with eyes dancing with excitement; 'come into the study, Charlie! Come, Susan, I want Charlie to assure himself, before me, that I deliver you a perfect maiden into his hands, and that you carry the warranty of your virginity in the pretty cushion between your thighs!'

Charlie put his arm round my waist and urged me towards the door through which Gladys and Lucia had passed, with eager but not unbecoming haste.

There was a large ottoman in this room (there were similar ottomans in every room in the house) and on this Lucia made us sit whilst she and Gladys stood before us.

'Now, first of all, Charlie, you must let me show Susan the Holy Saint who is to say his prayers in the niche prepared for him called her quim!'

Charlie laughed and said, 'Certainly.'

Lucia with rapid fingers undid his waistcoat, and his braces

before and behind; then she unbuttoned his trousers down to
the very last button, and, pulling up his shirt, produced what,
to my heated imagination, seemed something much larger than
I had ever expected to find a man's prick to be. Ah! how different is reality to imagination! I had had Charlie's beautiful prick
before me in a picture! I had heard it described! I had formed an
idea of its magnitude, bulk, length, and power, but ardent as my
imagination had been, minute as Lucia's descriptions had been,
the *reality* was vastly more splendid!

'There!' cried Lucia, as she put my hand on to the delicious
hot, hard, yet velvety-feeling weapon, round which my eager
fingers could hardly meet; 'there! that is the prick which took my
maidenhead, Susan! and which will take yours! Oh, beautiful
Saint John! oh, glorious Saint John! Is it not *grand*, Susan? Now,
is it not as delicious to feel as I told you it would be? But
wait until you feel it walking up and down your little silky
cunt, my dear. Oh! goodness! how I wish I had my first fuck to
do again. Now, here! put your hand in and get out the bag of
jewels.'

I did so as I looked at Charlie, who bent his head forward, and
as our mouths met, I had his magnificent balls in my hand. Oh!
how nice! how extra voluptuous they did feel. There is something
in the balls of a man which is more fascinating, more captivating
than even his glorious prick in all its glory. Is it because his balls
are the evidence of his manhood? I can't tell; but I only know
that I never tire of feeling a good pair; and I had, at that moment,
a splendid, full, hard, big pair of them in my fingers, and could
feel them slide from side to side, as I gently pressed them.

'Now, Charlie! Assure yourself of the existence of Susan's
maidenhead,' and Lucia lifted my dress, petticoats and all, high
over my knees.

Charlie needed no hand to guide his to my throbbing cunt. He
only held me a little more firmly whilst he just pressed his curved
hand and finger over my bushy motte and the soft lips of my
palpitating quim, and then, putting his tongue deep into my
mouth, he slipped his strong middle-finger as far as he could,
between the full, soft lips of a cunt which, except for Lucia's
fingers and twot, had been virgin, since it had been created.

Girls, dears! wait until a lover does the same to you, and then
you shall tell me if such caresses are, or are not exquisite!

'Well!' said Lucia, all avidity for Charlie's verdict.

'A perfect virgin,' he exclaimed. 'A first-class maidenhead. There can be no doubt about that.'

'And now has she not a delicious little cunt, Charlie?'

'Awfully good! awfully nice!' was the answer, as his finger gently and sweetly worked up and down, killing me with pleasure.

'Let me feel her maidenhead!' said Gladys, coming forward.

Charlie instantly withdrew his hand, and I saw Gladys give him what looked like a little packet of cigarettes. Then kissing me, she slipped her slender long finger in, and smiling and flushing at the same time, she said:

'Oh, yes! most distinct! a real and true maidenhead! and what a darling little quim. Charlie, I wish you every joy.'

'Now, Gladys, I was the original discoverer of this wonderful virginity. So let me have a last feel of it, for I think it won't see the light of another day!' This was Lucia, of course, her hand, oh! that dear little hand which had first made me aware of what immense resources of pleasure were concealed, unknown to me, in that dormant little cunt of mine, took the place of Gladys's.

But all these varying caresses, these different hands, these changing fingers, added to the state of intense excitement in all that highly susceptible region, produced a very natural, but apparently not expected, result. I had Charlie's glorious prick in my grasp again. It alone was capable, even so, of upsetting the equilibrium of my senses, but these fingers moving in and out . . .

'Oh! you naughty girl, Susan!' exclaimed Lucia, 'just look. Gladys, she has spent all over my hand.'

'I am very sorry, Lucia. Indeed I could not help it,' cried I, almost in distress.

'Never mind, darling,' they all cried together, and Charlie again taking posession of my quivering cunnie, kissed me really passionately. I heard the door shut, and when Charlie gave one a chance of seeing, I found that we were alone. Gladys and Lucia had left the room.

'Susan!' whispered Charlie, in a voice husky with excitement; dear boy, he was always excited, tremendously excited, when on the brink of a nice plump cunt. 'Will you give me your maidenhead now? Ah! say yes! I could not wait till bedtime.'

I raised my face and kissed him, and whispered, 'Yes.'

With a bound Charlie jumped up. He left me lying across the ottoman.

I heard a quick rustling of clothes, and there he was, with only his shirt and boots and socks on. Whilst I looked at him he tucked his shirt up so that all his body from his waist downwards to the top of his socks was absolutely and perfectly naked. Oh! how I longed to see him as Lucia had drawn him, with nothing on but his skin; what a handsome object a well-made naked man is. How different in every way was he from the slender softness of Lucia. Charlie's muscles seemed like engines of great force, as every movement of his made them play under his white and even skin, and how white his skin did look. I had no idea a man's skin could be so white, and it looked all the whiter from the contrast of the dark black hairs which grew in parts wonderfully thick over his body, down the outsides of his thighs and down his legs.

But what naturally attracted my most eager attention was that magnificent, glorious, handsome prick of his. To my astonished vision it appeared to have grown even longer, bigger, and more rigid than ever. It seemed to me, lying down as I was, to reach quite an inch up over his navel, and it was pointing straight up, apparently at his chin. I noticed then the curious shape of the under-side of its well-shaped head, as if it had been carved by nature into two curves meeting near the top, and gracefully sweeping down and asunder, one curve taking the right and the other the left. The shape of that head appeared to make the noble weapon it tipped perfectly irresistible, and I could see how admirably nature had formed it for penetrating. But, oh! could I possibly take in that huge (it did look so huge) thing?

Surely my cunt was neither deep enough, nor wide enough, to admit it all, and, as Lucia had told me, I noticed that it grew broader and broader as it approached its base. I saw too, all along the front, as it appeared to me, a kind of supporting rod under its tight-looking-skin, and of this Lucia had not told me anything that I could remember. And below, hanging in that curiously wrinkled pouch, which looked as if it had been sewn up all along the middle, were those delicious balls, which I had been feeling. How big they looked, and how beautifully even they seemed to hang, each in its own pocket as it were. And oh! what a splendid bush there was, out of which all these splendours grew. Far thicker and longer and much more curly than either Lucia's or mine.

Charlie saw admiration in my burning and excited glances, and he gave me time to note all, and then when he thought I had seen enough for the present, he said, 'Now, Susan let me clear *your* decks for action!'

Oh, the swiftness of his hands! He had my dress and petticoats over my face in a trice. He tugged at the band of my drawers, and without mercy burst it. I heard the ripping and felt the tearing, as his powerful fingers tore through the linen, and the fresh feeling of the air on my belly and thighs told me that he had stripped the lower part of my body as naked as his own! I could not see, for my face was covered.

'Susan, darling!' he cried, his voice trembling; 'here! look! take this and put it on me.'

He handed me a curious-looking little thing, which felt soft and elastic, and had a long deep line in it, for all the world like a little cunt. It was not thicker than an ordinary slate pencil, and about two inches long.

I looked wonderingly at Charlie, for I did not know what I was to do.

'There!' said he, 'take hold of me low down, near my balls, with your left hand. That's right. Now lay the letter on the top of my prick. So, only turn the other side (the cunt-shaped side) up. Now sweep your hand down, and that thing will open and cover me completely!'

I did exactly what he told me, and lo! there was his prick completely covered almost to its very end with a thin, transparent covering of india-rubber, which looked like another natural skin! This, then, was the covering of which Lucia had told me. I declare if it had not been for seeing this I should never have thought of the dangerous tadpoles! I was so eager, so anxious to be *fucked* that I had altogether forgotten the very serious lessons which dear Lucia had given me.

'Thank you, *dear* Charlie!' I cried. 'I know what this is for!'

'Lucia told you, I suppose?'

'Yes! She taught me everything!'

'You could not have a better instructor,' said Charlie; 'but now, my Susan, for experience!'

'Come!' cried I, lying back and opening my thighs wide, planting my feet firmly on the yielding ottoman.

In another moment Charlie was between them and on me. I felt with a thrill, not to be described for pleasure, as the soft-feeling yet powerful head, separating the lips of my throbbing little cunt, entered! The ease with which it penetrated astonished me. But it was in! in! I could feel it expanding and filling me, as far as it had gone. But something inside me checked it, and Charlie, instead of trying to push it in any further, kept pushing his prick in and out! tickling me in so ravishing a manner that I held my breath to enjoy it the more. All my soul seemed concentrated at that one spot. Little throbs began to shoot all about it, and I knew I was on the point of coming! I expected every moment Charlie would plump deeper in; but he still continued his play, which was on the point of becoming disappointing, when I suddenly came.

Charlie had apparently waited for this, for the moment he perceived it he grasped me to him tighter than ever.

I felt a violent struggle going on. It was the expiring effort of my poor little maidenhead! Then something rent inside me, an extraordinary sensation of neither pain nor pleasure followed, the obstacle was overcome, and with alternate movements backwards and forwards I felt Charlie's prick rapidly gaining ground, and for the first time knew the infinite joy of being filled and stretched to the utmost by the power of man!

'Ah! ah! ah!' cried Charlie at each stroke, and his breath poured hot down my neck inside my collar. His balls touched me! I felt them! I bucked! and he was *all* in!

'You *darling*!' he cried, and then began the splendid long strokes.

Gods! how nice it was! At first it did not tickle very much. The chief pleasure was feeling the alternating filling and contraction of my cunt! but after a few strokes the tickling, from end to end, began to grow more and more brilliant, until it seemed to me that I should faint from the excessive pleasure I experienced! There were perfect spasms, like electric shocks in their force and rapidity, which cannot be described, which, my dear girls, can only be experienced, and with all the most deliciously soothing sensations, indescribably delicious! oh, my God! was it not *Rapture? Rapture* with a very big '*R!*' But alas! the longest fuck is always too short! Charlie's time was come! All of a sudden he commenced those rapid, short digs which sent me wild with an agony of delight! My entire body glowed with the white heat of the glory of heaven! my senses reeled; all the room seemed to whirl round and round. I felt that in another moment I must faint, when, crushing me to him. Charlie for the last time dashed his prick into me to its very furthest limit, and I felt his whole weight on my pimping motte. I felt as if a powerful pump were sending streams in jets against me inside. One, two, three, four, I counted – there were more – but I went into a half-swoon of ecstasy, and seemed to be quite lifted out of all connecting me with earth. I was in a kind of dream in which I saw angels floating around me, *and felt the ineffable blessing of the peace of heaven.*

But Lucia's laughing voice recalled me to earth, and I found myself still in Charlie's arms, and could feel his glorious prick in me *working*, as if it were trying to burst my quivering cunnie by swelling itself out with repeated efforts.

'Well, Susan? Take your head out of the way, Charlie, and let me kiss *my* girl,' and I heard a smart slap on my lover's bottom, which vibrated all along his prick and made my cunnie quiver then. 'There, there, my own darling Susan!' as she kissed me with impetuous kisses, 'not much of a maidenhead left now I fancy. Did he hurt you, darling?'

'Hurt!' I exclaimed. '*Hurt!* oh, how could it hurt me, Lucia dear?'

'Oh, all right,' she exclaimed laughing. 'I am glad it did not, but sometimes it does.'

'By George, Lucia,' said Charlie, 'I can tell you it is well Susan has no teeth in her quim, or deuce a bit of a prick would I have left. Oh, if you could only feel her now!'

'Has she the nutcrackers, then?' exclaimed a voice which I knew to be that of Gladys.

'*Has* she? If you were like me, and *in* her, Gladys, you would soon know.'

'Oh, Susan, Susan, you *are* an acquition!' cried Gladys, moving from behind Charlie, where she had apparently been watching my behaviour, perhaps from the very beginning, for, once Charlie had begun to fuck me I had no senses to see or hear, and I don't know at what precise moment she and Lucia had returned to the room. She kissed me and petted me, and after a while, addressing Charlie, said, 'Is she still nipping you, Charlie?'

'I think that was the last,' said he.

'Very well. Get off her, then.'

'Ah! but Gladys, she has such an awfully nice quim. Let me enjoy it a little longer.'

'Nonsense, boy. Get up, I tell you. It is time we all bathed and dressed for dinner.'

'Ah well, I suppose I must. But oh, Susan, won't we just have a night of it? Do you like me, dear?'

Oh! I gave him such a kiss, and such a hug and such a sweet little buck, before he began to move, that he swore he never had had such a sweet, darling, responsive girl before in all his life.

'Did I not tell you she was a perfect diamond?' cried Lucia, delighted. Charlie slowly, slowly, withdrew his ardent prick, which as it issued sprang up as if it had been suddenly released from something holding it down, but the moment Gladys saw it she cried out –

'Why – oh, my goodness, Charlie! your letter has burst!'

And so it had. Charlie's prick was entirely through it. It was all rucked up about the middle of its shaft.

'Jump up, Susan; come with me,' cried Gladys; and Lucia, taking me by the arm, pulled me in a way which rather alarmed me.

'Don't be frightened, darling!' said Lucia; 'but the sooner we get Charlie's spend out of you the better!'

I felt a great deal of it running out of me then. I could feel it running down my thighs, but the recollection of the tadpoles frightened me a bit, and I ran upstairs following Gladys as quickly as I could. She and Lucia took me into a handsome little boudoir, and through it into a fine bathroom, where they made me tuck up my dress and petticoats, and sit on a small stool covered with American cloth, which felt very cool as I sat down on it. Lucia got a basin and put it between my feet, Gladys brought an enema and a bottle. Lucia got a small vessel and water, and in a wonderfully short time I had the tube in me, and a torrent of 'safety' liquid was cleaning me from that spend which had been so exquisitely pleasant to feel dashing into me.

Having tenderly wiped me between my thighs the two girls took me back into the boudoir. It was Gladys's, and oh, so beautiful. That it was intended for the offices of love was instantly apparent. The wall was hung with beautiful pictures, some in oils, some in watercolours, some engravings and some beautifully executed pencil or crayon drawings, but all, whether large or small, were of the most exciting erotic nature. Venus and Adonis, Diana and Endymion, Jupiter and Leda, Jupiter and Danae and many other mythological love scenes were there, with innumerable others representing amorous couples under almost every conceivable circumstance. Even love in a carriage in Rotten Row was depicted, showing the possibility of a rapturous fuck in the very midst of a crowd. And all were really beautifully painted or drawn, by no means the work of an indifferent artist. A choice collection of erotic literature, some hundred volumes or so of prose and poetry, was in full view in a handsome bookcase. The very letter-weights on the writing-table were erotic – either human couples in the very act, or animals, such as a stallion and mare, bull and cow and so forth. How often I wonder has Gladys given some active lover of hers joy on it.

There we sat and talked for a while until the handsome Annette came and announced that the bath was ready.

Oh, my dear male readers! if you only could have seen the three lovely naked nymphs who bathed their charms in that splendid marble basin; if you could but have seen the equally lovely handmaid, in all her beautiful nudity, plying soap and sponge and towel – I include myself, I know I am well made and pretty – I wonder which one of us would have made your blood boil the hottest and quickest. All four of us were dark-haired, and nature had been kind in giving us plenty of glory on our heads and on our mottes too.

Gladys's bush was the blackest, her hair was really black, she was most splendidly formed. Such shoulders, such arms. Such beautiful breasts and thighs. No wonder men delighted in her. She looked voluptuous from head to foot, and was as voluptuous as she looked.

Lucia had taught me what pleasure one girl can give another, but her caresses, ardent as they were, paled before the glory of those which Gladys could give. I learnt much from Lucia, but oh! how much more from my cousin Gladys!

After our bath Lucia introduced me to my own 'foutoir' and bedroom. Like Gladys's it was a very handsomely adorned room, with books, pictures, ornaments, and everything of a luxuriously and voluptuously erotic nature. There was the ottoman also, and well did I use it during the next few days. For our lovers soon heard of my arrival, and came running up to town to see and taste their new mistress. The ottoman was the consolatory article of those who could not immediately secure the night with me, or with Gladys, or Lucia; and came into play almost every afternoon. I have sometimes given delight to four different admirers in the course of two hours, I loved it, but I loved my bed much better.

And what a bed. I had never dreamt of one like it. It was immense and delicious in every sense. It was a four-poster of the most solid mahogany, its posts being of extra strength to support a huge mirror which formed its canopy. Mirrors also, slightly inclined inwards, formed three sides of it, so that I could see every movement of my lover, whilst I felt his action and his power. And my lover, whilst lying by my side, could see my naked charms in front of him, or as it were suspended over him. So that not only had I the pleasure of being fucked, but I could enjoy seeing myself enjoyed, and, as Lucia said, it was indeed a fetching sight.

We sat down eight to dinner. I was introduced to Allan MacAllan, and the other gentlemen, and although nothing very spicy was allowed in our conversation, we had a very merry party in which the very restrictions placed upon us made our wit all the more poignant. By degrees I felt the ants crawling again. Charlie's prick had driven them, away, but one fuck is by no means enough, and that a first one too. What added still more to the fire which consumed me was a small glass of some very delicate and delicious liqueur, which we all partook of. It contained some powerful aphrodisiac, and I would have been better without it, for I was burning. It took all I knew to prevent me making myself appear that I was randy beyond anything I had ever felt.

But, in Park Lane we, though late sleepers are early bed goers. At ten we said good-night to the gentlemen, and retired to our rooms. Annette came to assist me to undress, and when I was naked she produced my nightdress. What a dress! It was of some exquisitely fine and absolutely transparent silken material. It had no sleeves, but it fastened round my throat with a ribband which ran through eyelet holes. It was open from top to bottom, but fastened just above my breasts by ribbands which were tied, and again below my breasts, across my waist at my hips but so that the ribbands hid none of my bush, and again, but more loosely, at my knees. Its utility as an article of dress was nil, but it greatly added to the attractiveness of my charms by just veiling them.

I had no sooner donned this elegant costume than Charlie appeared, and Annette, wishing us a good-night, went off to prepare for her lover.

Oh Charlie! No! my nightdress might be very fetching, but my naked skin was much more so. The moment he was naked, and he stripped entirely, he untied all my ribbands, and there I was, as naked as himself.

Can I write down all the extravagancies of his behaviour – extravagancies which I, so far from finding outrageous, enjoyed to the uttermost. Ah, dear girls, dear readers believe me, my pen fails me. What a night we had! What kissing, caressing, fucking! If I had enjoyed what Lucia called No. 1, oh! how I revelled in *No. 2*! what extra bliss there was in *No. 3*! how superlatively delicious was *No. 4*! and we did not *end* with *No. 9*, because we began again on waking, and completed No. 12! After *that* Charlie acknowledged himself defeated! His proud prick begged for repose, and some time during the day be retreated to the country, having been, as he said, exhausted by the over-enjoyment of the naked charms of his charming cousin.

A NIGHT IN A COUNTRY HOUSE

FOR MANY YEARS I used to stay with some friends in their large country house in Yorkshire, for shooting, being often there seven or eight times in the season, and for periods of one or two weeks at a time. On this occasion I had arrived on the 9th of August, and on the twelfth, just before starting on the moors, I ran up to my bedroom for something I had forgotten, and found a very pretty housemaid in possession; she looked about five-and-twenty, and was a strapping fine girl. She smiled as I came in, and I thought looked 'cheeky', so I said to her, 'You frightened me, I thought you were a ghost.' She answered, 'Would you be afraid of a ghost?' 'No,' says I, 'if they will visit me at night, and I always leave my door a little open, so they can come in easily.' 'Take care, then you don't get visited soon, for this house may be haunted,' says she, bounding out of the room.

That night I got up to my bedroom about eleven, and did not shut my door, and soon after my light was out, to my joy, I saw a white figure glide noiselessly in, lock the door, and creep to my bedside. I at once put my hands out, and feeling a pair of plump firm breasts, knew it to be my pretty friend of the morning.

We were very soon cuddling each other to keep ourselves warm, and that was the commencement of many an enjoyable night. As the house was full of men, and many of them young bachelors, I asked her why she had picked me out of the lot, and not a bachelor.

She said she never went with a single man, for they were too reckless, and would think nothing of putting her in the family way; nor more would she go with a married man who had a family, as he probably did not know how to prevent it, but she always found out something about a man before she made up to him; that a married man knew the risk of putting a girl in the family way, that he never lost his head, etc.

One night after a delightful cuddle, and while we were resting, I asked her to tell me how she came first to lose her maidenhead.

'I was a big strong girl at eighteen, and had been a parlour maid in one or two small houses, which I had left at my own request. At last I was engaged by a Miss Watson, who kept a young ladies' school at Brighton, as housemaid. I went to the school and found Miss Watson was a lady of about thirty years of age, a well-built woman, of medium height, and with a very pleasant expression, if not pretty. She had managed the school by herself since her sister's death some three years previous. There was an old housekeeper, who kept every one in awe, two young maids who looked after the girls' rooms, and William, a lad of about eighteen or twenty. He was very fond of me, and nearly every evening after supper we used to stand for half an hour by the back door or in the arbour and have a chat, and for a long time he never did more than kiss me. At last he used to hug me, and thinking it no more harm for him than Miss W to rub me with his leg I used to let him. I don't know how he began it, but he did it very nicely, and afterwards he used to put my hands on his trousers, and I used to feel a big swelling, which I used to rub about, but I had never seen one, and was, I fear, very clumsy, however, one day he pulled it out in the arbour, and put it in my hand, it was the first weapon I had ever handled, and quite frightened me. It was summer time, so by the light I could examine it. I pulled him about as he showed me, now quicker, now slower, and with my left hand slowly feeling those marbles that hung down; but Mr. Bill's struggles became frantic, he drew his knees up, he sighed, he groaned and stretched his legs to their utmost length, his eyes half shut, his fingers clenched, and at last with many sighs and spasmodic movements of his legs, out shot the balmy liquid, but I stuck to my post till with a kiss he thanked me, and often was this repeated, he never once offering to have me, or I even dreaming of it, but it was bound to end so, and so it did. The first time was during the vacation. Miss W and the girls were all away, as were the maids, so the old housekeeper, William and I, were alone in the house. The housekeeper was in bed with rheumatism as usual, and Bill and I were cleaning up the girls' bedrooms. He was doing the windows, but soon gave up on that job to pull me about. Well, I did not mind, and seeing no harm in it let him throw me on the bed, and he began to rub about on top of me, and got me in such a state that I never noticed till too late that he had actually got my clothes up, and his weapon out, and was actually putting it into me; but it was too late, however he promised not to hurt me, and, dear boy, he did not, for at first he only buried the massive head between the lips, and with a few draws gently back and forward he drew from me an expenditure quite extravagant, but he had not finished yet, and with the assistance of what he called my home-made cream, he slowly pushed his way till his weapon was buried to the hilt. Strong as he was, he was very gentle, and though at times I was put to a little pain, I forgot all in the final throes of love's struggle, and between the two of us we could have floated a man-of-war. Now this all came of Miss W breaking me in to think her tricks were harmless. It ended by Bill putting me in the family way, and my having to leave; the child is since dead, and I got a place here, where I am not known, and no more men servants or bachelors for me.'

'But come on and do your duty, something has been banging against me for the last ten minutes, and I am dying for it.'

And what a performer she was, for as I buried my all into her, she clasped me to her warm breasts, and twining her legs round my back seemed to take more than was meant by nature to be admitted; then begging me to move, she in a most marvellous way chafed the extreme point of my weapon between two soft pads far hidden inside her.

But she could not last many minutes at this, for it always brought her to the melting moments, and then opening her thighs and straightening her legs she clasps me tighter with her arms, her body heaves, and she writhes, yet still I keep up the regular stroke, now buried to the hilt, now tantalizingly drawn till the soft head only remained between those pouting lips, and she in agony would say, 'Oh! don't leave me. Oh! quicker. Oh-h-h-h. I cannot bear it. Oh! darling. Oh,' often biting me on the shoulder, the marks remaining for days, and finally with some deep drawn 'Oh's,' that came from her heart, she would open her thighs quickly as I slipped, if possible, still further into her, and then I would feel that throb-throb, and a warm flow rewarded me.

With care we could continue one combat for thirty minutes by the clock, she often arriving at those moments of bliss two and three times before I considered it time to make a judicious ending to our pleasure.

Alas! those Arabian Nights are of the past.

Extract from

THE LOVES OF VENUS

OR

THE YOUNG WIFE'S CONFESSION*

My dear Frederica,

My promise to you before marriage shall be faithfully kept, but little did I think at the time you extracted it from me, that I should have to relate a confession by Ada, very similar, only far more piquante than the experiences that we as brother and sister indulged in when at home.

No apology is needed from me for getting married, and deserting a sister I always loved more than my life, a sister who sacrificed her honour, and everything we hold sacred to satisfy my incestuous lust, a sister whose loving wantonness would have always kept me with her, only being an elder son to a family of position, it was absolutely necessary for me to keep up the succession for fear that some day our hated relatives might reap the benefits of the fortune left by our ancestors.

You, too, my dearest pet sister, being engaged to be the bride of a special pal of mine, will soon be solaced for the loss of your dear Fred. Still we may confidently live in hope that some day Frederica and Fred, will again have a chance of feeling all the joys of love, which an incestuous connection imparts in an exceptional degree. Forbidden fruit is always so sweet.

How can I ever forget our parting on the eve of my wedding day, as we sat in the library of the old home at Cunnusburg, how

*The first edition, printed in 1881, was limited to 150 copies.

with tears in your eyes you kissed me in such an impassioned manner that I had to fuck you a fourth time, to the imminent risk of not being able to do my duty to Ada the next evening. How even then you would take a parting suck of my enervated pego, and again raised him in all his pride of life, till I spent even a fifth time, and swallowed every drop, as you said that the very essence of my being might go down to your heart.

Then, finally, I had to promise you a full account of my wedding night, and any discoveries I might make, or extract from Ada. At the time I thought you must know or guess at something, so you may be sure I was on the *qui vive*, especially as to the reality of the maidenhead I was to take. Now I write the result, and am sure that if you did know a little then, it cannot be a tithe of what I can now disclose.

The MSS is enclosed, and I trust that when your turn comes to be joined to your husband, you will repay my confidence, by equal candour on your part.

I remain, ever your most loving brother,

FRED.

London, 2nd June, 1879.

THE WEDDING NIGHT

'Darling Ada, the moment has come at last, when I am to have you all to myself, when our very souls and bodies can be commingled in the overflow of the essence of our life. In the carriage, in the train, and ever since we have arrived at this hotel, I have never felt we were alone, but it has now arrived that the supreme delights of love are within our grasp, have you any idea of their reality, my pet?'

This was how I addressed my bride, as the chambermaid of the Golden Lion at Uppington, closed the door behind us, as she bid us good night, with a most significant smile on her face.

By the way, what a nuisance it is, that everybody we meet, even waiters, chambermaids, and hotel people in general, all know a newly married couple, they seem fair game for every kind of extortion, in addition to which we have to put up with all, the funny looks, and suggestive speeches they may chose to indulge in, at our expense.

I made a mental resolve to have an explanation of the significant look from the pretty girl before we left the hotel.

But to return to Ada, she was all blushes, as crimson as a damask rose. You know she is hardly sixteen, and a most piquante little dark-eyed brunette, with full luscious lips constantly tempting you to kiss them, and sparkling blue-black eyes, full of the fires of an excessively ardent temperament.

'How should I, Fred, but I know there is something dreadful to go through at first, but don't hurry your little Ada, for I'm all in a tremble, now it's so near the realization of all my dreams of love,' as she threw her arms round my neck, and kissed me in a more impassioned way than she had ever done before. 'Let us sit down, and you smoke a cigar; don't you know sir, I ought to have retired to bed and got fairly between the sheets before you came into the room. I shall never be able to undress before you Fred. Ha! ha!! a fine joke, I'll make you, sir, go into that cupboard, and will only let you out, when I am ready to jump into bed, and have put out the light.'

'That's a fine idea, darling,' I replied, 'but I will humour your excessive and whimsical modesty for this once, Ada, and shall trust to make myself so free of your person presently that all mock modesty will be banished between us in future. But first I mean to read you an account I have got of a wedding night, in poetry; it is a delicious bit, and will enlighten you as to what you have to expect, my dear. Will you sit on my lap?

This she did, and I proceeded to read:

The Bride's Confession

Dear Bell, When we parted you begged me to write,
And inform you of all that occurred the first night,
When Frank and your Emma were joined hand in hand,
And allowed to perform all that love could command;
'But what language can tell,' as the wise man has said,
'Of the wonderful ways of a man with a maid?'
Be assured they can only be properly known,
By a lecture in bed, with a swain of your own.
Notwithstanding, I'll tell you as well as I can,
Of discoveries I've made in the secrets of man;
So that you and all curious damsels may learn
How the game may be played when it comes to your turn.
After breakfast was over, our carriage of four,
Well appointed and handsome, drove up to the door;

We started for Brighton exactly at noon,
To spend (as the phrase is) our sweet honeymoon;
Bright Phœbus shone o'er us the whole of the way,
The captain was amorous, ardent, and gay –
So much so that, although in the carriage,
He began to indulge in the freedom of marriage –
And ventured so far that I felt in a fright,
For fear the wild rogue would have ravished me quite.
We reached our hotel, and found all things prepared,
Our apartments were handsome, well furnished, and aired;
And the dinner was served so stylish and neat,
That 'twas really a sin not to fall to and eat;
But the feast we expected a little time hence,
So engrossed every thought and extinguished each sense,
That inferior desires seemed extinguished and gone,
And our appetites solely centred in one.
Frank praised the champagne – I though it delicious,
He swore 'twas enough to make Vesta propitious;
And indeed he was right, for between you and me,
I ne'er felt my spirits so jocund and free.
How the evening was passed 'tis needless to write,
For I know you'll skip all till you read the word 'night!'
And are now on the tip-toe of high expectation,
To come to the pith of my tale's consummation.
Well, attend, and I'll now draw the curtain aside,
And disclose all the sports of the bridegroom and bride;
Relating the whole of that process bewitching,
By which girls are cured of a troublesome itching,
And men, though at first impetuous and rude,
Are at length, by weak woman, quite tamed and subdued;
You remember how often we longed to discover,
All the joys to be found in the arms of a lover;
But now they approached I felt in a pucker,
And thought that my breast would have leaped from its
    tucker.
Frank saw my condition, and tenderly said –
'You are tired, dear Emma, so pray go to bed;
'Late hours are the bane and destruction of numbers,
'Make haste, and I'll soon come and watch o'er your
    slumbers.'
What a sly, wicked rogue! but I guessed what he meant,

So, covered with blushes, obeyed him, and went.
I was scarcely undressed, and prepared for my doom,
When I heard the dear fellow glide into the room;
And as listless I lay, between transport and dread,
He threw off his garments, and jumped into bed;
In an instant I felt myself clasped in his arms,
And as instantly lost all my girlish alarms,
For he soothed me so fondly, and gave me such kisses,
Which warmed my young blood for more exquisite blisses,
Whilst his bold daring hand, in pursuit of his game,
Pressed my bosom, and wandered all over my frame;
But most frequently trespassed – conceive my distress,
Where my pen dare not write, but I'm sure you can guess.
In tears I entreated him not to be rude,
But he sealed up my mouth, and his gambols pursued,
Declaring that 'if men might not do as they list,
'The world in a short time would cease to exist.'
This was all very true; then he bade me reflect,
That our parents, dear souls, so refined and correct,
Had done the same thing – and indeed 'twas quite clear,
If they had not, we surely should not have been here;
Moreover, he said, 'on that very day,
'I'd promised, in church, to love and obey;
'And the parson himself in a plain exhortation,
'Had stated that marriage and due copulation
'Were sent to check sin and prevent fornication;
'So that those whose desires were impetuous and randy.
'Might always have something to quiet them handy;
'Hence 'twas plainly quite wrong to preserve such a
    distance,
'And thwart his desires by a prudish resistance.'
This reserve was soon banished, and love unrestrained
By alarm, or by coyness, triumphantly reigned.
All his wanton endearments I freely returned,
'Till the flame of desire irresistibly burned.
Then proudly in arms, without further delay,
Like a lion he eagerly leapt on his prey,
And pursuing his course to the summit of friction,
His strong ample lance briskly pressed for admission;
But oh! such a weapon this wonderful lance is,
Surpassing by far our most juvenile fancies,

So resistless in power, and extended in length,
That so soon as I felt its dimensions and strength,
O'ercome with alarm, I exclaimed with a sigh:
'Oh! for God's sake forebear, or I am sure I shall die;'
But my pains and my prayers alike were unheeded,
For, bent on his purpose, the spoiler proceeded.
But although he was armed, as I thought, like a giant,
Dame Nature has made us young damsels so pliant,
That expanding, I yielded at every aggression,
Until he had obtained the completest possession;
Then I found my dear girl, that the saying's quite true –
That 'a man and his wife are but one, and not two,'
For a union so close, all description surpasses,
And can scarce be conceived by you innocent lasses.
Deep within me, so proudly, the conqueror swelling,
And kindled new life in his snug little dwelling,
While our limbs interwoven, in the primest position,
Completed the junction so well called coition.
The conflict now raged, and 'twas ravishing quite,
All my pain became pleasure, my terrors delight;
That great engine of bliss, in perpetual motion,
Played his part with such exquisite skill and devotion,
That as each eager thrust was impressively given,
I felt quite exhausted, and wafted to heaven;
Round his vigorous frame like a tendril I twined,
Whilst our lips in lascivious billings were joined,
And we revelled in joy, till our transport at last,
Reached the crisis of Hymen's delightful repast,
When, by, rapture's full tide, overwhelmed and oppressed,
With a strong closing effort he sank on my breast!
For some moments entranced, dissolving we lay,
While the fountains of pleasure were briskly at play,
And there thrilled through my veins an o'erpowering
    sensation,
And we gave the warm pledge of a new generation.
But, although the first tempest of passion was spent,
My young hero on further achievement was bent,
For he still kept possession, with power unsubdued,
And embracing me closely, his pastime pursued;
Delighted, I felt the keen impulse again,
And re-paid, with fresh ardour, the feats of my swain,

Who, more temperate now, played his amorous part,
And restrained the wild force of his soul-stirring dart.
Now halting – as if to prolong the delight –
Then again pressing on in the exquisite fight,
Till, panting with pleasure, my breath nearly gone,
I courted brisk action, and whispered, 'push on.'
All attention, he promptly the summons obeyed,
And again the rich tribute of ecstasy paid,
Till exhausted and spent with the genial emission,
We motionless lay in mere inanition.
Here the first act of wedlock was brought to a close,
And panting we sank into quiet repose;
But our slumbers were short, for warm fancy, impressed,
With the scenes which had passed, was destruction to rest,
And my dreams still reflected my amours again,
That I started, and woke with my blood in a flame;
Thus excited, I sought the renewal of bliss,
And impressed on my partner a warm ardent kiss,
Which, infusing fresh spirit through every vein,
Soon nerved him for love's sweet encounter again,
And he placed in my hand the dear source of my pleasure,
The pride of his manhood, and woman's best treasure.
The rogue, as I pressed him, grew stronger and stronger,
Till unable to bear my grasp any longer,
He flew to my arms, and with one active tilt,
Lodged his excellent weapon clean up to the hilt;
Then again we pursued our connubial employment,
And strained every nerve to increase our enjoyment.
Wild murmurs of ecstasy marked every stroke,
And the bed in its creaking our ardour bespoke,
Until, soon, we completed the blest operation,
And poured forth together our mutual libation.
Thus alternately sleeping and sporting we lay,
'Till bright Phœbus had mounted the chariot of day.
Five times we indulged in our amorous riot,
When my hero at length, seemed disposed to be quiet;
But, to tell you the truth, had he given me a score,
I still should have ardently coveted more;
But, more prudent, he thought it was time to observe
The maxim of keeping a corps in reserve,
And that he would not appear with 'eclat,'

If so soon, he was made a 'hors de combat;'
Still I clung fast around him with unquenched desire,
And fanned the warm embers of love's drooping fire.
Grown bold, I extended my warm roving hand,
And felt my dear playfellow gently expand,
Till he soon had attained the completest perfection,
And proudly stood forth in the grandest erection;
But my tormentor, laughing, still lay on his back,
And declared 'twas my turn to commence the attack;
So I mounted at once, and as something to brag on,
I acted the part of St. George and the Dragon;
And managed it, too, with such skill and address,
That it quickly was crowned with the wished for success.
This completed the sports of this wonderful night,
And put the last seal on this work of delight;
So we rose to perform our respective ablutions,
And wash off the stains of our frequent pollutions.
But words, after all, do but faintly reveal
The joys which, in wedlock, you're destined to feel;
Then lose not a moment, my dear Isabella,
But fly to the arms of some handsome young fellow,
Make haste and get married as soon as you can,
For life's quite a blank, till enjoyed with a man,
Who will quickly remove every girlish dilemma,
And make you as blest as your happy friend –

EMMA.

How she trembled and hid her face on my bosom, as the reading proceeded, whilst my prick was fairly throbbing with impatience under her bottom.

At last it was finished, and dropping the book, I took her face between my two hands, and bringing our lips together, we indulged in a long luscious kiss, which seemed to make her whole frame vibrate with emotion, especially when I thrust my tongue as wantonly as possible into her mouth, and she almost sucked my breath away.

At length she broke away, exclaiming, 'What a naughty, rude man you must be Fred, to bring that book to read to me, in fact you're dreadfully indelicate altogether, now get into that cupboard at once, sir!' opening the door, and motioning me to enter.

Willing to humour her for a little while, I stepped inside, but remarked as I did so, 'My idea, Ada, is in a hurry for me to be still more indelicate, but my darling can't be more impatient than I am.'

She did not answer, but I heard the key turned in the lock, and then a considerable rustling of dress, as she was evidently making haste for fear I should burst the door open to look at her.

'You are a good boy, Fred, to be so patient, and if always so obedient to your little wifey, I can never love you too much.'

'All right, dearest, but do make haste, for I'm really very impatient,' I replied, then I heard a faint trickling sound, and guessed she was at the moment performing the last necessary duty of nature, before being ready for bed.

A moment or two after the key was turned very softly in the lock, and pushing open the cupboard door I had to grope my way to the bed, for the little minx had drawn the thick window curtains quite close as well as putting out the wax lights.

I found my birdie safe between the sheets, only her head was buried out of sight, so throwing aside the bedclothes, my hand was upon her bosom in a moment, when she said softly, and evidently in a great flutter, 'Why, Fred, you're surely not coming to bed in your clothes, are you?'

'My darling you put out the lights, and made me forget all about that, certainly I must undress myself, but must light up to do so,' I answered, and soon the room was again illuminated by at least a dozen wax lights. The facetious hotel people had determined we should have enough candles to see well, and find our way into Hymen's bower of love, so I applied the taper to them all, especially as I knew they would be charged in the bill.

I was not bashful if she was, so soon stripped off everything, careless of whether she looked or not. My prick was in a fine state of erection, and you know it is a fair-sized instrument of its kind.

No doubt the sly puss had a good look at her fate, although pretending to hide her head.

For a moment or so I stood before the cheval glass, admiring my own manly beauty, especially the dart of love as I drew back the skin from its ruby head, and shook it triumphantly, so that she might have a good sight reflected in the glass.

Somehow the idea of exposing myself as much as possible to the little frightened creature, seemed to excite my lust to its utmost pitch of desire.

Next I slipped on my night shirt, and taking up the utensil, found my penis so distended that it was almost impossible to make water for a minute or two, till I had cooled it over the bidet with some cold water and a sponge. At length I managed to discharge a fine volume of water, the sound of which no doubt must have reached her ears, even if covered up.

Without putting out the lights I made my way to the bed, and opening the sheets, sprang in, and at once drew my trembling bride close to me, as I folded her in my arms, and took a long wanton kiss, tongueing and sucking each other's breath for a few seconds, till I felt my prick as hard as ever, throbbing against her belly, so slipping my hands down, I raised her *chemise de nuit*, and my own shirt, till we were both naked up to the arm-pits. What a delicious pair of hard, firm, round, little globes of love, her bosom now displayed to my delighted gaze, as the bedclothes were slightly thrown back. I moulded them with my fingers, kissed and sucked the pretty brown nipples, and made them feel my pretended bites, till the two little things were as stiff as little pricks. Then suddenly darting one hand lower down I felt the soft silky down on her *Mons Veneris*, and found her legs slightly open to give me a chance of attacking the grotto beneath.

'Darling, I must first ascertain that you are really a maid, that is a thing it is impossible I can be deceived in, has any one else ever been here?' I asked, placing one finger in her crack, which I found already quite moistened by a spend in anticipation, brought on no doubt by my attentions to her bubbies.

Her thighs closed convulsively at the instant, and as I could see her face quite plainly, the previous crimson flush was suddenly succeeded by an ashy paleness, and then as suddenly flushed up again, as the tears welled in torrents from her blue-black eyes.

'I'm undone, you'll never forgive me!' she sobbed as if her heart would break. 'Let me get up and go home to my uncle. Oh, oh, Fred, Fred, I never thought you could know. No, more you would,' she added, almost passionately, 'if you had acted in a manly way at once; but – but, of course your finger is a different thing. Oh, do let me go!'

She jumped out of bed, and would have been dressed in a very short time, sobbing all the while as if she would break her heart.

Her tears had an extraordinary effect upon me, I don't believe I had loved her before that moment, but now I yearned to comfort her, and felt how terrible it would be to lose such a darling.

'Ada,' I said, rushing to her, and folding her in my arms in spite of her resistance, 'I can forgive you everything if you tell me all – all – everything – what different are you now to what you would have been tomorrow morning, even if you had been a maid. Will you unbosom yourself, and love me as before, then nothing can interfere with our happiness?'

She fell on her knees, sobbing and crying more than ever, but presently composing herself a little, exclaimed, 'How good and generous of you, dear Fred, I will tell you all, and love you, and do everything you wish for the rest of my life. I won't even be jealous of other women as some foolish girls are. You shall have every freedom, and I will do my best to retain your love. But love me now, Freddy, I can't tell my tale till we feel one in every respect, tomorrow you shall know all.'

She was as passive as a lamb. I slipped off my night-shirt, and pulled every rag off her back as well.

What a beauty she was, so small, but perfect in every limb and part. In a frenzy of passion I carried her to the bed, threw her down and was between her legs in a moment, but she was awfully tight, and I had indeed to push hard to effect my entrance. She heaved up her bottom, and glued her lips to mine; I could not retain myself, but spent immediately. Then we lay in the ecstatic trance you know so well, till I felt the contractions of her cunt urging me to go on again. She is a perfect little devil for cock, and made me go on again and again, without withdrawing for a moment, till I had spent four times, and my prick was quite skinned.

When at last I did retire from the scene of my defeat, (for she had fairly exhausted me), I noticed a considerable stain of blood of the lips of her pussy, and on the sheet.

'I have really injured you as much as if I had taken your maidenhead, Ada dear,' I said.

A curious smile passed over her face, as she said, 'But for your threatening finger I should have cheated you, still I am far happier now, my Fred and will let you into the secret.

'I consulted a very clever old woman, who advised me to wash myself well with alum water, to tighten and harden my sheath, and then when the important crisis approached, to pass up a couple of good ripe red strawberries, which would give the proper stain – was it not clever, my pet; but I am indeed happiest as it is!'

We washed, and then before going to sleep, she first kissed my prick most affectionately for some minutes, and at last when I assured her that I was too sore for further play, she lubricated it with cold cream, hoping I should be all right in the morning.

What delicious dreams I had as I lay in the arms of my pet. It was all gone through again, only if anything with greater enjoyment, and at last I awoke in the act of spending, and found that my little wife had been gamahuching me in reality, till I quite unconsciously came in her mouth.

After breakfast we took a long walk over the lovely common, whilst far out of hearing of a living human being, she confided to me the following remarkable tale:

THE CONFESSION

When we had walked some distance, Ada said, 'Now, Fred, I will keep my word, and tell you all about my introduction to the ways of enjoyment, for I feel sure you must guess I am no novice.'

'Go on, dearest,' I answered, 'I only like you the better for your candour.'

She stopped and made me kiss her, again and again, and joked me about my prick getting stiff in my trousers, promising that her narrative would excite me tremendously, and that she really trembled for the consequences, when we should go to bed again.

'And perhaps long before that,' I replied with a laugh, 'but do go on, I'm all impatience.'

'You know I'm an orphan,' she began, 'and that I and my brother Ferdie have lived with our guardian, Uncle Harry, since our parents were lost in the City of Boston steamer, which was never heard of after leaving America, and you know uncle is still quite a young man, a year or two under forty; but, darling Fred, you must promise before I go further with my tale, to forgive every one I may mention, and remember too, dearest, that Uncle Harry is so rich, and besides he handed you my dower, did he not promise you another £20,000 if we lived happily together for five years, say you forgive them all as you have forgiven me?'

How could I do otherwise but promise, besides I have made up my mind to earn that £20,000, and perhaps may get it out of her uncle before the stipulated five years of kindness to Ada.

She continued, 'It is hardly four years since I went to live at uncle's place in Hertfordshire, you know the fine old hall standing in a large park; he was away in town, being an MP, but as soon as the session was over came at once to Curlington, and soon won my affections by his great kindness and consideration for our orphaned state.

'Ferdie used to come into my bedroom, (which was next to his), every night to kiss me before going to bed, and I soon began to notice that his embraces and kisses were getting more impassioned every day. One evening in particular he seemed as if he would never take his departure, so that when I had removed my dress, modesty prevented me continuing to disrobe until he was gone, "Now Ferdie, one more kiss and be off, I want to go to bed!"

'He was sitting by my side on the edge of the bed, and suddenly clasping me to his bosom, glued his lips to mine is such a warm sucking kiss, that I blushed and tried to get away from him, "Ah, for shame sir! you shan't come into my room again!" I gasped, almost choked by his kissing, as I found one of his daring hands on my thigh under my skirts.

'"I must, I will, never mind me Ada, I want to see if you are like a picture I have seen; would you like to look at it darling?"

'He spoke excitedly, and I was too astonished to answer, my skirts were thrown up, and he put his fingers in my little crack, which made me feel so funny, and then forcing my thighs apart, began to kiss me there in such a way, tickling the little button you know of with the tip of his tongue so lasciviously, that I was lost at once, and quite gave myself up to the delicious sensations aroused in me for the first time.

'"How nice, how lovely! Oh, Ferdie, what shall I do?" I exclaimed, "there's something coming, for heaven's sake leave me alone darling!"

'But he only redoubled his sucking and tongueing, whilst I squirmed and twisted about in ecstasy till I fairly came in his mouth.

'"May I sleep with you darling?" he asked, when we had got over the excitement a little, "I will show you a book of pictures belonging to Uncle Harry, and we can practise all the 'Loves of Venus', as it is called."

'"How can I refuse my dear boy," I replied, "only make haste and undress quietly in your room, so no one can hear us, and bring the book for me to see."

'He soon came back, with only his night shirt on, and made me take off mine, which was all I had on, as he wanted to admire my figure, and see if I had any little fur below yet, or if I was as beautiful as the girls pictured in the book.

'"What a little love my sister is, don't you think so, Ada?" he said smiling, then proceeded to kiss the firm round globes of my bosom, whilst his hand passed over and moulded every part of my person, making comments as he examined each part, such as, "Delicious bubbies! What a firm little rump, and what a lovely fat little cunny you have, sissy; how nicely it is getting covered with the soft downy hair just beginning to grow!"

'His touches fired the blood in my veins till I was quite beside myself, and yet without knowing what I wanted, he seemed to take such delight in handling me, that at last I thought it would be best to repay a few of his liberties, so I suddenly pushed him backwards, and noticing how his shirt stuck up over a certain part, just raised it to see the cause.

'"And pray what do you call this, sir?" I asked, taking the upright shaft in my left hand, as I was kneeling up between his legs, "and what pray do you call this bag with two lumps in it, which hangs below?"

'"Little simpleton," he said excitedly, "don't you know what they are? Why, to be sure, one is my cock, and the other my balls or bollocks, as some would call them; they also have other names, such as prick, pego, John Thomas, for a man's cock, which do you like best love?"

'"And is that what a man puts into a woman to make babies?" I asked.

'"Look at the book first, then if you are agreeable, Ada darling, we will try some of the designs, so Miss Impudence just cover up those jewels again with my shirt tail, and let us look at my prize."

'The book was a small oblong album, in half morocco and gilt edges, lettered outside "The Love of Venus".

'The first plate as he opened it, was a representation of Mercury catching Venus and Mars in a net, just as she was in the act of riding a St George and the God of War. It was a luscious scene, you could see her straddling over him with the shaft of love well up her cunny, but the idea was rather spoilt by the look of surprise caused by the sudden envelopment of the lovers in the treacherous net.

'The second representation was another beautifully soft steel plate, called "La Danza di Bacco e Arianna". This must have been before Bacchus grew into the bloated young man he is usually pictured to be. In this one the artist represents a lovely youth with standing pego, dancing with a lovely girl who also shows all her naked charms in front of his standard of love, which is almost close enough to touch her unfledged grotto.

'I remember all the plates in the book so well, because we often looked at them afterwards.

'The third was a swing scene, a lovely naked woman, her eyes almost closed by excessive emotion, clinging to the ropes by her hands, whilst her bottom projects in the most inviting manner towards her sweetheart, (also naked) who stands ready to meet and catch her luscious cunt right upon his standing prick, in fact he is steadying the swing so as to make sure of hitting the mark at every return.

'There were dozens of fine steel plates in the album, illustrating every possible position in which the passion of love could be enjoyed, but I will only describe one more of them. It represented a pretty girl seated in front of her youth, on a kind of rocking boat, with their toes just touching the floor to give the required motion; his prick is right in her bottom, and she is turning her face round to look at him, as he enjoys the sight of seeing his pego go in and out, at every rise and fall of the boat, a most luscious idea.

'"Now, Ada, which position do you like best?" my brother asked, as he put the book under the pillow.

'"I'm so afraid, dearest, to let you put that great thing into me, but I think the most affectionate and loving picture is where each one is kissing and sucking the other, you kissed me so nicely at first, may I now repay it to your cock, whilst you kiss me again?"

'He threw off his shirt, and then made me lay over him, so that my bottom was over his face, which he buried between my thighs, and at once commenced sucking my crack in the most exciting manner. How his tongue tickled that delicious sensitive spot you know so well, and then for a change he would draw it all along the crack once or twice, then thrust it right into me, and suck as if his life depended on it. How it fired every drop of blood in my veins, I pressed myself closer and closer to his dear lips as they gave me such exquisite bliss, and seized hold of his cock with both hands, as I brought the ruby head to my lips. Totally inexperienced as I was up to that moment, I instinctively rolled my tongue round the top, and even tickled the little hole from which he makes water, then imitating his motions, I licked all along the shaft, and even sucked his balls, when just as I was doing so I felt a sudden extra stiffening of the affair, and felt a lot of warm drops fall, or spout upon my neck; if I had had him in my mouth I should have had to swallow it.

'I knew something delicious had happened to him, as he gave such a deep drawn sigh, then ejaculated, "Darling – love – what pleasure you give me, dear sister."

'A sympathetic thrill of delight shot through my frame, and almost directly I inundated his mouth with quite a profusion of my own juice, which he seemed thoroughly to enjoy, for his tongue was so active he could not have missed a single drop.

'Our room was in darkness, as in the midst of our gamahuching the lamp had gone out, and I fancied as soon as I came to myself a little, that I heard a sigh and a rustling as if someone was moving about.

'"What's that, Ferdie?" I whispered, "oh, do run into your room and let me bolt the door, or I'm sure uncle, or someone will find you here!"

'Giving me a kiss, he took the album from under the pillow and slipped out of the room.

'I followed to bolt the door, and fancied I heard a whispering in the corridor; however, knowing I was now safe, I soon fell asleep after the extraordinary and enervating emotions I had experienced under Ferdie's tuition.

'During the next morning, whilst my brother was gone fishing, and I was sitting at work, making a smoking cap for our guardian, who should enter but uncle himself, a most unusual thing, and he looked so serious, my guilty conscience at once told me he knew all.

'Seating himself by my side on an ottoman, "Is my little girl doing that for Uncle Harry?" he asked.

'"Who else should I make it for, uncle?"

'"But you might have a sweetheart, Ada!"

'"For shame, uncle, I don't even know a boy of my own age!" I said with a laugh.

'"Isn't Ferdie your lover, I caught him slipping out of your bed-room at two o'clock this morning!"

'My face crimsoned, and I burst into tears, sobbing as if my heart would break, as I sprang up and tried to rush from his sight. He was after me in a moment, and grasping me round the waist, carried me back to the ottoman, and placed me upon his lap, kissing my forehead tenderly at the same time.

'"Perhaps things are not quite so bad, Ada; Uncle Harry can forgive anything if you love him."

'"How kind, how good of you, dear uncle!" I cried, sobbing on his breast, "you know we both love you so dearly!"

'"Then I will tell my birdie," he went on, "that I peeped into the room and saw all, in fact the sight made me sigh so, you were startled, and I had to slink away; now all I want is to join in your love gambols, and for you to be as free with me as you are with Ferdie, only think of him taking my little album to show you, but I can show you a lot more beautiful pictures as well as books, if you come to my library. You have read the history of Rome, but never saw an account of the private lives of the Emperors, how some loved their own sons and daughters, whilst Nero had his mother, and Caligula his horse, the latter in fact had a kind of platform in the stable with a pair of low shafts, into which his horse was backed, and so harnessed that he could neither kick or get away, whilst his Imperial master made love to his bottom behind, but that was a dirty fancy, sons and daughters, or better still nephews and neices are more in my way, but you shall see the book for yourself, and can read it, as you know French."

'Whilst he was speaking his hand wandered under my clothes, and already got possession of my slightly fledged crack.

'"What a beautiful little plump thing you have, Ada, how it excited me to see you and Ferdie kissing each other's affairs, I felt quite overcome, and had to frig myself, which made me sigh when I came, that was what you heard, darling!"

'"What is frigging, uncle?" I asked in my simplicity.

'"Rubbing my cock up and down with my hand, till I make the seed spurt, will my little love do it for her uncle?" he asked.

'"Anything to give you pleasure. You love us so I know, shall I put my hand into your trousers and find him?"

'"Yes darling," he replied, kissing me ardently, "you couldn't please me better."

'I slipped down on my knees, and with trembling hands unbuttoned his trousers; there was a great hard thing under his shirt, and I soon exposed a fine manly weapon about nine inches long and thick in proportion.

'How proudly it stood, as I measured its length by grasping it one hand over the other, drawing the skin downwards, till the fiery red head was fully exposed, projecting quite two inches beyond what my little hands could hold of its length.

'My first impulse was to imprint a gentle kiss on its beautiful top, my tongue shot out instinctively to tickle and give him pleasure.

'He gave a deep, long drawn sigh, as he murmured, "Go on, Ada, my little love, kiss and rub me both at once, you will soon give me most exquisite pleasure! Ah – oh – go on – suck me – rub me quick – take it all in your mouth – don't be afraid, darling! Ah – that's grand – what a love – oh, oh, oh – there!" he ejaculated as I went on, and at last I felt the same sudden spasm shoot along the shaft as I was handling him, and my mouth was flooded with his warm creamy emission, which would have choked me if I had not greedily swallowed it all, yes, and enjoyed it too dearie!'

As Ada was telling me her confession we had settled upon a bank, and just at this point she had my trousers undone, as you may guess my prick was in a fine state. She took it into her little mouth at once, and racked me off deliciously, never stopping for a moment till she had drained the last drop, then looked up in my face with a smile, and said, 'Dear Fred, you didn't know I was so accomplished, did you? I do enjoy that so, and I know it gives you pleasure. I have often kissed your sister Frederica, and you can tell her I've told you if you like. That was when she came to see us at uncle's, and happened on days when we were left alone by ourselves, only she used to say she liked a man best, and so do I darling love!'

She continued, 'I need not tell you much more about our doings at Curlington; uncle took my maidenhead, and used to delight in seeing Ferdie have me. Other times he would have me himself, whilst Ferdie laid by our side on the bed, so that uncle could suck his cock, whilst my brother played with his big affair as it worked in and out of little Ada. My hands would also be busy frigging Ferdie's prick into uncle's mouth. Don't you think it was awfully grand, even if so dreadfully wicked, as people would say if they knew? Do you know, Fred, I am longing to see you take the impudence out of the chambermaid at the hotel, as I believe she is as knowing as she looks.'

'Do you really mean that you would like to see me have that girl, Ada?'

'Yes, to be sure, and especially as I believe it would give you pleasure,' she replied.

Of course it suited me, but I determined to make Ada lay the trap herself, so I just communicated to her a little plan which I thought would work admirably, which she readily agreed to carry out, whilst I should be hidden in the same closet, in which I had waited the previous night whilst she undressed and got into bed.

Next morning I purposely made my arrangements for being away all day, in the presence of our intended victim when she came into our sitting room at breakfast time to receive Ada's orders, about several things she required during the morning, notably, a bath she wished to have in our bedroom with Sophy for attendant.

About one o'clock I was put away in the closet, with a tall stool to sit upon, and a nice little peephole, so that I could see and hear everything done in the room.

Enter Miss Sophy in answer to Ada's ring.

'Is the bath ready to be brought in, and have you plenty of time to attend to me Sophy? You can tell them you are engaged with me, and they can charge it in the bill, if they please to do so, for your extra attendance,' said Ada.

'Certainly ma'am,' and away trotted the chambermaid.

Then two of the hotel servants brought in the bath and all the necessary requirements for it, and Ada ordered Sophy to bolt the door.

Then my wife was undressed and bathed, after which she insisted upon Sophy stripping and having a bath also.

I had enjoyed the sight of Ada being wiped down by the chambermaid, who even applied the towels to the most interesting chink of love, seeming to take a peculiar kind of interest in my wife's cunny.

And now I was doubly pleased to see Sophy strip as Ada helped her to do so, ever and anon complimenting the girl on her different beauties and contrasting them with her own.

Sophy was a finely moulded girl of medium height, with dark red auburn hair, hazel eyes and rosy cheeks, whilst, as to her crack, it looked deliciously small and tight, with only just a shade of rather golden hair upon the mount, her skin was as white as alabaster, and the girl was evidently proud of herself.

She was soon into and out of the bath, then Ada attended to her with the towels, and I could see considerably excited Miss Sophy by occasional funny touches, making her blush all over every now and then.

'What a love you are, Sophy, how I should like to cuddle you in bed, do you think you could love me, dear?' she asked.

'Oh, ma'am, your husband might come back and catch us; pray don't, its so rude, you make me so ashamed!'

By this time Ada was standing with one arm round the girl's waist, kissing her mouth, whilst the other hand had got its forefinger on the sensitive spot just inside Sophy's crack, and was gently frigging her as their naked bellies touched one another.

'Isn't that nice, Sophy dear? Doesn't it make you love me a little?' she whispered.

'Yes, yes, it's beautiful, but, oh ma'am, how can you do so to me?' she answered with a sigh, blushing deeper than ever.

'You know, Sophy, that girls often love other girls as much or more than they do men; here, sit on my lap on the sofa, and I will tell you of something which has just happened in Paris, and for printing which the editor of a French newspaper is now undergoing a sentence of twelve months imprisonment.

'It was an article calling public attention to this incident, and pretended to expose the secret practices of young ladies whose morals were supposed to be above suspicion.

'The names were fictitious of course, but everyone believes the story is founded on actual facts.

'A member of the old nobility, Monsieur St. Roque, wishing to marry, determined not to select a wife from the frivolous young beauties of Parisian society, the lightness of whose morals he hadn't the greatest possible horror of, but selected a young girl of sixteen, whose parents had had her brought up and entirely educated at a convent, of the strictest possible reputation, in fact she only left the religious establishment on the morning of her marriage.

'Everything went on smoothly for a short time, excepting that Monsieur found his bride so cold, and evidently pining for something or some one.

'One night, in bed, he elicited from Celestine, in answer to his enquiry of what she wanted to make her really happy, that she was *triste* on account of having been parted from Mlle. Sapho, her most intimate friend and bedfellow at the convent.

'"Is that all, my darling, then we will invite her to pay us a long visit at once," replied Monsieur, only too happy to think that such a trifle would make his little wife happy, and attributing her sadness, in his innocence of mind, to the extreme youth of his spouse, and the extraordinary affection of two young girls for each other (he was quite right, but little guessed the nature and foundation of such loving attachment).

'Mlle. Sapho's presence seemed to bring him all the access of happiness he had wished for, the young bride's coldness was at once changed to a warm loving demeanour; in fact he found she was almost too exacting in her constant demands upon his vigour, and found himself regularly kept to the "whole duty of a man", i.e. a constant worship at the shrine of Venus.

'He also noticed that the two loving girls were very fond of repairing by themselves to a little pavilion in a very secluded part of the garden, so his curiosity prompted him to spy out their secret, and placed himself in ambuscade in a shrubbery at the back of the pavilion, so that when his birds entered their cage he could both hear and see all that passed between them.

'"How dull I am without you, Celestine, you quite forget me, now you can enjoy your husband every night," said the young wife's friend.

'"You do me great injustice dear, dear, darling Sapho, you know I would not be happy till I got Monsieur to invite you to stay with us, and now you complain that I am forgetful of you, when the fact is that I burn more and more for your love every day. Let me love you now, and I promise this very night to make my husband agree to all you wish, can I do more to show my love?" replied the young wife, kissing and taking all sorts of loving liberties with her friend, as they assisted each other to divest themselves of their clothing, till both were perfectly naked.

'The sight drove Monsieur St. Roque almost beside himself, when he found that Celestine was a confirmed young tribade, but restraining himself, he witnessed all their salacious and indelicate games, sucking, kissing, and toying till with a positive groan of horror, he beheld them in the last listless state of prostration which succeeds for a short time the attainment of forbidden joys.

'It was only by putting the greatest possible restraint upon himself that he was able to rest till night should disclose what his wife had promised to ask of him.

'They had retired to bed, and his wanton little wife was more loving than ever, so much so that she almost drove from his mind the disagreeable incidents of the morning, the denouement of which he had been so anxiously awaiting, and he was just about to mount upon the throne of love when she exclaimed, with a slight laugh at his impetuosity, "Ah, no, no, not yet love, you must promise me something first."

'"You know I will refuse you nothing, Celestine, that is proper for my wife to have," he replied.

'"But it is not exactly proper, sir, although very nice, especially for you; you can't refuse me, or I won't kiss your affair in the way you are so fond of having me do. Make up your mind at once, or I will take away my hand and turn my back; do you promise or not, whatever it may be it won't hurt you, but only add to our pleasure?"

'He consented, and breathlessly awaited her explanation, which was, that Sapho and herself, when at the convent, had been taught by one of the nuns all the ways of procuring pleasure for each other, and that afterwards being bedfellows, made them so fond of each other that they bound themselves by a most fearful oath, that neither of them should enjoy a sensual pleasure without the full participation of her friend, in fact the first one who got married was to share her husband with the other, and if both had husbands they would exchange, or have them altogether in the same room.

'"And, now darling, let me run and fetch Sapho, she is dying for you to have her, then we will both kiss you in every possible way, and always have our love together, won't it be delicious?" saying which she sprang from the bed and left the room.

'Imagine the husband's horror at finding his wife such a filthy-minded debauched creature, all faith in her purity gone, and himself wretched, dishonoured, disgraced, how could he live?

'When Celestine returned with Sapho she found Monsieur St. Roque gone, so they amused themselves in the best way they could, expecting him to surprise them every moment, till at last, after about an hour, a loud report of firearms startled them from their lascivious frolics.

'The noble husband had blown out his brains, but not before leaving a letter to his banker, which fully explained his reasons for so doing.'

'What do you think of that story, Sophy, I don't think my husband would shoot himself if I asked him to have you, and what would you say?' asked Ada of the chambermaid, as her rude touches fairly made the girl shiver with sensuous delight.

'For shame, ma'am, you would kill me, and besides if he could but see us now, it would disgust him,' was the blushing answer.

'Not so long as you don't encourage him to make love on the sly; the only thing to disgust him is a mock modest girl who wants a bit of cock, and pretends not to. I must run to the w.c. dearie, in the next room, so please get my clean things out of that closet by the time I come back,' and Ada ran out laughing.

Now was the moment, and I was as naked as the first day I was born, excepting of course, a little hair on my prick, as I had let everything, dressing gown, etc., drop off me in anticipation of my turn soon arriving. Mr. Pego was in a glorious state, fit for any young lady's inspection.

Sophy advanced to the closet, and opened the door, 'My God, sir, what shall I do! What a shame!' she screamed, and I heard Ada laughingly call out from the next room, 'Make the best of him, dear, you are welcome!'

In a moment Sophy flew to the bed, and hid her face in the pillow, but I seized hold of her buttocks at once, and soon got into her dog fashion, and had a most glorious fuck, which she evidently enjoyed immensely, being so well prepared and excited by my little wife beforehand.

She spent so profusely that it fairly dropped down the inside of her thighs, still she pretended to be so bashful and would not even look at me.

'This is too hard work, Sophy,' I said, 'if you want to hide your face, I shall put you on the bed, and then I don't mind,' so suiting the action to the word I hoisted her up, and soon had her kneeling in front of me with her face still in the pillow, and determined to give her a treat she little dreamed of.

My prick was as stiff as ever, and at once took his place again in the girl's cunt to her evident delight, to judge from the way she wriggled her bum, and met me at every lunge.

My plan was to go on that way a little till she was tremendously excited, then slyly applying some spittle to her other tight little pink hole, I changed from one to the other, and was fairly into her bottom before she could remonstrate, and in a moment or two she hardly knew the difference except by the great increase of excitement, and we soon spent again with cries of delight, which for her part she found it quite impossible to repress.

I was fairly pumped out for a time, but Ada came into the room and asked Sophy what she thought of me, then she jumped on the bed by the side of us, and commenced playing with my late partner, never giving the girl a moment's rest, frigging her and slapping her buttocks, till poor Sophy almost groaned with renewed excitement. Ada kissed her and hugged her to her bosom, tipping the velvet with her tongue, and doing everything she could think of to stir all the fires of Sophy's warm temperament.

At last she exclaimed, 'Oh, ma'am, how you excite me, and you haven't got a prick, that's what I want, and look at your husband, he's quite used up, poor man, no doubt you took a lot out of him before you got up this morning!'

'Silly girl, why you're actually jealous of me, I do believe,' laughed Ada. 'You don't know that thing so well as I do, it only wants a little coaxing Sophy. Now take my advice, just get over him, and take it in your hand and help yourself. A true man like my husband never refuses to pity a girl who wants it.'

Saying which she again left us alone, and Sophy proceeded to act upon her advice. Her face was flushed with blushes, whilst the dark red masses of her hair fell in dishevelled locks over those alabaster shoulders, and those otherwise soft hazel eyes were full of humid lustful fire, as she put her left leg across me, then taking hold of my limp affair in her right hand, she essayed to bring its head to her longing gap. Her fruitless efforts both amused and excited me, especially when I noticed how chagrined she looked at the result of her first efforts, I smiled, and drawing her face down to mine, gave the dear girl a luscious kiss that she fairly quivered with emotions from head to foot.

'Keep it in your hand Sophy, and keep kissing me as you rub its head against your crack, and I shall soon be ready to oblige you darling, once more,' I whispered.

Didn't she kiss me, that's all, I never knew a girl seem to want me so much; she thrust her tongue into my mouth, she rubbed her cunt down on the head of my cock, till in a minute or two he gradually got firm enough to keep his place, then throwing her arms around me, she rode me famously, there was such a delicious contraction in the folds of her vagina, that she gave me the most exquisite pleasure, and to judge by her actions she was almost beside herself with wanton desire, and at last when she spent, went into screaming and laughing hysterics.

Next day Ada's brother Ferdie came down from London, to see how we were getting on, and he was enlightened as to all she had confessed to me. He is such a lovable young fellow. I took to him more than ever, and by the introduction of Sophy, we made up a most happy quartette every night, as we got him a room next to ours, and Ada obtained permission for the chamber-maid to sleep in our little ante-room, in case she was required to attend my wife, who pretended to be very delicate.

There are many who consider incest such a dreadful crime, but I would just ask such persons what can be more natural than for brothers and sisters to love each other, and allow all those freedoms which only strangers who may happen to marry them are supposed to have a right to.

How could I help loving you to distraction, my darling Frederica, it always seemed to me the most natural thing in the world that I should possess all those charms of my beautiful sister, which had ripened under my very eyes as it were. You always seemed my property, and why should I have left for a stranger the fruit which had, as it were, grown under my own eyes?

Adam's children must have married brothers and sisters, and their parent himself must have been something more than incestuous if the bible is to be believed, for Eve was even part of himself, bone of his bone, and flesh of his flesh; did not Abraham have his own sister Sarah for wife, from whom descended God's own special people, and even the Messiah of the Christian World. In fact we are all the offspring of incest, or the globe would never have been peopled.

The ancient Egyptian Ptolemys always had their sisters for wives.

The wickedness of incest is a manufactured article, made a sin, not by God, but by the restlessness of mankind, ever on the move to make fresh offences out of harmless things, and continually piling up the burden of over government which the growing instinct of liberty in the present generation will soon, I hope, sweep away.

But to go on, I loved Ferdie soon quite as much as his sister, and almost every night our first programme would be for him to have his sister. They are both small but so beautifully propor-tioned, and seemed so thoroughly to enjoy fucking each other, that it was the greatest treat I could have to see them in the act.

I would sit with Sophy on my knee, as I tickled her clitoris with my fingers, making her spend over and over again, as I would talk to her thus: 'Isn't it lovely, dear, to see such a pretty pair in action? Look at Ferdie's beautiful prick as it slips in and out of his sister! Don't you wish you had a brother to fuck you

Sophy? Now they're coming; look, look, how they strain, and shove to get in even another quarter of an inch. It's over, my God, how they must have spent, look at it oozing and dripping on the bed. Frig me quick, I'm coming now. Ah, you darling, how delightfully your hand does it; kiss me, give me your tongue quick!'

My favourite plan was to get Ferdie's bottom well spitted on my prick, as he sat on my lap, whilst his sister and Sophy gamahuched him by turns, till we both came again at the same time. Another way was to lay both girls on the bed, on their sides, face to face, then I would straddle over them so that my prick could be kissed by both of them at once, whilst I also had my head buried between their bellies, with a cunt on each side of my nose, then Ferdie would get into me behind, and altogether we carried out such a voluptuous fancy that on more than one occasion the excess of excitement was greater than I could bear, and I fairly fainted in the act of emission.

Sophy told us a funny story of an elderly couple, brother and sister, who were staying in the hotel last summer. They were Scots, Mr. and Miss McLachlan, the brother a man of nearly seventy, whilst his sister was only a year or two younger.

They had two bedrooms communicating, as Mr. McLachlan said his sister was liable to frights in the night, and could not sleep unless she was close at hand to him, and able to run into his room when a sudden fright came.

She was curiously excited to find out more about them, especially as one or other of the beds always seemed unusually tumbled, and once she found several spots and smears of blood on the lower sheet.

The weather was very warm, and Mr. McLachlan used to have his bedroom window partially open, although the blind was always drawn down, so as their rooms were on the first floor, it occurred to Sophy that the gardener's light ladder, which he used for trimming the grape vines, etc., would just enable her to see all that was going on. Bob, the gardener, being her sweetheart, she easily persuaded him to place the ladder for her, and mind it whilst she went up to peep at the old people. To further her purpose she had fixed the blind so that when pulled down it would just leave about half an inch of space at the bottom, and so afford every facility for both seeing and hearing everything from the outside.

It was rather a dark night when she and Bob put their plan in operation, and this is her description of the scene.

'Mr. McLachlan is seated in an easy chair, apparently absorbed in reading several letters, which the old gentleman would kiss as he finished reading each of them.

'Enter his sister on tiptoe, till she stood behind the chair glaring at the letters he was so taken up with, grinding her teeth, and shaking a birch rod over his head.

'At last she snatches a letter, "Ha, ha! caught you again, sir, reading that minx's letters. Have you not promised me over and over again that you will give her up, you faithless wretch, I'll teach you to love any one but your sister! Eh – you're frightened, are you? Take down your breeches, sir, this moment."

'The brother looks awfully frightened, but she takes him by the wrist, and leads him to the bed, and I could see the old girl had only her chemise and drawers on under her dressing gown. She tied both hands by the wrists, with a piece of cord which depended from the top frame of the four-poster, then one ankle to the right and the other to the left leg of the bed, so that he was most comfortably fixed up, indeed to judge by his looks he really dreaded her. I heard him frequently appeal for mercy.

'"Oh, Maria, you won't now, pray don't, I can't stand it, you cut me up so the night before last, do forgive me, and I'll burn the letters."

'"You would, would you, sir; how often James have I caught you reading them, after the same broken promises. Do you still correspond with that designing girl? You know she only wants your money. I'll birch you out of that fancy, my boy, till you again love poor Maria, you shall never marry whilst I can hold a rod, sir. I only wish I had the girl here, her bum should smart, I'll warrant!"

'She now pulled his breeches down, and tucked up his shirt so as to expose a fairly plump rump, which she patted admiringly, then her face seemed to get stern, and reaching the rod off the dressing table she again began to lecture him as she applied the twigs vigorously, so much so that he fairly screamed for mercy, "I'll never think of her again, Maria, indeed I won't, you know I love you so! You have such a sweet grey-haired cunt."

'"What insult! How dare you say that to your sister. You shall get me at once Mrs. Allen's Hair Restore, Rowland's Kalydor, Breidenbach's Macassarine, and Ross's Extract of Cantharides. Ha, ha you shall pay to make my hair its natural colour, sir! But now I think of it, I'll get a Ross's Nose Machine for your poor old cock, its awfully down in the world, and will only stand for little featherless chits, such as you correspond with."

'All the while her cuts were something painful to see, yet the sight had a most exciting effect upon me, so much so that when Bob in his impatience crept up the ladder behind me, to see what was keeping me so long up there, and he slipped his hand up my thighs behind till he got hold of you know what, instead of boxing his ears, I positively allowed him to finger me at pleasure, till I came down with my love juice all over his hand.

'This so excited him that I believe had it been possible he would have fucked me on the ladder. However he managed to get up on to the same step with myself and clasped his other arm round my waist, as he peeped over my shoulder to see what was going on, for I had now got one corner of the blind nicely up, as the parties inside were far to busy to notice it. I repaid his caresses by momentarily turning my head for a kiss, and feeling his prick with my left hand, giving it a loving squeeze, as I whispered, "Look, Bob darling, did you ever see such a sight, I believe she is going to birch him till he is fit to have her, only fancy brother and sister, did you ever?"

'I was quite right in my conjecture, his bottom was all over deep red, fiery looking weals and scratches, and I could even see drops of blood oozing from the lacerations here and there; he seemed to writhe and twist about in a peculiar manner, as if he wanted to attract her attention, so much so that I soon caught glimpses of all he possessed.

'"Look," whispered Bob in my ear, "did you ever see such a teazer as the old fellow's got, and as grey as a badger, by Jove!"

'I nudged him with my elbow to keep quiet.

'"You're showing me your impudence, are you, sir? It doesn't want a nose machine now, have I brought it to love its Maria, then?" said the old woman, as she first threw away her worn out rod, then quickly untying one ankle she turned him round, and knelt down and caressed his tremendous affair.

'"How I love you now, darling!" she said, handling and kissing his prick, till I expected he would spend in her eye, but she was too clever to go too far, so loosening his other ancle and hands, she slipped off her dressing gown and sprang on the bed, whilst he threw off everything but his shirt, and was on to her in a moment.

'"My James, my love, come to my arms, you do love me now," she said excitedly, opening her legs at the same time, and giving us a fair glance at a fat pair of thighs, at the top of which we could see a lovely pouting cunny, but as grey as possible. One of her hands directed his rampant prick to the longing receptacle, whilst her other arm thrown round his neck, drew his face to hers, and they indulged in a most loving kiss at the same moment, as he was fairly sheathed to the hilt, and she threw a fine pair of legs over his buttocks.

'I had never seen such a pretty sight before, although old and grey, they were both plump and good figures, and the sight of his rump working furiously, whilst her feet drummed on his posteriors to hasten his action (they were set off by silk stockings and pretty Turkish slippers), had such an effect on me that whispering to Bob we hastily slipped down our ladder, and indulged in al *al fresco* uprighter, under a fine tree close by; then removing our ladder we slipped into the hotel and found our own rooms.

'You may be sure we often had a peep at James and Maria, but their proceedings had so much sameness about them that we came to the conclusion it was a regular get up affair on his part, and that playing at punishment was for the purpose of getting Mr. James up to the proper pitch of excitement, and so enable him to oblige his sister's voluptuous propensities, for she was a hot old girl, and actually made love tomy Bob, which I repaid by spooning Mr. McLachlan, and as neither of us were jealous it paid very well. I don't know how much the old woman gave him; I had nearly £50 from Mr. James, and gave it all to Bob to bank, but the faithless wretch has run away to New Zealand with all the money and another girl, and left me still chambermaid at the hotel.'

Now, my darling sister, I must end this long letter, and trust some other time to tell you more, and only add that we all wish you were here.

Your affectionate brother,
FRED

BOUND FOR INDIA
ON BOARD A P&O STEAMER
from THE CABINET OF VENUS

AFTER A ROUGH start from Southampton, which kept most of the passengers below for three or four days, we got some fine weather, and found that among our number were three brides; one having been married only two days before we sailed, and the other two within the last fortnight. It is with one of the latter, I may say, more experienced ones, that I got mixed up with in a little midnight adventure during the twenty-four hours we were at anchor off Malta.

This good lady, Mrs. M was barely eighteen, with a pretty face, short, but well-knit figure, and as plump a little partner as any man could wish for.

The spooning on board of all three of these married couples was painful to behold, and with such limited space as a steamer affords, we could not give them that solitude they longed for, and it was not until we were running into Malta harbour that their spirits and hopes began to rise.

On arrival, off we bachelors rushed with our little baggage to the nearest hotel, got our rooms, and roamed all the afternoon about Malta, dining mostly at the club, then going to the opera.

At the opera were all our fellow passengers, including Mrs. M and her well-built hubby, a captain in an infantry regiment.

After the opera I returned to my hotel, not feeling well enough to enjoy a round of Malta at midnight. I was not long tumbling into my virtuous couch, and had just put out the candle when I heard the door of the next room open and two people enter.

Judge of my amusement when I discovered that the wall between us consisted only of thin canvas, papered over, and that it was almost possible to hear, even a pin dropping in the next room, and that its occupants were Mrs. M and her husband.

After a few remarks to each other about the opera, Malta, etc., during which I could hear they were undressing, I heard Captain M say, 'I don't think we will put the candle out just yet.'

Which was answered by a laugh, followed immediately by a short scuffle and 'Oh, don't, dear.'

It was not hard to determine that their bed was next to the canvas wall, and so within a few inches of mine.

'Oh! don't, dear,' seemed to have no effect, for after some rustling, and a few minutes silence, Mrs M began to breathe heavily, and broke out into murmurings of 'Oh! oh! darling, you will kill me,' and deep sighs proclaimed her to be suffering the most exquisite pain, and by the soft noise I heard at intervals I knew that Captain M was giving his young bride a kiss which once a woman experiences is never forgotten.

After a most prolonged kiss, in which Mrs. M must have rolled all over the bed, and tried its bearing powers to the utmost, she exclaimed.

'Fred, darling, do stop now, or I will faint.'

Fred laughed and said, 'Girls only faint for want of it, never when they are having it, so I will revive you.'

Mrs M laughed and said, 'Oh! don't hurt me, will you? and be very gentle.'

After some rustling, and 'Oh! do be gentle – that hurts me. Oh! oh! darling. Oh! oh-h-h-h,' and the regular creak from the bed, I knew Master F, was in 'the very lists of love', and that his kissing had somewhat excited him, for the exclamations came quicker and deeper from Mrs. M and very soon after, with almost a shriek, and a very deep sigh, and some involuntary exclamations from Fred I knew the fiery liquid had darted forth, and set the young blood in their veins tingling.

In about half an hour the latter part of this scene was again enacted, and after a prolonged and most exciting encounter, all was still for the night, but little sleep could I get.

At last I did, and in the morning found that the young lovers must have heard me cough or move in bed, and so discovered the thin wall, for they never spoke out of a very low whisper.

They also must have found out who their neighbour was, for

Mrs. M could not look me in the face again, and Captain M was so very anxious to find out what time I really did go to bed.

In the cabin with Mrs. M was a Mrs Stuart, an aged lady, whose husband was on board, and who was a merchant at Port Said, and a Mrs. Jenkins, whose husband was a Bengal civilian, and who was to meet her on arrival at Bombay.

Mrs. Jenkins was about thirty; she was a good-looking woman, and was decidedly plump, though she declared she was very thin when she had left Bombay with her only child not a year ago.

She had had only one child, she told me, since her marriage, and the child was now nine years old, and, being a boy, she did not mind leaving him at school.

And I did not think she did take it much to heart, as she was of the 'frisky' sort. We two had become great chums on the voyage to Malta, and had got to the stage of 'calling a spade a spade', but no further.

The night after we left Malta, when sitting on the deck after dinner, she said, 'I notice that something peculiar has happened between you and Mrs M.'

'There has,' said I, laughing, 'and she won't tell you what it is, I bet?'

'Well, dear boy, you will I am sure?' says she.

In the end I did, and most graphically described what I had heard, and before the end of my yarn, which I told her as she lay in a long bamboo chair under the darkness of a double awning, and I in a short deck chair with my feet resting upon the edge of hers, found our bloods so fired that I scarcely realized that I had at last broken the ice, and that my hand, though in hers, and on her lap, was rubbing her thighs, and at last, that sacred spot.

I dare not put my hand under her clothes, as so many passengers were continually perambulating the deck, but being no novice, I was able to give her some satisfaction, and when she lay back with closed eyes, compressed lips, and an upheaving of the body, combined with unsuccessfully suppressed sighs, I knew she had had some satisfaction, but I had none.

However, the next morning about noon, when we were sitting on deck together, I told her that her pocket should be like, 'the widow's cruse,' and to it there should be no bottom.

She looked at me for a minute with a twinkle in her eye and said, 'Well, now, after lunch to-day I shall think of what you have said, and see if I can make out what you mean.'

I did not see her again until dinner-time, and after dinner we settled down on our chairs in the shade with our rugs over us.

After a few idle remarks I said, 'I shall now proceed to pick your pocket,' and after a little chaff and hesitation on her part, she let me find the pocket, and I quickly found she had taken my hint, and made a way through her petticoats by which I could, without observation of passers-by, put my hands on her bare thighs, and need I say more?

I was delighted at this discovery, and while drawing my hand just to moisten my fingers, I whispered to her, 'Now, be a good girl, and let us have all the pleasure that can be got under these difficult circumstances.'

'You are a dear boy,' said she, and laying a little more on her back, she opened her thighs, and I was able to get my hand conveniently on her warm spot, and a warm spot it was, for though she had not yet spent, there was the warm dew on it which always foretells a randy woman.

My finger was quickly on the opening, and then running it upwards I had no difficulty in finding the clitoris, and that hard firm cord which with her was very well developed, and felt more like a cable than the thin whip-cord size that most women boast of.

How I toyed with it, and how it delighted me to feel it now hard, now soft, now disappearing, now thicker than ever, my fingers roaming along it, now across it, and she with closed eyes, her fingers clutching the basket work of the chair, her feet outstretched, her hips heaving, and with difficulty suppressing her sighs, would at last with a few short convulsive struggles proclaim to me my victory and her defeat, by a warm flow.

As she lay heavily back in the chair in a sort of stupor, I could tell her pleasure had indeed been acute.

Before we parted for the night, and when most of the passengers had gone below, she would turn on her side, steal her hand under my rug, and clasp that staff she would have loved to bury elsewhere.

All women's hands are soft, but hers were the softest I ever knew, and her touch most electrifying. She knew so well how to tantalizingly bring on that feeling that I felt as though its poor head must burst, and then without its doing so, the sensation pleasantly died away; the palm of her hand as it pressed the already overheated point felt like that indescribable grip that alone can be given by a truly well-formed pussy.

If darkness favoured us our lips were glued together, and after a sharp struggle the end came, alas only too soon, and with a faint goodnight we struggled below to our berths.

About this time an amusing incident took place on board. A Mrs. A had accidentally left her sponge in the ladies' bathroom, and about twelve o'clock one morning she hastened to the bath room to get it for fear one of the stewards would appropriate it, but no sooner had she pushed open the door than a sight met her eyes that made her hastily and quickly close it, and pale and breathless with excitement, she rushed upstairs to tell the other ladies what she had seen, and these were her words.

'Why, when I opened the bathroom door I saw on the floor a pair of electrified pink silk stockings, and a strange bottom in convulsions.'

Need I tell you the ladies hurried down and concealed themselves to see who the owners of these articles might be, and enjoyed as only women would, the discomforted appearance of one of the poor little brides and her husband, and as the poor little thing ever afterwards went by the name of the 'red-legged partridge', and was well chaffed, I hope it will be a lesson to her through life to lock the door herself in future.

My dear friend, Mrs. Jenkins, had struck up the greatest friendship with Mrs. M who had even confided to her how I must have overheard her and her husband at Malta, but Mrs. J told her she knew I could be trusted, and never to think of it again, so I was once more in Mrs. M's good graces.

The old lady, Mrs. Stuart was greatly in the way of these two friends, and Mrs. J, who slept in the adjoining berth to Mrs. M used to excite me by her accounts of Mrs. M's lewdness, and how the young bride never missed a morning without tossing herself off, which she could plainly see by the heaving of the clothes, and short quick breathing; but one morning Mrs. Stuart took it into her head to go first to the bathroom, and by her movements in the cabin had temporarily stopped Mrs. M's selfish game.

Dear Mrs. Jenkins, unable to resist it, jumped out of bed as Mrs. Stuart shut the door, bolted it, and rushing to Mrs. M who was lying on her back with a flushed face, with only a sheet over her, as the weather was very warm said, 'You little darling, I can stand it no longer, I will be your husband,' and taking no refusal, nor waiting for one, she leapt into bed, and laying on her, made her clasp her feet round her back, and the tender spots meeting, with very little rubbing the already heated Mrs. M was soon in a pleasant faint. But this was not enough for Mrs. J who was a real artiste, and having tired of the true lovers' kisses, with which she had nearly choked Mrs. M she rapidly transferred them to that still warm corner, and after a fierce encounter, in which Mrs. M. struggled as it were for life, she expired with deep sighs, and then had to beg Mrs J to desist, and only in time, for Mrs Stuart shortly after appeared.

But Mrs. J confided to me, that in all her experience of women, she had never come across one with so very large a clitoris, and that the cord when inflamed was fully the size of many men's pegoes, making it one of the easiest and most delightful to kiss. How I longed for an opportunity.

In a few days we arrived at Port Said, where Mrs. Stuart left us, and now these two friends had the cabin to themselves.

One afternoon Mrs. J confided to me that she had arranged to leave Mrs. M and her husband in undisputed possession of the cabin every afternoon, but that of course it was a profound secret, and Captain M would have to go in and out without discovery.

'Why should not you and I have the cabin to ourselves sometimes,' said I.

'Oh! it would never do, suppose you were seen entering, how dreadful!'

'But why not at night?' said I.

'Tell Mrs. M to sleep very sound, and that I will promise never to disturb her slumbers, and all will be well.'

'This is an idea,' said Mrs. J 'but I am sure it is impossible.' However to make a long story short, it had only to be hinted to Mrs. M and she jumped at the idea, and so delighted was she at the thought of being so close to Mrs. J when a man was really having her, and perhaps in the dull light to be able even to distinguish the forms, that she made Mrs. J arrange for my visit that very night.

About midnight I crept into the cabin, and it having been carefully explained where to find Mrs. J's berth, I was soon alongside her, and noticed that Mrs. M's pillows were at the foot of Mrs. J's berth, however, what cared I.

On lifting the sheet and finding myself at last in bed with Mrs. J who had only a thin nightdress on, my feelings were indescribable.

How I choked her with kisses, played with her firms breasts, and finally with a few lover's bites on her plump thighs, I made her open her legs, and the kiss that I gave her caused such a sigh to escape that it made Mrs. M move in her bed.

Need I describe her wild struggles, how she ground her teeth, and clenched her hands; but I was no novice, and with a lovely woman I was not likely to let her off very easily, but at last that strong cord showed signs of softening, so I gave her a little rest preparatory to her undergoing another ordeal.

While we rested she gave me a nudge, and drew my attention to poor Mrs. M who I could see was sadly in want of a bedfellow, and was doing the best she could to make up for one, and Mrs. J whispered to me, she will never be able to get through the night, you have no idea what a hot woman she is.

However, I was not going to let Mrs. J off so easily the first night, as I told her, and being able to wait no longer, I laid her across the berth, and putting one of her pretty feet on each of my shoulders as I stood on the floor, I was soon into her, and found her to be one of the most perfectly made women, and a perfect artiste at that internal and most fetching of nipping that comes natural to some, and if not natural can never be acquired.

With the previous excitement I was not long coming to the point, but sea-air, little exercise, and the good living on board, was all in my favour, and without drawing I was able to wait till the new erection was almost stiffer than the last.

I now played the royal game of push-pin in real earnest, and she joined me heart and soul. Fearing I might come before her, she stole down her hand and with her finger was actively whittling her strong cord, so between us she was soon heaving, sighing and struggling, but though she flooded me I had not yet joined her, and now she saw her mistake, and took her hand away leaving me to do the work alone. I drove it home in her to her very vitals, and soon she flooded me once more, so much so that I had to draw and wipe my weapon so that he might have a better grip, and now we really fought tooth and nail for the end; she quite lost her head, bit and scratched in her excitement, and I was more like a brute beast in the roughness I used to prevent her in her struggles from dislodging me. After a desperate finish nature came to our assistance, and simultaneously we lay helpless on the bed.

We were at last brought to our senses by a long drawn sigh,

and kind-hearted Mrs. J said, 'Oh! how selfish of me to forget that poor girl, this night will kill her.'

With that she slipped out of bed, telling me to lay quiet, and with a little whispering soon got under Mrs. M's sheet, but I knew Mrs. J was not now good for much, so was not surprised when I heard her say, 'Charlie, you may come and kiss us if you like, but, mind, nothing else.'

I was quickly with them, and it was then for the first time I felt the swollen cord that had startled Mrs. J. It was quite as large as many pegoes, very firm, and longer than anything I ever knew; in fact I felt for its end, fearing it might be a man in disguise, but I quickly found it was not, and so after some gentle kisses and soft strokings, which made the little woman move, I seized the firm cord between my lips, and between mumbling it, biting it, and soft caresses, she soon came to a climax, and this extraordinary woman now again surprised me by sending her first tribute of love from her with the force of a man.

At her desire, I, nothing loath, continued my kisses, but at last she said to Mrs. J.

'Oh! darling Nina, do let him finish properly, I cannot go on like this.'

'Yes, do,' said Mrs. J to me, and while Mrs. J continued toying with poor M's breasts, I drove my staff home, and it had now been erect so long it seemed quite numbed, and without any feeling, which bode ill for poor Mrs. M who I now knew was in for a long bout, but she bore up well, in fact was a perfect glutton, and though I kept her spending at frequent intervals, I was at last able to reward her with a plenteous tribute of love, after a violent and noisy encounter, during which Mrs. Jenkins kept telling us we would wake all the crew, but it was of no use, we were wound up, and for days I carried the marks of the bites and scratches I received, and I fear in turn left some ugly bruises.

As we at last lay exhausted, Mrs. J said, 'Well, I did think you two would never have enough of it.'

I stole back to my cabin, but before the voyage was over we had many pleasant nights, and Mrs. J who was not looking forward to meeting her old husband at Bombay, as he was such an old fumbler, confided to me her great ambition was to have one other child, and she was sure her husband never could get one.

However, a short time after landing, I got a letter from her to say the old fumbler was as proud as a peacock, but you naughty boy, I am sure I ought to have told you that I did not want twins.

Extract from

THE NEW EPICUREAN*

GENTLE READER,

Before transcribing my correspondence with my fair friends, it is necessary to describe the scene of the amours alluded to in the letters, and also to say a few words regarding the chief actor, myself.

I am a man who, having passed the Rubicon of youth, has arrived at that age when the passions require a more stimulating diet than is to be found in the arms of every painted courtezan.

That I might the better carry out my philosophical design of pleasure without riot, and refined voluptuous enjoyment without alloy, and with safety, I became the purchaser of a suburban villa situate in extensive grounds, embosomed in lofty trees, and surrounded with high walls. This villa I altered to suit my taste, and had it so contrived, that all the windows faced towards the road, except the French ones, which opened on the lawn from a charming room, to which I had ingress from the grounds at the back, and which was quite cut off from the rest of the house. To render these grounds more private, high walls extended like wings from either side of the house and joined the outer walls. I thus secured an area of some five acres of woodland which was

---

*The full title of this publication was *The New Epicurean, or The Delights of Sex facetiously and philosophically considered in graphic letters addressed to Young Ladies of Quality.*

not overlooked from any quarter, and where everything that took place would be a secret unknown to the servants in the villa.

The grounds I had laid out in the true English style, with umbrageous walks, alcoves, grottoes, fountains, and every adjunct that could add to their rustic beauty. In the open space, facing the secret apartment before alluded to, was spread out a fine lawn embossed with beds of the choicest flowers, and in the centre, from a bouquet of maiden's blush roses, appeared a statue of Venus, in white marble. At the end of every shady valley was a terminal figure of the god of gardens in his various forms; either bearded like the antique head of the Indian Bacchus; or soft and feminine, as we see the lovely Antinous; or Hermaphroditic – the form of a lovely girl, with puerile attributes. In the fountains swam gold and silver fish, whilst rare crystals and spars glittered amidst mother o'pearl at the bottom of the basins.

The gardeners who kept this happy valley in order were only admitted on Mondays and Tuesdays, which days were devoted by me entirely to study; the remaining five being sacred to Venus and love.

This garden had three massive doors in its walls, each fitted with a small lock made for the purpose, and all opened with a gold key, which never left my watch guard.

Such were the external arrangements of my Caproe. Now, with a few words on the internal economy of my private *salle d'amour*, and I have done.

This apartment, which was large and lofty, was in its fittings and furniture entirely *en Louis Quinze*, that is to say, in the latest French mode; the walls were panelled, and painted in pale French grey, white and gold, and were rendered less formal by being hung with exquisite paintings by Watteau. Cabinets of buhl and marqueterie lined the sides, each filled with erotic works by the best authors, illustrated with exquisite and exciting prints, and charmingly bound. The couches and chairs were of ormolu, covered *en suite* with grey satin, and stuffed with down. The legs of the tables were also gilt, the tops were slabs of marble, which, when not in use for the delicious collations (which were from time to time served up, through a trap door in the floor) were covered with rich tapestries. The window curtains were of grey silk, and Venetian blinds, painted a pale rose colour, cast a voluptuous shade over the room.

The chimney piece was of marble; large, lofty, and covered

with sculpture in relief, representing beautiful naked children of both sexes, in every wanton attitude, entwined with grapes and flowers, carved by the hand of a master. The sides and hearth of this elegant fireplace were encrusted with porcelain tiles of rare beauty, representing the Triumph of Venus, and silver dogs were placed on either side to support the wood, according to the style in vogue in the middle of the last century.

To complete the *coup d'oeil*, my embroidered suit of garnet velvet, plumed hat, and diamond hilted sword were carelessly flung upon a chair, while the cabinets and sideboards were covered with costly snuff boxes and China. Such were some of the striking features of this delightful chamber. As for the rest of the house, it was furnished like any other, respectable domicile of our times.

My establishment consisted of a discreet old housekeeper, who was well paid, and not too sharply looked after in the little matters of perquisites and peculations; a bouncing blooming cook, and a sprightly trim housemaid; who were kept in good humour by an occasional half guinea, a holiday, and a chuck under the chin. Beyond these innocent liberties they were not molested. As for the gardeners, they lived out of the house, and being as well paid for their two days' work as if they worked all the week, it followed that they knew their own interest too well to manifest any undue or indiscreet curiosity as to what passed in the grounds, when their services were not required.

Having thus given a sketch of the premises, I proceed at once with the letters, only expressing a hope that you, most courteous reader, will quietly lay down the book, if it is too strong for your stomach, instead of falling foul of.

Your humble servant

THE AUTHOR.

TO LESBIA

You ask me, most charming Lesbia, to relieve the ennui which your too venerable and too watchful lord causes you to suffer, with his officious attentions, by a recital of some of those scenes which are not visible to the uninitiated; and I, having always been your slave, hasten to obey.

You must know then, *chère petite*, that I have certain convenient ladies in my pay, whom I call pointers, forasmuch as they put up the game.

Last Thursday, as I lay stretched on a sofa, absorbed in that most charming of Diderot's works 'La Religieuse', the silver bell which communicates with the southern gate, gave tongue, and roused me from my lethargy. I sprang to my feet, and wending my way through that avenue of chestnut trees, which you and I, Lesbia, know so well, made direct for the gate. Here the well-known chariot met my eye, and it only required a glance at the smart coachman to show me that jehu was none other than Madame R . . . herself; and a devilish handsome groom she made, I can assure you.

An almost imperceptible raising of the eyebrows, and a gesture with her whip handle towards the interior of the carriage, told me all I wanted to know; so first looking up and down the road, to see that we were not observed, I whispered 'ten o'clock' and then opened the door. 'Come my little darlings', said I, to two delicious young creatures, who coquettishly dressed, with the most charming little hats in the world, and full petticoats that barely reached their rose-coloured garters, sprang, nothing loth, into my arms. The next minute we were all three standing in the garden, the door was locked, and the chariot drove off. The elder of my little pets was a blooming blonde, with soft brown hair, that shone like gold, melting eyes of the loveliest blue, and cheeks tinted with the softest blush of the rose. A pert little nose slightly retroussé, carmine lips, and teeth like pearls, completed a most delicious face. She was, she said, just sixteen years old. Her companion, a sparkling brunette, with dark eyes, raven hair, and a colour that vied with the damask rose, was about fifteen. They were charming children, and when I tell you that their limbs were moulded in the most perfect symmetry, and that their manners were cultivated, elegant, and gay, I think you will agree with me that Madame R . . . had catered well.

'Now my little loves,' said I, giving each a kiss, 'what shall we do first; are you hungry, will you eat?'

This proposal seemed to give great satisfaction, so taking each by the hand I led them to my room; and patties, strawberries and cream, apricots, and champagne disappeared with incredible rapidity. While they were eating, I was exploring; now patting the firm dimpled peach-like bottom of the pretty brunette, now inserting a finger into the pouting hairless cleft of the lovely blonde. The latter was called Blanche and the former Cerise. I was beside myself with rapture, and turning first to one and then to the other, covered them with kisses. The collation finished at last, we all went into the grounds, and having walked them round and shown them everything curious, not forgetting the statue of that most impudent god Priapus, at whose grotesque appearance, with his great prick sticking out, they laughed heartily, I proposed to give them a swing. Of course in putting them in, I took care that their lovely little posteriors should bulge out beyond the velvet seat, and as their clothes were short, every time they swung high in the air, I had a full expansive view of those white globes, and the tempting rose colored slits that pouted between them; then, oh! the dear little feet, the fucktious shoes, the racy delectable legs; nothing could be finer. But the sight was too tantalizing. We were all heated; I with the exertion of swinging them, they with the wine, so they readily agreed to my proposal to proceed to a retired spot, where was a little lake lined with marble, not more than four feet deep. We were soon naked, and sporting in the water; then only was it that I could take in all their loveliness at a glance. The budding small pointed breasts, just beginning to grow; the polished ivory shoulders, the exquisite fall in the back, the tiny waist, the bulging voluptuous hips, the dimpled bottoms, blushing and fresh, the plump thighs, and smooth white bellies. In a moment my truncheon stood up hard and firm as a constable's staff. I put it in their hands, I frigged and kissed their fragrant cunnies, I gamahuched them, and then the saucy Cerise taking my ruby tipped ferrule in her little rosy mouth, began rolling her tongue round it in such a way, that I nearly fainted with bliss. At that moment our position was this. I lay stretched on my back on the grass; Blanche sat over me, a leg on either side, with my tongue glued to her rose. Cerise knelt astride of me also, with her posteriors well jutted out towards me, and one of my fingers was inserted in her rosebud. Nor were the hands of the delicious brunette idle; with her right she played with my balls, and with the forefinger of her left hand she exquisitely titillated the regions beneath. But human nature could not stand this long; so changing our position I placed Blanche on her hands and knees, while Cerise inserted my arrow, covered with saliva from her mouth, into the pretty Blanche. She was tight, but not a virgin, so after a thrust or two, I fairly went in up to the hilt. All this while Cerise was tickling me, and rubbing her beautiful body against me. Soon Blanche began to spend, and to sigh out: 'Oh! oh! dear sir, give it me now! Shoot it into me! Ah! I faint! I die!' and as the warm fluid gushed into her, she fell prone on the ground.

When Blanche had a little recovered herself, we again plunged into the lake, to wash off the dew of love, with which we were drenched.

Thus sporting in the water, toying with each other, we whiled away the hot hours of the afternoon, till tired, at length, we left the lake and dressed ourselves. The sun had long disappeared behind the trees, and the shades of evening began to close in, I therefore proposed to adjourn to the villa, where for some time I amused my little friends, with bawdy books and prints. But you are not to suppose that my hands were idle, one being under the clothes of each.

Cerise had thrust her hand into my breeches, and was manipulating with great industry, which amused me very much; but I soon found out the reason, for presently she said, pouting out her pretty mouth, 'You like Blanche better than me!'

'I love you both, my angels,' said I, laughing heartily at the little puss's jealousy.

'Ah, it's all very well to laugh,' cried Cerise, 'but I don't see why I am not to be fucked as well as her!'

'Oh! I exclaimed, 'that's the way the wind blows, is it!' And drawing the sweet girl to a couch, I tossed up her clothes in a moment.

'Quick, quick, Blanche!' cried Cerise, 'come and gamàhuche the gentleman, and make his yard measure stiff before he begins, for you know how tight I am at first.'

The little Blanche flung down the book she was looking at, and running up to me, placed herself on her knees, then clasping my naked thighs with her milky arms, she seized upon the red head of my thyrsus, and worked her mouth up and down upon it, in the most luscious manner possible. In a few minutes more I could certainly have spent on her tongue, had not Cerise, fearful of being baulked, made her leave off. Then guiding the randy prick into her opening rosy little cunny, she began to bound and wriggle and twist, until she had worked it well in, then twining her legs around my loins, and thrusting her tongue in my mouth, she gave way unrestrained to the joys of sensation. I was astonished that so young a creature could be so precocious, but

I learnt from Madame R . . ., who had brought her up, that every pains had been taken to excite those passions in this girl; first with boys, and subsequently with grown-up persons. Blanche I had thought most delicious, but there was a furore in Cerise's fucking which carried you away, as it were, out of yourself.

So great was the delight I experienced with this amorous girl, that I held back as long as possible, but she bounded about with such energy, that she soon brought down another shower of dew, and all was over. I was glad to hide the diminished head of poor Pego, in my white silk breeches, and it being now nearly ten o'clock, I rang for chocolate, which soon appeared, through the trap door, served up in pretty little porcelain cups, with ratafia cakes and bonbons, to which the girls did ample justice. The bell having announced Madame R . . . at the gate, we went forth hand in hand, having first placed in their pockets a bright new guinea apiece.

Arrived at the gate, I gave her ladyship a pocket-book containing twenty pounds, with which she seemed well content.

'Adieu, my dear children,' said I. 'I hope before long you will pay me another visit.'

'Good bye, sir,' cried both the girls in a breath, and the chariot drove off.

Quite tired by this time, I locked the gate, and going round to the front of the villa, I knocked and entered, as if I had just come home, retiring soon after to bed, to dream over again of the joys of that delightful evening.

TO LAIS

I am afraid, my pretty Lais, I am in disgrace with you for not writing before, so to excuse my seeming neglect, I will now narrate to you an adventure I have lately had here, which will amuse you very much. You may remember, possibly, pretty Mrs H . . ., the wife of an old prig of a grocer, whom you met here once. Well, she came to see me the other day, when, after I had done justice to her charms, which indeed are not to be despised, sitting on my knee, and sipping some old Burgundy, for which the fine dame has a great liking, she told me the cause of her visit.

'As you are so generous,' she began, 'it always gives me great pleasure to oblige you, and throw anything in your way that is worthy the notice of such a true Epicurean. Now I have just received from the country, a niece whose father has been long dead, has now lost her mother, so the good people of the place where they lived, to get rid of the orphan have sent her up to me. This has vexed my good man not a little, as you know he loves his money dearly; not able to get a child for himself, he has no fancy to be saddled with other people's. But I quieted him with the assurance that I would get her a place in a few days. The girl is just seventeen, as beautiful and fresh as an angel, and innocent as a baby, so I thought what a nice amusement it would be for you, to have her here and enlighten and instruct her. You have I know, a little cottage fitted up as a dairy, engage her as your dairymaid, buy a cow or two, and the thing is done.'

'But,' said I, 'won't she be afraid to live in the cottage all alone, and if the gardeners should find it out, what would they think!'

'Nay, sir,' said the tempter, 'your honour knows best, but it seems to me that these difficulties can easily be got over. I know an old crone, a simple poor, humble creature, who would do anything for half-a-crown, and be delighted to live in that cottage. She alone, will be seen by the gardeners, and my niece will be kept close during the two days they work in the grounds.'

'That will do capitally,' said I, 'you arrange it all.' Accordingly, old mother Jukes and the blooming Phoebe were duly installed. Two Alderney cows occupied the cowhouse, and the new dairy maid set to work. After two or three days had passed, I went one afternoon to see her milk the cows. She jumped up from her three-legged stool in confusion, and blushing deeply, dropped me a rustic curtsey.

'Well Phoebe,' said I gently, 'what do you think of the dairy? Do you think you shall like the place?'

She dropped me another curtsey, and replied, 'Yes, an't please ye, sir'.

'You find the cottage convenient?' said I.

'Oh! la sir, mighty,' cried Phoebe.

'Very good,' said I, 'now when you have done milking, I will show you the poultry yard, and my pet animals, all of which are to be under your care.'

As soon as the fair creature had drawn off as much milk as she required, she placed her pails in the dairy, and smoothing down her white apron, attended me. First to the poultry yard, when Phoebe espied the cock treading one of the hens.

'Oh, my,' she exclaimed, 'that cruel cock, look at him,

a-pecking, and trampling upon that poor hen, that is just the way they used to go on at feyther's, but I wont let un do it.' And she ran forward to drive away the cock.

'Stop, stop, Phoebe,' I exclaimed. 'Do not drive him away, for if the cock does not tread the hen, how are we to have any chickens?'

'Sure, sir, the chickens will come from the eggs, and if he treads upon the poor hen that gate, he will break them all in her belly, other while.'

'Not at all,' said I. 'It is true pullets lay eggs, and very good are such eggs for eating, but they will never come to chickens. It is the cocks who make the chickens.'

Phoebe opened her large blue eyes very wide at this, and ejaculated, 'Mighty!'

'Don't you see, Phoebe, that while he is treading, he is also doing something else?'

'Noa, sir, I doan't,' said Phoebe, demurely.

'If you look at the hen's tail, Phoebe, you will see that it is lifted up and spread open, there; now look; and you will see the cock is putting something in the opening under her tail.'

'Oh, la, yes,' cried she, blushing as red as a peony; I see now, well I never.'

'You see, Phoebe, you have much to learn; but come to the stable, and I will show you something more extraordinary. Where, may I ask, do you suppose foals come from? And kittens, and puppies?'

'Lawk sir, from their mothers, I suppose.'

'Yes, but they would not come, without they were made; now you shall see what my little stallion pony will do, when I let him into the stall of the mare, and some months hence you shall see the foal he has made.'

To this Phoebe could only respond, 'Mighty.'

We went to the stable. The ponies were beautiful little creatures, of a fine cream colour, and pure Pegu breed, sent to me from Burma by a friend.

Like all horses of that colour, their noses, pizzle, etc., were flesh colour; and therefore at once caught the eye. Removing the bar that divided the loose box, I let the stallion pass into the other side. The little mare received him with a neigh of welcome.

'Oh, my,' cried Phoebe, 'she seems to know him quite nat'ral loike.'

The stallion began nibbling at different parts of the mare, who raised her tail, and again neighed. Her lover answered the neigh. Soon he began to scent her sexual beauties, which he caressed with his lips, his enormous yard shot out, and banged against his stifle. I pointed it out to Phoebe.

'Oh, good lud! yes, sir, I sees it!' cried she, blushing up very red, and trembling all over.

I passed my arm round her taper waist, and gently kissing her, whispered, 'Now observe what he will do.'

Presently the stallion mounted on his hind legs, embracing the mare with the fore ones, his great pizzle began to enter; the mare stood firm and did not kick. He laid his head along her back, nibbling her coat. He moved backwards and forwards. Phoebe trembled and turned red and pale by turns. The mare whinnied with delight, the stallion responded.

'See, Phoebe,' said I, 'how these lovers enjoy themselves. *Mon Dieu!* how happy they are!'

'La, sir,' cried the girl, 'what pleasure can there be in having that great long thing put into her body?'

'The pleasure,' said I, sententiously, 'which nature gives to those who propagate their kind, and some day my little Phoebe will feel the same pleasure; but look! He has finished, and is out again. See how the female parts of the mare open and shut with spasms of delight. Observe how she cocks her tail – see how she turns her head, as if asking for more. There now, she neighs again.'

But Phoebe was not listening; she had seated herself on a truss of hay, and with her eyes fixed on the again stiffening pizzle of the stallion, had fallen into a reverie. I guessed what she was thinking about, so seating myself by her side, I stole a hand up her clothes. She trembled, but did not resist. I felt her firm plump thighs, I explored higher, I touched her feather; soft and silky as a mouse's skin was the moss in which I entwined my fingers. I opened the lips, heavens! could I believe my senses. She was spending, and her shift was quite wet. Whether it was accident or not, I cannot say, but she had dropped one of her hands on my lap.

My truncheon had long been stiff as iron; this additional aggravation had such an effect, that with a start, away flew too material buttons, and Jack sprang out of his box into her hand. At this she gave a little scream, and snatching away her own hand, at the same time pushed away mine, and jumping up, began smoothing down her rumpled clothes, and with great vehemence exclaiming: Oh, la; fie, sir: doantee, doantee, Oh, I'm afeard, etc., etc.

But I was not going to lose such a chance, and began to soothe her and talk, until at length we got back to the same position again. I grew more bold, I kissed her eyes, and her bosom; I handled her lovely buttocks; I frigged her clitoris – her eyes sparkled; she seized upon that weapon which had at first so frightened her, and the next minute I had flung her back on the hay, and was frigging away at her maidenhead, but she made a terrible outcry and struggled most violently. Fortunately, Mrs Jukes had a convenient attack of deafness, and heard nothing; so that after a good deal of trouble, I found myself in possession of the fortress, up to the hilt. Once in, I knew well how to plant my touches, and ere long a soft languor pervaded all her limbs, pleasure succeeded pain. She no longer repulsed me, but sobbing on my shoulder, stopped now and then to kiss my cheek.

Her climax came at length, and then she threw all modesty aside; entwined her lovely legs around my back, twisted, wriggled, bit, pinched, and kissing me with ardour, seemed to wake up to the new life she had found.

Thrice we renewed the seraphic joys; and then and not till then, did I leave her to her poultry yard and her dairy.

She is still with me; an adept in the wiles of love; not the least jealous, but very useful to me in all the other little affairs which I have on hand. As for Mrs H . . ., I gave her fifty guineas for her niece's maidenhead; and although I have bought many much dearer, I never enjoyed it as I did with Phoebe.

So now good-night, and if you can sleep without a lover after such a recital, it is more than I can; so I shall seek the arms of this unsophisticated country lass, to allay the fires that recording this narrative has lit up in my veins.

TO SAPPHO

You complain, my sweet girl, that it is long since you heard from me, and remind me that I, of all men, am the only one who could ever give you delight. In reply to your complaint, I must assure you that had there been anything to relate which would have been likely to interest my young philosopher, I should have written, but I know too well that ordinary love affairs between men and women do not much amuse you, and that the loves of girls for each other are more to your taste. By your other remark I am much flattered; and if you can frame some excuse to your aunt for leaving home, and will come here, I think I can show you how to pass an agreeable afternoon. In the interim I will detail an adventure, which I met with the other day, and I think will vastly please your fancy.

I was strolling out in one of those thick woods which abound in this neighbourhood, when in a secluded dell, I espied two young ladies seated very lovingly together, engaged in earnest conversation. They were so absorbed in their discourse, that I found no difficulty in approaching softly to within a yard of the spot, and, concealing myself in a thicket, sat down on the turf to listen to them.

The elder of the two was a fine handsome woman of about five or six and twenty, with lustrous dark eyes, black hair, an aquiline nose, and noble figure, yet rather too masculine looking to be altogether pleasing. Her companion was a lovely girl of sixteen, a most exquisite face of a perfect oval; laughing blue eyes shaded with long black lashes, and a profusion of the most beautiful hair of a light auburn, which wantoned in the breeze in a hundred lovelocks, forming a most charming picture; her figure was exquisitely rounded in all the witchery of early girlhood, and its undulations raised certain strong desires in my heart to be better acquainted with its beauties.

I now set myself to listen to their conversation.

'I assure you,' the dark-eyed woman was saying, 'there is nothing in it; these men are the most selfish creatures in the world; and besides what pleasure, think you can they give us, that we do not have already without their aid?'

'Well, dear friend,' laughed the girl, in a sweet silvery voice, 'I am sure you talk very sensibly, but yet there must be something in the joys of love, if we are to believe the poets, who have so often made it their theme; besides, I do not mind telling you that I know a little more about the subject than you may suppose.'

'*Mon Dieu*,' ejaculated the dark beauty, who I now began to think was a Frenchwoman, especially as I had already noticed a slight foreign accent in her voice; '*Mon Dieu*,' (and she turned pale) 'how is it possible you should know anything of love at your age?'

'Shall I tell you?' replied the young girl.

'Ah! yes, yes; tell me, *ma chère*.'

'Well then, dear; you know young Mrs Leslie?'

'Certainly.'

'She was a former schoolfellow of mine; and a month or two after her honeymoon, I went on a visit to that pretty country seat of her husband's, Harpsdeen Court, in Bedfordshire. While there she not only told me all about the secret joys of matrimony, but permitted me to witness her bliss.'

'To witness it? Incredible!'

'"Tis a fact, I do assure you; shall I tell you what I saw, and how I saw it?'

'Oh yes, *ma petite*, I do not mind what you may have seen, I was only afraid one of these perfidious men had captivated your poor little heart; as it was a mere girlish frolic, it will amuse me very much to hear all about it.'

The young girl, first giving her friend a sweet kiss, which I envied, thus began:

'My friend Clara Leslie, though not strictly handsome, has a pleasing amiable face, but nature you know is full of compensations, as her husband found out to his great satisfaction. She has a shape that vied with the Venus de Medici, the most lovely figure you ever beheld. When quite a girl at school, she could show a leg that any woman might envy, but now at twenty years of age, she surpassed the finest statue I ever saw. I will not trouble you with a recapitulation of all that passed on her wedding night, and subsequently, up to my arrival at Harpsdeen, because you, my sweet friend, doubtless know all that occurs on such occasions, but will confine myself to what I saw. She proposed to me to sleep in a room adjoining theirs, divided only by a thin oaken wainscot, in which one of the knots in the wood could be taken out at pleasure, and thus command a full view of the nuptial couch. Clara told me she would place a pair of wax lights on a table near the bed, and out of regard to me, would so manage matters, that I should see all that passed between her and her handsome husband, the squire. Accordingly, we all went to bed about ten o'clock one night, and I having undressed and wrapped myself in my *robe de chambre*, placed myself on an ottoman over against the panel. Assisted by her husband, Clara was soon reduced to a state of nature, and stood naked like a beautiful Eve, with her lovely hair meandering down her alabaster back and shoulders.'

'"Charles, dear," said my sweet friend, "do you lie on the foot of the bed, and let me mount you, a la St. George, you call it, I believe. I do so love that position."

'He kissed her tenderly, and being now himself naked, flung himself back on the foot of the bed.

'Then, dearest Maria, I saw, for the first time, that wondrous ivory staff, with its ruby crested head, rising from a nest of glossy black curls. Having waited a moment to give me an opportunity of seeing it, she pressed her face in his lap, and took the head of his noble toy in her mouth, then after moistening it for a few seconds, she mounted astride him, displaying to my delighted gaze, her large beautiful dimpled bottom, and lily-white thighs, between which I could clearly discern the mark of her sex; then grasping his wand in her little hand, she guided it in, and immediately began to move up and down a la postillion.

'He clasped those white hemispheres with his hands, he squeezed them together, he held them open, he thrust his finger into the nether rosebud, he kissed her breasts, while mutual sighs of delight escaped the fond pair. As for me, I was so excited, as to be almost beside myself, and felt almost suffocated. At length, I sought relief in the schoolgirl's substitute, and used my finger for want of something better. Though this was but a poor expedient, it relieved the burning heat, and caused a flow of love's dew, which allayed the itching desire which had taken possession of me. Meantime, Clara's climax and Charlie's came simultaneously, and they lay panting in each other's arms. In a very short time, however, he was again ready for action, and making Clara kneel upon the bed, he stood behind, and again the amorous encounter was renewed. Four times in various attitudes did he repeat the play, and then putting out the candles they retired to rest.

'As for me, I could scarcely sleep at all; all night I was tossing about, trying in vain with my finger to procure myself that satisfaction which I had seen her enjoy.

'Now my dear Marie, inveigh as much as you please against love; for my part the sooner some nice young fellow takes a fancy to me, the better I shall like it.'

'My dearest child,' cried the dark beauty, 'I daresay it is very true that your friend has made a very excellent match, and is quite happy in her husband, but what I want to impress upon you is, that for one such marriage as that, there are ten wretched ones. Besides, I will, if you like, soon demonstrate to you that there is more pleasure to be derived from the love of woman for woman than any that the male can give. We are all alone here in this lovely glen; let me show you how I will make love.'

'You!' cried the young girl, 'What? Are you going then to make love to me?'

'To yourself, my pet,' hoarsely whispered the salacious woman, as her dark eyes gleamed, and her hand passed up the clothes of her companion.

'Oh; but – ' said the younger, 'this is very droll, good heaven, what are you about! Really, Marie, I am surprised at you.'

'Do not be surprised any longer then, my little angel,' cried her friend, 'give me your hand,' and she passed it up her own clothes. 'Now, I will show you how to touch that little secret part. It is not by putting the finger within, that the pleasure is to be gained, but by rubbing it at the top, just at the entrance, there it is that nature has placed a nerve called by doctors the clitoris, and it is this nerve which is the chief seat of bliss in our sex. All this while, the libidinous creature was manipulating with skill.

The colour came and went in the cheeks of her beauteous companion, who faintly sighed out, 'Ah, Marie, what are you doing? Oh, joy; oh blissful sensation! Ah, is it possible – oh – oh – ur – r – r – r,' she could no longer articulate.

The Tribade saw her chance, and waited no longer; so throwing up the clothes of the young girl, she flew upon her like a panther, and forcing her face between the thighs of her friend, gamahuched her with inconceivable frenzy. Then, not satisfied with this, she pulled up her own clothes, and straddled over the young girl, presenting her really symmetrically formed posteriors close to her face, nearly sitting down upon it, in her eagerness to feel the touch of the young girl's tongue. Nor had she to wait long, wrought up to the last pitch of lascivious ecstasy, her friend would have done anything she required, and now gamahuched her to her heart's desire.

I continued to watch these Tribades for some time, revolving in my mind how I could get possession of the young one, for whom I had conceived a most ardent longing.

Suddenly it occurred to me that, as they were strangers in the neighbourhood, it was not likely they had walked, and that possibly, on the outskirts of the wood, I should find a coach waiting for them.

Full of designs upon the pretty young creature, I left the amorous pair to their amusement, and soon reached the margin of the road. Here, ere long, I espied a coach and six, with servants in rich liveries, and approaching nearer, saw from the coronet on the door, that it belonged to some person of quality. As I came up, I accosted one of the lacqueys, and tossing him a crown, asked whose carriage it was.

'His Grace the Duke of G——'s, your honour,' said the man, touching his hat respectfully, as he glanced at my embroidered coat, sword and diamond buckles, and pocketing the crown.

'Then you are waiting, I presume, for the two ladies in the wood?' said I.

'Yes, sir,' replied the lacquey; and being a talkative, indiscreet person, he added, 'Lady Cecilia Clairville, his grace's daughter, your honour, and Madame La Conte, her governess.'

'Ah, indeed!' said I, with as indifferent a manner as I could assume, and passed on.

At a turn of the road, I again dived into the wood, and soon reached my own demesne.

'A very pretty affair, truly,' said I to myself, as I took a glass of wine. Madame La Conte, engaged by the Duke to complete the education of his daughter, takes advantage of her position to corrupt her, and by making a Tribade, renders her wretched for life; for let me tell you, Sappho, there is no more certain road to ill health, loss of beauty, pleasure, and all the zest of life, than this horrid lust for the wrong sex.

'Very well, Madame La Conte,' I soliloquised, 'I shall turn this discovery to account, you may depend,' and with that resolve I went to bed.

Next morning I sent a billet in French, by a trusty messenger, to his grace's mansion in Cavendish Square. It was as follows:

'Madame, to all that passed between you and the Lady Cecilia in the wood yesterday, I was a witness. I am a man of position, and if you do not wish me to call upon the Duke, and acquaint him with your nefarious proceedings, you will come tomorrow afternoon, at three o'clock, to the big oak at the east end of the same wood, in a hackney coach, which you will alight from at the west side. To avoid discovery, you had better both be masked.

Yours, as you behave yourself,

ARGUS.'

Punctual to the appointment I had made, I placed myself beneath the shade of the oak, and as there was no saying what might happen, or what ambush this devil of a Frenchwoman might lay for me, I, besides my sword, put in my pocket a brace of loaded pistols. Soon the fair creatures approached, hand in hand. I raised my hat to the young girl, but as for madame, I merely honoured her with a contemptuous stare.

'Do not be alarmed, Lady Cecilia,' said I; 'you are with a man of honour, who will do you no harm. As for you, madame, you may make a friend or an enemy of me, which you will.'

'Really, monsieur,' said the governess, 'your conduct in this affair is so singular, that I know not what to think; but let me tell you, sir, that if you have any improper designs in inveigling us to this place, I shall know how to be avenged.'

'Doubtless, doubtless, madame, I know the French well, and have well prepared for all contingencies. But allow me, ladies, to offer each an arm, and do me the honour to walk a little further into the wood.'

The alacrity with which the wily Frenchwoman complied, told me at once what I had to expect.

She had resolved to assassinate me. Having made up my mind how I should act, I allowed her to lead me which way she pleased, keeping, however, a sharp look out on all sides, as we strolled along. I was about to enter upon the subject of their coming, when suddenly, three masked highwaymen sprang out, and demanding: 'Your money or your life,' levelled their horse-pistols at us. The ladies screamed; I shook them both off, and as one of the scoundrels sent a bullet through my wig, I drew my pistols from my pocket, and shot him dead; his companions then both fired, one of the bullets grazed my shoulder, but the other, curious enough, pierced the head of Madame La Conte, who, casting a glance full of fury upon me and clenching her hands, fell back a corpse.

The remaining rascals turned to flee; but before they could escape, I brought down a second, and attacking the third with my sword, soon passed it through his lungs.

The enemy being now utterly defeated, I turned towards the lovely Lady Cecilia, who had fainted; and raising her light form in my arms, bore her off to the spot where the coach had been left. But it was gone. The jarvey, doubtless hearing the firing, and anxious to save his skin, had driven away. My resolution was taken in a moment. So carrying my fair burthen to the nearest gate that opened into my grounds, I bore her to my secret chamber, and having fetched old Jukes and Phoebe to her assistance, with strict orders not to tell her where she was, but to pay her all needful attention, I saddled a swift horse, and rode off to the nearest town, one of the magistrates there being an old friend.

He was much pleased to see me, but wondered at my being covered with dust, and at my sudden arrival. I told him a most dreadful affair had happened; that returning home, I heard cries for assistance in the wood, and found three ruffians robbing and ill-using some ladies, that they had fired at and wounded me, and killed one of the ladies; as for the other she escaped.

That in the end, I had succeeded in dispatching the rascals, more in consequences of their want of skill in the use of their weapons, than from any extraordinary valour on my part, and finally requesting him to give orders to have the bodies removed with a view to a coroner's inquest. All which he promised to do; and in spite of his earnest request that I should stay and drink a bottle of wine, I made my excuses, and returned home.

I found my fair guest much better, and having consoled her as well as I could for the loss of Madame La Conte, I then gradually unfolded to her all the wickedness of that vile woman, and after delicately touching upon the scene in the wood the day before, I told her I had been a witness of it all and heard all the conversation.

At this denouement, Lady Cecilia covered her face with her hands to hide her blushes; and when I enquired whether Madame La Conte had shown her my letter, she said she knew madame had received a letter, which was very unpleasant, which she tore up and burnt in a great rage, but as to its contents she was ignorant.

This was very satisfactory news for me, as my handwriting might have been recognized. So turning to the young girl with a cheerful countenance, said, laughing, 'Well, my dear young friend, all is well that ends well; now let us make our plans for the future. In the first place, it seems to me that you are formed for the joys of love. It is true I am not quite so young a lover as you might desire; but I am more fit for amorous combats than many younger men. I am rich, and though not absolutely a man of rank, I am a scion of a noble house. What do you say? I know your secret. I have already seen all your charms; shall we make a match to it? Will you marry me?'

'Indeed, sir,' said the dear girl, 'your gallantry in attacking those ruffians, and defending my honour, would alone have been sufficient to win my heart; but as my father, the Duke, has designs of wedding me to a man older than himself, an old creature, whom I detest, I deem this meeting with you a most fortunate one, and will accept your offer with the same ingenuous frankness with which you have made it. You say, truly, that you have already viewed my person with pleasure; take it, dear sir, and do what you please with me. I am yours for ever.'

I was quite enraptured with this decision, and it being determined that the duke should be written to in the morning, and informed that his daughter, entertaining an insuperable objection to the match he had in store for her, had eloped with the man of her choice.

This affair settled, and Phoebe, with many sly glances, having made up a bed on one of the sofas, I shut the windows, and hastened to undress my future bride. She was exquisitely formed, with the most lovely breasts in the world; and as for her bottom and thighs, nothing could be finer.

We were soon in bed, and all that her finger and the wanton tongue of madame had left of her maidenhead, I soon possessed myself of. Dawn found us still in dalliance; but at length, being both quite fatigued, with a last sweet kiss, we fell asleep. The next day we were to be privately married by licence.

So now, my dear Sappho, I must conclude this long letter, by saying to you, 'Do thou go and do likewise.'

TO JULIA

Your letter, giving me an account of your adventure with the Marquis at Ranelagh Gardens, diverted me vastly. Meantime I have not been idle.

Since you were last here, I have colonised one corner of my grounds. A discreet old creature called Jukes, has been placed in charge of that pretty cottage covered with roses and jasmine, which you admired so much; and in the dairy she is assisted by the freshest and most charming of country girls. Positively you must come and pay me a visit, if only for the pleasure you will experience in the sight of Phoebe's perfections; but this is a digression, and I know you hate digressions, therefore to proceed.

Phoebe and I, you must know, quite understood each other, but she is so pretty, brisk, loving and lively, and time, place and opportunity so frequently present themselves, that I have nearly killed myself with the luscious fatigue, and having fucked her in every imaginable attitude, having gamahuched her, and been gamahuched in return, I at length cloyed, and began to look out for some new stimulant, but alas, Madame R ... did not call, I saw nothing of Mrs H ... To write to them was not in accordance with my usual prudence. What was to be done? I was in despair. At this juncture, that dear old Jukes came to my aid, though very innocently, as I believe. With many curtseys and hope 'your honour's worship won't be offended at my making so bold' etc., she told me that she would be greatly beholden if I would allow her to have a little orphan grandchild of hers, to live with her and Phoebe in the cottage.

She told me that her little girl was a sweet pretty creature, fifteen years of age, and she thought I might like to have her.

I at once consented, and in a few days arrived one of the sweetest flowers that ever blushed unseen in the woods of Hampshire. I was charmed, and lost no time in providing suitable clothes for the little pet, and, with the aid of Phoebe, her frocks were so contrived that they only reached her knees. This, you will readily understand, was for the purpose of giving me facilities for seeing her young beauties, without doing anything that might alarm her young innocence. We soon became great friends, and she took at once to Phoebe, the swing, the gold fish, strawberries and cream, the rambles in the woods, and above all her handsome new clothes, combined to render little Chloe as happy as a princess; while her old granddam would follow her about exclaiming, 'Lawk-a-mercy! well I never!' and so on.

In the course of a few days, our young rustic had quite rubbed off her first shyness, would run in and out of my room, sit on my knee, hide my snuff box, kiss me of her own accord, and play all sorts of innocent tricks, like other children, in swinging, climbing up trees, and tumbling about on the grass; the little puss not merely showing her legs, but everything else besides.

At first Mrs. Jukes tried to stop it, and told her it was rude to behave so before the gentleman, but I begged she would take no notice in future, as I did not mind it, and liked to see the little girl unrestrained and happy.

Now old Jukes always went to bed at sunset. I therefore

arranged with Phoebe, that after the old crone was gone to rest, she should wash Chloe all over every night before putting her to bed, and that it might be done properly, I used to go and witness the operation, for it gave me a pleasurable sensation to see the girl naked when Phoebe was present.

Phoebe was a clever girl, and did not require much telling, so that none of the most secret charms of my little Venus were concealed from my lascivious gaze.

At one moment Phoebe would lay Chloe across her lap, giving me a full view of her little dimpled bum, holding open those white globes, and exposing everything beneath. Then she would lay the girl on her back, and spread out her thighs as if to dry them with the towel. In fact she put her into almost every wanton attitude, into which she had seen me place herself. The little innocent girl meanwhile, seemed to think this washing process capital fun, and would run and skip naked about the room, in the exuberance of her animal spirits.

In this amusement I found all the excitement I desired, and should perhaps have been content with viewing her beauties, without attacking her innocence, but for a circumstance that occurred.

One evening, after the usual performance of washing, skipping about, etc, the little saucebox came and jumped on my knees, putting a leg on either side of them, and began courting a romp. Had I been a saint, whereas you know I am but a sinner, I could not have resisted such an attack on my virtue as this.

Only imagine, my dear Julia, this graceful lovely creature in all the bloom of girlhood, stark naked, except her stockings, her beautiful brown hair flowing over her exquisite shoulders, imagine her position, and how near she had placed herself to the fire and then, say, can you blame me?

In fine, I slid my hand down, and released that poor stiff prisoner, who for the last half hour had nearly burst open his prison; as a natural consequence he slid along between her thighs, and his crested head appeared (as I could see by the reflection in an old mirror) impudently showing his face, between her buttocks on the rear side. She would perhaps have noticed it, were it not that my finger had long been busy in her little slit already 'tickling' she called it, and laughed heartily, tickling me under the arms in return.

Suddenly, as if a thought struck her, she said,

'Do you know that, – '

She paused. Never did man wait with more exemplary patience.
'That – that – '
Another pause.
'That I saw – '
Pause again.
'The cock – '
Here Phoebe tried to stop her; but she squeezed her interrupter's
two cheeks, so that she could not speak, and hurriedly concluded.
'Making chickens – there.'
This was too much for my gravity, and I was convulsed with
laughter; when I had a little recovered, I asked, 'And how does
the cock do that, my dear?'
'Why,' said Chloe, with the most artless manner in the world, 'he
tickles the hen, and when she lays eggs they come to chickens.'
'Tickles her! I do not understand,' said I.
'But he does,' insisted the little girl.
'But the cock has no fingers; how can he tickle?'
'Why,' cried Chloe triumphantly, 'he has got a finger, and a
long one too, and I saw it shoot from under his tail, when
he was treading the hen, and he tickled her, just as you are
tickling me now, but putting it right into her body. Now, am
I not right in saying the cock makes chickens, by tickling the
hen?'
'Well reasoned, my little logician,' cried I, really pleased with
her wit, 'I see though you have lived in the country, you are no
fool, and I will tell you something, which girls are always very
curious about, but which their mothers and grannies will never
tell them anything of. But first tell me, why you thought the cock
tickling the hen, made the chickens?'
'Why, because Phoebe told me, to be sure.'
'Oh, ho!' said I, laughing, 'you told her, Phoebe, did you?'
Poor Phoebe looked frightened out of her wits.
'I hope you will forgive me, sir, but Chloe did worrit so, and
keep all on about that ere beast of a cock, that at last I up and
told her.'
'God bless you, my dear girl. What if you did? There is no harm
in that, I hope. There can never be anything wrong in what is
natural.'
Then turning to Chloe, whose little cunny I had not let go of
all this while, 'Would you like to know, my dear, where the
babies come from, and how they are made?'

'Oh, yes; that I just should,' exclaimed Chloe, hugging and kissing me.

'Very well; now you know, I suppose, that you are not made exactly like a little boy, do you not?'

'Yes, I know that down here, you mean,' and she pointed to where my finger was still tickling.

'Just so. But did you ever, by chance, happen to see a man?'

'Never.'

'And you would like to?'

'Of all things.'

'There then!' cried I, lifting her up and allowing the rampant yard to spring up against my belly.

'Oh, the funny thing!' said Chloe, then taking hold of it, 'how hot it is. That is what I have felt against my bottom, these last ten minutes, and could not think what it was; but what has that to do with making babies?'

'I will show you,' said I, 'but I cannot promise you that I shall make one, as I am too old for that, but it is by doing what I am going to do to Phoebe, that children are begotten.'

'Oh, I see!' cried the little girl, clapping her hands, 'you are going to serve Phoebe, as I saw the stallion serve the mare to-day. That will be capital fun.'

'Serve the mare,' I ejaculated, glancing over my shoulder at Phoebe, 'how's this?'

'Well, the truth is, sir,' said the conscious girl, 'ever since your honour showed me that trick, I have often gone to see them do it, and I was watching them today, when this little scapegrace came running into the stable. So I was obliged to tell her all about it, as I did about the chickens.'

'Well,' said I,' if she has seen that, I see no harm in her seeing the other, so pull up your clothes, my dearest creature.'

In a moment Phoebe had tucked up her petticoats, and kneeling on the truckle bed, and jutting her white posteriors well out, presented a full view of all her charms.

'Oh, my,' cried Chloe, 'why Phoebe, you have got hair growing on your – '

She stopped, and with a charming blush, hid her face in my bosom.

'And so will you have, my little maid,' I whispered, 'when you are as old as she is; but now observe what I am going to do, and mind you tickle me underneath, all the while.'

This she did in the most delightful manner, occasionally laughing to see Phoebe wriggling about. As soon as all was over, I sent Phoebe to my room for some refreshments and wine, and while she was gone, I gamahuched the lovely little Chloe, which operation, coming, as it did, after all the frigging she had undergone, roused at once her dormant passions into precocious energy. With eagerness, she seized my again erect wand, and putting it into her little mouth, worked it up and down, so that, just as Phoebe returned, I sent a spurting shower over her tongue, while her virgin dew drenched my own.

'Oh, my! how salt it is,' sputtered the little girl, spitting, and making a wry face.

'And is it that stuff, sir, that makes the babies?'

'One drop of it, my dear, is sufficient to make a little girl, as pretty as you.'

'Or a little boy?'

'Yes; or a little boy.'

After supper, Chloe, who said she was not at all sleepy, wanted Phoebe and me to perform again, but I told her that was quite enough for one night, and that she was on no account to say anything of what she had seen to her granddam.

Now I think, my dear Julia will say, I have related a most interesting adventure; but really, I wish you would come and stay a few days, and share in our sports. I shall confidently expect to see you before long.

THE WHORE'S CATECHISM*

Question. – What is a Whore?

Answer. – A girl who, having laid modesty entirely aside, no longer blushes at yielding herself to the promiscuous gratification of sensual pleasures with the opposite sex.

Q. – What are the most requisite qualities for a whore to possess?

A. – Impudence, complaisance, and metamorphosis.

Q. – What do you mean by impudence?

A. – I mean that a girl who gives herself up to libidinous commerce should be ashamed of nothing. All parts of her body are to be exposed to the men with as little ceremony as she would expose them to herself, viz., her breasts, her cunt, and her backside, are to be thought no more of when with a strange man whom she has to amuse, than a modest woman of the palm of her hand, which she does not blush to expose.

Q. – What do you mean by complaisance in a whore?

A. – It is an allurement by which she artfully retains the most casual customers. Assuming the air of thorough good nature, she yields herself cheerfully to the various whims, desires, leches, and caprices of men, by which means she retains them as in a net, and obliges them, in spite of themselves, to return another time to the object who has so well gratified a momentary passion.

*The Whore's Catechism from *The Voluptuous Night*.

Q. – What do you mean by metamorphosis?

A. – I mean that a perfect whore should, like the fabled Proteus of old, be able to assume every form, and to vary the attitudes of pleasures according to the times, circumstances, and temperaments. A thorough-bred whore has made her particular study for the various methods of giving pleasure to men for there is a difference between amusing a man of a cold constitution and a man of a warm one – between exciting a vigorous youth and a worn-out debauche. Nature, more impressed with the one, requires only to be relieved in the regular way; and, more moderate with the other, requires different degrees of titillation, situations more voluptuous, coaxings and frictions more piquant and more lewd. The whore who only exposes her bottom to a young Ganymede, will make him discharge almost to blood, while the same action shall produce but an ordinary sensation in another. The jerks and heaves of a strong lustful woman will plunge the man of vivid temperament into a torrent of delight, while they would be death to the effeminate strokes of the decrepit old lecher.

Q. – What are the characteristics by which you discover a whore from another woman?

A. – Her dress is gay and flaunting – her manners loose and unreserved, her looks bold and lascivious – and her conversation voluptuous and enticing. By these means her trade is known. Were she to affect modesty, there are many men so timid and bashful they would be afraid to accost her, and she would lose much good practice by assuming a decorous demeanour which might be misunderstood.

Q. – But is it not possible for a whore to imitate the decency and reserve of a modest woman?

A. – Yes; and those of this class are most subtle. They allure by that means the simpletons they wish to dupe. They affect to be greatly enraged at their propositions, in order to entrap them the more securely: and how many are there caught in this snare who flatter themselves they have got something choice and safe, until they find themselves well poxed. Some whores make great profits by this kind of commerce, but it is only those who can move in a respectable style that can conveniently act this hypocritical part.

Q. – Have all women a decided penchant to become whores?

A. – Yes; all are, or desire to be whores, and it is nothing but pride or fear that restrains the greater part, and every girl who yields for the first time, is from that moment a decided whore. The smock once lifted, she is as familiarized to the game as if she had played it for ten years.

Q. – Ought a whore to give herself up to the pleasure whenever she submits to the embraces of a man?

A. – There is a medium in everything. It would be very imprudent in a whore to indulge herself in stroking to excess, as it would soon make the flesh soft and flabby; but there is a refinement in pleasure, which an accomplished whore should know how to use. A word, a gesture, a touch at the critical moment, produces in men the illusion of pleasure; and as the heart is an impenetrable abyss, the crafty courtesan often fulfils, by a fictitious enjoyment, the luxurious views of the men who content themselves with the appearance.

Q. – Ought a whore to administer as much pleasure to the man who only gives her a crown as to him who pays her liberally?

A. – It is certain that a whore ought to live by her vocation, and as the sperm which is injected into her will not serve for food, she ought to act with such a stroker as with the Father Zorobadel, and tell him –

'Nescio vos.'

'I live by my cunt, as you do by the altar.'

Nevertheless, the great art of a courtezan who would acquire a reputation, is to avoid appearing mercenary. She must study her men, and with some refuse the proffered fee. She will meet with those who will be susceptible of this delicacy, and be touched by the apparent disinterestedness shown them, imagining that she is more taken with their person than their money. The pleasure which does not appear to them to be bought, is more piquant and more thought of; and a whore is often a great gainer by this kind of artifice.

Q. – How ought a whore to conduct herself when her charms have attracted a customer?

A. – She must make him feel himself perfectly at home. The first thing a man does, when entering the lodgings of a girl, is to explore her bubbies, then her buttocks, and next her 'bush'. While he is doing this, she ought to unbutton his breeches, and play with his tool, which is most probably in a state of erection, produced by the examination of her person. Now is the time to use endearing expressions and exciting titillations, and now is also the proper period for demanding her fee, which will be the more readily given to prevent delay between the preludes and the moment of enjoyment. It will not be amiss to mention in this place the rapacious custom of many courtezans. If a gentleman offers them a crown, they will demand two. If he yields, their importunity increases, they want a ribbon or a ring, in short, they are never satisfied. This conduct, however, is very injurious to them, because the men's minds being intent on pleasure, are greatly disgusted by being so long baulked through the avarice of the women.

Q. – What are the attributes and utensils requisite for the chamber of a woman of pleasure!

A. – She ought to have some good rods hung up in sight; also in her drawers she ought to have scourges of different kinds of leather, a cat-of-ninetails made of knotted whip cord, and one with pins fastened to the thongs, together with straps, bandages, and cords, strong enough to bind a powerful man.

Q. – What are the uses of all these things?

A. – They are of very great importance in the profession of a courtezan, because many men would never visit her if she did not keep rods and know how to use them. Flagellation is one of the most powerful excitements that can be resorted to when friction and coaxing have not been able to procure an erection. Give a man twenty or thirty hard cuts on the backside with a good rod, and it will soon rouse his energies, and make him fit for action. The passion for birch discipline is not confined to persons advanced in life, you will meet with candidates for it of all ages, from eighteen to eighty. Some will only require it gently, whilst others will not be satisfied unless you wear out two rods upon them, and cause the blood to run down at their heels. They generally like to be strapped down to a couch or horse, or to have their hands tied firmly to a bed post. Courtezans in good practice have curious machines made on purpose to confine these votaries of discipline hand and foot while they receive the torture. Some copulate immediately afterward, others only wish to be tossed off by a female hand; whilst a third class obtain all the pleasure they desire during the period of fustigation. They are brought to their crisis by the intensity of the smart and the sperm flies from them spontaneously. Some are frigged by one woman while another flogs them: others like to be horsed on the back of an athletic female and discharged through the friction against her back. You will find this class of customers have more odd whims, strange fancies, and fantastical caprices than any others. Some will require to be flogged in woman's clothes; and before they undergo the operation, will call in the aid of great variety of preludes and ceremonies, without which their imagination will not be sufficiently worked upon.

Q. – Ought a courtezan to demand a double fee for the execution of so fatiguing operation?

A. – Certainly; for although she may derive a degree of pleasure in flogging a handsome backside, and may sometimes even 'spend' whilst engaged in a flagellation, yet there are *paillards* who would tire out the arm of the most vigorous woman who might herself have a passion for this kind of excitement. She ought, therefore, to be well paid for the rods she uses in this tragic-comic ceremony.

Q. – What language ought a courtezan to using during flagellation?

A. – Her conversation ought to be suited to the character and humor of the *paillard* whom she fustigates. Some like to be sworn at and assailed with the most violent and blackguard terms of abuse while their flesh is being cut to pieces. This class will often have an erection like a jackass, and the sperm will fly from them with fury whilst under the operation. Others again, whose passions and humours are more mild, are desirous that you should renew with them the innocent sports of childhood, and pretend to administer juvenile corrections, calling them naughty boys, little scoundrels, mischievous rogues, dunces, ordering them to put down their breeches, and threatening to whip them until the blood comes. These, and many other phrases of a similar nature, which a skilful courtezan knows how to use, have a wonderful effect in procuring an erection and making them discharge.

Q. – Can you give me any other information relative to this strange lech?

A. – Some men instead of being whipped themselves by a female, have a desire to be the operator. Their lech is to flog a girl who has a fine plump bottom. They like to have her hands tied to a sofa or horse, but generally prefer having her legs left at liberty, as her kicking, wriggling and plunging, adds much to their amusement. The quivering and reddening of her buttocks under the rod, is to them a powerful source of excitement. They sometimes discharge whilst in action, or release the girl and spend with her; others have no connection with the woman, but will be 'tossed off' by another female hand. There are, in all establishments devoted to venereal pleasures, women trained on purpose to receive severe whippings, many of whom make fortunes entirely by the hardness of their posteriors. There is also a third class of *paillards* connected with this singular lech, who neither wish to whip nor to be whipped, but are satisfied with the sight of it. These would give any money to peep through a window and see a great girl of fourteen or fifteen horsed and flogged by a schoolmistress. They often set women up in schools in order that they may witness such exhibitions.

Q. – What other attributes and utensils should adorn the chamber of a *fille de joie?*

A. – She ought to have a collection of lascivious pictures and bawdy books, illustrated with prints, some *baudruches* and two or three dildoes.

Q. – What am I to understand by *baudruches?*

A. – They are little bags or sheaths made from the blind gut of the lamb, with which a man envelopes his pego when he strokes a woman of whom he is not sure. By this means he is protected against the pox; but the precaution, thought prudent, is often displeasing to women of a lustful temperament, as it deprives them of the boiling injection. They are also used to prevent getting modest women with child, and are of great importance to married women whose husbands are abroad?

Q. – What do you mean by 'dildoes'?

A. – A dildoe is an artificial prick, intended originally for the use of those who could not get the real thing. It is of very great antiquity, being well known to the ancient Hebrews, Chaldeans, Persians, etc. The Egyptians made them of porcelain; the Greeks of wood and ivory; the Roman ladies preferred them of glass, and called them 'Phalli'. We, however, make them of india-rubber, and cause them to perform as well, if not better than the real thing. They are much used by nuns in convents, and by widows and old maids; but the use a courtezan has for them is only to gratify the caprices of her visitors. For this purpose it is necessary to have two sorts, some to use with the hand, as when a gentleman wishes to see a girl frig herself with a dildoe: and some made with stomacher and bands, for one woman to strap on in order that she might roger another woman, which gentleman often order to be performed in their presence, and pay well for seeing it.

Q. – Ought a courtezan to go with a man when she knows she is diseased?

A. – No. She ought to consider it unpardonable to communicate her corruption to one who seeks nothing but pleasure in her embraces. She ought to prefer losing her practice, but a candid avowal of her situation will often gain her the esteem of her customer, who, in such cases, will not baulk her of her fee, and will content himself with the use of her hand.

Q. – Ought a courtezan to go with a man when she has her courses?

A. – No. It is necessary to observe a strict degree of decency even in debauchery, to prevent the opposite sex being disgusted. I am aware that women are apt to be more lustful during the period of their 'menses,' but they must not let their passions overcome their prudence. Nevertheless, if a man persist in his determination to stroke a girl after she has apprised him of her situation, she ought no doubt, to profit by the violence of his desire. Men are very different in their tastes and desires. Some are very delicate and particular, others very gross and sensual, and careless of cleanliness which are necessary to tempt and provoke the appetites of the former class. Some like high-seasoned 'things', others would have them washed every hour in the day. You will occasionally meet with very strange animals among them; but you may take as a general rule, that neatness and propriety will be most universally esteemed. Cleanliness ought to be the religion of every woman, but more particularly of the courtezan whose livelihood is to administer pleasure promiscuously.

Q. – Ought a courtezan to submit to the embraces of a man who is diseased?

A. – If it is not permitted her to go with a man when she herself is contaminated, she has of course, the privilege of refusing the embrace of a man who is infected. Indeed, it is a duty every courtezan owes herself, to examine minutely the state of a man's vessel before she suffers it to enter her port. It ought to undergo the quarantine of a strict investigation. She ought to lug out his tool, shake it, rub the foreskin up and down, and squeeze the gland of the penis to see if there are any relics of disease. She ought, moreover, to cast an inquisitive eye at his shirt, in order to ascertain if there are any indications of a geographical chart on it.

Q. – May a girl avail herself off all the finesses of her sex, and whatever arts of fascination she possesses, in order to obtain as much money as possible from those who visit her?

A. – Yes. As long as no fraud is made use of, and good faith directs the temptations, she may employ the art of a syren. In doing this she is only following her vocation, and the man has nothing to complain of but his own weakness in yielding to her fascination.

Q. – To what age can a courtezan exercise her profession with honour and profit?

A. – That depends a great deal on temperament. The fair women ought to quit this trade before the dark ones, as their flesh is more subject to become flabby. A woman who has been in the seraglios until she is forty, must be very much the worse for wear, and will find it prudent to retire.

Q. – What then must a courtezan do who has grown old in the combats of Venus, without having laid anything by to support her declining years?

A. – That fault, which is almost universal with women of pleasure, is not then to be remedied. Plutus generally flies from the boudoirs which are deserted by love; and an old whore has no alternative but to be either a bawd or servant to another whore; for no longer able to make dupes, she must content herself with holding the candle, and being sometimes the patient spectatress of certain pleasures, the remembrance of which must cause the most painful regrets. Her only hope can be the chance of occasionally cajoling a gouty old codger, or a young fellow rendered stupid through drunkenness. The courtezan on the contrary, who, during the prosperity of youth, has laid by a competence, shall still have as much sensual pleasure as she can wish, even under wrinkles, and old age, for her money will procure her as many strokers as she pleases. She may often in the embraces of a robust operator forget her decrepitude and enjoy the pleasure of youth over again; for a woman can never be too old to receive delight, if rogered by a vigorous young man: While life is in her body she is capable of enjoyment. Therefore if she has money, she may be stroked till the day of her death; and what death can be more sweet than that of a whore who dies while she is spending?

Extract from

CLARA ALCOCK:
HER INITIATION IN THE WAYS OF LOVE AND FULL ENJOYMENT OF ITS SWEETS

CLARA'S ENLIGHTENMENT, RELATED BY LORD FERRARS

Our party consisted of myself, Queenie; my husband, Dr Harpur, better known as Dick; our young friend Miss Jemima Bond, commonly called Jim: and our guest Lord Ferrars, accompanied by Miss Frances Gipton, who although occupying the position of his mistress made herself so generally pleasant and agreeable that she was esteemed a favourite by us all.

Time did not hang heavy on our hands, for one had plenty of occupation, my husband with his professional duties, Lord Ferrars with his yacht, I with household cares, and our two young ladies with gardening and various kinds of ornamental work.

Pleasure however was the great object of our pursuit, and we neglected no means by which it might be obtained and secured; for instance, we all had our own bedrooms, but it was understood that every door was to be left open at night and every bed free to each individual of the party.

The consequence of this arrangement was that a large portion of every night was pleasantly passed in a friendly interchange of visits, leading to most delightful reciprocity of sexual excitement, followed by multiform embraces, either in couples, or more frequently, all together.

During the day we had to be more cautions and circumspect, yet a day seldom passed without some of that sly petting and feeling of the secret parts of each other, which is as pleasant to the one who gives as to the one who receives the attention.

In short, our house was a true Liberty Hall, everybody did as they pleased but then, the ruling desire of each was to gratify the rest. Accordingly happiness prevailed and mutual enjoyment was the order of the day. My good husband not only accorded me the most unbounded freedom but actually took special delight in assisting me to obtain the highest pleasure in the arms of others. Indeed his favourite position was lying with his prick soaking in the cunt of either Frances or Jim, while with his hands he held and directed the prick of Lord Ferrars in the act of prodding my cunt. As I lay at his side with my bottom turned up for the satisfaction of his friend, and within easy reach of my husband's fond inspection and pleasing titillation.

I confess that, while I always enjoyed the entrance of Lord Ferrars' experienced tool into my furrow of delight, I felt a pleasure far beyond the power of words to express when I know that my husband was not only looking approvingly, but doing all he could to urge on the fierce delight and deepen the penetration of his friend's prick in his wife's cunt.

Whenever I felt my husband's hand pressing the borders of my throbbing recess, as he held Lord Ferrars' prick and rubbed its head up and down between the lips, an unusual thrill was sure to pervade the entire region of love: and as soon as he had guided it to the sensitive entrance at the end of the slit, I used to give a sudden spring with my loins and at once engulf the luscious morsel: then as I felt it separating the clinging folds of my cunt and causing every nerve inside to tingle with approaching rapture, I could hardly refrain from shouting out with delight.

Sometimes, I would exclaim: 'Oh dear Dick, that is delicious! I do so love to feel your hand on the lips of my cunt while his Lordship drives in his prick!'

Then Dick would change his hands, placing one under my bottom, and with the other grasping his Lordship's cods all the time heaving away over his own fair partner who held him tightly clasped in her wanton arms. There we would cry alternately: 'Oh my cunt! – Oh my bottom! – Fuck Lord Ferrars! Fuck Dick! – Fire away, Fred! – Shoot it in, Dick!' until we were all bathed in that rich flood which alone brings relief.

A note was received about this time from Major Ormund, announcing that he was coming to pay us his promised visit and asking leave to bring with him a young Creole girl, named Myra, whom he described as being highly accomplished, pleasing in manner, and beautiful in person, while her temperament was lascivious beyond all description, so that he expected that both Lord Ferrars and my husband would have additional enjoyment.

The gentlemen were of course delighted, and we accordingly made no objection and sent the young lady a cordial invite.

Our friends soon afterwards made their appearance, and Myra quickly, won all our hearts by the freshness of her youth, the simplicity of her manner, and the genial warmth she manifested in all her actions.

The more inquisitive of our party speedily made themselves familiar with the beautiful roundness of her buttocks, the luxurious smoothness of her belly, and the marvellous beauty of her plump and rosy cleft.

After supper a general fucking scene was enacted, which Myra enlivened by declaring that she would not be satisfied unless her cunt was poked by each prick in succession.

We then reposed in a variety of attitudes, but with every cunt and prick open to view and ready for any amount of petting and manipulation: and all now agreed that this was the time when we could listen with special enjoyment to the promised continuation of Lord Ferrars' interesting and very exciting narrative.

His Lordship readily complied, and having prepared himself by placing his hand on my cunt and inviting Jim to sit between his knees and play with his prick, he produced a manuscript and read as follows.

During one of my later visits to my Aunt, the wealthy and distinguished Colonel Alcock came to reside in our neighbourhood.

He had only one child, a blooming girl of fifteen, named Clara. Since her mother's death about three years before, she had been at a first class boarding-school where she acquired many accomplishments and made some schoolgirl acquaintances with whom she still carried on a desultory correspondence.

Her father, considering that she was now sufficiently educated, had lately brought her home to take charge of his household and cheer him in his lonely life.

An intimacy with my Aunt was quickly established, and alternate visits between the two families became frequent.

Colonel Alcock, although one of those who lay great stress on the conventional proprieties which regulate modern society, yet seemed powerfully acted on by the attractive character of Lady Flora's voluptuous nature, and accordingly, while showing no intention of seeking her hand in marriage, he yielded himself without reserve to the sweet influence of her seductive charms.

I am not certain whether at first she entertained any amorous thoughts concerning himself, for so far as I could observe, it was the daughter she had chiefly in her mind; but at all events, she soon put forth her well-practised arts to draw him also to her feet, with a view, no doubt, of leading him on to ascend to that sweet furnace of love, which maintained an ever glowing heat in the luscious corner higher up; while at the same time she neglected no opportunity to win the confidence and secure the affection of his lovely daughter.

She herself told me that she was longing to gain free access to Clara's hidden charms, that from the appearance and manner of the young girl, she was certain that she possessed a little love chink of peculiar softness and beauty, and endowed with unusual sensibility. 'I have prevailed on her father,' she continued, 'to allow her to come to us and stay for a few weeks. She is a sweet girl Freddy and you may try your hand with her if you like; but one must be careful not to startle her at first, for she has probably been brought up, not only in ignorance of all these subjects, but taught to regard the very thought of them as wrong and injurious. However, for her own advantage and for our satisfaction, we will do what we can to enlighten her. With this view I have appointed Susan to be her waiting-maid, and among the three of us, it will be strange if we do not succeed.'

In due time, Clara came accompanied by her father. He dined with us, and we passed a pleasant evening together, my Aunt and the Colonel, evidently getting more and more in rapport. On his departure, he left his daughter in Lady Flora's charge, directing her to be good and obedient.

My Aunt made everything very comfortable for her in a room adjoining her own, and when she was bidding her good-night, told her that she had desired Susan her own maid to get ready a warm bath and attend her, as she was in the habit of doing for herself before going to bed; and that if she felt sleepless or lonely in the night, she might run in to her, as there was a door opening into her room. She then kissed her and retired, merely drawing the door to, so that it might be opened with a push.

My Aunt had thus arranged with her usual cleverness that Susan, as being less likely to excite suspicion, was to make the first attempt on the innocent Clara, and to commence that night when assisting at her bath.

She accordingly invited me to come to her room and watch with her the progress of the undertaking.

When I entered, I found her in her chemise and dressing-gown. She at once put out the light, placed a large easy chair in a suitable position, and pushed the door slightly open.

She put me into the chair and sat herself between my legs to play with my prick while we listened and watched together.

Through the opening of the door we had a full view of all that part of the inside room where Susan placed the bath, and we could also hear every word spoken.

Susan having set the bath in order said, 'Now, Miss Clara, the bath is just at the right temperature; shall I assist you to undress as I do her Ladyship? She takes a bath almost every night, and I always help to undress her, as that makes it more pleasant for her; and she told me to do everything for you as I would for herself.'

'Well Susan, I really don't require any assistance, but if you think that Lady Flora would like it, you may remain.'

'I am sure she would like me to do everything for you just as I would for herself. She lets me take off everything – this way.' But Clara held her chemise and said she was ashamed.

'You surely don't mind taking off your chemise before me, Miss Clara! Women don't usually feel ashamed of one another. I see Lady Flora naked almost every night. There. That's right, now step in. Is the bath as you would like it?.'

'Yes, it is very comfortable.'

'Now, lean back, let me sponge you as I do her Ladyship;' and taking the sponge she passed it up and down over her body as she lay in the bath.

'Open your thighs, Miss, it is here that her Ladyship likes to be well sponged.' She told us afterwards that, in order to excite her without her knowing it, she fairly frigged her little cunny with the sponge while she was still in the bath.

'Now Miss, step out, I have placed a towel for you to stand on while I rub you all over.'

She first threw a sheet round her, and then laying that aside, commenced rubbing her with a fine towel. While doing so she turned her to face the door through which my Aunt and I were peeping, thus presenting us with a charming view of the fair and beautifully formed figure of the young girl. The well-rounded prominence of her cunt stood out in bold relief at the bottom of her belly, and as Susan opened her legs when drying the inside of her thighs, the rosy line of her sweet chink became apparent. Then she rubbed between the cheeks of her bottom, after which turning her attention altogether to the sweet little cunt she managed very skilfully to frig the clitoris so as to produce, seemingly without design, a very pleasing sensation in Clara's region of love.

'Oh! Susan! Oh ah! you are tickling me so! Does Lady Flora let you rub her there too?'

'Oh dear yes, this is what her Ladyship enjoys beyond anything. She even likes me to rub the inside, in here, with my finger. It makes a body feel nice and warm after the bath. Sit down now on the couch. Miss Clara, lean back, open your legs, and I will do for you just what I do for Lady Flora.

Clara was now so thoroughly excited that she readily complied with Susan's direction besides, was she not following the example of the elegant and accomplished Lady Flora!'

Susan sat on the floor between Clara's legs, with her face close up to her delicious little love-chink, so plump, so smooth, and so fair! My Aunt admired it greatly, and whispered, 'What a dear innocent little cunt she has, Freddy! Would you not like to be where Susan is? To kiss it, and suck it, and fuck it. I shall have great fun by and by putting this saucy little fellow into it. It will just suit your size,' she said, as she gently frigged my prick with her hand and pressed its head between her lips.

'It is a very pretty little cunt,' I replied 'and looks so soft and smooth with only a little down in place of hair, but somehow, I think the fine luxuriant bush you have here, Auntie is more suggestive and more exciting,' and putting my hand down, I felt and poked her cunt.

'That will do now, Freddy, or you will make me rise and get across you for a fuck. Let us listen.'

Susan spread open the plump lips of Clara's cunt, and rubbing her finger up and down the rosy chink asked, 'Ain't that pleasant, Miss Clara? Does not that make you feel nice and warm.'

'Oh yes it does, Susan, but I never felt anything like it before,' she said, as she twisted her bottom from side to side.

Susan kissed the sweet little cunt, and drawing the clitoris into her mouth gently nibbled it with her teeth.

'Oh Susan! are you kissing it? What an extraordinary thing to kiss a body there!'

'Not at all, dear Miss Clara, this is the nicest spot in a young girl's body, and it is the part which men are always thinking of and longing to get at.'

'Why Susan? Why should men think about that part of us at all?'

'Just because it is the part that gives them the most pleasure.'

'But surely, they would not wish to kiss it!'

'Aye, that they would, and put something into it too – their article, you know – just in here,' and she pushed her finger up the as yet unbroken passage of Clara's maiden cunt.

'Oh! Susan! That makes me feel so queer – Oh! Ah! Yes, you may go on – I like it. But tell me, Susan, would a man's article, as you call it, feel as nice as your finger?'

'Oh dear yes, and a great deal nicer. But he would call it his prick. Did you ever hear that name? Would you mind saying it?'

'No Susan I never heard that name before; but I will say it for you – prick Susan – prick; and now dear Susan, tell me what a man's prick is like. I have sometimes thought of it when I felt down there, and longed for someone who could tell me about it.'

'Well, dear, Miss Clara. I will try to please you, for this nice little slit of yours has so much life and feeling, that I am sure it will be a source of the greatest pleasure and enjoyment to you when you know what it is made for, and are not afraid to use it as nature intended.'

'Thanks, dear Susan, I shall be so much obliged to you, for I feel such heat now in my little slit, as you term it, that I am sure I shall never rest satisfied until I have had a taste of that part of man which you call his prick. Now tell me all about this prick – what it is like, and what a man does to a woman with his prick.'

'Well, the prick is something like a big finger, as thick as three of mine put together, and a good deal longer. It has a large round head, smooth and rosy like a ripened plum; round the back of it there is a ridge that is meant to rub against the inside of the cunt, which you know is the name given to this little slit, and this rubbing in and out – this way, is called Fucking; say fucking, Dear.'

'Fucking; a man's prick fucking a woman's cunt.'

'That's a dear girl. I would so like to have a nice prick myself, and I would get over you and push it into your cunt, and jerk my bottom up and down – so – and then – Oh then – you would feel so nice, and you would press up and hug me in your arms and cry: "Drive your prick into my cunt and fuck me well; fuck harder – as hard as ever you can – fuck me. Oh fuck, fuck, fuck."'

'Oh Susan, you are setting me wild! I never felt so funny in my life! Why haven't you a prick? I would so like to be fucked now. – Oh – Ah – Oh! I don't know what is coming but, I feel a luxurious kind of melting all through my cunt and bottom.' Then throwing up her legs, she said: 'Rub me, Susan, rub, me hard – push your finger up. – Oh! – Oh!!!'

Susan seized the young girl round the body, and pressing her face in between her wide-spread thighs glued her lips on the slit of her throbbing cunt and eagerly supped up the ambrosial dew, which now for the first time distilled from Clara's fount of love.

Clara closed her eyes and lay back apparently quite exhausted, while Susan continued sucking and mumbling at her little cunt. The only signs of life which she exhibited were an occasional twinge of her bottom and gentle up heave of her loins.

After a few moments, she looked up at Susan and said:

'What a new world you have opened to me, Susan! I never dreamt that any one could enjoy so much pleasure. It is very strange but very delicious. Does every woman feel the same?'

'Yes, Miss Clara, every woman that lets nature have fair play; but the greater number are so constrained by custom and prejudice that they do all they can to stifle these feelings until the time for enjoyment has passed away.'

'Well Susan, that's not the case with you, I am sure. Now tell me, have you much feeling there yourself!'

'Where Miss? '

'Ah! you want me to name it again.'

'I do, Miss Clara, it is far pleasanter and much more exciting to give up all squeamishness in these matters, and call everything by its right name.'

'Well then, Susan, have you as much feeling in your cunt as I have in mine?'

'I suppose I have, Miss; when it is frigged or fucked, it feels alive with pleasure.'

'Would you mind showing me your cunt Susan?'

'Not in the least, Miss,' and Susan pulled up her petticoats and exhibited a fine bush tuft at the bottom of her belly; then separating the hair with her fingers she opened the rosy cleft between the fat pouting lips of her cunt.

'Oh my! What a lot of hair on your cunt, Susan! Sit down here in my place and let me play with it for a while.'

Susan sat on the couch and submitted her cunt to the curious investigation of the young girl, then spread it open, and said: 'What a grand slit you have here, Susan! So long and deep! And all between these fat lips is surprisingly hot and moist! Will my cunt ever be like yours, Susan?'

'Very likely it will, Miss, especially if you use it well, that is, allow it to be well kissed, and sucked, and fucked.'

'But who is there, to kiss, and suck, and fuck, Susan?'

'Oh there are plenty who would be only too glad, if you let them try and give them the opportunity.'

Clara stooped until her face was close to Susan's gap, and rubbing her nose over the clitoris, as if she was thinking said:

'Your cunt has a great deal of smell, Susan, and though I did not like it at first now I begin to find it both pleasant and exciting. Has my cunt the same smell? And do you like it Susan?'

'Yes, it has a little; every cunt has that smell, more or less; most men like it, and even women when they are excited find it pleasant and agreeable. I quite enjoyed both the smell and taste of your cunt, Miss Clara, when I was petting it just now, but it will have a more racy smell by and by when it has been fucked as often as mine has.'

'And has your cunt been often fucked Susan?'

'Yes, Miss, very often.'

'And by different men.'

'Yes by a great many different men.'

'How strange! And did you like having different men? I should have thought that a woman would only like to have one man, at least at one time.'

'That's the common notion, but my opinion is that most women keep to one man, not because they are satisfied with one, but because they are afraid of the judgement of others. Any woman that really understands and enjoys fucking will desire a change of pricks, and the more frequent the change the greater will be her enjoyment.'

'But is it not fucking that makes a woman get with child?'

'Certainly; and if she keeps to one man she is almost certain to get in the family way, but if she goes with several she will have a fair chance of escaping.'

'Were you ever fucked by anyone in this house, Susan?'

'Well, Miss Clara, I think I may trust you,' here she lowered her voice, as if speaking in the greatest confidence, 'I was.'

'Would you mind telling me which, Susan?'

'I may tell you, Miss Clara, for I am sure you will be careful not to make mischief, but remember it is in the strictest confidence. Lady Flora's page, James often fucks me. He comes to my bed at night, pulls up my shift and feels my cunt then he gets over me, with his legs between mine, you know, and as soon as I feel his prick poking against me, I put down my hand, take hold of it and frig it for a few moments.'

'How do you frig a prick, Susan?'

'The prick has a soft skin about it which slips easily up and down, and when you pass your fingers round it and move your hand up and down, this skin moves too, and that gives the man, a pleasant feel as if he was fucking; then the prick grows hard and stiffens up, and if you went on you would soon make the seed flow; but as I do not want it to come that way, I always stop frigging after a few turns.'

'I would so like to have a prick in my hand now, Susan, and to frig it up and down, so as to make it grow hard and stiffen up. But tell me what you and James do next.'

'Well, when I feel his prick in working order, that is, strong enough to force its way up my cunt, I direct its head to the entrance, just here, and hold it in my hand while he pushes it up; then when it is all inside he begins to fuck, working his bottom up and down, as he drives his prick in and out of my cunt, while I heave up to meet every thrust he gives with his prick,' and Susan worked her cunt up and down, making it open and shut, while Clara observed it attentively and said:

'What does he do with his hands while he is fucking you?'

'He generally has one round my waist and the other under my bottom pressing me up to him, or else at the back of my neck holding my head for his kisses.'

'And what do you do with yours?'

'Oh! I have them clasped round his body or on his bottom, which he likes me to squeeze as hard as I can while he is fucking me.'

'What does he say when he is fucking you?'

'He does not say much himself, but he tries to make me talk, and delights in hearing me use the words, prick, cunt, fucking, and such like: and so when he pushes up his prick, I cry: "Oh my c-u-n-t!" dwelling on word cunt, when he draws it back, I say: "Oh pr-i-c-k!" another push, "Fu-c-k!" then: "ar-s-e!" and that usually sends his spunk flying up my cunt.'

'Does he ever come to you by day?'

'Yes, when her Ladyship is not at home and there is no chance of his attendance being required.'

'And what does he do then?'

'If it is in my own room, he places me on the bed and gets me to lean back and frig my cunt while he watches it; and when I tell him I am near spending, he darts upon my cunt, sucks it first and then licks it all round inside. Then I frig and suck his prick, while we talk of all kinds of bawdy subjects.'

'How I would enjoy watching you, Susan!'

'Well, perhaps I might let you see me fucked some day.'

'What else does he do?'

'All sorts of queer things: he is very fond of looking at my bottom, or as he likes me to call it, my arse, and he takes great pleasure in tickling and even sucking the little hole there. Now Miss Clara, say arse for me.'

'Arse, Susan, do you like having your arse sucked?'

'Yes, Miss Clara, it is very delicious and makes your cunt as randy as anything. Turn up your little arse now, Miss Clara, I will suck it, and then you will know how pleasant it feels.'

They now changed places, and Susan placed Clara on her back across the sofa, and lifting her legs she separated them widely and pressed them back on her belly, thus presenting us with a most ravishing view of her sweet little cunt, with its lips stretched open and showing all its glowing interior. It seemed in a state of continual spend, for we could see a thick stream like milk oozing out at the end of the slit. Susan pulled up her skirts as she knelt down, so as to bare her own bottom to our view, and after wiping Clara's cunt with the towel she kissed and licked it all over. Then pressing lower down she applied her mouth to the nether entrance, and sucked it so with her lips and tongue, that Clara writhed with rapture, and at last moaned out:

'That will do, dear Susan, I can bear no more – I feel as if I was all dissolved away. Put me to bed now; tomorrow we can continue our conversation, and you can tell me more of these wonderful things.'

Clara then betook herself to her couch while Susan emptied the bath and tidied up the room. But when she was bidding good-night, Clara caught her in her arms, kissed her and said: 'Dear Susan, I feel quite fond of you for all you have told me tonight. You have opened my eyes and given me such ideas as I never had before, but often felt a craving for, although I did not know the reason why. I shall be longing in the morning to hear more: and perhaps with your help I shall be able to obtain some of these enjoyments without which I now feel that life would be a mere blank. You will have to manage to give me half an hour in the early part of the day. So now, again good-night, and thanks, dear Susan.'

You will all easily understand what a very exciting effect the foregoing scene had on my Aunt and myself. My prick remained in unceasing erection, with a little drop of spunk perpetually oozing out, which my Aunt always sipped up but carefully avoided stirring the prick itself which would at once have brought on a full emission. Her own cunt was in a similar state of constant flow, and I afterwards found that her thighs were wet down to her very knees. She repeatedly whispered her commendation ...

'What a delicious little cunt Clara has, Freddy! I am longing to kiss and suck it! How well Susan humours her and makes her twist her bottom! Good girl! I must give her a handsome present. She has managed this case with wonderful cleverness! Her success has far exceeded my expectation. We must let her work it out her own way, and nature will give the finishing touch.'

When Susan wished Clara good-night, my Aunt closed the door on her side, gently but firmly, and going over to the bed, sat down as she said: 'Oh Freddy, my cunt and bottom are in a terrible glow! You must give me some relief.'

I leaned over her and asked: 'Shall I fuck you, dear Auntie?'

'Yes, but let us wait for Susan, she will be here in a minute.'

Susan quickly entered, looking very bright and animated.

'Well my Lady, are you pleased?'

'Exceedingly so, dear Susan, you did your part well. Lie down here across the bed and I will give your own cunt a little petting while Freddy fucks mine over your face; and after that you may get a good poke from either Tomkins or James, whichever you like.'

Susan at once complied and stretched herself on her back across the bed with her head projecting slightly over the edge. My Aunt then straddled over her face with her naked bottom cocked up, and rubbing her bubbies against Susan's belly, embraced her hips with her arms, and bent her head down between her separated thighs; thus opening the lips of her cunt she drew the soft clitoris into her mouth, and worked her tongue about in the moist sensitive slit.

Susan then placed her hands on my Aunt's wriggling bottom and looking up from between her thighs, she said, 'Now, Master Freddy, see her Ladyship's bottom is spread for your admiration, press these soft cheeks and I will introduce your prick into her Ladyship's cunt.' Susan not only handled my prick most deliciously as I pushed it up the hot sheath of my Aunt's cunt but gently squeezed my balls, and pushing her finger into my bottom tickled it in the most lubricious manner.

Lady Flora now lifted her head, as she muttered, 'Good Susan, talk plenty; and Freddy, don't hurry, give me that slow steady lunge which I love – it gives my cunt time to relish both the taste and feel of your prick – that's the way. Now pinch my bottom well: that makes my cunt hotter and able to hold your prick more tightly.'

Thus exhorted, Susan continued, 'Now Master Freddy, fuck her Ladyship well, push your prick slowly up her cunt, pinch her Ladyship's bottom and rub your bollocks over my face. Press down your cunt, my Lady, so that I may reach the clitoris with my tongue, while Master Freddy is fucking you?'

I had now come to the short strokes and commenced crying, 'Oh Auntie! Oh sweet cunt! Oh delighted prick! Oh Susan, your tongue is grand! Lick my bollocks; bite em – Oh!!!'

This emission considerably weakened my strength; and I was not sorry when Lady Flora said, 'Fred, you must be tired; go to bed now, get a good sleep, and you will be ready for any fresh demands that may be made on you tomorrow.'

I certainly was glad to lay my wearied limbs to rest, and soon passed unconsciously into a sweet and refreshing sleep.

My Aunt however, as I afterwards learned, did not finally go to rest until she had been twice poked by Tomkins, while she watched Susan enjoying a similar treat at the hands of James.

CLARA'S FIRST EXPERIENCES,
RELATED BY LORD FERRARS

Clara appeared very bright and cheerful next morning, and much more talkative than usual. When speaking to me, I observed that her eyes were often directed to the fork of my trousers, and also that she seemed particularly impressed with the well-developed lump which Tomkins, the butler, exhibited in the same interesting locality. She asked my Aunt to let her have Susan in her room for an hour in the fore-noon to alter one of her dresses. My Aunt of course willingly gave her consent. In fact, knowing already Clara's intended request, she had given Susan instructions and supplied her with books and pictures to use on the occasion. Thinking it wiser to leave them altogether by themselves, she went out with me soon after breakfast to superintend some improvements she was making in the grounds; first however, telling Susan to meet us in one of the enclosed gardens, as soon as her interview with Clara was ended, that she might report what additional progress she had made.

In due time, we found Susan awaiting us, and my Aunt having secured the garden door, led the way to a mossy bank, on which we three reclined together. Susan made her account more interesting by performing her usual duty of petting her Mistress' cunt, at the same time placing herself, so as to afford me a full view of her own region of love.

She told us that she found Miss Clara even more lubriciously inclined than she was the night before. That she readily permitted her again to examine her cunt, and freely admitted that she was longing to be fucked and know by experience all the sweet pleasures which a man's prick and balls could afford her, she was delighted when Susan opened before her a book of French prints, and the spend moistened her cunt, as she questioned Susan, about the various attitudes and modes of procuring sexual gratification. Pointing to one of the pictures, she exclaimed: 'Oh Susan! What a love of a prick that man has! How I envy the girl he is going to fuck! And look at this one, how she cocks up her naked bottom before all these men! I wonder she is not ashamed! Were not you ashamed the first time a man looked at your naked cunt and bottom?'

'Yes, perhaps a little at first, but I soon came to enjoy being looked at. Does not the thought that I am looking at your cunt now increase the sensation of pleasure? And with a man it would be still more so.'

'Yes, I like to have you looking at my cunt, Susan, but I am certain I should feel greatly ashamed before a man.'

'Ah, that feeling would soon wear off, especially after you had handled his prick and felt it in your cunt.'

'Very likely, at all events I am convinced from the effect of these pictures on my self that fucking must be very delightful. I never understood until now, why men and women like to sleep together. I suppose they keep fucking all night. But if the pictures are so pleasant to look at, how much more enjoyable it must be to see the reality itself. You said something last night, Susan, about letting me see you fucked, could you manage it to day? It would be such a treat.'

'Well, dear Miss Clara, I would like very much to please you, and Lady Flora gave me special directions to gratify you by every means in my power. She is out now and will not return until luncheon time, and therefore James won't be wanted, and he is always ready for a fuck. So come with me into her Ladyship's room. It opens into the boudoir, and you can look into it without being seen yourself. I will bring James by another door into the boudoir, and show him some of these pictures, and that will set him on for a fuck.'

'Thanks, dear Susan, but I hope her Ladyship won't find me in her room.'

'You need not mind if she did. There is nothing that would please her more than to see and pet your little cunt. She is very good and loves to see people happy and enjoying themselves, especially in that way. Now Miss, sit here, keep your finger in your cunt, and open both your eyes and ears.'

Susan quickly appeared in the boudoir and James with her.

They sat down on a broad sofa right opposite to and facing the door through which Clara was peeping.

Susan was speaking, and the first words which Clara could distinguish were: think, James, we may count on half an hour without interruption, so come tell me what you have been doing with yourself since you left me last night?' And she began unbuttoning his trousers and slacking off his suspenders. She then drew down his prick, and looking at it, said: 'This roving prick looks as if he had not been idle' and making him lean back, she put one hand under his balls to raise them and show their size, and with the other frigged up his prick into standing order, as she continued: 'Now tell me, James, whom did you fuck last?'

'Well Susan, I have promised to hide nothing from you. The last who favoured me in that way was the new cook.'

'What! that great fat woman! I wonder her cunt did not swallow you up. But how did you manage to get at her so soon?'

'I brought her some of her Ladyship's spiced wine last night after the other servants had gone to bed. She relished it greatly, and soon grew so jolly that she let me kiss her and, handle her fat bubbies, and at last make my way to her hot and randy slit; which is not by any means so large as one might expect. In fact, her cunt is as tight and close as that of a young girl. Then I got her to lean over the kitchen table, and throwing her clothes up over her back exposed a pair of the most splendid posteriors I ever looked at. Oh! it was delicious to press my belly against them and rub my prick up and down the soft furrow between! And though it was scarcely an hour since I left you, my prick soon recovered its usual size and strength. When I shoved it up she held the table with her hands, and pushing back her arse kept on grinding her teeth and muttering: "Pound my arse – my arse – my arse – Oh! that's good! – fuck – fuck – fuck."'

While James was giving this account, Susan continued manipulating his prick with her hands, kissing it, and rubbing it to her nose and about her face, until he cried, 'Stop Susan, let me into your cunt before I spend.'

Susan helped him to take off his trousers, then throwing herself on her back, she heaved up her legs so as to display all her cunt and bottom to Clara's peeping eye! and when James leaned over her she caught hold of his prick and said, 'Leave him to my management – I'll put him in.'

Susan still arranged matters so that Clara might see the prick pass in between the close clinging lips of her cunt and bury itself in its hidden depths; and when James commenced that prodding movement natural in such cases, she so twisted about as to cause him to vary his strokes, and occasionally exhibit the greater part of his smoking tool outside, then by a sudden bound she would re-engulf it in her amorous sheath. Sometimes she even threw him out altogether, that she might have the pleasure of putting it in again. But this pleasing operation came to a speedy end – much too speedy, thought Clara – and James lay panting on Susan's belly, with his prick soaking in the humid folds of her cunt. When she had allowed him a few moments of this luxurious rest she got up and as she shook down her clothes said: 'I must now return to Miss Clara, who is waiting for me. She is a fine cocklesome girl, and I expect will turn out as fond of the sport as any of us.'

'I thought so myself from the look in her eye, and she is in good training with you and her Ladyship. But listen, Susan, if you ever get me a twist at her, you will be tenfold more the delight of my life than you are.'

'Oh! you villain, will nothing satisfy you? You have fucked the maid, and you have fucked the mistress, and you have fucked the cook, and now you want to fuck the young lady visitor!! Nevertheless, if I can help you, I will. Now clear out, I must put this place to rights before her Ladyship comes in.'

When she returned to Clara, she asked, whether she had seen all that passed, and whether the sight had pleased and excited her?

'Oh yes, dear Susan; I enjoyed it immensely, and all your funny talk! and how you promised to help him to get me. But dear Susan, watching James' fine prick rushing in and out of your hairy cunt made my heart beat and almost took away my breath. I was envying you the whole time he was fucking you, and kept frigging my cunt with my finger; but though I spent more than once I felt no real satisfaction. You were quite right, I feel now as if I never could live without a a prick; and I don't think I should find two or three too many. You said that you were fucked by more than one man, tell me, dear Susan, were you ever fucked by any one else now in the house besides James?'

'I was, Miss, Tomkins has fucked me several times.'

'Tell me all about it, dear Susan, I could not help observing this morning that he seems very big there; when does he go to you?'

'He generally comes to me in the early morning when I first go into the drawing-room to open the shutters. He slips in behind me, catches me in his arms and kisses me: then he shoves his hand up under my petticoats and feels my cunt and bottom, that of course excites me, and I respond by taking out his prick and petting it with my hands: sometimes I kiss it and take its head into my mouth: you know, there is nothing a man enjoys more than to have his prick sucked by a woman. It is a certain way of making him long for a fuck. Then he places me on my back on the carpet, and I nothing loath lift my legs and turn up my bottom. He takes a good peep and perhaps another kiss, and then kneels between my thighs with his prick in his hand, then having opened the lips of my cunt with his fingers, he pushes in the head of his prick and drives it slowly up. Tomkins has a fine big prick, large and longer than that of James, and I enjoy his fucking very much. Oh Miss! if you only saw it standing up with its top all swollen and red, your cunt would water to take it in and suck it like a mouth.'

'It must indeed be fine to be fucked by such a fine prick as you say Tomkins has, but tell me, Susan, has anyone else in this place besides Tomkins and James ever fucked you?'

This was leading up to what was evidently the uppermost thought in her mind, for when I replied: 'Yes, Master Freddy sometimes looks for my favours and seems pleased when I gratify him.' She smiled, and said, 'I thought so: now dear Susan, tell me how he gets on with you, and all about his prick, and how you like being fucked by him.'

I was amused at her eagerness, and replied, 'Master Freddy has a wonderful prick for his age, and knows right well how to use it; and his manner is so gentle and kind that any woman might be glad to give it a welcome in her cunt. I am confident, Miss Clara, that if you let him, you will find him both ready and able to please you in every way.'

'Well Susan, I won't be sorry if he makes the attempt, I only fear he will find the task too easy, for my cunt will be longing for his prick the whole time. But are you quite certain that he will be anxious for it himself?'

'Of that I have not the slightest doubt, for he loves fucking more than anything in the world, and her Ladyship told me that he said you were the sweetest girl he ever met. If you only give him the opportunity and are not too coy when he makes advances, you will be surprised how rapidly he will proceed.'

'Very well dear Susan, I hope he won't be slow about it, for my cunt is burning at the mere thought of his fucking it. Lady Flora asked him this morning to drive me in the pony and trap. This will be opportunity if he is inclined to avail himself of it, and I will tell you everything to-night.'

Lady Flora again commended Susan for her wise and successful management of this delicate affair; and turning to me, said: 'The next advance devolves on you, Freddy; Susan has prepared the soil, cast in the seed, and a luxuriant crop already covers the ground, it only remains for you to thrust in the sickle and reap the harvest. I envy you the work – you will find it as easy as it is delightful; and I trust you will be very careful to make it as painless and enjoyable as possible to the sweet girl. Let us now go in.'

My Aunt's design was duly carried out, and shortly after luncheon, Clara and I were seated side by side in the pony trap on our way to see a neighbouring ruin. She was very amiable and friendly and we chatted pleasantly together. I addressed her as Clara, and she made an equal approach by calling me Freddy.

I placed the reins and whip in her hands and offered to teach her to drive. In doing so my arm passed round her waist, and our cheeks frequently touched. I remarked, how pleasant it was to be sitting closely together. She agreed, and I pressed her still more closely to my side. I though I felt a slight trembling, but she made no objection; then, making a bold advance, I said, 'These thick skirts of yours, Clara, are rather in the way, may I lift them up a little?'

She nodded, so I drew them up, and as I did so, said, 'Now, sweet Clara, let me place your leg resting on mine, and we shall be able to sit still more comfortably together.'

She did not object, and I accordingly lifted up her soft and shapely leg over my knee. As I put my hand under, I touched for a moment the satin surface of her thigh just above her stocking. As she did not seem to notice it, I replaced it there, and while we kept on talking of the various objects of interest we passed on the road, I gradually pushed it higher and higher.

Her warm skin felt deliciously smooth and soft; and as her drawers were capacious, my hand soon attained a position very near that sweet angle where Love holds his court. We were driving over a rough part of the road, which rather facilitated my movements, and the next bound of the vehicle caused my hand, as if involuntarily to press against two pulpy down-covered lips. On which, she exclaimed in a tone in which surprise and gratification were strangely blended: 'Oh! Freddy, your hand is something more than friendly!'

'Yes, darling Clara, it is more than friendly, it is full of admiration and love Let it stay, dearest. It is delicious to press these soft lips; and this lovely chink! – so moist and warm! How exquisitely made you are! Open your legs a little more; tell me, Clara, like a dear girl, what do you call this little mouth?'

'I have no name for it; what would you call it?'

'It is commonly called cunt, Dear, and if we use that name when we are talking familiarly together, we shall find it agreeable and exciting – say it now, my love.'

'Cunt, Freddy; why do you like putting your hand on my cunt?'

'In the first place, I want to give you pleasure; now, tell me truly, does not the rubbing of my finger on this part of your cunt give you pleasure?'

'It does, Freddy, I like to feel your fingers moving about in my cunt.'

'Good, and in the next place it gives me pleasure, very great pleasure, for it excites the corresponding part of my body. I have not got a cunt, but I have what exactly corresponds to it, and is in fact especially made for its use and enjoyment. Do you know what it is like, Clara?'

'No, dear Freddy; how could I.'

'Well, lay down the whip and give me your hand for a moment.' She allowed me to take the whip out of her hand and then carry her hand to the front of my trousers which I had already unbuttoned. I placed it inside on my prick standing up with uncovered head. It was delicious to feel how readily her soft fingers closed around it.

'Take it out, my pet, and look at it,' I said, opening my trousers to the greatest extent.

She drew it out and looked down on it with admiring glances.

'Move it up and down, Dear, that will make it grow bigger.'

She smiled, and moved her lily hand up and down its shaft.

'Now, I am certain you know what it is for.'

She blushed, but said nothing.

'Do you know what it is called?'

'No, Freddy, what is its name?'

'Prick, Dear, and you see it is made just to fit the cunt. This soft shelving head slips so easily and nicely into the little hole at the lower end of the cunt and makes its way so pleasantly up the passage inside, that it fills a woman's belly with rapture and delight. Now say prick for me, and tell me what you think of mine.'

'I am no judge of pricks, Freddy, but I like to hold yours in my hand and to move it up and down, as that seems to give you pleasure.'

'That's a good girl, but you would like for better to feel it in this nice little cunt, fucking you – But here we are arrived. I will take the pony from the trap and let him graze in this paddock while we go over the ruins.'

We then wandered about through old passages and doorways and up broken stone steps until we came to an open space thickly covered with mosses and lichens; when I said: 'Let us rest here awhile. Clara, you have had a great deal of climbing and must be tired.' She replied that she did feel somewhat tired and would enjoy a little rest. I chose a soft place for her to sit upon and then threw myself at her side. I looked into her eyes, they seemed melting with love and tenderness, and as I slipped my hand under her clothes, I whispered: 'My darling, I feel as if we were made for one another let us enjoy ourselves together while we may. Favour me now with a view of the dear little cunt I have been petting as we drove along.'

'Oh no, dear Freddy, you may feel it if you wish, but I cannot let you see it, I should be so ashamed.'

'You need not be ashamed of me now, Clara. See I am not ashamed to have you looking at my prick,' and I again took it out and placed it in her hand. 'Besides I want you to let them kiss – it would be so nice, and you would like it so. Won't you let me try.'

'I may some day, but I can't now.'

'Why not now, Dear? There is no time like the present – there – lean back,' and I gently inclined her backwards.

She made a slight attempt to keep down her petticoats as I pulled them up, but at last I drew them all up; and when I had opened her snowy drawers, and with gentle force separated her yielding thighs I got a full view of the rising mound and voluptuous lips of her maiden cunt. How beautiful it looked, so fair and soft, and so redolent of sweetest perfume!

At first I felt almost overpowered by its excessive loveliness, but on opening the lips I perceived a tiny drop of pearly spend trembling at its lower extremity, and I longed to taste it! So throwing myself at full length between her legs, I applied my mouth to the luscious chink. The contact of my lips seemed to have an electrical effect: her thighs at once spread themselves out to their widest extent, her cunt was thrust up in little gentle heaves, and her hand placed on my head, as if playing with the hair, pressed it strongly down. In short, I never observed more evident symptoms of the highest pleasurable emotion.

After a few moments, I looked up and said, 'You have a sweet cunt, Clara, do you like me to kiss it?'

'Yes, dear Freddy, the suction of your lips and movement of your tongue makes my cunt thrill so that I cannot keep quiet.' I kissed it again, and said: 'Now let me put my prick to it and make them kiss, and then perhaps you will let me put it in.'

'You may, Freddy, but only a little way.'

I pushed it up to her and said, 'Put your hand on it, Dear, and show me how far I may put it in.'

She smiled as she took it in her hand, and said, 'I think you might put in the head, but not any more.'

'Very well, Dear, you can tell me when you feel the head in and when you wish me to stop.'

I held my prick to her cunt, rubbed it over it, and up and down the slit, then placing it at the true opening I very gently urged it forward; the head slipped easily in, and I asked, 'Do you feel it, Clara? Is it hurting you.'

'I do feel it, Freddy; it did hurt me at first, but not now.'

'Shall I stop pushing?'

'No, Freddy; I like it – you may push it in a little more – push a little more still – Oh! It feels very nice – you may push it in as far as ever you can.

I now gave her thrust after thrust, as I said, 'Hold me in your arms, Darling – heave up your dear cunt, and tell me how you like it!'

'Oh, it is delicious! Freddy, you may fuck me as much as you like. Oh! how your prick fills my cunt! I feel it ever so far up my belly! Are you going to spend now? Do it – pour it into my cunt. Oh my darling Freddy, I cannot tell you what pleasure you are giving me,' and with a prolonged Oh!!! her grasp of me released, her eyes closed, and she lay back powerless on the bank. I felt her cunt however closely pressed round my prick, as with loving throbs it seemed to suck out every drop of love juice that remained.

After this, all reserve was thrown aside by Clara, and she allowed her generous nature full play in the free exercise of a variety of little wanton acts and lascivious expressions. This imparted to the young girl such an air of innocence and freshness as made her still sweeter and more charming than ever.

There is nothing more attractive or delightful to a man than to meet a woman of warm temperament and loving disposition who so fully confides in him as to manifest before him, the secret working of her newly kindled desires, and to tell forth the innermost feelings of her loving heart. Such were the thoughts which passed through my mind, when as I laid myself back to rest she took hold of my languid tool and said: 'I wish, Freddy, you would teach me how to bring to life again this poor little prick. He seems very tired, and is only half his former size.'

I showed her how to frig it and pet the balls. She bent over it with marked interest, she kissed it, and finally took its head into her mouth and sucked it. It was not insensible to her kind attentions and soon began to swell and get stronger. She continued her gentle and stimulating touches, and lifting her head said, 'Do you like to hear me speak of pricks, cunts, and bottoms while I am frigging you?

'Yes, Darling, it has a great effect on my prick.'

'Are there any other words of that kind which you would like to hear me say?'

'Yes, Dear, there is spunk.'

'Oh, that is what your prick darted into my cunt when you were fucking me. What else?'

'Bollocks. And that is the name of these round balls at the root of my prick that hold the spunk.'

'Then there is the common expressive word arse. And that,' she said with a laugh, 'is the vulgar name for this part,' placing her delicate fingers first on the cheeks, and then sweetly touching the hole of my bottom.

'Now my pet I want you to uncover all your lovely arse, and straddle over me with a knee on each side, so as to place your cunt on my mouth, and if you like you can then bend forward and play with my prick while I suck your cunt.'

'Oh,' she said; 'that will be very nice, and I will suck your prick while you are kissing my cunt.'

Very soon I had her luscious little cunt melting over my mouth, while my prick was sucked and my balls petted with so much fervour that a stream of seed poured forth a second time, every drop of which Clara swallowed with apparent relish and satisfaction. She continued playing with my prick all the way back and told me how Susan had frigged her cunt for the first time the night before, and had described the pleasure of fucking; but she added, giving me a kiss and a fond squeeze of the prick, the reality far exceeds the description.

I praised Susan to her and asked would she be very jealous if she saw me making free with her?

She replied: 'Sometime ago, I am afraid I should, but now that I understand more of these matters I see things in quite another light; so, if I felt sure that your making free with her would not cause you to love me less, then I would rather be pleased to know that you were enjoying yourself with her, and especially if I thought that you would regard my acquiescence as a proof of my confidence and affection.'

'Why Clara, you are quite a little sage! You are perfectly right, Dear. The fact of you allowing me to go with others, or to speak plainly, to fuck them before you and with your help, would not only be the most convincing proof of your confidence and affection, but be the surest means of binding me to you for ever.'

She answered with a kiss, a pleasant little way she had, and I responded with a loving hug.

On reaching home, my Aunt called me into her boudoir, and taking out my prick, she examined, kissed, and smelt it, while I gave her a minute account of my success with the sweet and trustful Clara.

'She is indeed a dear girl. Freddy, be very careful not to do her harm, and prize her love, for you won't find many so loving and confiding as she is.'

CLARA'S EXPANDING DESIRES

That night before going to bed, Clara gave Susan a full account of all our doings in the afternoon, and described how pleased she was when she first perceived my hand on her thigh, and the exquisite sensation in her cunt when she felt my fingers groping between the lips. Then the intense delight that thrilled through her frame when at last I placed her on her back with her legs wide apart, and commenced pushing the head of my prick against her cunt; and how she hugged and squeezed me in her arms while the dear prick was working deliciously in and out of her throbbing recess.

'Did it hurt you much when first forcing its way in?'

'Yes it did, but I scarcely minded that, I was so anxious to get it in and the short pain was so quickly turned into such excessive pleasure that I could hardly distinguish between them. In fact judging from my own experience, I would say that the pain caused by the first entrance of the prick is much overrated.'

'Ah but remember. Master Freddy's prick is not so large as that possessed by older and bigger men; and besides, he has such a deft way of handling his tool, that I don't think he would hurt even a child. But if your cunt had been entered for the first time by the prick of a man like Tomkins, for instance, you might have had a different story to tell.'

'Then I suppose,' Clara said, with a rosy blush over her face, 'that if a bigger prick gives more pain, it also gives more pleasure.'

'I am not so sure of that. Certainly Tomkins gives a grand fuck, and his prick stretches your entire cunt and seems to fill up all your belly but somehow, I rather prefer Master Freddy's quiet deliberate style of fucking, and Lady Flora, who I may tell you is a thorough connoisseur in these matters, says that is the perfection of this most delightful art.'

'Well Susan, although at present I have no wish to be fucked by Tomkins yet the thought of his big prick, pushing up into my cunt, fills my mind with peculiarly lascivious fancies and ideas. Look at my cunt now, Dear, and tell me, whether you think it has been much opened up by the entrance of Freddy's tool to-day. Though it stretched me a good deal at first, I did not seem to feel it much afterwards.'

She then lay back on the bed and spreading her legs allowed Susan to push a pillow under her bottom that she might inspect her cunt more freely.

'Yes, dear Miss Clara, your cunt is very much more open than it was, and it could now take in with ease a prick very much larger than that which Master Freddy can boast of. It looks very pretty now, it is so soft and red. I am sure that Lady Flora will admire it very much when she sees it, and I think she intends to come to you tonight; and take my advice, Miss, don't be at all coy with her, just talk to her as you do with me, that is what she likes. Speak freely of pricks, cunt, bottoms, and fucking, and all things of that kind; in fact, the more lascivious you show yourself, the more she will be pleased with you and like you.'

'What time do you think she will come, Susan.'

'After you have had your bath and before you get into bed.'

'Let us hurry then, Susan, and make me as nice as you can for her Ladyship.'

Lady Flora had brought me into her room, and we listened with much pleasure to the interesting conversation between Clara and Susan, which I have related with the greatest fidelity and minuteness.

At the time indicated my Aunt said, 'I must now go into this sweet girl, but you had better stay here and be ready to come whenever I call you.'

Susan had just finished drying Clara, whose whole body looked as fresh and fragrant as that of the fabled Hebe, when the door opened and my Aunt entered. Going up to Clara, she said, 'My dear Clara, I have come to see that you have everything you wish for. What a fair sweet girl you are! I am delighted to find you in a state of nature. It enables me to view and admire all your charms. Come, sit on the bed with me while Susan removes the bath,' and putting her arm round her, she drew her naked as she was towards the bed.

'Thanks, dear Lady Flora, I have everything I can wish for, and Susan is most attentive. Your Ladyship is very fortunate in having a maid so clever and obliging. She anticipates my every wish.'

'I am glad you are pleased dear Clara, and I am glad to observe that you have sufficient good sense not to mind my seeing you undressed. Many young girls are foolishly weak in feeling over-powered with shame at being seen naked even by a woman.'

'But dear Lady Flora is not that a natural feeling; at best, what we are all taught to regard as such?'

'Yes, but a great many of our conventional notions are clearly opposed to nature. At all events, our first parents so long as they were innocent had no sense of shame. It is all very well, to cover up the old and ugly, but when nature has carved out a form like yours, radiant with health and beauty, there can be no just reason to hide it at least from another woman. But I want to see a little more of your maiden charms.' Here Lady Flora, who had her left arm round Clara's waist, put her right hand gently on her soft swelling mons. 'Lean back, my love, open your thighs – that's a dear girl; you are deliciously formed here; and if you have full confidence in me, I will teach you how to use this little love-chink. So as to obtain the greatest pleasure without danger or risk. Do you know any name for it?'

'Yes, Lady Flora, Susan told me it was my cunt.'

'And you know why your cunt has this mouth-like shape?'

'Yes, because it is meant to take in a prick; and to be fucked,' she added with a blush and a smile.

'Right, my pet, a cunt is never satisfied until it gets a prick; but your little cunny feels to me as if it had been already entered by something in the shape of a prick. Now show confidence in me, dear Clara, and tell me honestly if you were ever fucked and by whom?'

'Dear Lady Flora, I have the greatest confidence in you, and I will tell you everything. I never saw a man's prick, and was never fucked until today. Freddy succeeded in getting his hand on my cunt while we were in the pony-trap, and when he had placed me sitting on a mossy bank inside the ruins, he coaxed me to let him see my cunt, then he prevailed on me to handle his prick, and one thing led on to another, until he got between my legs and fucked me. Are you very angry?'

'Not in the least, dear Clara, it was the most natural thing that could have happened to you; and I consider Freddy a very lucky fellow to have been the first to draw honey from this sweet little tulip. It is indeed a dear little cunt. Do you like to have me looking at it and petting in this way?'

'Yes, now that I have got over the shame I felt at first, I like to see you looking at my cunt, and you are rubbing it so nicely that I feel as if I was just going to spend.'

'You are a good sensible girl, Clara, and I will now give you all the pleasure I can. I am going to kiss and suck your little cunt, and I want you to spend while I am sucking it. And now I will let you into a secret; if you wish to make the pleasure still more delightful, go on talking of pricks, cunts, and fucking, and you will find that every time you use these and such-like words, you will get an additional feeling of pleasure in your cunt. So while I am sucking it, tell me exactly how Freddy fucked you to-day and everything you both said and did.'

'I will, dear Lady Flora, oh! how nice your tongue feels in my cunt! I like your hands on my bottom too! Oh Lady Flora! I am dying with pleasure! Freddy sucked my cunt before he fucked me. He asked me how much of his prick he might push into my cunt? At first I told him to push in only the head, but when that got in, it made me long for the whole, and I told him to push all his prick into my cunt as far as he could, and fuck me-fuck me-fuck me fast and hard. And I pressed him in my arms and felt his prick very strong and hard in my cunt, and he cried that he was going to spend, but I did not need him to tell me that, for I felt his hot seed shooting up into my belly. Afterwards when he drew out his prick, it was quite soft and only half as big as it was before he fucked me. So I petted and coaxed it, and then placed its head in my mouth and sucked it, and I played with his bollocks too and petted his bottom, which he told me was commonly called his arse. Then he got me to kneel over him and place my naked arse, on his face and he sucked my cunt and bottom, while I stooped forward sucked his prick, tickled his bottom, and then we both spent together. He supped up my spending and I drank his spunk. – Oh! Dear Lady Flora! Its coming – its coming so nice – squeeze my bottom suck my cunt – Oh!! that's delicious!!'

Clara at first seemed quite overpowered by the sweet sensations she experienced as Lady Flora sucked out the spermy juice which flowed from her throbbing recess. But she soon recovered, and throwing her arms round my Aunt, kissed her and said, 'It is now your Ladyship's turn to gratify me with a view of your own chink of love.'

'Certainly, my pet: see, here it is – behold a matured specimen of woman's great charm. You may feel it, or kiss it, or do anything else that you like.'

My Aunt reclined back with her beautiful thighs at their widest stretch, and heaving her bottom with little wanton jerks presented her cunt in the most lascivious and enticing aspect.

As soon as Clara obtained a full view of Lady Flora's large bushy cunt, she exclaimed: –

'Oh, it is grand! Such great fat lips! And such a profusion of golden-brown hair! Susan showed me her cunt last night, it was very nice, but your Ladyship's is far nicer. And how hot it feels inside! Has it been often fucked, Lady Flora?'

'Yes, dear Clara, it has enjoyed that felicity very often.'

'Are you fond of fucking, Lady Flora?'

'I consider fucking the most delightful sensation in the world, Clara.'

'If you would excuse my being so inquisitive, I would like to ask how you are able to obtain such a gratification when you are still unmarried?'

'You may ask any thing you like, Dear, and I will always answer you as freely as I can. Although I have not married again. I should neither be happy nor enjoy good health, unless I satisfied the craving of nature by allowing my cunt to have an occasional poke which it demands and requires.'

'But, dear Lady Flora, you have not told me how you manage to get it, that occasional poke.'

'My dear child, that's the easiest thing in the world. Men are so awfully fond of fucking, that a woman never has the least difficulty in having her cunt poked as often as she likes. There are however two real difficulties which must be carefully avoided. The first is scandal, involving loss of reputation. Reputation is dearer to most women than even life itself, while there are plenty of envious and evil minded people whose chief pleasure is to injure and destroy that of their neighbours. Now I have succeeded in avoiding this by confiding only in my own tried and trained domestics and a few safe friends. The second is that danger which naturally arises from intercourse with the male sex. This risk may be obviated in two ways: either by not allowing the man to deposit his seed inside the cunt, by making him withdraw his prick just as he is going to spend, or compelling him to cover his prick with a little hood made of some thin substance, such as the skin cases called French letters. Both these ways however tend to lessen the pleasure, and are often vexatious in the use; so that I prefer another plan, which though not absolutely sure, reduces the danger to the smallest possible degree and is vastly more enjoyable. And that is, to go with two or three men at the same time. Physiologists tell us that the mixing of different men's seed in our cunts, tends to neutralize its impregnating power and render it inert. Taking a man's seed in the mouth and swallowing it has also the same tendency. The semen thrown into the stomach seems to inoculate the system and render it seed-proof. It is by these means that I have hitherto avoided a big belly, which I abhor.'

'Thanks, dear Lady Flora, what you say seems reasonable enough, but you have made me very uncomfortable about myself, Freddy poured a lot of spunk into my cunt to day. What a terrible thing it would be if he got me in the family way. I should die with shame, and Papa would be so angry! Oh Lady Flora, can you help me in any way? Would you advise me to get myself fucked by somebody else?'

'Well, my darling, that might avert the danger if it were quickly done, and in any case could not make matters worse. But I don't think you need be much afraid of what happened today. The first time a girl is fucked, she is in such a state of trepidation that she seldom conceives, no matter how much seed is thrown into her cunt. It is on subsequent occasions when her nerves have quieted down and she resigns herself more thoroughly to the full partici-pation of the sweet joy, that her womb becomes most susceptible.

But if you are neither ashamed nor afraid to trust yourself to my guidance, and will permit Freddy to fuck you again before me I will see that he is followed at once by my own two favourites, James and Tomkins. The first has a larger prick than Freddy, and coming after him, he will afford your cunt a new and extended treat; while the second has a tool of really grand proportions, which will so stir you up, that every nerve inside your cunt will thrill with the highest degree of voluptuous gratification.'

'Very well, dear Lady Flora, your description has fired my imagination, and I place myself in your hands without reserve.'

My Aunt is now delighted beyond measure. She had reached the goal towards which all her efforts had been directed. Nothing pleased her more than to have the management of a fucking transaction between those who were comparatively fresh to the soft encounter; and now her desire was to be fully gratified.

Nor was she altogether selfish in this gratification. Her peculiar tact and great experience enabled her both to increase and prolong the sweet of coition; but her highest delight consisted in exercising her talent for the benefit of others, and in watching with prurient interest the manifestations of their pleasure.

So she replied with ardour: 'You are a sweet girl, Clara. You seem to be formed by nature for voluptuous exercises and enjoyment. And your delicious little cunt is the very abode of blissful love. Let me kiss it once again before I go to prepare for its fullest gratification.' And placing her hands under Clara's bottom she raised her up, and ravenously kissed and sucked her dear little arse-hole.

Then getting up, she said: 'Stay just as you are, my pet, with your lovely bottom turned up and your delicious cunt full in view. I won't be long.'

Susan first came in, she smiled when she saw the lascivious posture in which my Aunt had placed her docile pupil and said, 'Oh, Miss Clara, how enticing you look! Let me give you a view of your own secret charms,' and bringing the lights nearer she placed a tall mirror at each side, so that Clara, on turning her naked bottom could view the rosy cleft which gleamed in the luxurious furrow between its beautifully rounded cheeks. 'Now, whoever comes in will have a treat.'

To please Lady Flora, I had taken off everything even my shirt, while she had also disrobed, retaining only a light dressing gown open in the front. We entered together, and as we came up to the bed my Aunt said, 'Now Freddy, here is Clara's sweet cunt ready to receive your prick. Let me put him in, and Susan and I will watch you and pet you both, so that we shall all share in the pleasing operation. Oh there! How easily Freddy's prick slips in! Now, Clara, heave your little arse, is he fucking as you like?'

'Oh yes – I like that – Fuck me, Freddy fuck me. – Dear Lady Flora, how nicely you rub my clitoris! And your finger Susan is setting my bottom on fire. Freddy, how is your prick feeling now? Do you enjoy fucking me with your dear Aunt looking on and holding your prick?'

'Yes, Darling, your cunt is heaven to my prick, and my dear Aunt's fingers are like angels helping me in – hot – there – Clara – isn't that nice?'

'Yes – oh! yes – shoot it in – oh Lady Flora! My cunt is full – Oh!!!' and Clara's head fell back and her arms lay extended by her sides, but her pretty round bottom kept twitching as the frothy spunk oozed out of her overflowing cunt.

Her rest was not long, for in a moment, Freddy was replaced by another, and she was aroused by feeling a large firm prick making its way with delicious thrusts through the soft and yielding folds of her cunt.

My Aunt's fingers again resumed their amorous play as she said: 'Fuck steadily James. This is the greatest proof of confidence and affection I have ever given you. Be sure to treat this sweet young lady with the utmost tenderness and respect. And never forget your solemn promise of perfect and unbroken silence,' and stooping forward she kissed Clara and asked, 'Dearest pet, how are you enjoying your second fuck? Is James' prick, giving you satisfaction.'

'Yes, dear Lady Flora; I like the feel of James' prick in my cunt. He works it well. Are you fond of fucking, James?'

'Yes, dear Miss Clara, I love fucking. I would like to fuck every pretty girl, but I never was in a nicer cunt than yours – Oh! oh!! – your Ladyship! – I have discharged.'

'Get off then, James. Now, Tomkins, it is your turn, your prick feels in good order – Oh! – it's in! without the slightest difficulty! Now Clara, your cunt looks stretched a little.'

'Oh yes, I feel it – oh! I feel it – but it is delicious! – Fuck me Tomkins – don't be afraid – ram your big prick – all the way into my cunt – Hoh? That's a grand fuck – Fuck – Oh!! What a gust! – That will do – I have got enough – Surely I must be safe now.'

CLARA'S DESIRES BECOME INSATIABLE

The enjoyment of three pricks in succession appeared to stir up Clara's excitable nature to its very depths. From that day forward she seemed to think of nothing but fucking. The gratification of her itching cunt occupied all her thoughts by night and by day. She commenced in the morning by getting Susan to frig and suck her cunt until she spent, at the same time throwing her body into the most wanton postures and repeating all the bawdy words she had ever heard. She would turn up her naked bottom, flying her legs in the air and cry, 'Now Susan, come look at my cunt. Gamahuche me, spread my cunt open with your fingers, push in your tongue as far as you can. Suck my cunt, Susan, suck it, put your finger in the hole of my bottom.' Then jerking up her arse. 'Oh Susan! – that's nice. I love to have my cunt looked at and then kissed and sucked. I also greatly enjoy petting and sucking a nice prick; and I know you like it too. Which do you enjoy most, Susan, sucking the prick of a man or his sucking your cunt?'

'Both are very nice', replied Susan. 'I like one at one time, and the other at another time, according to circumstances.'

'I have never sucked but one prick, and that was Freddy's; but when James and Tomkins were fucking me last night, I could not help thinking that as their pricks felt so very nice in my cunt, how pleasant it would be to hold them in my hand, rub them up and down with my fingers, and then put them to my lips and suck them in my mouth. I had the whole head and shoulders of Freddy's prick in my mouth, the fingers of one hand were closed firmly round the root, and with the other hand I gently squeezed his cock, and he looked so pleased as he jerked his bottom, I should say his arse, and fucked me in the mouth; all the while, his hands were on my head playing with my ears and curls, and then when his spunk began to shoot he roared like a bull, and seemed as if he wanted to ram his prick down my throat. I swallowed all his spending every drop. It had rather a mawkish taste, but seemed to warm me inside, and certainly increased the feeling of pleasure in my cunt.'

'You did quite right, when a girl does take a man's seed in her mouth, it is better to swallow it, for it increases the pleasure on both sides and has other good effects besides. Most men like occasionally to spend in the mouth of a woman, and they enjoy her cunt all the more afterwards. I nearly always suck the prick of every man that fucks me.'

'Yes, I have seen you suck James' prick, and you told me that you have sucked Tomkins' also; but what a mouthful his must be!'

'It certainly does stretch one's lips, but I only sucked what I could get into my mouth, and the part round the head-nut or glands, as they call it is the most sensitive part of the prick; and besides, I tickled his bollocks and even his arse-hole until he spent. But there is a way of making this operation vastly more interesting and enjoyable, in fact; doubling the pleasure.'

'What way is that, Susan? Tell me all about it.'

'Well, let us suppose you are going to suck Master Freddy's prick; we will place him sitting in an arm-chair, and having let down his trousers and made him open wide his legs, we will set you on your knees before him, so that you can hold his prick in your hand and suck its head in your mouth. Then we will lift you skirts and lay your pretty bottom perfectly bare. We will then get James, suppose, to kneel behind you. He will have your delicious arse spread out before him. How he will admire its full round plumpness! How he will pass his hands over its smooth cheeks! How he will press his fingers down the voluptuous furrow! How he will play with the lips of your longing cunt? How he will pinch the rosy nob at the top and dart his fingers into the randy slit below, until you are forced to take the luscious morsel from your mouth and cry: Fuck me, James, fuck me, my cunt is all on fire, thrust your prick into it and quench the flame with a flood of spunk: Then as you felt James' prick prodding your cunt and his belly rubbing your bottom, you would realize how much the pleasure is increased by being engaged with two different men at the same time, and you would suck Master Freddy's prick, squeeze his bollocks and tickle his arse as you never did before.'

'Oh, Susan, that would be grand! and I will try it too; but meanwhile you have got my cunt into a terrible state – it does feel just on fire – suck it, dear Susan – suck it – put your finger well into my bottom – stir it round about – Oh my – I am going wild – my arse – my cunt – my arse – Oh Susan! – my arse – my arse!!' and Clara lay back thoroughly exhausted.

Clara and I used to wander about the gardens in the forenoon; while my Aunt wrote letters and transacted her other business. As she was known to be both liberal and good, she was much sought after as Patroness for various Charitable Institutions, and received numerous applications for relief.

Meanwhile Clara and I amused ourselves in whatever way the fancy of the moment inclined it to go; but our fancy always led to one result – the gratification of our sexual desires. There was a capital swing hung in a sheltered part of one of the enclosed gardens, which seemed very attractive to Clara. She delighted in placing me on it and then striding across me and drawing up her skirts would bury my prick in her soft aperture of love. Our joint efforts to keep the swing going were sufficient to produce such new and varied motions of my prick in her cunt as caused us both peculiarly agreeable sensations. She would cry: 'Stir it again, dear Freddy, now a little push, now, another jog – Oh! that's delicious!' and she twisted about, grinding the satin cheeks of her bottom against my belly and thighs until she pumped me dry, and I had to get off the swing and crave a little rest.

Another time when sitting on a bank toying with one another, she happened to see James passing through the garden with a basket of fruit which he had gathered, and was about to carry to a neighbouring farmhouse by his Mistress direction. She whispered: 'Dear Freddy, I have quite tired you out, and yet my cunt is not satisfied, would you mind if I ran after James and made him give me one little poke?'

'Not in the least, Dearest, twenty, if you like; only manage it so that I may see your sweet cunt while you are giving it the desired gratification.'

'All right,' she said with a smile, and started off.

'James, I want you here for a moment – what were you and Susan doing last night?'

'Oh, the old game. I felt her cunt, she lugged out my prick and drew me towards her. I pulled up her petticoats, she spread her legs, I pushed forward my prick, she placed it in her cunt, I pushed it up, she jogged her rump, I heaved back and forward, she caught me by the bollocks. I grasped the cheeks of her arse, and stroked her until my spunk was all spended, and ever she cried: "Enough."'

'Then, I suppose, you are thoroughly drained now.'

'Not at all, Miss; see here,' and he drew out his prick, erect and in fair fucking order, 'may I give you a trial of it, Miss?'

'Yes, if you can do it to me standing up.'

'Why not, throw your right arm over my shoulders, hold up your clothes with the left; press your bottom into me while I lift your thigh, there, it is going in, how do you like this manner of fucking?'

'It is wonderfully good, push James, push,' and making a succession of little springs with the one foot resting on the ground, she spun him round, all the while urging him on by saying: 'Drive up your prick, James, up my cunt. Fuck, squeeze my bottom – now – I feel it coming let your spunk fly fuck – fuck – fuck –'

I sometimes took my gun and walked to a wood near us to shoot rabbits.

She would mount her pony and ride round to meet me there. Probably she would find me sitting under a tree to rest. Having quickly dismounted and tied up her pony, she would advance towards me, her golden curls fluttering in the summer breeze, her rosy face smiling with anticipated joy and her bright eyes beaming with wanton merriment and lustful desire.

Seated by my side, and with my hand in hers, or more likely playing with the silky hair which was now beginning to over-shadow her sweet cunt, we would talk of such amorous subjects, as Jupiter's assumption of the form of a bull in order that he might obtain possession of Europa. She was curious to know whether it was as a bull that he ravished her? 'For' she said, 'Susan and I were looking this morning through a window in one of the out houses into the back yard, and we saw the bull mounting several cows, and when I watched his long red thing pushed up into their bellies it made my cunt itch for it too.'

I laughed and replied: 'The Latin Poets do not inform us on the subject, but there is an account of how Pasiphae, the wife of the Minos, one of her grandsons was enabled, by means of an ingenious support contained by Doedalus, to sustain the weight and receive into her wanton cunt the pizzle of a famous white bull, given by Neptune to her husband, and that she afterwards gave birth to a monster, half man, half bull, which was called the Minotaur.

I also told her how Jupiter gained access to the arms of Leda in the shape of a swan and enjoyed her in that guise, so that she afterwards brought for the eyes and that many ancient statues and pictures representing this curious fucking scene had been preserved, showing the amorous swan fluttering in the arms of a naked woman, his bill snatching kisses or thrust under her arm, his webbed feet separating her legs, and his hinder parts pressed in between her thighs and his red tool darting into her moist and open cunt. 'Oh Freddy! it must be very nice to be fucked by a swan, to hold the dear white fellow in one's arms and feel his slippery tool playing in one's cunt.'

During this conversation she would manage to get my trousers unbuttoned down the front, and soon her kind efforts would be repaid by my prick showing signs of strong erection, bobbing to her kisses and standing up boldly amid her encircling fingers.

Then she would say: 'Now Freddy, you have been working too hard of late. Sit perfectly still, I will do it all myself,' and rising up she would place herself astride on my lap, and nestling the head of my prick between the warm lips of her cunt would press slowly down, saying: 'Now – dont stir – keep your hands on my bottom as I move up and down, and give me a pinch if you wish to hurry me.'

Then as she worked her body up and down, wriggling her arse and twisting from side, she would keep on kissing me and muttering: 'Good boy, your dear prick – fills my cunt so nicely – oh! isn't that good?' Then pressing down and rubbing her bottom on my thighs, she would stoop and clutch my balls with her hand, saying: Good bollocks – now they swell – shoot in your spunk – Oh – there – I feel it – pinch my arse – fuck – fuck – fuck.'

On another occasion, we were walking by the cottage of one of my Aunt's labourers named Madden. He was standing at the door with his baby in his arms and saluted us as we passed.

He was a fine burly-looking fellow, the very picture of manly strength and good temper. I perceived that Clara was immediately struck with the unusually large protuberance that swelled out between his legs. Her eyes were fastened on it as she said: 'Will you excuse me for a few moments, Freddy. I want to go and play with Madden's baby.'

I laughed for I knew it was a baby without legs or arms, and with hair at its tail that she was thinking of.

'Go,' I said, 'and enjoy yourself with his baby as long as you like. I will walk about until you come out.'

Going up to the cottage door she said: 'What a fine baby you have, Madden. How is it you are acting as nurse?'

'His mother has gone to the village to make some purchases, and she asked me to mind him until she returned.'

'If you are as good a nurse as you are a gardener, the child will be well cared for. Let me hold him for a moment.'

'Thankee, Miss, the wee chap resembles his mother, and I like him for her sake?'

'I think he takes more after you, for he has your good humoured smile and roguish eye,' and she gave him a wicked glance, 'but he seems sleepy now, where is his cot?'

'Come in, Miss, and I will show you.'

She followed him into the inner room, and having placed the baby in his little cot threw off her hat and her neck-kerchief as the day was very warm. Then she leaned over the child and began to hum a time to make him go to sleep.

Madden remained standing by her side, looking down on her graceful figure as she stooped over the cot. She was conscious of his admiration, and to increase the effect she slowly stirred her bottom from side to side so as to display its voluptuous curves to more advantage. The man's lustful nature warmed at the sight. He came a step nearer – then bent forward to settle the baby's pillow, and as if to steady himself placed his hand gently on Clara's beautiful bottom. To his great delight he perceived no shrinking from his hand, it felt very soft indeed, but met his touch with a fleshy firmness that seemed to invite him to further advances; so he muttered: 'It was very good of you, dear Miss Clara, to come in here to put baby into his cot.'

'I always wish to be kind to those whom I like; and you are one of my special favourites, Madden.'

'Dear Miss Clara, I would do anything to please you,' and he pressed up against her, and spreading his fingers moved them about over her bottom.

She evidently did not object to this little innocent familiarity, for she only stooped more over the child and stirred her bottom in time with the tune she was humming.

He gently pressed one soft cheek, then he moved to the other. Then passing his fingers down the indentation between those luxurious prominences he reached what he knew was the lower end of her sweet little slit. He could hardly believe it possible, but surely he felt it pressing out a little and the thighs getting gradually more open. His lust was now thoroughly aroused, and he scarcely knew what he was doing as he said: 'Oh, dear Miss Clara, my heart burns for you. What a lovely young lady you are!' And stooping suddenly he ran his hand up between her thighs and seized her moist and gaping cunt.

'Oh Madden! What do you mean? You must not put your hand up my clothes, you must not uncover me.'

'Dear Miss, stay as you are,' and he put one hand on her back to keep her down, and with the other directed the swollen head of his enormous prick to her eager and longing cunt.

'Oh stop, stop, I beg of you. What do you want to do?'

'To fuck you, Miss Clara – to get my prick into your sweet cunt and fuck you, there, it has got in, let me push it all the way up.' And shoving his hands under her clothes on each side he grasped her round the loins, and began working his great prick with such vigour that his hairy belly smacked against her smooth bottom and made her whole body vibrate with the violence of his shocks.

'Oh Madden, you are a terrible man, and your prick is enormous. Yes, I like it now – push – fuck – yes, fuck away, as hard as you please. – Oh! that's grand! Hold me up while you push – I'm coming too – now – fuck – fuck – fuck.'

I had crept up to the open window and watched the foregoing scene with much interest and amusement, but just at this moment, to my horror as well as theirs, the door of the room suddenly burst open and a shrill voice cried: 'Hollo, Madden! what are you doing? Who is that impudent slut you have brought into my bedroom as soon as my back was turned? Get out, you strumpet.'

This was dreadful, so I rushed to the front door and bounding into the room caught Mrs Madden by the shoulders, and pulling her back, said: 'Don't speak that way to Miss Alcock. She is not to blame, for she only came in to see your fine handsome baby.' That softened her a little. 'And I suppose Madden must have taken a drop too much and mistook her for your charming self; so cool down I pray you. And after all, what great harm has Madden done you? You have him as often as you like, and it is very selfish to keep such a fine man all to yourself. Give him liberty to enjoy himself, and I am sure he won't care how many lovers are attracted by your own undoubted charms. Madden, would you mind a body kissing your wife, if it was done openly and with your consent?' And placing my arm round her I drew her beside me on the bed.

All this time, poor Clara having shaken down her tumbled skirts sat on a chair sobbing with her face covered by her hands. Madden stood at her side looking very foolish but making some awkward attempts to soothe her. But on hearing my proposal to kiss his wife, he at once brightened up and said: 'Not in the least, Master Freddy, you may kiss her as much as you like, on the face or any where else that you wish, so far as I am concerned.'

On this, I placed my hands on each side of her pretty face and tried to turn it up for a kiss. She said nothing, but seemed determined not to let me. Madden, however, winked at me to persevere; then he said in a louder and more commanding tone: 'Margery, don't be a fool, let Master Freddy kiss you. It is the only amend you can make for your dreadful abuse of this dear young lady who was not to blame at all.'

Mrs Madden now began to show signs of yielding, and allowed me to kiss her cherry lips and then put my hand on her full and exuberant bubbies. I pressed on, still encouraged by the approving looks of her husband, and leaning hard against her gradually forced her back on the bed. I pushed my knee in between hers, but when I attempted to pull up her petticoats, she suddenly squealed out and said: 'Madden, do you mean to say, you are going to allow this young gentleman to make free with your wife here in your very presence and on your own bed too – Fie Sir – I wont let you – take your hand.'

'Don't mind her, Master Freddy, you have better my full consent. Pull up her coats and dont heed her squalls.'

Considering that Madden knew his wife better than we did, I tugged away, and soon had a pair of great fleshy thighs laid bare and, in spite of her struggles and outcries, a fine bushy tuft of dark brown hair that completely covered the temple of love.

Madden laughed: 'Bravo, Master Freddy, you have got to the right place at last; get into it now and take possession, and this dear young lady will repay me by letting me stroke her own sweet pussy once again.'

Clara smiled as he again put his immense prick in her hand and groped his way to her well-moistened cunt.

Meanwhile I had got my own prick out, and as Mrs Madden began to understand that, under the circumstances, it was wiser not to prolong her opposition too far, I succeeded in pushing in between her thighs and directing its head to the luscious opening of her cunt. A sudden push introduced it without difficulty, and I commenced to fuck her with a firm but gentle stroke.

As soon as her husband observed this, he felt that, having advanced so far, a bold finish would be best. So without saying a word he took up Clara in his arms, carried her to the bed, and placed her by his wife.

Then, lifting her clothes, with one plunge drove his prick up to the root into her cunt and said: 'Now, Master Freddy, let us jog together. How do you like Margery's cunt? She was a maid, at least she said so, when I first fucked her before our marriage, about this time last year, and you are the first besides myself that has tried her since. Is not that the truth Margery?'

'Mind your fucking and don't be asking silly questions.'

'Anyway, Master Freddy, I trust she is giving you satisfaction.'

'Your wife – has a splendid cunt, Madden – and you have taught her well – how to site it – for she fucks like a hero – You are a fine and very sensible woman, Margery and your husband is a brave fellow too – Do I fuck to your liking?' I gasped out between my strokes.

'Why yes, Master Freddy. I don't fault your fucking, but it does seem queer to be fucked this way before one's husband; but as he is content and you have got in your prick, fuck away as hard as you like – but look at Ned – how he wags his bottom! and stretching out her hand she felt her husband's prick as it plunged in and out of Clara's cunt, and asked her: 'Do you like how Ned fucks you, Miss Clara? You have a dear little cunt; she added as she felt her clitoris and the thick pouting lips which clung round her husband's tool. I hope Ned is filling it with pleasure and delight.'

'Thanks, dear Mrs Madden – you are really kind – your husband has a grand affair – it feels delicious in my cunt – fuck me – oh Ned! fuck me – fuck me, hard!' and Clara wagged her beautiful arse with wanton energy and effect.

Meanwhile, Margery clasped me in her arms, crying: 'Fuck me, fuck me, Freddy dear,' and pressed up her quivering cunt to receive the spunk I was darting into her salacious womb.

Before I left I slipped a few guineas into Margery's fist. Her face glowed when she saw the coins. She thanked me, and turning to Clara, entreated her to forgive the foolish words she had used in anger, and before she was aware to whom she was speaking, and she told her to come again as often as she liked, and that she might have the use of Ned's article whenever she felt inclined; then looking towards me, with a rosy blush she added: 'You will be welcome too.'

I kissed her and shook hands with Madden, commending him for his liberality and good sense, and wished them good bye.

I am pretty certain you will all agree that both Madden and his wife acted wisely and judiciously in the matter.

He was really an excellent husband, and valued his wife at a high rate, and treated her with the greatest affection and respect; but like many another her husband was led astray by the force of strong temptation, and discovered in the act. This seemed a great misfortune, but swung to their mutual forbearance and good sense, it led to the happiest results.

Henceforth they each conceded absolute freedom to the other, and thus being no longer galled and irritated by restraining bonds they were drawn really closer to one another, and having nothing to conceal there was no longer room for bitter jealousy nor foolish recrimination. As a matter of fact, I have never known a happier or more prosperous couple.

I used to visit them occasionally, and often enjoyed the pleasant embraces of sweet Margery before her husband, who generally helped with his own hand and followed me by plunging his prick into his wife's prepared and highly excited cunt.

They have now a flourishing progeny, and one curly headed urchin takes so much after me that Madden declares there can be no mistake as to his father. Be that as it may I have accepted the responsibility and have invested a sum the interest of which his parents receive for his education and benefit.

Extract from

A NIGHT IN A MOORISH HAREM

ABDALLAH PASCHA'S SERAGLIO

HER BRITISH MAJESTY'S SHIP *Antler*, of which I was in command, lay becalmed one afternoon off the coast of Morocco. I did not allow the steam to be raised for I knew the evening breeze would soon make toward the land.

Retiring to my cabin I threw myself upon the sofa. I could not sleep for my thoughts kept wandering back to the beautiful women of London and the favours which some of them had granted me when last on shore.

Months had elapsed since then and months more would elapse before I could again hope to quench, in the lap of beauty, the hot desire which now coursed through my veins and distended my genitals.

To divert my mind from thoughts at present so imperative I resolved to take a bath. Beneath the stern windows which lightened my cabin lay a boat, into which I got by sliding down a rope which held it to the ship. Then I undressed and plunged into the cool waves. After bathing I redressed, and, reclining in the boat, fell asleep. When I awoke it was dark and I was floating along near the shore. The ship was miles away.

The rope which held the boat must have slipped when the breeze sprang up, and the people on the ship being busy getting underway had not noticed me. I had no oars and dared not use the sails for fear the Moorish vessels in sight would discover me. I drifted towards a large building which was the only one to be seen; it rose from the rocks near the water's edge. The approach to the place on which it stood seemed to be from the land side, and all the windows which I could see were high above the ground.

The keel of my boat soon grated on the sand and I hastened to pull it among the rocks for concealment, for it was quite possible I might be seized if discovered and sold into slavery. My plan was to wait for the land breeze just before dawn and escape to sea. At this moment I heard a whispered call from above. I looked up and saw two ladies looking down on me from the high windows above, and behind these two were gathered several others whom I could just see in the gloom.

'We have been watching you,' said the lady, 'and will try to assist you. Wait where you are.'

She spoke in French, which is the common medium of communication among the different nations inhabiting the shores of the Mediterranean, and which had become familiar to me. I now thought this isolated building was a seraglio and I resolved to trust the ladies, who would run even more risk than myself in case of discovery.

After waiting some time, a rope of shawls was let down from the window and the same voice bid me climb. My discipline when a midshipman made this easy for me to do; I rose hand over hand and safely reached the window through which I was assisted by the ladies into the perfumed air of an elegant apartment richly furnished and elegantly lighted.

My first duty was to kiss the fair hands which had aided me, and then I explained the accident which had brought me among them and the plan I had formed for escape before dawn. I then gave my name and rank.

While doing this I had an opportunity to observe the ladies; there were nine of them and any one of them would have been remarked for her beauty. Each one of them differed from all the others in the style of her charms: some were large and some were small; some were slender and some plump, some blonde and some brunette, but all were bewitchingly beautiful. Each, too, was the most lovely type of a different nationality, for war and shipwrecks and piracy enable the Moorish Pashas to choose their darlings from under all the flags that float on the Mediterranean.

A lady whom they called Inez and whom, therefore, I took to be a Spaniard, answered me by bidding me in the name of all of them the warmest welcome.

'You are,' she said, 'in the seraglio of Abdallah, the Pasha of this district, who is not expected until tomorrow, and who will never be the wiser if his ladies seize so rare an opportunity to entertain a gentleman during his absence.' She added, 'We have no secrets or jealousy between ourselves,' smiling very significantly.

'That is very unusual,' said I. 'How can any of you know whether he has any secrets with the one he happens to be alone with?'

'But one of us is never alone with him,' said Inez. The blank look of consternation I had set them all laughing.

They were brimful of mischief and were evidently bent on making the most of the unexpected company of a young man. Inez put her hand on my sleeve. 'How wet you are,' said she. 'It will not be hospitable to allow you to keep on such wet clothes.'

My clothes were perfectly dry, but the winks and smiles that the young ladies exchanged as they began to disrobe me led me cheerfully to submit while they proceeded to divest me of every article of clothing.

When at length my shirt was suddenly jerked off they gave little affected screams and peeped through their fingers at my shaft, which by this time was of most towering dimensions. I had snatched a hearty kiss from one and all of them as they had gathered round to undress me.

Inez now handed me a scarf which she had taken from her own fair shoulders. 'We can none of us bear to leave you,' she said, 'but you can only kiss one at a time; please throw this to the lady you prefer.'

Good heavens! Then it was true, that all of these beautiful women had been accustomed to be present when one of them was embraced.

'Ladies,' said I, 'you are unfair. You have stripped me, but you keep those charms concealed which you offer to my preference. I am not sure now if you have any imperfections which you wish to keep covered.'

The ladies looked at one another, blushed a little, then nodded and laughed, then began undressing. Velvet vests, skirts of lawn and silken trousers were rapidly flung to the floor. Lastly, as if at a given signal, every dainty chemise was stripped off and some of the most lovely forms that ever floated through a sculptor's dream stood naked before me. Was I not myself dreaming, or had I in truth been suddenly transported amid the houses of the seventh heaven?

For a while I stood entranced, gazing at the charming spectacle. 'Ladies,' said I at last, 'it would be immodest in me to give preference when all are so ravishingly lovely. Please keep the scarf, fair Inez, and when I have paid a tribute to your fair charms, pass it yourself to another, till all have been gratified.'

'Did he say all?' cried a little brunette.

'All indeed!' cried the rest in chorus, bursting into laughter.

'Every one,' said I, 'or I will perish in the attempt.'

Inez was standing directly in front of me; she was about nineteen, and of that rarest type of Spanish beauty, partly derived from Flemish blood. Her eyes were sparkling brown, but her long hair was blonde. It was braided and coiled round the top of her head like a crown which added to her queenly appearance, for she was above the ordinary stature; her plump and well-rounded form harmonized with her height. Her complexion had the slight yellow tinge of rich cream, which was set off by the rosy nipples which tipped her full breasts and the still deeper rose of her lips and mouth.

She happened to be standing on one of the silken cushions which, singly and in piles, were scattered about the room in profusion. It made her height just equal to my own. As soon as I had made the speech last recorded. I advanced and folded her in my embrace.

Her soft arms were wound round me in response; and our lips met in a delicious and prolonged kiss, during which my shaft was imprisoned against her warm, smooth belly. Then she raised herself on tiptoe, which brought its crest amid the short, thick hair where the belly terminated. With one hand I guided my shaft to the entrance which welcomed it; with my other I held her plump buttocks toward me. Then she gradually settled on her feet again, and, as she did so, the entrance was slowly and delightfully effected in her moist, hot and swollen sheath. When she was finally on her feet again I could feel her throbbing womb resting on my shaft.

The other ladies had gathered round us; their kisses rained on my neck and shoulders, and the presence of their bosoms and bellies was against my back and sides – indeed they so completely sustained Inez and myself that I seemed about to mingle my being with them all at once. I had stirred the womb of Inez with but a few thrusts – when the rosy cheeks became a deeper dye, her eyes swam, her lips parted and I felt a delicious baptism of moisture on my shaft.

Then her head sank on my shoulder, the gathered sperm of months gushed from my crest so profusely that I seemed completely transferred with waves of rapture into the beautiful Spanish girl. Her sighs of pleasure were not only echoed by my own, but by those of all the ladies gathered around us in sympathy. They gently lowered us from this sustaining embrace to a pile of cushions. As they did so, with hardly any aid on our part, my diminished shaft was drawn out of Inez and, with it, some of my tributary sperm, which splashed on the floor.

'It was too bad of you, Inez, to take more than you can keep,' said one of the others. She said it in such a pitiful tone it convulsed us all with laughter. As for me, I now realized the rashness of the promise I had made them all, but they gaily joined hands round Inez and myself and began a circling dance, their round, white limbs and plump bosoms floating in the lamplight as they moved in cadence to a Moorish love song, in which they all joined. With my cheeks pillowed against the full breasts of Inez, I watched the charming circle, which was like a scene in fairy land. Bracelets and anklets of heavy fettered gold glittered on their arms and legs; rings, necklaces and earrings of diamonds and rubies, which they had in profusion, glistened at every movement.

Each one had her hair elaborately dressed in the style peculiarly becoming to herself and there were no envious garments to conceal a single charm. I urged them to prolong the bewitching spectacle again and again, which they obligingly did. Then they gathered around me, reclining to rest on the cushions as near as they could get, in attitudes which were picturesque and voluptuous.

When we were thus resting I frequently exchanged a kiss or caress with my fair companions, which I took care to do impartially. Then it occurred to me that I would like to hear from the lips of each the most interesting and voluptuous passage from their lives. Again these interesting ladies, after a little urging, consented, and Inez commenced.

THE SPANISH LADY'S STORY

We lived in Seville. When I attained the age of sixteen my parents promised me in marriage to a wealthy gentleman, whom I had seen but twice and did not admire. My love was already given to Carlos, a handsome young officer who had just been promoted to a lieutenant for bravery. He was elegantly formed, his hair and eyes were as dark as night and he could dance to perfection. But it was for his gentle, winning smile that I loved him.

On the evening of the day that my parents had announced their determination to me, I had gone to be alone in the orange grove in the farthest part of our garden, there to sorrow over my hard fate. In the midst of my grief I heard the voice of Carlos calling me. Could it be he who had been banished from the house and whom I never expected to see again?

He sprang down from the garden wall, folded me in his embrace and covered my hair with kisses for I had hidden my blushing face on my bosom. Then we talked of our sad lot. Carlos was poor and it would be impossible to marry without the consent of my parents; we could only mingle our tears and regrets.

He led me to a grassy bank concealed by the orange trees and rose bushes, then he drew me on his lap and kissed my lips and cheeks and eyes. I did not chide him, for it must be our last meeting, but I did not return his kisses with passion. I had never felt a wanton desire in my life, much less now when I was so sad.

His passionate kisses were no longer confined to my face, but were showered on my neck, and at length my dress was parted and revealed my little breasts to his ardent lips. I felt startled and made an attempt to stop him in what I considered an impropriety, but he did not stop there. I felt my skirts being raised with a mingled sensation of alarm and shame which caused me to try to prevent it, but it was impossible – I loved him too much to struggle against him, and he was soon lying between my naked thighs.

'Inez,' he said, 'if you love me, be my wife for these few moments before we part.'

I could not resist the appeal. I offered my lips to kisses without any feeling save innocent love, and lay passive while I felt him guide a stiff, warm object between my thighs. It entered where nothing had ever entered before and no sooner was it entered than he gave a fierce thrust which seemed to tear my vitals with a cruel pain. Then he gave a deep sigh and sank heavily upon my bosom.

I kissed him repeatedly, for I supposed it must have hurt him as much as it did me, little thinking that his pleasure had been as exquisite as my suffering had been. Just at that moment the harsh voice of my duenna resounded through the garden, calling, 'Inez! Inez!'

Exchanging with my seducer a lingering, hearty kiss, I extracted myself from his embrace and answered the call. My duenna eyed me sharply as I approached her.

'Why do you straddle your legs so far apart when you walk,' said she, and when I came closer, 'Why is the bosom of your dress so disordered and why are your cheeks so flushed?'

I made some excuse about climbing to get an orange and hurried past her to my room. I locked the door and prepared to go to bed that I might think uninterruptedly of Carlos, whom I now loved more than ever. When I took off my petticoat I found it all stained with blood. I folded it and treasured it beneath my pillow to dream upon, under the fond illusion that Carlos's blood was mingled there with my own.

For weeks afterwards I was so closely watched that I could not see Carlos. The evening preceding my marriage I went to vespers with my duenna. While we were kneeling in the cathedral a large woman, closely veiled, came and knelt close beside me. She attracted my attention by plucking my dress, and, as I turned, she momentarily lifted the corner of her mantle and I saw it was Carlos in disguise. I was now all alert and a small package was slipped into my hand. I had just time to secure it in my bosom when my duenna arose and we left the church.

As soon as I regained the privacy of my own room I tore open the package and found it contained a silken rope ladder and letter from Carlos requesting me to suspend it from the window that night after the family was at rest.

The note was full of love. There was much more to tell, it said, if I would grant the interview by means of the ladder. Of course, I determined to see him. I was very ignorant of what most girls learn from each other, for I had no companion. I supposed when a woman was embraced as I had been she necessarily got with child, and that such embraces therefore occurred at intervals of a year or so. I expected, consequently, nothing of the kind at the coming interview. I wanted to learn of Carlos if the child, which I supposed to be in my womb, would be born so soon as to betray our secret to my husband.

When the family retired I went to my room and dressed myself elaborately, braiding my hair and putting on all of my jewellery. Then I fastened one end of the rope ladder to the bedpost and lowered the other end out of the window; it was at once strained by the ascending step of Carlos. My eyes were soon feasted with the sight of my handsome lover, and we were soon locked in each other's arms.

Again and again we alternately devoured each other with our eyes and pressed each other to our hearts. Words did not seem to be of any use; our kisses and caresses became more passionate, and for the first time in my life I felt a wanton emotion. The lips between my thighs became moistened and torrid with coursing blood; I could feel my cheeks burn under the ardent gaze of my lover; I could no longer meet his eyes – my own dropped in shame.

He began to undress me rapidly, his hand trembling with eagerness. Could it be that he wanted to pierce my loins so soon again, as he had done in the orange garden? An hour ago I would have dreaded it; now the thought caused a throb of welcome just where the pain had been sharpest.

Stripped to my chemise, and even that unbuttoned by the eager hand of my lover, I darted from his arms and concealed my confusion beneath the bedcover. He soon undressed and followed me – then, bestowing one kiss on my neck and one on each of my naked breasts, he opened my thighs and parted the little curls between. Again I felt the stiff, warm object entering. It entered slowly on account of the tightness, but every inch of its progress inward became more and more pleasant.

When it was fully entered I was in a rapture of delight, yet something was wanting. I wrapped my arms around my lover and responded passionately to his kisses. I was almost tempted to respond to his thrusts by a wanton motion of my loins. My maidenhead was gone and the tender virgin wound completely healed, but I had still some remains of maiden shame.

For a moment he lay still and then he gave me half a dozen deep thrusts, each succeeding one giving me more and more pleasure. It culminated at last in a thrill so exquisite that my frame seemed to melt. Nothing more was wanting. I gave a sigh of deep gratification and my arms fell nerveless to my sides, but I received with passionate pleasure two or three more thrusts which Carlos gave me, at each of which my sheath was penetrated by a copious gush which soothed and bathed its membranes. For a long time we lay perfectly still; the stiff shaft which had completely filled me had diminished in size until it slipped completely out. Carlos at last relieved me of his weight by lying at my side, but our legs were still entwined.

We had now time to converse. My lover explained to me all the sexual mysteries which remained for me to know, then we formed plans which would enable us after my marriage to meet often alone. These explanations and plans were mingled so freely with caresses that before my lover left me we had melted five times in each other's arms. I had barely strength to drag up the rope ladder after he departed.

The day had now begun to dawn. I fell into a dreamless sleep and was awakened by my duenna pounding on the door and calling that it was nearly ten o'clock and that I was to be married at eleven. I was in no hurry but they got me to church in time. During the whole ceremony I felt my lover's sperm trickling down my thighs.

We all applauded Inez as she thus finished her story. While she was telling the story one of the ladies, whom I noticed to be the most fleshy of the number, cuddled up close to my side and suffered me to explore all her charms with my hand. During the description of the scene in the orange garden my fingers toyed with the curls between her thighs, and, as the story went on, parted the curls and felt of the lips beneath. She was turned partly on her belly against me so that this by-play was not observed.

My fingers were encouraged by the lady's hand until two of them made an entrance and were completely enclosed in the hot, moist tissue. The little protuberance which all women have within the orifice, and which is the principal seat of sensation, was in her remarkably developed. It was as large as the end of my little finger. I played with it and squeezed it and plunged my fingers past it again and again; she manifested her pleasure by kissing me on the neck, where she had hidden her face.

When Inez described her first thrill in the bedroom scene my fingers were doing all in their power to complete the other lady's gratification, and this, too, with success, for they were suddenly bathed with moisture, and, at the same time, the lady drew a deep sigh, which was not noticed, for all supposed it to be in sympathy with Inez's story. Then she withdrew my hand and lay perfectly still. Inez was about to give her the scarf, but she lay so motionless that she handed it to another.

'This,' said Inez, 'is Helene, a Grecian lady. She will tell you a story and then she will do anything you wish.'

My head was still pillowed on Inez's breast. Helene smiled, then stooped and kissed me. She was about medium height, very slender, but graceful and well rounded, and her skin was as white as alabaster. Her features were of the perfect antique mould and were lighted with fine grey eyes. Her glossy black hair was all brushed back to a knot just below the back of the neck, from which but a single curl escaped on either side and toyed with her firm but finely rounded bosom.

The deep vermilion of her lips compensated for the faint colour of her cheeks, whose tinge was scarcely deeper than that of her finely cut ears. She was about twenty-two, and ripe to yield a charming embrace. I drew her down to a seat on my loins and begged her to begin her story.

THE GRECIAN LADY'S STORY

I entered the bridal bed a virgin. When the bridesmaids left me I trembled with apprehension and covered up my head under the bedclothes. It was because I had heard so many stories of the trials and hardships of a virgin on her marriage night and not because I had any antipathy towards my husband. On the contrary, I liked him.

His courtship had been short, for he was a busy man in the diplomatic service of the Greek government. He was no longer young, but he was good-looking and manly, and I was proud that he had selected me from all the other Athenian girls. My heart beat still more violently when he entered. He came to the side of the bed and, turning down the clothes from my head, he saw how I was agitated. He simply kissed my hand, and then went to the other side of the room to undress. This conduct somewhat reassured me.

When he got into bed and took me in his arms my back was turned towards him. He took no liberties with any part of my person but began to converse with me about the incidents of the wedding I was soon so calm that I suffered him to turn me with my face towards him, and he kissed me first on the forehead and then on the lips.

After a while he begged me to return his kisses, saying that if I did not it would prove that I disliked him; thus encouraged I returned his kisses. When I had so long lain in his arms that I began to feel at home, he turned me upon my back and unfastened the bosom of my chemise and kissed and fondled my breasts. This set my heart beating wildly again, but we kept exchanging kisses till he suddenly lifted the skirt of my chemise and lay between my thighs.

Then I covered my face with my hands for shame, but he was so kind and gentle that I soon got so accustomed to the situation that I suffered him to remove my hands and fasten his mouth to mine in a passionate kiss. As he did so I felt something pushing between my thighs. It entered my curls there and touched the naked lips beneath. I felt my face grow hot with shame and lay perfectly passive.

He must have been in bed with me two hours before he ventured so far. He had his reward, for a soft desire began to grow in my brain, the blood centred on my loins and I longed for the connection which was so imminent. I returned him a kiss as passionate as he gave; it was the signal for which he had been waiting. I felt a pressure on the virgin membrane, not hard enough, however, to be painful. The pressure slackened and then pushed again and again.

By this time I was wanton with desire and not only returned the passionate kisses, but I wound my arms around him. Then came the fateful thrust, tearing away the obstruction and reaching to the very depths of my loins. I gave a cry of mingled bliss and agony, which I could not help repeating at each of the three deep thrusts that followed. Then all was still and an effusion like balm filled my sheath in the place of the organ that had so disturbed it. A delightful languor stole over my frame and I went to sleep in my husband's arms.

In less than six months circumstances compelled me to deceive him. After we had been married awhile our position required us to go a great deal in company. Card playing was very fashionable and the stakes got higher and higher. One night the luck ran terribly against me; I proposed for the party to double.

My husband had gone on a journey a few days before and had left a large sum of money in my charge. It was nearly all his fortune. A portion of this money I now staked, thinking that the luck could not possibly go against me again, but it did. I was rendered desperate. Again I proposed to double – it would take all I had left if I lost.

The ladies who were playing withdrew; the gentlemen were too polite to do so. The cards went against me. I felt myself turn dreadfully pale. The French ambassador, Count Henri, who was sitting beside me, was disposed to conceal my terrible embarrassment. He was a handsome man, but, unlike my husband, he was very stalwart. His manners were very engaging He kept up a stream of small talk till the others had dispersed to other parts of the room, then he offered to bring me on the morrow the amount I had lost.

I turned as crimson as I had before been pale. I knew the price of such assistance. I made him no reply, my look dropped to the floor and I begged him to leave me, which he politely did. All next day I was nearly distracted; I hoped Count Henri would not come. My cheeks would burn as on the evening before and the blood all rush back to my heart.

At three o'clock he came; the valet showed him into the parlour, closed the door and retired. Count Henri must have known he was expected, for I was elegantly dressed in blue silk and my shoulders were set off with heavy lace. I was so weak from agitation that I could not rise from the sofa to greet him.

'May I have the happiness,' he said, 'of being your confidant?' as he seated himself beside me, holding in one hand a well-filled purse and dropping the other around my waist. I could not reject the purse. If I kept the purse I could not ask him to remove his arm. I was giddy with contending emotions.

'For God's sake, spare me,' I murmured. My head dropped, he caught it to his heart – I had fainted away.

When I again became conscious I was lying on my back upon the sofa in the arms of the Count, the lace on my bosom was parted, my heavy skirts were all turned up from my naked thighs and he was in the very ecstasy of filling my sheath with sperm.

It was this exquisite sensation which had restored me to consciousness, but I was too late to join in the ecstasy. His shaft became limber and small and I was left hopelessly in the lurch. Then I beseeched him to go as it was no time or place for this. 'Will you receive me in your bedroom tonight?' asked the Count, kissing my bare bosoms. He had so excited my passions that I no longer hesitated. 'The front door will be unfastened all night,' I replied, 'and my room is directly over this.' Then he allowed me to rise. I adjusted my disordered dress as quickly as possible, but I was not quick enough. The valet opened the door to bring in the card of a visitor. He saw enough to put me in his power.

After the Count had gone I found the purse in my bosom, it contained more than I had lost, but my thoughts were not of money. My lips had tasted the forbidden fruit; I was no longer the same woman; my excitement had culminated in lascivious desire. I could hardly wait for night to come.

When finally the house was still I unfastened the front door, retired to my room, undressed and was standing in my chemise with my nightgown in my hand ready to put on when the door of my room opened and Alex, the valet, stood before me with his finger on his lips. He was a fine looking youth of seventeen, a Hungarian of a reduced family, who acted half in the capacity of secretary and half in that of valet for my husband. I could not help giving a faint scream, while I concealed my person as well as possible with the nightgown I held in my hands.

'My lady,' said he, 'I know all, but I shall be discreet. I only ask you to give me the sweetest proof of your confidence.'

There was no help for it. With a murmured 'For shame,' I sprang into bed and hid under the bedclothes. He quickly undressed and followed me. My object was to dismiss him before the Count came; I therefore suffered him to make rapid progress. He took me in his arms and kissed my lips and breasts and, as he raised my chemise, our naked thighs met. He was much more agitated than myself. I had been anticipating a paramour all the afternoon and he could not have known what reception would be accorded him. He could hardly guide his shaft to the lips that welcomed it.

As for myself, I began where I had left off with the Count. My sheath with wanton greediness devoured every inch that entered it and at the very first thrust I melted with an adulterous rapture never felt in my husband's embrace. Just at that moment I heard the front door softly open and shut. I pushed Alex away with force that drew his stiff shaft completely out of me.

'Gather up your clothes quickly and get into the closet,' I said. Madly eager as he must have been to finish, he hurried with his clothes into the closet as the Count entered.

The Count came up and kissed me. I pretended to be asleep. He undressed hastily, and, getting into bed, took me in his arms. But I delayed his progress as much as possible. I made him tell me everything that had been said about my losses at cards. I used every artifice to keep him at bay until his efforts should arouse my passions.

Then he mounted me and his stalwart shaft distended and penetrated me so much deeper than that of young Alex that it was more exquisite than before. Again the wild, adulterous thrill penetrated every part of my body. I fairly groaned with ecstasy. At that moment the front door loudly opened. It must be my husband unexpectedly returning.

'Good heavens, Count!' I cried, 'under the bed with you.' He pulled his great stiff shaft out of me with a curse of disappointment that he could not finish and scrambled under the bed, dragging his clothes after him.

My husband came in all beaming with delight that he had been able to return so soon. I received him with much demonstration. 'How it flushes your cheeks to see me,' he said.

When he had undressed and come to bed I returned his caresses with so much ardour that he soon entered where Alex and the Count had so hastily withdrawn. I felt pleasant, but feigned much more rapture than I felt.

To console the Count I dropped one of my hands down alongside the bed, which he was so polite as to kiss, and, as my husband's face was buried in my neck, while he was making rapid thrusts I kissed my other hand to Alex, who was peeping through the closet door. Then I gave a motion to my loins which sent my husband spending and repeated it till I had extracted from him the most copious gushes. It was too soon for me to melt with another thrill; my object was to fix him for a sound sleep, but the balmy sperm was so grateful to my hot sheath after the two fierce preceding encounters that I felt rewarded for my troubles.

He soon fell sound asleep. Then I motioned for the Count to go. With his clothes in one hand and his stiff shaft in the other he glided out. Soon after, we heard the front door shut and the disconsolate Alex cautiously came forth. With his clothes under his arm and both hands holding his rigid shaft, he too disappeared.

RANDIANA

OR

EXCITABLE TALES BEING THE EXPERIENCE OF AN EROTIC PHILOSOPHER*

A FIRST EXPERIENCE

Those of my readers who peruse the following pages and expect to find a pretty tale of surpassing interest, embellished with all the spice which fiction can suggest and a clever pen supply, will be egregiously mistaken, and had better close the volume at once. I am a plain matter of fact man, and relate only that which is strictly true, so that no matter how singular some of my statements may appear to those who have never passed through a similar experience, the avouchment that it is a compendium of pure fact may serve to increase the zest with which I hope it may be read.

I was born some fifty years ago in the little town of H — , about seven miles from the sea, and was educated at the grammar school, an old foundation institute, almost as old as the town itself.

Up to the age of fifteen I had remained in perfect ignorance of all those little matters which careful parents are so anxious to conceal from their children, nor, indeed, should I then have had my mind enlarged had it not been for the playful instincts of my mother's housemaid, Emma, a strapping but comely wench of nineteen, who, confined to the house all the week, and only

*First printed in 1884

allowed out for a few hours on Sunday, could find no vent for those passionate impulses which a well-fed full-blooded girl of her years is bound to be subject to occasionally, and more especially after the menstrual period.

It was, I remember well, at one of these times that I was called early by my mother one morning and told to go and wake Emma up, as she had overslept herself, and the impression produced on me as barefooted and in my night shirt I stepped into the girl's room and caught her changing the linen bandage she had been wearing round her fanny was electrical.

'Good gracious, Emma,' said I, 'what is the matter? you will bleed to death,' and in my anxiety to be of assistance I tried to get hold of the rag where the dark crimson flood had saturated it worst.

In my anxiety and hurry my finger slipped in, rag and all, and my alarm was so great that had it not been for Emma laughing I believe I should have rushed down stairs and woke up the house.

'Don't you be a little fool, Master Jimmy,' said Emma, 'but come up tonight when your father and mother are both gone to bed, and I'll show you how it all occurred. I see you're quite ready to take a lesson,' added she, grinning, for my natural instinct had supervened on my first panic, and my night shirt was standing out as though a good old-fashioned tent pole were underneath.

I had been frequently chaffed at school about the size of my penis, which was unnaturally large for a boy of my years, but I have since found that it was an hereditary gift in our family, my father and younger brothers all boasting pricks of enormous build.

I turned reluctantly to leave the bedroom, but found it impossible to analyse my feelings, which were tumultuous and strange.

I had caught sight of a fairy little bush of hair on the bottom of Emma's belly, and it perplexed me exceedingly.

Impelled by an impulse I could not then comprehend, but which is understandable enough now, I threw myself into Emma's arms, and kissed her with fond ardour, my hand resting on two milk white globes, which just peeped above the edge of her chemise, when I heard my mother's voice.

'James, what are you doing up there?'

'Nothing, mamma; I was only waking Emma up,' and I came down stairs hurriedly, with my boy's brain on fire, and longing for the night, which might, I thought, make plain to me all this mystery.

That day at school appeared a dream, and the time hung heavily, I went mechanically through my lessons, but seemed dazed and thoughtful; indeed so much so that I was the subject of general remark.

One of the boys, Thompson, the dull boy of the class, who was nearly fifteen, came to me after school was over, and enquired what was the matter.

I suddenly resolved to ask Thompson. 'Can you tell me,' said I, 'the difference between a boy and a girl?'

This was too much for Thompson, who began to split with uncontrollable laughter.

'Good God, Clinton,' said he (he swore horribly), 'what a question, but I forgot you have only one sister, and she's in long clothes.'

'Well,' replied I, 'but what has that to do with it?'

'Why, everything,' said Thompson, 'if you'd been brought up among girls you'd have seen all they've got, and then you'd be as wise as other boys. Look here,' suddenly said he, stopping and taking out a piece of slate pencil, 'you see this,' and he drew a very good imitation of a man's prick upon his slate, 'do you know what that is?'

'Of course I do,' said I, 'haven't I got one.'

'I hope so,' replied Thompson, with a smartness I hadn't up to that time conceived him to possess.

'Well, now look at this,' and he drew what appeared to me at the time to be a lengthy slit, 'do you know what *that* is?'

After what I had seen in the morning I could form a shrewd guess, but I feigned complete ignorance to draw Thompson out.

'Why that's a woman's cunt, you simpleton,' observed my schoolmate, 'and if you ever see a chance of getting hold of one, grab it my boy, and don't be long before you fill it with what God Almighty has given you,' and he ran away and left me.

I was more astonished than ever. I had lived fifteen years in the world and had learnt more since six o'clock that morning than all the preceding time.

The reader may depend that although I had to go to bed tolerably early, I kept awake until I heard my father and mother safely in their room.

My mother always made it a special point to come and see that I had not thrown the clothes off, as I was a restless sleeper, and on this occasion I impatiently awaited the usual scrutiny.

After carefully tucking me up I watched her final departure with beating heart, and heard her say to my father, as the door closed –

'He was covered to-night; last evening he was a perfect sight, his prick standing up as stiff and straight as yours ever did in your life – and such a size, too; I can't imagine where my boys get them from. You are no pigmy, dear, it is true, but I'm sure my brothers as boys were – ' and I lost the rest of the sentence as the door closed, Now, thought I, is about the right moment, and I slid softly out of bed, and across the landing to the staircase, which was to lead me to heaven.

How often since then have I likened that happy staircase to the ladder which Jacob dreamed of. I've always considered that dream an allegory, Jacob's angels must have worn petticoats, or some Eastern equivalent, and the patriarch doubtless moistened the sands of Bethel thinking about it in his sleep.

I ASCERTAIN THE MEANING OF 'REAL JAM'

Her bedroom door I reached without any mishap, and found her safely ensconced in bed, but with the candle still burning.

'Come here, dear,' said she, throwing back the clothes, and for the first time in my life I saw a perfectly naked woman. She had purposely left off her chemise, and was stretched there, a repast for the Gods.

I do not know that with all my experience of paphian delicacies since, have I ever viewed any skin more closely resembling the soft peach bloom which is the acmé of cutaneous beauty.

Her plump breasts stood out as though chiselled by some cunning sculptor, but my eyes were not enchained by them, they wandered lower to that spot which to me was such a curious problem, and I said, 'May I look?'

She laughed, and opening her legs, answered me without saying a word.

I examined it closely, and was more and more puzzled.

Her menses had passed, and she had carefully washed away the stains.

'Put your finger in,' said she, 'it won't bite you; but haven't you really, Master Jimmy, ever seen one of those things before.'

I assured her that I had not.

'Then, in that case,' said Emma, 'I shall have some virgin spoil to-night,' and passing her hand under my night shirt, she took hold of my prick with a quick movement that surprised me, and although it was proudly erect, and seemed ready to burst, she worked it up and down between her thumb and forefinger till I was fairly maddened.

'Oh! for God's sake,' murmured I, 'don't do that, I shall die.'

'Not yet awhile, my darling,' said she, taking hold of me, and lifting me, for she was a girl of enormous muscular power, on to the top of her. 'Not until I have eased my own pain and yours too.'

Emma called passion pain, and I have since proved her to be in some sort a philosopher. I have carefully analysed that terrible feeling which immediately precedes the act of emission, and find pain the only proper word to express it.

I struggled with her at first, for in my innocence I scarcely knew what to make of her rapid action, but I had not long to remain in doubt.

Holding my prick in her left hand, and gently easing back the prepuce, which had long since broken its ligature, though through no self-indulgence on my part, she brought it within the lips of her orifice, and then with a quick jerk which I have since thought was almost professional, I found myself burried to the extreme hilt in a sea of bliss.

I instinctively found myself moving up and down with the regular see-saw motion that friction will unconsciously compel, but I need not have moved, for Emma could have managed the whole business herself.

The movement of her hips and her hands, which firmly grasped the cheeks of my fat young arse, soon produced the desired result, and in my ecstasy I nearly fainted.

At first I thought that blood in a large quantity had passed from me, and I whispered to Emma that the sheets would be stained red, and then mamma would know, but she soon quieted my fears.

'What an extraordinary prick you have got, Master James, for one so young, why it's bigger than your father's.'

'How do you know that?' asked I, surprised more than ever.

'Well, my dear, that would be tellings,' said she, 'but now you have tried what a woman is like, what do you think of it?'

'I think it's simply splendid' was my response; and indeed, although long years of varied experience may have dulled the wild ardour of youth, and a fuck is hardly perhaps the mad excitement which it has been, I should find it difficult to improve upon the answer I gave to Emma.

Twice more I essayed to valiantly escalade the fortress of my *inamorata*, and each time she expressed astonishment to think a mere child should have such 'grit' in him.

All at once I heard a slight noise on the stairs, and thinking it was my mother, hastily slunk under the bed, the candle was still burning.

'Are you asleep, Emma?' whispered a low voice. It was my father's.

'Lor, sir,' said she, 'I hope the missus didn't hear you coming up. I thought you said it was to be tomorrow.'

'I did,' replied my father, 'but to tell you the truth I couldn't wait. I put a drop of laudnum in your mistress's glass of grog just before retiring, so she's safe enough.'

And this man called himself my father. I need scarcely say I lost all my respect for him from that moment.

Not another word was passed, but peeping from my hiding place I saw by the shadow on the wall that my father was preparing for immediate action, yet he went about it a very different way to me.

He insisted upon her taking his penis into her mouth, which at first she refused, but after some little solicitation and a promise that she should go to the 'fairing' which was to be held on the following Friday, she finally consented, and to see my father's shadow wriggling about on the wall, while his arse described all manner of strange and to me unnatural contortions, was a sight that even at this distance of time never fails to raise a smile whenever I think of it.

Presently the old man shouted out, 'Hold on, Emma, that's enough, let's put it in now.'

But Emma was shrewd, she knew what a frightfully drowned-out condition her fanny was in, and felt sure my father, with his experience, would smell a rat, so she held on to his tool with her teeth, and refused to let go, till my father, between passion and pain, forced it away from her. But judge of his disgust when he found himself spending before he could reach the seat of bliss.

His curses took my breath away.

'You silly bitch,' said he, 'you might have known I couldn't stand that long,' and still muttering despondent oaths, he got out of bed to make water.

Now, unfortunately, the chamber was close to my head, and Emma's exhaustion after the quadruple performance was so great that for the moment she forgot me.

The exclamation of my father as he stooped down and caught sight of his eldest boy recalled her to herself.

I would rather draw a veil over the scene that ensued. Suffice it to say that Emma received a month's wages in the morning, and I was packed off to a boarding school.

My mother had *not* slept so soundly as my father had fondly hoped. Whether the laudanum was not of first-rate quality, or her instincts were preternaturally sharp, I have never been able to determine, but I do know that before my father had skulldragged me from underneath Emma's bed on that eventful night he was saluted from behind with a blow from a little bedroom poker, which would have sent many a weaker constitutioned man to an untimely grave.

MORAL AND DIDACTIC THOUGHTS

Having in the last two chapters related my first boyhood's experience in love, I think for incident it will equal any to be found in works of greater fame, but I do not intend to weary you with any further relations of my early successes on the Venusian war path.

I pass over the period of my youth and very early manhood, leaving you to imagine that my first lesson with Emma and my father as joint instructors was by no means thrown away.

Yet I found at the age of thirty I was only on the threshold of mysteries far more entrancing. I had up to that time been a mere man of pleasure, whose ample fortune (for my father who had grown rich, did not disinherit me when he died) sufficed to procure any of those amorous delights without which the world would be a blank to me.

But further than the ordinary pleasures of the bed I had not penetrated.

'The moment was, however, approaching when all these would sink into insignificance before those greater sensual joys which wholesome and well-applied flagellation will always confer upon its devotees.'

I quote the last sentence from a well-known author, but I'm far from agreeing with it in theory or principle.

I was emerging one summer's evening from the Café Royal, in Regent-street, with De Vaux, a friend of long standing, when he nodded to a gentleman passing in a 'hansom', who at once stopped the cab and got out.

'Who is it?' said I, for I felt a sudden and inexplicable interest in his large lustrous eyes, eyes such as I have never before seen in any human being.

'That is Father Peter, of St Martha of the Angels. He is a bircher, my boy, and one of the best in London.

At this moment we were joined by the Father, and a formal introduction took place.

I had frequently seen admirable *cartes* of Father Peter, or rather, as he preferred to be called, Monsignor Peter, in the shop windows of the leading photographers, and at once accused myself of being a dolt not to have recognized him at first sight.

Descriptions are wearisome at the best, yet were I a clever novelist given to the art, I think I might even interest those of the sterner sex in Monsignor Peter, but although in the following paragraph I faithfully delineate him, I humbly ask his pardon if he should perchance in the years to come glance over these pages, and think I have not painted his portrait in colours sufficiently glowing, for I must assure my readers that Father Peter is no imaginary Apollo, but one who in the present year of grace, 1883, lives, moves, has his being, eats, drinks, fucks, and flagellates with all the *verve* and dash he possessed at the date I met him first, now twenty-five years ago.

Slightly above the middle height, and about my own age, or possibly a year my senior, with finely chiselled features, and exquisite profile, Father Peter was what the world would term an exceedingly handsome man. It is true that hypercritics might have pronounced the mouth a trifle too sensual, and the cheeks a thought too plump for a standard of perfection, but the women would have deemed otherwise, for the grand dreamy Oriental eyes, which would have outrivalled those of Byron's Gazelle, made up for any shortcoming.

The tonsure had been sparing in its dealings with his hair, which hung in thick but well-trimmed masses round a classic head, and as the slight summer breeze blew aside one lap of his long clerical coat, I noticed the elegant shape of his cods, which in spite of the tailor's art, would display their proportions, to the evident admiration of one or two ladies who, pretending to look in at the windows of a draper near which we were standing, seemed rivetted to the spot, as the zephyrs revealed the tantalizing picture.

'I am pleased to make your acquaintance, Mr. Clinton,' said Father Peter, shaking me cordially by the hand. 'Any friend of Mr. De Vaux, is a friend of mine also. May I ask if either of you have dined yet?'

We replied in the negative.

'Then, in that case, unless you have something better to do, I shall be glad if you will join me at my own home. I dine at seven, and am already rather late. I feel half-famished and was proceeding to Kensington, where my humble quarters are, post haste, when the sight of De Vaux compelled me to discharge the cab. What say you?'

'With all my heart,' replied De Vaux, with alacrity, and since I knew him to be a perfect sybarite at the table, and that his answer was based on a knowledge of Monsignor's resources, I readily followed suit.

To hail a four-wheeler, and get to the doors of Father Peter's handsome but somewhat secluded dwelling, which was not very far from the south end of the long walk in Kensington Gardens, did not occupy more than twenty minutes.

En route I discovered that Father Peter possessed a further charm, which added to those I have already mentioned, must have made him (as I thought even then, and as I know now) perfectly invincible among womankind. He was the most fascinating conversationalist I ever listened to. It was not so much the easy winning way in which he framed his sentences, but the rich musical intonation, and the luscious laughing method he had of suggesting an infinity of things without, as a respectable member of an eminently respectable church, committing himself in words.

No one, save at exceptional intervals, could ever repeat any actual phrase of Monsignor's which might not pass current in a drawing room, yet there was an instinctive craving on the part of his audience to hear more because they imagined he meant something which was going to lead up to something further, yet the something further never came.

Father Peter was wont to say when questioned upon this annoying peculiarity: 'Am I to be held answerable for other people's imaginations?'

But then Father Peter was a sophist of the first water, and a clever reasoner could have at any rate proved that his innuendoes had in the first place created the imaginings.

Daudet Belot, and other leaders of the French fictional school have at times carefully analysed those fine *nuances* which distinguish profligate talk from delicate suggestiveness, Monsignor had read these works, and adapted their ideas with success.

'My *chef*,' said Monsignor, as we entered the courtyard of his residence, 'tyrannizes over me worse than any Nero, I am only five minutes behind, and yet I dare not ask him for an instant's grace. You are both dressed. I suppose if I hadn't met you it would have been the "Royalty" front row; Florina, they say, has taken to forgetting her unmentionables lately.'

We both denied the soft impeachment, and assured him that the information about Florina was news to us.

Monsignor professed to be surprised at this, and rushed off to his dressing-room to make himself presentable.

A SNUG DINNER PARTY

Before many minutes he rejoined us, and leading the way, we followed him into one of the most lovely little bijou *salons* it had ever been my lot to enter. There were seats for eight at the table, four of which were occupied, and the *chef*, not waiting for his lord and master, had already sent up the soup, which was being handed round by a plump, rosy-cheeked boy, about fifteen years old, who I afterwards found acted in the double capacity of page to Monsignor and chorister at St. Martha of the Angels.

I was briefly introduced, and De Vaux, who knew them all, had shaken himself into his seat and swallowed half of his asparagus soup before I had time to properly note the appearance of my neighbours.

Immediately on my left sat a complete counterpart of Monsignor himself, save that he was a much older man, his name, as casually mentioned to me, was Father Boniface, and although sparer in his proportions than Father Peter, his proclivities as a trencherman belied his meagreness. He never missed a single course, and when anything particular tickled his gustatory nerve, he had two or even more helpings.

Next to him sat a little short apoplectic man, a Doctor of Medicine, who was more of an epicure.

A sylph-like girl of sixteen occupied the next seat. Her fair hair, rather flaxen than golden-hued, hung in profusion down her back, while black lashes gave her violet eyes that shade which Greuze, the finest eye painter the world has ever seen, wept to think he could never exactly reproduce. I was charmed with her lady-like manner, her neatness of dress, virgin white, and above all, with the modest and unpretending way she replied to the questions put to her.

If ever there were a maid at sixteen under the blue vault of heaven, she sits there, was my involuntary thought, to which I mechanically nearly gave expression, but was fortunately saved from such a frightful lapse by the page, who placing some appetizing salmon and lobster sauce before me, dispelled for the nonce my half visionary condition.

Monsignor P. sat near this young divinity, and ever and anon between the courses passed his soft white hands through her wavy hair.

I must admit I didn't half like it, and began to feel a jealous pang, but the knowledge that it was only the caressing hand of a Father of the Romish Church quieted me.

I was rapidly getting maudlin, and as I ate my salmon the smell of the lobster sauce suggested other thoughts, till I found the tablecloth gradually rising, and was obliged to drop my napkin on the floor to give myself the opportunity of adjusting my prick, so that it would not be observed by the company.

I have omitted to mention the charmer who was placed between De Vaux and Father Peter. She was a lady of far maturer years than the sylph, and might be as near as one could judge in the pale incandescent light which the pure filtered gas shed round with voluptuous radiance, about twenty-seven. She was a strange contrast to Lucy, for so my sylph was called. Tall, and with a singularly clear complexion for a brunette; her bust was beautifully rounded with that fullness of contour which, just avoiding the gross, charms without disgusting. Madeline, in short, was in every inch a woman to chain a lover to her side.

I had patrolled the continent in search of good goods, I had over-hauled every shape and make of cunt between Constantinople and Calcutta, but as I caught the liquid expression of Madeline's large sensuous eyes, I confessed myself a fool.

Here, in Kensington, right under a London clubman's nose, was the *beau ideal* I had vainly travelled ten thousand miles to find. She was sprightliness itself in conversation, and I could not sufficiently thank De Vaux for having introduced me into such an Eden.

Lamb cutlets and cucumbers once more broke in upon my dream, and I was not at all sorry, for I found the violence of my thoughts had burst one of the buttons of my fly, a mishap I knew from old experience would be followed by the collapse of the others unless I turned my erratic brain wanderings into another channel, so that I kept my eyes fixed on my plate, absolutely afraid to gaze upon these two constellations again.

'As I observed just now,' said the somewhat fussy little Doctor, 'cucumber or cowcumber, it mattes not much which, if philologists differ in the pronunciation surely we may.'

'The pronunciation,' said Father Peter, with a naïve look at Madeline, 'is very immaterial, provided one does not eat too much of them. They are a dangerous plant, sir, they heat the blood, and we poor churchmen who have to chastise the lusts of the flesh, should avoid them *in toto*; yet I would fain have some more,' and suiting the action to the word, he helped himself to a quantity.

I should mention that I was sitting nearly opposite Lucy, and seeing her titter at the paradoxical method the worthy Father had of assisting himself to cucumber against his own argument, I thought it a favourable opportunity to show her that I sympathized with her mirth, so, stretching out my foot, I gently pressed her toe, and to my unspeakable joy she did not take her foot away, but rather, indeed, pushed it further in my direction.

I then, on the pretence of adjusting my chair, brought it a little nearer the table, and was in ecstacies when I perceived Lucy not only guessed what my manoeuvres meant, but actually in a very sly puss-like way brought her chair nearer too.

Then, balancing my arse on the edge of my seat as far as I could without being noticed, with my prick only covered with the table napkin, for it had with one wild bound burst all the remaining buttons of my breeches, I reached forward my foot, from which I had slid off my boot with the other toe, and in less than a minute I had worked it up so that I could just feel the heat of her fanny.

I will say this for her, she tried all she knew to help me, but her cursed drawers were an insuperable obstacle, and I was foiled. I knew if I proceeded another inch I should inevitably come a cropper, and this knowledge, coupled with the fact that

Lucy was turning wild with excitement, now red, now white, warned me to desist for the time being.

I now foresaw a rich conquest – something worth waiting for, and my blood coursed through my veins at the thought of that sweet little bower nestling within those throbbing thighs, for I could tell from the way her whole frame trembled how thoroughly mad she was at the trammels which society imposed. Not only that, the moisture on my stocking told me that it was something more than the dampness of perspiration, and I felt half sorry to think that I had 'jewgaged' her. At the same time, to parody the words of the Poet Laureate:

"'Tis better frigging with one's toe,
Than never to have frigged at all.'

Some braised ham and roast fowls now came on, and I was astonished to find a poor priest of the Church of Rome launching out in this fashion. The Sauterne with the salmon had been simply excellent, and the Mumms, clear and sparkling, which accompanied the latter courses had fairly electrified me.

By the way, as this little dinner party may serve as a lesson to some of those whose experience is limited, I will mention one strange circumstance which may account for much of what is to come.

Monsignor, when the champagne had been poured out for the first time, before any one had tasted it, went to a little liqueur stand, and taking from it a bottle of a most peculiar shape, added to each glass a few drops of the cordial.

'That is Pinero Balsam,' said he to me, 'you and one of the ladies have not dined at my table before, and, therefore, you may possibly never have tasted it, as it is but little known in England. It is compounded by one Italian firm only, whose ancestors, the Sagas of Venice, were the holders of the original recipe. Its properties are wonderous and manifold, but amongst others it rejuvenates senility, and those among us who have travelled *up and down* in the world a good deal, and found the motion rather tiring as the years go on, have cause to bless its recuperative qualities.'

The cunning cleric by the inflection of his voice had sufficiently indicated his meaning, and although the cordial was, so far as interfering with the champagne went, apparently tasteless, its effect upon the company soon began to be noticeable.

A course of ducklings, removed by Nesselrode pudding and Noyeau jelly, ended the repast, and after one of the shortest graces in Latin I had ever heard in my life, the ladies curtsied themselves out of the apartment, and soon the strains of a piano indicated that they had reached the drawing room, while we rose from the table to give the domestics an opportunity of clearing away.

My trousers was my chief thought at this moment, but I skilfully concealed the evidences of my passion with a careless pocket handkerchief, and my boot I accounted for by a casual reference to a corn of long standing.

THE HISTORY OF FLAGELLATION CONDENSED

'Gentlemen,' said Monsignor, lighting an exquisitely aromatized cigarette, for all priests, through the constant use of the censer, like the perfume of spices, 'first of all permit me to hope that you have enjoyed your dinner, and now I presume, De Vaux, your friend will not be shocked if we initiate him into some of the mysteries with which we solace the few hours of relaxation our priestly employment permits us to enjoy? Eh, Boniface.'

The latter, who was coarser than his superior, laughed boisterously.

'I expect, Monsignor, that Mr. Clinton knows just as much about birching as we do ourselves.'

'I know absolutely nothing of it,' said I, 'and must even plead ignorance of the merest rudiments.'

'Well, sir,' said Monsignor,' leaning back in his chair, 'the art of birching is one on which I pride myself that I can speak with greater authority than any man in Europe, and you may judge that I do not aver this from any self-conceit when I tell you that I have during the last ten years, assisted by a handsome subsidy from the Holy Consistory at Rome, ransacked the known world for evidence in support of its history. In that escritoire,' said he, 'there are sixteen octavo volumes, the compilation of laborious research, in which I have been assisted by brethren of all the holy orders affiliated to Mother Church, and I may mention in passing that worthy Dr. Prince here, and Father Boniface have both contributed largely from their wide store of experience in correcting and annotating many of the chapters which deal with recent discoveries, for, Mr. Clinton, flagellation as an art is not only daily gaining fresh pupils and adherents, but scarcely a month passes without some new feature being added to our already huge stock of information.'

I lighted a cigar, and said I should like to hear something more about it.

'To begin with,' began Father Peter, 'we have indubitable proof from the Canaanitish stones found in the Plain of Shinar, in 1748, and unearthed by Professor Bannister, that the Priests of Baal, more than three thousand years ago, not only practised flagellation in a crude form with hempen cords, but inculcated the practice on those who came to worship at the shrine of their God, and these are the unclean mysteries which are spoken of by Moses and Joshua, but which the Hebrew tongue had no word for, therefore it could not be translated.'

'You astonish me,' said I, 'but what proof have you of this?'

'Simply this, it was the age of hieroglyphics, and on the Shinar Stone was found, exquisitely carved, a figure of the God Baal gloating over a young girl whose virgin nakedness was being assailed by several stout priests with rough cords. I have a facsimile in vol. 7, page 343 – hand it to Mr. Clinton, Boniface.'

Boniface did so, and sure enough there was the Caananitish presentment of a young maiden with her lovely rounded arse turned up to the sky, and her hands tied to the enormous prick of the God Baal, being soundly flogged by two stout-looking men in loose but evidently priestly vestments.

'The fact that the Israelites and Men of Judah were constantly leaving their own worship, enticed away by the allurements of the Baalite priests, is another proof of the superior fascination which flagellation even in those days had over such unholy rites as sodomy, and the bottom-fucking also too frequently the foibles of the priests of Levi.'

'Your deductions interest me as a matter of history,' I said, 'but nothing more.'

'Oh, I think I could interest you in another way presently,' said Dr. Price.

Monsignor continued: 'The races all, more or less, have indulged in a love of art, and it is well known that so far as Aryan lore will permit us to dive into the subject, both in Babylon and Nineveh, and even in later times in India also (which is surely something more that a mere coincidence) flagellation has not only thrived, but has been the fashionable recreation of all recorded time.'

'I really cannot see,' interrupted I, 'where you get your authorities from.'

'Well, so far as Nineveh goes, I simply ask you to take a walk through the Assyrian Hall of the British Museum, where in several places you will see the monarchs of that vast kingdom sitting on their thrones and watching intently some performance which seems to interest them greatly. In the foreground you will perceive a man with a whip of knotted thongs, as much like our cat-o'-nine-tails as anything, on the point of belabouring something, and – then the stone ends, or, in other words, where the naked-arsed Assyrian damsel would be, is *nil*. Of course this has been chipped off by the authorities as likely to demoralize young children, who would begin to practise on their own posteriors, and end by fucking themselves into an early grave.'

'Well,' I said, in unbounded surprise, 'your research is certainly too much for me.'

'I thought we should teach you something presently,' laughed Dr. Price.

'I have thousands of examples in those sixteen volumes, from the Aborigines of Australia and the Maoris of New Zealand to the Esquimaux in their icy homes, the latter of whom may be said to have acquired the art by instinct, the cold temperature of the frozen zone suggesting flagellation as a means of warmth, and, indeed, in a lecture read by Mr Wimwam to the Geographical Society, he proved that the frigidity of Greenland prevented the women from procreating unless flagellation, and vigorous flagellation, too, had been previously applied.'

'The patristic Latin in which the books of the Holy Fathers are written,' went on Monsignor, 'contain numerous hints and examples, but although Clement of Alexandria quotes some startling theories, and both Lactantius and Tertullian back him to some extent, I cannot help thinking that so far as practical bumtickling is concerned, we are a long way ahead of all the ancients.'

'But,' mildly observed Dr. Price, 'Ambrose, and Jerome knew a thing or two.'

'They had studied,' replied the imperturbable Father Peter, 'but were not cultured as we moderns are, for example, their birches grew in the hills of Illyria and Styria, and in that part of Austria we now call the Tyrol. Canada, with its glorious forests of birch were unknown. Why, sir,' said Monsignor, turning to me, his eyes lighted up with the lambent flame of enthusiasm, 'do you know the King Birch of Manitoba will execute more enchantment on a girl's backside in five minutes than these old contrivances of our forefathers could have managed in half an hour. My fingers tingle when I think of it. Show him a specimen of our latest consignment, Boniface,' and the latter worthy rushed off to do his master's bidding.

To tell the truth I scarcely appreciated all this, and felt a good deal more inclined to get upstairs to the drawing room, when just at this moment an incident occurred which gave me my opportunity.

The bonny brunette, Madeline, looked in at the door furtively and apologized, but reminded Monsignor that he was already late for vespers.

'My dear girl,' said the cleric, 'run over to the sacristy, and ask Brother Michael to officiate in my absence – the usual headache – and don't stay quite so long as you generally do, and if you should come back with your hair dishevelled and your dress in disorder, make up a better tale than you did last time.'

Or else your own may smart, thought I, for at this moment Father Boniface came in to ask Monsignor for another key to get the rods, as it appeared he had given him the wrong one.

Now is my time, reflected I, so making somewhat ostentatious enquiries as to the exact whereabouts of the lavatory, I quitted the apartment, promising to return in a few minutes.

I should not omit to mention that from the moment I drunk the sparkling cordial that Father Peter had mixed with the champagne my spirits had received an unwanted exhilaration, which I could not ascribe to natural causes.

I will not go so far as to assert that the augmentation of force which I found my prick to possess was entirely due to the Pinero Balsam, but this I will confidently maintain against all comers, that never had I felt so equal to any amorous exploit. It may have been the effect of a generous repast, it might have been the result of the toe frigging I had indulged in; but as I stepped into the brilliantly lighted hall, and hastily passed upstairs to the luxurious drawing room, I could not help congratulating myself on the stubborn bar of iron which my unfortunately dismantled trousers could scarcely keep from popping out.

Veni, vidi, vici!

Fearing to frighten Lucy if I entered suddenly in a state of *déshabillé*, and feeling certain that a prick exhibition might tend to shock her inexperienced eye, I readjusted my bollocks, and peeped through the crack of the drawing room door, which had been left temptingly half open.

There was Lucy reclining on the sofa in that *dolce far niente* condition which is a sure sign that a good dinner has agreed with one, and that digestion is waiting upon appetite like an agreeable and good-tempered handmaid should.

She looked so arch, and with such a charming pout upon her lips, that I stood there watching and half disinclined to disturb her dream.

It may be, thought I, that she is given to frigging herself, and being all alone she might possibly – but I speedily banished that thought, for Lucy's clear healthy complexion and vigorous blue eyes forbade the suggestion.

At this instant something occurred which for the moment again led me to think that my frigging conjecture was about to be realized, for she reached her hand deliberately under her skirt, and lifting up her petticoats, dragged down the full length of her chemise, which she closely examined.

I divined it all at a glance, when I toe-frigged her in the dining room she had spent a trifle, and being her first experience of the kind, could not understand it.

So she really is a maid after all, thought I, and as I saw a pair of shapely lady-like calves encased in lovely pearl silk stockings of a light-blue colour, I could retain myself no longer, but with a couple of bounds was at her side before she could recover herself.

'Oh! Mr. Clinton. Oh! Mr. Clinton; how could you,' was all she found breath or thought to ejaculate.

I simply threw my arms around her, and kissed her flushed face, *on the cheeks*, for I feared to frighten her too much at first.

At last, finding she lay prone and yielding, I imprinted a kiss upon her mouth, and found it returned with ardour.

Allowing my tongue to gently insinuate itself into her half-open mouth and touch hers, I immediately discovered that her excitement, as I fully expected, became doubled, and without saying a word I guided her disengaged hand to my prick, which she clutched with the tenacity of a drowning man catching at a floating spar.

'My own darling,' said I, and waiting for no further encouragement, I pushed my right hand softly up between her thighs, which mechanically opened to give it a passage.

To say that I was in the seventh heaven of delight, as my warm fingers found a firm plump cunt with a rosebud hymen as yet unbroken, is but faintly to picture my ecstasy.

To pull her a little way further down on the couch, so that her rounded arse would rise in the middle, and make the business a more convenient one, was the work of a second; the next I had withdrawn my prick from her grasp and placed it against the lips of her quim, at the same time easing them back with a quick movement of my thumb and forefinger, I gave one desperate lunge, which made Lucy cry out 'Oh, God', and the joyful deed was consummated.

As I have hinted before, my prick was no joke in the matter of size, and upon this occasion so intense was the excitement that had led up to the fuck, it was rather bigger than usual, but thanks to the heat the sweet virgin was in the sperm particles of her vagina were already resolved into grease, which mixing with the few drops of blood caused by the violent separation of the hymeneal cord, resulted in making the friction natural and painless. Not only that, once inside, and I found Lucy's fanny was internally framed on a very free-and-easy scale, and here permit me to digress and point out the ways of nature.

Some women she frames with an orifice like an exaggerated horse collar, but with a passage more fitted for a tin whistle than a man's prick, while in others the opening itself is like the tiddiest tiniest wedding ring, though if you once get inside your prick is in the same condition as the poor devil who floundered up the biggest cunt on record and found another bugger looking for his hat. Others again – but why should I go on in this prosy fashion, when Lucy has only received half-a-dozen strokes, and is on the point of 'coming'.

Heavens what a delicious process I went through, even to recall it after all these years, now that Lucy is mother of two youths verging on manhood, is bliss, and will in my most depressed moments always suffice to give me a certain and prolonged erection.

The beseeching blue eyes that glanced up at Monsignor's

drawing room ceiling, as though in silent adoration and heartfelt praise at the warm stream I seemed to be spurting into her very vitals. The quick nervous shifting of her fleshy buttocks, as she strove to ease herself of her own pent-up store of liquid, and then the heartfelt sigh of joy and relief that escaped her ruby lips as I withdrew my tongue and she discharged the *sang de la vie* at the same moment.

Oh! there is no language copious enough to do justice to the acmé of a first fuck, nor is there under God's sun a nation which has yet invented a term sufficiently comprehensive to picture the emotions of a man's mind as he mounts a girl he knows from digital proof to be a maid as pure in person, and as innocent of prick, dildo, or candle as arctic snow.

Scarcely had I dismounted and reassured Lucy with a 'serious' kiss that it was all right, and that she need not alarm herself, when Madeline came running in.

'Oh! Lucy,' cried she, 'such fun,' then, seeing me, she abruptly broke of with – 'I beg your pardon, Mr. Clinton, I did not see you were here.'

Lucy, who was now in a sitting posture, joined in the conversation, and I saw by the ease of her manner that she had entirely recovered her self-possession, and that I could rejoin the gentlemen downstairs.

'Do tell those stupid men not to stay there over their cigars all day. It is paying us no great compliment,' was Madeline's parting shot.

In another moment I was in my seat again, and prepared for a resumption of Monsignor's lecture on birch rods.

'Where the Devil have you been to, Clinton?' said De Vaux.

'Where it would have been quite impossible for you to have acted as my substitute,' I unhesitatingly replied.

My answer made them all laugh, for they thought I referred to the water closet, whereas I was of course alluding to Lucy, and I knew I was stating a truism in that case as regarded De Vaux, for he was scarcely yet convalescent from a bad attack of Spanish glanders, which was always his happy method of expressing the clap.

A VICTIM FOR THE EXPERIMENT

Now, my dear Mr. Clinton, I wish you particularly to observe the tough fibre of these rods,' said Monsignor Peter, as he handed me a bundle so perfectly and symmetrically arranged that I could not help remarking on it.

'Ah!' said Monsignor, 'that is a further proof of how popular the flagellating art has become. So large a trade is being done, sir, in specially picked birch of the flogging kind, that they are hand sorted by children and put up in bundles by machinery, as they appear here, and my own impression is that if the Canadian Government were to impose an extra duty on these articles, for they almost come under the heading of manufactures, and not produce, a large revenue would accrue; but enough of this,' said the reverend gentleman, seeing his audience were becoming somewhat impatient. 'You saw at the dinner table the young lady I addressed as Lucy.'

I reflected for a moment to throw them off their guard, and then said, suddenly, 'Oh, yes, the sweet thing in white.'

'Well,' continued Monsignor Peter,' her father is a long time since dead, and her mother is in very straitened circumstances; the young girl herself is a virgin, and I have this morning paid to her mother a hundred pounds to allow her to remain in my house for a month or so with the object of initiating her.'

'Initiating her into the Church?' enquired I, laughing to myself, for I knew that her initiation in other respects was fairly well accomplished, and my prick wagged a responsive hear, hear, in a most appreciative fashion.

'No,' smiled Monsignor, touching the rods significantly; 'this is the initiation to which I refer.'

'What,' cried I, aghast, 'are you going to birch her?'

'We are,' put in Dr. Price, 'her first flagellation will be tonight, but this is merely an experimental one. A few strokes well administered, and a quick fuck after to determine my work on corpuscular action of the blood particles, tomorrow she will be in better form to receive second class instruction, and we hope by the end of the month – '

'To have a perfect pupil,' put in Father Peter, who did not relish Dr. Price taking the lead on a flagellation subject, 'but let us proceed to the drawing room, Boniface, put that bundle in the birch box, and bring it upstairs.'

So saying, the chief exponent of flagellation in the known world led the way upstairs to the drawing room, and we followed, though I must confess that in my case it was with no little trepidation, for I felt somehow as though I were about to assist at a sacrifice.

As we entered the room we found Lucy in tears, and Madeline solacing her, but she no sooner saw us than, breaking from her friend, she threw herself at Monsignor's feet, and clinging to his knees, sobbed out, 'Oh, Father Peter, you have always been a kind friend to my mother and myself, do say that the odious tale of shame that girl has poured into my ears is not true.'

'Good God!' muttered I, 'they have actually chosen Madeline as the instrument to explain what they are about to do.'

'Rise, my child,' said Monsignor, 'do not distress yourself, but listen to me,' half bearing the form of the really terrified young thing to the couch, we gathered round in a circle and listened.

'You, doubtless, know, my sweet daughter,' began the wily and accomplished priest, 'that the votaries of science spare neither friends nor selves in their efforts to unravel the secrets of nature. Time and pains are of no object to them, so that the end be accomplished.'

To this ominous introduction Lucy made no response.

'You have read much, daughter of mine,' said Monsignor, stroking her silken hair, 'and when I tell you that your dead father devoted you to the fold of Mother Church, and that your mother and I both think you will best be serving her ends and purposes by submitting yourself to those tests which will be skilfully carried out without pain, but, on the contrary, with an amount of pleasure such as you cannot even guess at, you will probably acquiesce.'

Lucy's eyes here caught mine, and although I strove to reassure her with a look that plainly intimated no harm should come to her, she was some time before she at last put her hand in the cleric's, and said, 'Holy Father, I do not think you would allow any thing very dreadful, I will submit, for my mother, when I left her this morning, told me above all things to be obedient to you in everything, and to trust you implicitly.'

'That is my own trump of a girl,' said Monsignor, surprised for the first time during the entire evening into a slang expression, but I saw his large round orbs gloating over his victim, and his whole frame trembled with excitement, as he led Lucy into the adjoining apartment, and left her alone with Madeline.

'Now, gentlemen,' said Monsignor, 'the moment approaches, and you will forgive me, Mr. Clinton, if I have to indulge in a slight coarseness of language, but time presses, and plain Saxon is the quickest method of expression. Personally, I do not feel inclined to fuck Lucy myself. As a matter of fact I had connection with her mother the night previous to her marriage, and as Lucy was born exactly nine months afterwards, I am rather in doubt as to the paternity.'

'In other words,' said I, astounded, 'you think it possible that you may be her father.'

'Precisely,' said Monsignor. 'You see that the instant the flagellation is ended, somebody must necessarily fuck her, and personally my objection prevents me. Boniface, here, prefers boys to women, and Dr. Price will be too busy taking notes, so that it rests between you and De Vaux, who had better toss up.'

De Vaux, who was stark mad to think that his little gonorhoeic disturbance was an insuperable obstacle, pleaded an engagement later on, which he was bound to fulfil, and, therefore, Monsignor Peter told me to be sure to be ready the instant I was wanted.

Madeline entered at this moment, and informed us that all was ready, but gave us to understand that she had experienced the greatest difficulty in overcoming poor Lucy's natural scruples at being exposed in all her virgin nakedness to the gaze of so many of the male sex.

'She made a very strange observation too,' continued Madeline, looking at me with a drollery I could not understand, 'she said, if it had been only Mr. Clinton, I don't think I should have minded quite so much.'

'Oh! all the better,' said Father Peter, 'for it is Mr. Clinton who will have to relieve her at the finish.'

With these words we proceeded to the birching room, which it appears had been furnished by these professors of flagellation with a nicety of detail, and an eye to everything accessory to the art that was calculated to inspire a neophyte like myself with the utmost astonishment.

On a framework of green velvet was a soft down bed, and reclined on this full length was the blushing Lucy.

Large bands of velvet, securely buckled at the sides held her in position, while her legs, brought well together and fastened in the same way, slightly elevated her soft shapely arse. The elevation being further aided by an extra cushion, which had been judiciously placed under the lower portion of her belly. Monsignor bent over her and whispered a few soothing words into her ear, but she only buried her delicate head deeper into the down of the bed, while the reverend Father proceeded to analyse the points of her arse.

THE EXPERIMENT PROCEEDS

Having all of them felt her arse in turn, pinching it as though to test its condition, much as a *connoisseur* in horseflesh would walk round an animal he was about to buy, Monsignor at length said, 'What a superb picture,' his eyes nearly bursting from their sockets, 'you must really excuse me, gentlemen, but my feelings overcome me,' and taking his comely prick out of his breeches, he deliberately walked up to Madeline, and before that fair damsel had guessed his intentions, he had thrown her down on the companion couch to Lucy's, and had fucked her heart out in a shorter space of time than it takes me to write it.

To witness this was unutterably maddening, I scarcely knew what to be at, my heart beat wildly, and I should then and there have put it into Lucy myself, had I not been restrained by Father Boniface, who, arch vagabond that he was, took the whole business as a matter of course, and merely observed to Monsignor that it would be as well to get it over as soon as possible, since Mr. Clinton was in a devil of a hurry.

Poor Lucy was deriving some consolation from Dr. Price in the shape of a few drops of Pinero Balsam in champagne, while as for De Vaux he was groaning audibly, and when the worthy Father Peter came to the short strokes De Vaux's chordee became so unbearable that he ran violently out into Monsignor's bedroom, as he afterwards informed me, to bath his balls in ice water.

To me there was something rather low and shocking in a fuck before witnesses, but that is a squeamishness that I have long since got the better of.

Madeline having wiped Monsignor's prick with a piece of *mousseline delaine*, a secret only known to the sybarite in love's perfect secrets, retired, presumably to syringe her fanny, and Monsignor buttoned up and approached his self-imposed task.

Taking off his coat he turned up his shirt cuffs, and Boniface handing him the birchrods, the bum warming began.

At the first keen swish poor Lucy shrieked out, but before half a dozen had descended with that quick tearing sound which betokens that there is no lack of elbow grease in the application, her groans subsided, and she spoke in a quick strained voice, begging for mercy.

'For the love of God,' said she, 'do not, pray do not lay it on so strong.'

By this time her lovely arse had assumed a flushed, vermillion tinge, which appeared to darken with every stroke, and at this point Dr. Price interposed.

'Enough, Monsignor, now my duty begins,' and quick as thought he placed upon her bottom a piece of linen, which was smeared with an unguent, and stuck it at the sides with a small modicum of tar plaster for to prevent it from coming off.

'Oh!' cried Lucy, 'I feel so funny. Oh! Mr. Clinton, if you are there, pray relieve me, and make haste.'

In an instant my trousers were down, the straps were unbuckled, and Lucy was gently turned over on her back.

I saw a delicate bush of curly hair, a pair of glorious thighs, and the sight impelled me to thrust my prick into that divine Eden I had visited but a short time before with an ardour that for a man who had lived a fairly knockabout life was inexplicable.

I had scarcely got it thoroughly planted, and had certainly not made a dozen well-sustained though rapid strokes before the gush of sperm which she emitted drew me at the same instant, and I must own that I actually thought the end of the world had come.

'Now,' said Dr. Price, rapidly writing in his pocket book, 'you see that my theory was correct. Here is a maid who has never known a man and she spends within ten seconds of the entrance being effected. Do you suppose that without the birching she could have performed such a miracle?'

'Yes,' said I, instanter, 'I do, and I can prove that all your surmises are but conjecture, and that even your conjecture is based upon a fallacy.'

'Bravo,' said Father Peter, 'I like to see Price fairly collared.

Nothing flabbergasts him like facts. Once get him in a corner and he's completely coopered. Dear me, how damnation slangy I am getting tonight. Lucy, dear, don't stand shivering there, slip on your things, and join Madeline in my snuggery, we shall all be there presently. Go on, Clinton.'

'Well,' said I, 'it is easy enough to refute the learned Doctor. In the first place Lucy was not a maid.'

'That be damned for a tale,' said Father Boniface, 'I got her mother to let me examine her myself last night while she was asleep, and previous to handing over the hundred pounds.'

'Yes, that I can verify,' said Monsignor, 'though I must admit that you have a prick like a kitchen poker, for you got into her as easy as though she'd been on a Regent-street round for twenty years.'

'I will bet anyone here £50,' said I, quietly taking out my pocket book, 'that she was not a maid before I poked her just now.'

'Done,' said the Doctor, who upon receiving a knowing wink from Father Peter, felt sure he was going to bag two ponies, 'and now how are we to prove it?'

'Ah, that will be difficult,' said Monsignor.

'Not at all,' I observed, 'let the young lady be sent for, and questioned on the spot, where you assume she was first deflowered of her virginity.'

'Yes, that's fair,' said De Vaux, and accordingly he called her in.

'My dear Lucy,' said Monsignor, 'I wish you to tell me the truth in answer to a particular question I am about to put to you.'

'I certainly will,' said Lucy, 'for God knows I have literally nothing now to conceal from you.'

'Well, that's not bad for a *double entendre*,' said the Father, laughing,' but now tell us candidly, before Mr. Clinton was intimate with you in our presence just now, had you ever before had a similar experience?'

'Once,' said Lucy, simpering, and examining the pattern of the carpet.

'Good God,' said the astonished Churchman, as with deathlike silence he waited for an answer to his next question.

'When was it and with whom?'

'With Mr. Clinton himself, in the drawing-room here, about an hour ago.'

I refused the money of course, but had the laugh at all of them, and as we rolled home to De Vaux's chambers in a hansom about an hour later I could not help admitting to him that I considered the evening we had passed through was the most agreeable I had ever known.

'You will soon forget it in the midst of other pleasures.'

'Never,' said I. 'If Calais was graven on Mary's heart I am quite sure that this date will be found inscribed on mine if ever they should hold an inquest upon my remains.'

A BACHELOR'S SUPPER PARTY

Becoming after this a frequent visitor at 'The Priory', the name Monsignor's hospitable mansion was generally known by, and had numberless opportunities of fucking Lucy, Madeline, and two of the domestics, but somehow I never properly took to flagellation in its true sense.

There certainly was a housemaid of Monsignor's, a pretty and intelligent girl called Martha, the sight of whose large, fleshy bum, with an outline which would have crushed Hogarth's line of beauty out of time, used to excite me beyond measure, but I was not an enthusiast, and when Monsignor saw this, and found that as a birch performer I laid it on far too sparingly, his invitations were less pressing, and gradually my visits became few and far between.

De Vaux, on the other hand, had become a qualified practitioner, and would dilate for hours on the celestial pleasures to be derived from skilful bum scoring. In fact so perfect a disciple of Monsignor's did he get to be in time that the pupil in some peculiar phases has outstripped the master, and his work now in the press, entitled 'Bumtickling, or Heaven on Earth', may fairly claim, from an original point of view, to be catalogued with the more abstruse volumes penned by the Fathers, and collated and enlarged by Messrs. Peter, Price, and Boniface upon the same subject.

As, however, I stated before, I could not enter so thoroughly into the felicity of birching. I saw that, physically speaking, it was productive of a forced emission, but I preferred cunt more *au naturel*. The easy transition from a kiss to a feel, from a feel to a finger frig, and eventually to a more natural sequence of a gentle insertion of the jock, were a series of gradations more suited to my unimaginative temperament, and I, therefore, to quote the regretful valediction of De Vaux, relapsed into that condition of paphlan barbarism in which he found me.

But I was by no means idle, my income, which was nearly £7000 per annum, was utilized in one direction only, and as you shall hear, I employed it judiciously in the gratification of my taste. In the next suite of chambers to mine lived a young barrister, Sidney Mitchell, a dare devil dog, and one whose *penchant* for the fair was only equalled by his impecuniosity, for he was one of that many-headed legion who are known as briefless.

I had occasionally, when he had been pounced upon by a bailiff, which occurred on an average about once a month, rescued him by a small advance, which he had gratefully repaid by keeping me company in my lonely rooms, drinking my claret and smoking my best havanas.

But this was to me repayment sufficient, for Sydney had an inexhaustible store of comic anecdotes, and his smartly told stories were always so happily related that they never offended the ear, while they did not fail to tickle the erective organs.

One morning Sydney came to me in a devil of a stew.

'My very dear Clinton,' said he, 'I'm in a hell of a scrape again; can you help me out of it?'

'Is it much?' said I, remembering that I had paid £25 for him a few days before.

'Listen, and you may judge for yourself. I was at my Buffalo lodge last night, got drunk, and invited about half a dozen fellows to my chambers this evening to dinner.'

'Well,' I remarked, 'there's nothing very dreadful about that.'

'Yes, there is, for I have to appear as substitute for a chum in the Queen's Bench in an hour, and my wig is at the dresser's who won't part with it until I've paid up what I owe, which will swallow up every penny I had intended for the dinner.'

'Oh, that's easily got over,' said I, ask them to dine here instead, say you quite forgot you were engaged to me, and that I won't let you off, but desire they will accompany you.'

'I'm your eternal debtor once more,' cried Sydney, who really was fathoms deep in gratitude, and he rushed off to plead as happy as a butterfly.

I ordered a slap-up dinner for eight from the neighbouring restaurant, and as my 'Inn dinners' were well known by repute, not one of the *invités* were missing.

We had a capital dinner, and as Sydney's companions were a jolly set, I made up my mind for a glorious evening. Little did I know then how much more glorious it was to wind up than ever I had anticipated.

When the cigars and the O.P. came on, and the meeting was beginning to assume a rather uproarious character, Sydney proposed that his friend Wheeler should oblige with a song, and after that gentleman had enquired whether my fastidiousness would be shocked at anything *ultra* drawing room, and had been assured that nothing would give me greater pleasure, he began in a rich clear voice the following:

As Mary, dear Mary, one day was a lying,
As Mary, sweet Mary, one day was a lying,
She spotted her John, at the door he was spying,
With his tol de riddle, tol de riddle, lol de rol lay.

And then came the chorus, rolled out by the whole company, for the refrain was so catching that I found myself unconsciously joined in with –

His tol de riddle, tol de riddle, lol de rol lay.

Oh Johnny, dear Johnny, now do not come to me,
Oh Johnny, pray Johnny, oh do not come to me,
Or else I'm quite certain that you will undo me,
With your tol de riddle, tol de riddle, lol de rol lay.

Chorus – With your tol de riddle, &c.

But Johnny, dear Johnny, not liking to look shady,
But Johnny, sweet Johnny, not liking to seem shady,
Why he downed with his breeches and treated his lady,
To his tol de riddle, tol de riddle, lol de rol lay.

Chorus – To his tol de riddle, &c.

Oh, Johnny, dear Johnny, you'll make me cry murther,
Oh, Johnny, pray cease this, you'll make me scream murther,
But she soon changed her note, and she murmnred 'in further'
With your tol de riddle, del de riddle, lol de rol lay.

Chorus – With your tol de riddle, &c.

Now, Mary, dear Mary, grew fatter and fatter,
Now Mary's, sweet Mary's, plump belly grew fatter,
Which plainly did prove that her John had been at her,
With his tol de riddle, tol de riddle, lol de rol lay.

Chorus – With his tol de riddle, &c.

Moral
Now all you young ladies take warning had better,
Now amorous damsels take warning you'd better,
When you treat a John make him wear a French letter,
On his tol de riddle, tol de riddle, lol de rol lay.

Chorus – On his tol de riddle, &c.

The singing of this song, which I was assured was quite original,
was greeted with loud plaudits, then one of the young gentlemen
volunteered a recitation, which ran as follows:

On the banks of a silvery river,
A youth and a maiden reclined;
The youth could be scarce twenty summers,
The maiden some two years behind.

Full lip and a neck well developed,
That youth's ardent nature bespoke,
And he gazed on that virtuous maiden,
With a look she could hardly mistake.

But the innocent glance of that virgin,
Betokened that no guile she knew,
Though he begged in bold tones of entreaty,
She still wouldn't take up the cue.

He kissed her and prayed and beseeched her,
No answer received in reply,
Till his fingers were placed on her bosom,
And he crossed his leg over her thigh.

Then she said 'I can never, no never,
'Consent to such deeds until wed;

'You may try though the digital process,'
That maiden so virtuous said.

And he drew her still closer and closer,
His hand quick placed under her clothes,
And her clitoris youthful he tickled,
Till that maiden excited arose.

'F – k me now, dear, oh, f – k me,' she shouted,
'F – k me now, f – k me now, or I die.'
'I can't, I have spent in my breeches,'
Was that youth's disappointing reply.

Monsignor Peter had, after an infinite amount of persuasion, given me the address where Pinero Balsam was to be obtained, and I had laid in a decent stock of it, for though each small bottle cost a sovereign, I felt morally sure that it was the nearest approximation to the mythical *elixir vitoe* of the ancients that we moderns had invented. Some of this I had secretly dropped into the port wine, and the effect upon my guests had already become very pronounced.

'I say, Clinton,' said the junior of the party, who had only 'passed' a month, and who might be just turned twenty, 'your dinner was splendid, your tipple has a bouquet such as my in-experience has never suggested, have you anything in the shape of petticoats about half so good? if so, give me a look in.'

The youth was rapidly getting maudlin and randy; just then came a faint rap at the door, it was the old woman who swept and garnished the 'diggings'.

'I thought I might find Mr. Mitchell here, sir,' she said, apologetically, 'here's a telegram come for him,' and curtseying, the old girl vanished, glad to escape the fumes of wine and weed which must have nearly choked her.

'No bad news, I hope,' said I.

'Not at all,' said Sydney; 'what's the time?'

'Nearly 8.30' replied I, consulting my chronometer.

'Then I shall have to leave you fellows at nine, my married sister Fanny arrives at Euston from the north by the 9.30.'

'What a pity!' said the Callow Junior, 'if it were a sweetheart now one might be overjoyed at your good fortune – but a sister!'

'Is it the handsome one?' put in Wheeler.

'Yes,' said Sydney, showing us the face in a locket the only piece of jewellery, by the way, he boasted.

There was a silence as all clustered round the likeness.

'By Jove,' said Tom Mallow, the *roué* of the party, 'if I had a sister like that I should go clean staring mad, to think she wasn't some other fellow's sister, so that I might have a fair and reasonable chance.'

I said nothing, but I fell over head and ears in love with that face to such an extent that I felt there was nothing I would not do to possess the owner.

I, of course, presented a calm exterior, and under the guise of a host who knew his duty, plied them with rare old port, and proposed toast after toast, and health after health, until I had the satisfaction of seeing in less than three-quarters of an hour every member of the crew so dead drunk that I felt I could afford to leave the chambers without any fear of a mishap; then rolling the recumbent Sydney over, for he was extended prone upon the hearthrug, I subtracted the wire from his pocket, and saw that his sister's name was Lady Fanny Twisser.

'Oh,' said I, a light breaking in upon me, 'this then is the girl Sydney's plotting mother married to a rich baronet, old enough to be her grandfather; this doubles my chances,' and locking the door I made my way into the street. It was by Greenwich mean 9.19, and I was a mile and a quarter from the station.

'Hansom!'

'Yes, sir.'

'A guinea if you can drive me to Euston Station in ten minutes.'

That man earned his guinea.

THE EFFECTS OF SHELLFISH

From the booking office I emerged on to the arrival platform, and hailing a superior-looking porter, placed a sovereign in his hand, whispering in his ear, 'The train coming in the distance contains a Lady Twisser, engage a good cab, put all her luggage on it, and if I should happen to miss the lady, as I might do in this crowd, conduct me to her.'

He obeyed my instructions *au pied de la lettre*, and in less than two minutes I was shaking hands on the strength of a self-introduction to Lady Fanny.

I explained that her brother was engaged in consultation with a senior counsel at the bar, and that had it not been a very important case, he would have met her in person, but my instructions were that she was to come to his chambers where he would probably be by the time we arrived.

Lady Fanny's portrait had by no means exaggerated her loveliness.

A stately Grecian nose and finely cut lips suggested to me that she was a mare that might shy, but then her soft, brown, dreamy eyes told a sweeter tale, and as I thought of diviner joys I leaned back in the cab, and almost wished I had not touched the Pinero cordial, for I was in momentary fear of spending in my trousers.

'This, I think is your first visit to London.'

'Scarcely,' replied she, in a voice whose gentle music made my heart bound, 'I came up with my husband six months ago to be "presented", but we only stayed the day.'

'London is a splendid city,' I rejoined, 'so full of life and gaiety, and then the shops and bazaars are always replete with every knick-nack, that for ladies it must seem a veritable paradise.'

Lady Fanny only sighed, which I thought strange, but before my cogitations could take form we were at my chambers.

'Had not my boxes better be sent to some hotel,' said Lady Fanny, 'I am, of course, only going to make a call here.'

'Yes,' returned I, 'that is all arranged,' and feeing the cabman handsomely, I directed him to take them to a quiet hotel in Norfolk-street, Strand, and conducted her ladyship to her brother's rooms.

Here I left her for a few moments to see after my drunken guests, but found them all snoring peacefully, some on the floor, others on chairs and sofas, but all evidently settled for the night.

After knocking at Sydney's door I again entered his sitting-room, and found it empty.

Damn it, I thought to myself, the bird hasn't flown, I hope.

My ears were at this moment saluted with the gurgling which betokened that her ladyship was relieving herself in the adjoining apartment, and I quietly sat down and awaited her return.

On seeing me she started and turned as red as a full blown peony, the flower being a simile suggested by the situation, and said, 'I had no idea, Mr. Clinton, that – '

'Pray, Lady Fanny, do not mention it; I know exactly what you were about to say.'

'Indeed?'

'Yes, you as a matter of fact didn't know what to say, because you thought I heard you – a-hem – in the next room – but, my dear Lady Fanny, in London we are not so mighty particular as the hoydenish country folks, and as an old friend of your brother's, you will pardon my saying that I do not think you have treated me over well.'

'Treated you – really, Mr. Clinton, you amaze me; pray what have I done.'

'Rather, my dear Lady Fanny, what have you left undone.'

'Nothing, I hope,' said she, hastily, looking down as though she expected to see a petticoat or a garter falling off.

'No, I don't mean anything like that,' said I, coming closer to her, until the flame which shot from my eyes appeared to terrify her, and she moved towards the bedroom, as if to take refuge there.

Now this was the very height of my ambition, I knew once in that apartment all struggles and cries would be of little avail, for the walls were thick, the windows high, and there was no other door save the one she was gradually backing into.

'What does this conduct mean, Mr. Clinton?' said the lovely girl, for she was only two-and-twenty at the time of the *rencontre*.

'I surely am in my brother's chambers, and with his friend, for he has often written and told me of your kindness to him. You are not an impostor? you are not one of those dreadful men of whom one reads in romances, who would harm a woman?'

'No,' said I, 'Lady Fanny, do not mistake the ardour of devotion for any sinister motive, but sit down, after your fatiguing journey, while I order in some refreshment.'

'Doubly locking the door, on the principle of safe bind, safe find, I gave an order to the restaurateur round the corner which astonished that gentleman, and in less than ten minutes I had overcome Fanny's scruples, got her to take off her Moiré mantle and coquettish bonnet, and had placed before her a bijou supper in five courses such as I knew would make a country demoiselle open her eyes.

'Good gracious me,' said Lady Fanny, 'does my brother always live like this, if so, I am not at all surprised at his frequent requisitions on my purse.'

'Yes,' said I, nonchalantly, 'this is generally our supper, permit me,' and I poured out a glass of champagne, taking care, however, that six drops of Pinero had been placed in the glass.

A DISAPPOINTED WIFE'S FIRST TASTE OF BLISS

Really magical was the effect, for her conversation, hitherto so constrained, became gay and lively, and as this vivacity added to her other charms, I grew more and more enamoured of her.

'What capital oysters these are,' said she, swallowing her ninth 'native'.

'Yes,' said I, 'in your Cheshire home you would find it difficult to procure such real beauties.'

'We should, indeed,' replied she, 'and for the matter of that it is perhaps better that shellfish are so scarce with us,' and she heaved another sigh.

This beautiful woman is decidedly a conundrum, thought I, but determining to probe the puzzle, I enquired the meaning of her last remark.

She blushed and simpered, then fixing her eyes on her plate said, 'I have always understood that shellfish are exciting, and stimulate the passions.'

'That is perfectly correct,' retorted I, 'and therefore all the more reason why a married lady should patronize them.'

She sighed again, and then at last I guessed the reason. Fool that I was not to have divined it before this time. Hope now was succeeded by a certainty.

After disposing of some chicken and another glass of champagne, into which I insidiously dropped some more balsam, she sank back in the arm chair and murmured, 'How long do you think my brother's consultation is likely to last?'

'Pray heaven,' ejaculated I, fervently, 'that it may last all the night through.'

'Why do you say that, Mr. Clinton?'

'Because to see you and to listen to your voice is ravishing delight, which to dispel would seem to me the precursor of death,' and I flung myself upon my knees before her, and seizing her hand pressed it to my lips, and covered it with burning kisses.

She gently tried to withdraw it, and pointing to her wedding ring, said, 'Dear Mr. Clinton, I am a wife, have pity on me, I am but a weak woman, and – '

But I caught her in my arms, and stifled the rest of the sentence with a long and ardent mouth embrace, which, repulsed at first, was at length returned.

Two seconds afterwards my finger had softly glided into her willing cunt, and as it encountered the clitoris I found that

that membrane was as stiff as my own penis, which was now at bursting point.

'Oh, Mr. Clinton, for God's sake forbear. If my brother should come in there would be blood spilled, I should be lost.'

'Fear nothing, my darling,' said I, rubbing her vagina with the point of my finger, and feeling the beginning of the pearly trickle exuding all over my hand.

'Come this way,' and leading her ladyship unresistingly by the hand, never, however, leaving hold of her sweet cunt the while, I placed her on her own brother's bed, and, oh, how can I write further, since to say that she was superb is but faintly to describe the joy I felt as, straightening my throbbing prick, I gently insinuated it into her.

She gave one loud sigh, then lifted her strong country arse, and I plunged in up to the hilt. At each thrust I gave her lady-ship sighed, and returned the shove with a rapid promptitude which showed how fresh and spunky her vigorous constitution was.

'Go on, my own precious,' whispered she, as I put my tongue into her panting hot mouth. 'Faster, for Christ's sake, faster,' and as she said the words I shot into her a discharge which must have clean emptied my cods, for although Fanny still faintly struggled to emit some more, the last lingering spark of vitality appeared to have flown from me.

I did not seem to have even the strength left to take it out, but lay there on her rounded breasts (for she had undone her stomacher before commencing) supine and nerveless.

'Do try again, love,' she murmured, toying with my hair. 'You will never guess, dear Mr. Clinton, what this has been to me, my old husband never did such a thing, he always uses a beastly machine, shaped like that which is in me now, but made of guttapercha, and filled with warm oil and milk.'

'You mean a dildo, dear?'

'I have never heard its name,' said Fanny, but it is nothing near so nice at this dear sweet thing of yours. Oh! I never knew what real happiness was before; could you manage it once more,' and again her ladyship wriggled her bottom.

In my waistcoat pocket I had a *petite* flask of Pinero. I took this out, and removing the stopper, drank about half a tea spoon-ful, the result was electrical.

Drawing my prick nearly out of my lady's passage I found it

swelling again, and just giving the potent charm time to work, I softly began once more.

It may almost seem romancing, but I can assure my readers that the second fuck was more enjoyable than the first.

For having made coition a long study, I have always found that, given a cool brain, I can get more pleasure out of a slow connection than a gallopade, where the excitement gets the business over before you can absolutely realize the details.

I revel in a slow friction, gradually warming up to fever heat, and quite agree with that exquisite stanza of the immortal native of Natal

'Who was poking a Hottentot gal,'

And who upon being remonstrated with, or in the words of the bard

'Said she, oh! you sluggard,'

Replied most correctly

'You be buggered,
'I like fucking slow, and I shall.'

To resume, we both seemed to be so *au courant* of each other's little ways and modes of action as though we had mutually performed the 'fandango de pokum' for years, instead of only a few short minutes.

Presently, to vary the bliss, and to give her ladyship a few wrinkles, I suggested her mounting me, à la St. George.

But she begged of me not to take it out, and on my assuring her that that was by no means a necessary concomitant, she agreed.

I have always been distinguished as particularly *au fait* at the St. George, so I managed to roll over very gradually, first one leg and then the other, till I had got Fanny fairly planted on the top of me.

But I had gauged her ladyship's cunt power at too low an estimate, for she no sooner found herself mistress of the situation than she took in the position at a glance, and ravished me with such terrible lunges that I fairly cried a 'go'.

But nothing daunted, Fanny held on, and I stood no more chance of getting my poor used up 'torch' out of her vagina than if it had been wedged into a vice.

At last I felt the hot *créme de la créme* pouring down over my balls, and with a last despairing gasp of mingled pleasure and regret to think she could hold out no longer, Fanny once more sank into my arms about as thoroughly spent as a woman should be who has been most damnably twice fucked in a quarter of an hour.

Hastily putting on her things, and making herself shipshape, I drove with her to the hotel, where her boxes had arrived safely, and in the morning informed her brother, as I had previously arranged with Fanny, that she had sent a messenger to his chambers overnight, saying where she was to be found.

I also told him how I had excused him in a return message by the hotel porter, and his gratitude to me knew no bounds.

I deemed it prudent not to see her ladyship during her stay in town, though she sent me three pressing letters, but I feared we should be bowled out, and wrote her so.

Twelve months after this I heard she had separated from her husband, having presented him, nine months from that blissful evening, with a son and heir, which the old man, not believing in miracles, could scarcely altogether credit the dildo with.

THE INFLUENCE OF FINERY

Now my next essay was of a totally different character, and may, perhaps, be stigmatized by the fastidious reader as an escapade, degrading to one whose last *liaison* had been with the wife of a baronet, but to tell the truth, and judging cunt from a strictly philosophical standpoint, there is so little difference between a chambermaid and a countess, that it would take a very astute individual indeed to define it.

It is, perhaps, true, that the countess's opening may be, by frequent ablutions kept sweeter, and the frangipanni on her ladyship's fine cambric chemisette may possibly make the entrance more odoriferous for a tongue lick, but Dr. Johnson's admirable impromptu definition will apply to the vagina of a Malayese or a China girl equally with that of our own country-women. He said, if you remember, on the occasion when poor Oliver Goldsmith was troubled with the venereal, and came to him for sympathy:

'Cunt, and what of it? –
A nasty, slimy, slobbery, slit,
Half-an-inch between arse and it;
If the bridge were to break 'twould be covered with – '

So that any twitting my reader feels inclined to bestow upon my next venture should be judiciously seasoned with a little reflection.

I have already in the course of this narrative mentioned the duenna who cleaned my chambers. She was a cast off mistress of one of the old serjeants of the Inn, who had procured her this situation for life, and supplemented it with a small allowance, which enabled her to live in comparative comfort.

Two of her bastard daughters were married, and a younger one, the pretty one as she called her, had just returned home from boarding-school, whither the old woman by dint of careful frugality had managed to send her.

She was barely turned sixteen, as upright as a dart, had a fine full face, with plenty of colour in it, and a form so shapely that I scarcely gave credence to the mother's statement that she was only sixteen. The old woman was very garrulous, annoyingly so sometimes, but on the subject of her darling daughter I used to let her tongue run on till further orders.

'She's a fine, strapping, wench, sir, just the kind of girl I was at her age, though I think if anything she's a trifle more plump than I was.'

'Yes, by God, and so should I,' was my involuntary exclamation, as I looked at the aged frump's wizened features.

'I don't know what I shall do with her,' muttered her mother. 'I shall have to send her to service, this place won't keep two of us, and not only that, sir, I've been thinking that it's hardly the thing for a giddy girl like her to be brought into contact with gentlemen like you.'

Of course the mother was thinking of her own youthful transgressions with the serjeant, so I merely remarked that I was surprised such thoughts should run in her head, but I inwardly resolved that come what may I would see if a girl of sixteen with such a full fleshy face had got a cunt to match.

Noticing that the daughter was fond of dress, I bought a small parcel of ribbons one day at a draper's, and had them addressed to her without saying a word as to my having sent them.

The following morning I met her on the stairs, gaily decked out, and I asked her where she was going.

'Only for a walk in this silly old inn,' she replied. 'I have a beau, sir, an unknown beau, who has sent me all these beautiful ribbons, and a lot more besides, and I thought by going out he might see that I had appreciated his gift, that is if he were watching for me,' added she, with an arch smile.

'That's right, my girl, perhaps he will send you something else; by the way, what is your name?'

'Gerty,' said the young lady, smiling.

'Well, Gerty, you'll excuse me saying so, but that splendid ribbon with which you have decorated your hat, makes the hat look quite shabby.'

'Alas! sir, I know it, but mother is poor, and I can't afford to buy another one just yet.'

'If you'd promise not to tell your mother, promise me sacredly not on any account to tell her, I will take you to a shop where I saw a lovely one yesterday that would suit your style admirably, and I shall only be too happy to purchase it for you.'

'Oh, sir, you are very kind, but I could not impose – '

'Tut, child, don't speak like that, but go out into the street, and walk to the corner of the Great Turnstile, and I will join you in three minutes.'

Of course I did this to avoid observation. Presently I went out myself, and took her to the very drapers where I had bought the ribbon.

'Good morning, sir,' I have now got that particular shade of ribbon you wanted yesterday.'

The cat was out of the bag, Gerty glanced quickly up at me, and I saw I was discovered.

'So *you* are the unknown beau,' she whispered, 'well, I am surprised.'

'And, I hope, pleased, too, Gerty?'

'Well, I hardy know,' said she, 'but what about the hat?'

To cut a long story short I rigged her up from top to toe, and before I left the shop I had expended nearly £20 on her.

'How on earth am I to account for having this to mother?'

'We'll have it sent like the ribbons, and, of course, you can't form a guess where it came from. The shop people must put no address inside,' and giving all the necessary instructions, I shook hands with Gertrude and bade her good morning.

In the evening a gentle tap at my door ushered in the young lady herself, who, closing it softly after her, said, 'Those things have come, sir, and mother went on like anything, but I vowed I didn't know who had sent 'em, so she told me in that case I'd better thank God, and say no more about it.'

'Then it's all right,' said I, looking intently at her large rounded bust, which, confined as it was by a tightly fitting dress, showed to singular advantage.

'I'm afraid, sir,' said, she, 'that I didn't thank you sufficiently this morning, and so I thought as mother has gone down to Peckham to see her brother I'd call in and do it now.'

'My dear Gertrude,' said I, 'there's only one way of showing your gratitude to me, and that way you are as yet I fear too young to understand. Come here, my dear.'

I was sitting by a blazing coal fire, and although I had not lit the gas the light was ample, she stepped forward, and seemed, as I thought, rather timorous in her manner.

'My dear Gerty,' said I, placing my arm round her waist, 'you are heartily welcome to what my poor purse can afford. As for those petty matters I purchased to-day, one kiss from those pouting lips will repay me a thousand fold,' so saying I lifted her on to my knee, and kissed her repeatedly.

At first she tried to disengage herself, but soon I found my caresses were not unwelcome. Presently I began undoing the buttons of her frock, and although she fought against it at first, she gradually allowed herself to be convinced, and as her swelling bubs disclosed themselves to my view I felt transported.

'Oh! Mr. Clinton, you will ruin me, I'm sure you will. Pray stop where you are, and do not go any further.'

Her beautiful little nipples, as the firelight threw them into relief on her lily breasts looked like a pair of twin cherries, and before she could prevent me, my mouth had fastened on one, and I sucked it with avidity.

'Oh! Mr. Clinton, I shall faint. Do let me go. I never felt anything like this in my life.'

'My darling,' said I, suddenly placing my prick in her hand, 'did you ever feel anything like that?'

Her thumb and fingers clutched it with a nervous clasp, and I felt that her hands were moist with the hot dew of feverish perspiration. Before, however, I could prevent her, or, indeed, fathom her motives, she had slid from my grasp, and was kneeling on the floor between my extended legs.

'What is the matter, Gerty dear?' said I.

I got no answer, but the hand which still held my penis was brought softly forward, her mouth opened, and drawing back my foreskin, she tongued me with a sweet solacing suck that almost drove me frantic.

For at least two minutes I lay back in the arm chair, my brain in a delirium of delight, till not able to bear it any longer, for she had begun to rack me off. I got my prick away, pushed back the arm chair, and with mad, and, I may add, stupid haste, broke her maidenhead, and spent in her at the same instant with such force that for the moment I expected (contrary to all anatomical knowledge) to see the sperm spurting out of her mouth.

It would be unjust to Gertrude were I to accuse her of want of reciprocity, for my hearthrug gave pretty good proof that she was by no means wanting in juice, since to say it was swamped would be but mildly to describe its condition.

Hardly had Gertrude wiped out her fanny, and just as I was in the act of pouring her out a glass of brandy and water, to prevent the reaction, which in a maid so young might I thought possibly set in, when, without announcing her entrance, the mother rushed into the room like a tigress. She had returned to fetch her latch key.

'So this is what I brought you up for like a lady, is it,' she began; 'and this is the conduct of a gentleman that I thought was a real gentleman. Don't deny it, you brazen bitch,' she continued, seeing that Gertrude was about to try a lame explanation, for she was ready witted enough. 'I've got a nose of my own, and if ever there was a maidenhead cooked its been done in this room since I've been out. Why, even the staircase smells fishy. I discard you for ever. Perhaps the gentleman,' laying a sneering stress on the word, 'now that he's ruined you, will keep you,' and she bounced out of the room.

I took the old woman at her word, and rented a little cottage at Kew, where I kept Gerty in style for about three months, and should have done so to the end of the chapter if I had not caught her one Saturday afternoon *in flagrante delicto* with one of the leading members of the London Rowing Club, so I gave her a cheque for £100, and she started as a dressmaker, or something of the kind, at which business she has I understand done very well.

A PARAGON OF VIRTUE

One morning, as the summer was waning, and August warned us to flee from town, De Vaux called upon me at my new chambers, for prudence had suggested my removal from my late quarters, and found me dozing over a prime Cabana, and the latest *chic* book from Mr. — , the renounced smut emporium.

'Glad to see you,' said De Vaux. 'My friend Leveson has asked me down to Oatlands Hall for a week's shooting, and wishes me to bring a friend, will you come?'

'Is there anything hot and hollow about,' asked I, 'for to tell you the truth, my boy, knocking over grouse is a very pleasant occupation, but unless there is some sport of another kind on as well, the game is not worth the candle.'

'Clinton, you are incorrigible, I never remember to have met such an incurable cunt hunter in my life. Well, there may be some stray 'stuff' drop in while we are there, but I warn you not to try it on with Mrs. Leveson, for though she might give you the idea at a first glance that she was fast and frivolous, she's in reality as true as steel to her husband, and I would not give a brass farthing for the chance of the veriest Adonis that ever stood in a pair of patent leather boots.'

'I should immensely like to have a slap at this dreadful Diana of yours, De Vaux. Is she a beauty?'

De Vaux sighed heavily.

'I was hard hit myself that quarter once,' he said, 'but it was no go. Her eyes are wandering orbs, like a gipsy's. She has the finest set of teeth I ever saw in my life, and a form, well – I'd rather not go into it, for it upsets me.'

'I'd rather go into it, for my part,' said I, laughing. 'Why you're a very Strephon, De Vaux, in your poetic keep-at-a-distance style of admiring this divinity. Did you seriously try it on now, left no stone unturned, eh?'

'I did, indeed,' said De Vaux, 'both before and after she was married, but it was love's labour lost. I got my hand on her leg once, and she froze me with a few curt words, and wound up by telling me if I did not instantly go back to town, and foist some lying excuse on Leveson for going, she would expose me mercilessly, and by God, Clinton, I am sufficiently learned in womankind to know when they mean a thing and when they do not.'

'Really, I must see this paragon of yours, De Vaux. The more obstacles there are in the way, the better a Philosopher in Cunt enjoys it.'

'You can come with me and welcome, Clinton, but I tell you candidly Mrs. Leveson is beyond your reach or that of any other man. She is simply ice.'

'But, my dear De Vaux, ice can be made to thaw!'

'Not the ice of the poles.'

'Yes, even that, if you apply sufficient heat. Bah! my friend, I'll wager you twelve dozens of my finest Chateau Margaux to that emerald pin you wear, for which I have often longed, that I will fuck your pearl of chastity before this day week.'

The bet was instantly accepted, for although I had previously offered him £50 for his pin, and he didn't want to part with it, still he felt no danger in the present instance, and went home and probably drank in his imagination half of my wine in anticipation.

'Clinton, my boy,' said I, apostrophizing my prick, as I got into bed that evening, if you don't disturb her ladyship's ice-bound repose before many nights have gone over your proud red head may you be damned to all eternity, and, in response, my noble, and, I may add, learned friend, perked himself up straight, and though he didn't speak, his significant and conceited nod assured me that he at any rate had no misgivings.

OTHER GAME PREFERRED TO GROUSE

HAVING arrived at Oatlands Hall about five o'clock in the afternoon, after a delightful journey, for it was the 11th August, and the mellow corn just fully ripened for the sickle greeted our city-worn eyes all along the line. So really picturesque was the view that I lost several opportunities of getting well on with a buxom young chit who wanted fucking worse than anything in petticoats ever did between London and York.

De Vaux slept most of the way, and if without committing murder I could have got the girl's mother out of the carriage window, I should certainly have landed a slice of fifteen, for she could not have been over that age.

I may, however, mention that I had an after opportunity in the year that followed, which will come in its turn, as, like most of the fashionable novelists, I must decline to anticipate.

Leveson was a very jolly fellow, about thirty-eight or forty, and Mrs. Leveson, a really grand creature, at least ten to twelve years his junior, but although De Vaux had prepared me for something above the common, I must confess the reality far surpassed my expectations.

Figurez vous, as our lively neighbours would put it, a sweet smiling Juno, with an oval face, coloured prettily by nature's own palette, and a pair of finely arched eyebrows surrounding eyes so dazzling in their lustrous black that I fell a victim to the very first glance.

Poor De Vaux seemed half in doubt, half dread, for this was the first time he had seen her since the *fiasco*. She, however, stretched out her hand and welcomed him cordially. We had a fine, old-fashioned country dinner, and then Mrs. Leveson proposed a stroll round the grounds. She took a great pride in the garden and orchard, and the exquisite fascination of her manner as she described lucidly all the various differences between plants, shrubs, greenery, exotics, and all the thousand and one trifles that interest a botanical student showed me that she was no ordinary woman.

Again I was compelled to silent admiration when we walked through the stables, which Caligula's could scarcely have excelled for cleanliness, and as she patted the horses in their boxes I envied them, for they neighed and whinnied with delight at her very touch.

I was glad when she and her husband had gone into the house, and left De Vaux and me to finish our smoke alone.

'Well,' said he, 'what do you think of her?'

'Think of her,' muttered I, 'I'd rather not think of her, she has excited me to such an extent that if I don't get into something in the house I shall really have to go into the village and seek out an ordinary 'pross'.

'Well, my dear boy, then you'd better do that at once, for unless some of the chambermaids are amenable, I'm perfectly certain that you've no time to lose. You might as well dream of fucking the moon as Mrs. Leveson. She's quite as chaste and just as unattainable.'

'That be damned,' said I, 'De Vaux's constant reiteration of this Dulcinea's chastity was gall and wormwood to me.

We were the only guests who had arrived for the 12th, and as grouse shooting meant getting up at dawn, we had one rubber at whist, and retired to bed early.

On the first floor of this large old mansion there were at least a dozen rooms. My own bedroom door immediately faced our host and hostess's; De Vaux slept in the next room to mine.

'How frightfully hot it is,' said Leveson. 'I should say we're bound to have some rain.'

'I hope not,' said I, 'for it will spoil our morning, though this temperature is simply insufferable' I had been all round the world in my father's yacht, and had spent a considerable time in the tropics, but had never remembered such an intense dry heat.

Taking with me to bed a French novel I had picked out of the library shelves, and getting the servant to bring in a large glass of lemonade, I was soon asleep, in spite of the heat, though I had to forego sheets, blanket, and counterpane, and simply sleep in my night shirt.

In the gray of the morning I was aroused, and could scarcely believe my eyes. There was a young woman standing by the side of the bed, and I recognized her as a shapely lass who had taken my portmanteau upstairs the previous evening.

I have always had an unpleasant habit in my sleep of twisting and turning until my shirt rucks up under my armpits, thus it appears that as this hot night had proved no exception to the rule, Hannah, for such was the filly's name, had knocked at the door to awaken me, but receiving no response, and fearing she should get into trouble if I overslept myself, had opened the door, and the sight of my magnificent prick had simply transfixed her so that she stood there like one bewitched.

I rubbed my eyes once more, then sprang up, and before the girl could, like a frightened fawn, reach the door I had gently but firmly closed it, and set my back against it.

'Oh! Mr. Clinton, missis would be so angry if she heard me in here.'

'Has your mistress yet been called?'

'No, sir.'

'Have you roused Mr. De Vaux?'

'Not yet.'

'Who knows then of your being here?'

'The cook, sir, and she's a spiteful old thing as hates gentlemen, because they don't never look at her.'

'Hannah,' said I, 'didn't I hear you called by that name last night.'

'Yes, sir; please let me go downstairs.'

'Hannah, is there light enough for you to see this?' and I quietly raised my night shirt.

'Oh, Mr. Clinton, how can you be so rude.'

'Now, look here, Hannah, we needn't mince matters. Your mistress doesn't know of your being here, but if you cry out she's bound to know it, and of course you'll get sacked for being found in a gentleman's bedroom. I shan't be blamed for trying to get into a girl who actually comes to ask me for it.'

'But, my God, I haven't, sir.'

'No, but don't you see that that is what I should be obliged to say if any awkward questions were put to me.'

'Oh! please, sir, I'll never come into your bedroom again, sir, indeed I won't.

'My dear Hannah,' said I, 'I hope you will every night of my stay; but I must have my first taste now.'

With a sudden movement I caught her in my arms, and threw her down on the bed.

The silly stupid fool struggled with the strength of a giantess, and I saw that it was going to be a fair fight for it.

This is what I enjoy, provided the struggle is not too exhausting, and in this case it was fortunately only of sufficient duration to give the proper zest, for no sooner in the course of her efforts to keep my hand away from her 'fanny' had her own touched the top of my splitting jock than she was powerless as a kitten.

I will not dilate upon my fuck with Hannah, for she was in too frightened a state to give me much pleasure at that time.

I have, however, under more favourable conditions, since amused myself with her during a spare half-hour, and although her cunt has not got that tenacity of grip which distinguished Lady Fanny, for example, yet there was that general spunkiness about her final throw off which places her in the front rank for one in her station of life.

To again quote dear old Sam: 'A man's imagination is not so inflamed with a chambermaid as a countess,' and, besides, Hannah was not a maid, the coachman having settled her hash about six months before.

CHECKED AT FIRST

But after this Hannah kissed me and bolted off, and I drank a tumbler of water with a few drops of balsam in it, and felt none the worse for my *affaire par hazard*, but at once joined the shooting party.

I did a fair share of bagging, though the birds were scarcly wild enough to my taste.

I hate the fashionable *battue* business of today, but do not mean to imply that it was anything like that, for I am speaking of more than twenty years ago, but still Leveson's keepers had fed them too well, and they scarcely rose to the tramp of a foot near their cover.

We returned to the hall to lunch, and Mrs. Leveson enquired as to the result of our morning's work.

We told her it had been fair, but I half hinted at my preference for seeing a bit of the country, as I was a fickle sportsman, and one morning's shooting was enough for me. She, without a moment's hesitation, offered to become my *cicerone*, and procuring two horses from the stable I sallied forth with her.

'Now, you must be my mentor in everything, please Mrs. Leveson. I must admit to being dreadfully ignorant of country matters.'

She rode with me fully fifteen miles, and although I felt my way cautiously, I began to see there was an iron bar between us, which would probably prove impassable.

The instant there was the slightest hint or suggestion which implied a *double entendre*, her cheek flushed, and she looked full in my face with her sparkling eyes, and a gaze of steady searching frankness as who should say, 'do my ears deceive me, or are you trying to covertly insult me'.

'Damn it,' thought I, James Clinton, you've met your match this time, and a still small voice never left off whispering, 'see what the balsam will do, try a few drops of it,' but I never got the opportunity, and as we cantered down the broad gravel walk that led to the front lawn, she with her face flushed with the excitement of riding, mine flushed also, but with the excitement of a 'horn' which I had now the satisfaction of knowing could be relieved without quitting the mansion, De Vaux met us.

'Well,' said he, in an undertone to me, after he had assisted Mrs. Leveson to dismount, 'how does the bet stand?'

'Blast the bet,' said I, 'I'll give you six dozen to let me off.'

He laughed and said he would take one hundred and forty three bottles, and leave me the other to get drunk upon and drown my disappointment.

FORTUNE FAVOURS THE BRAVE

Hannah did not come up to my room that night, though she had promised to, still the weather was again so damned hot that I was in one sense rather glad of it. About four a.m., however, she came up to call the indefatigable sportsmen, but Leveson had already risen, and had entered my room in his shirt and trousers, so that when Hannah gently opened my door she was petrified at finding her master there trying to persuade me to go with them.

'What the devil do you mean, you minx, by coming into a gentleman's room without knocking first?'

I immediately interposed, and told him what a sound sleeper I was, and spoke of the difficulty the girl had experienced the previous morning.

Mr. De Vaux is up, so you needn't trouble to call him, and you needn't bring up any coffee to your mistress, for she's as sound asleep as a rock. So you won't come, Clinton?'

'Not this morning, old boy; I'm deuced tired and sleepy.'

'Very well, then,' said he, 'I suppose we must manage without you,' and presently I heard both the noble sportsmen quietly taking their departure.

I at first tried to compose myself to sleep, but found it impossible, for my prick had become a cursed incumbrance. The advent of Hannah had excited it to start with, and now there was the tantalizing fact that within a few yards of me was lying the lady of the mansion, yet, in respect to approachability, as far off as if she had been at the Antipodes.

Still the old proverb of 'faint heart never winning fair lady' came to my rescue, and I quietly arose and softly opened my door, just to see if there was a ghost of a chance.

As I previously mentioned, my room faced that of Mr. and Mrs. Leveson's, judge then my delight when I saw that mine host had actually, and I presumed by inadvertence, left his door ajar.

Stealthily and silently as a cat I crossed the corridor, scarcely daring to breathe, and pushing the door open, inch by inch, I put my head inside.

There, lying on the bed with nothing but a sheet to cover her splendid form, was the woman for whose possession I so madly longed, but the knowledge that her chastity was an insuperable bar to the ordinary preliminaries of a fair fuck, suggested my attempting the siege in another fashion.

Stooping down, and going on all fours, I approached the bed side, and gently lifting up one end of the sheet I revealed her naked form, for, like me, she had got her night chemise rolled up as far as her titties. Her legs were lying temptingly open, and, as little by little, I worked myself under the sheet, my face drew nearer to the lovely little cunt whose pouting lips looked only fit to be kissed.

Gradually, and without sufficient movement to alarm or even awaken my sleeping beauty, I got my head well between her legs, and my smooth face, for I only had a moustache, rested on her right thigh, without altering her posture.

She did move once, and passed her hand down over my head, murmuring the while, 'Oh, George, wait until the morning,' and then as I remained perfectly quiescent, she dozed off again.

Presently I got well into position, and putting out my tongue, gave the lips a gentle lick. I could feel that there was a slight tremor, but as that was only the natural effect of the electrobiology, I knew that she was not yet awake.

Another lick, this time a trifle further in, and the next second I plunged my tongue far up, until it touched the clitoris. She was instantly awake.

'Oh, George, darling, it is years since you did this, why, you dog, you haven't thought of such a thing since our honeymoon.'

I renewed my licking, thrusting her splendid thighs aside, though, in reality, there was no need to thrust, for she opened them as far as ever she could, until my tongue was in right up to the root, and I found from the rapid up and down movement of her bottom that unless I speedily withdrew it, she would most certainly come.

In my excitement I muttered 'my darling,' and she hearing a strange voice threw back the sheet, and I suppose looked down.

She must have seen at a glance that it was not her husband, for she put her hands on my head, and in a low voice, half of anguish, half pleasure, said, 'Oh, who are you? How could you?' but the matter had gone too far now to be remedied, and she must have felt this, for the movement of her arse continued, and was getting more violent.

I could stand it no longer, so taking out my tongue, I looked up at her.

'I guessed it was you, Mr. Clinton, you are doing a very wicked thing, but I really must have it now, I can't wait,' and pulling me on to her, my prick found the already well-greased hole, which was full of slobber from my own mouth, and with several quick movements, long thrusts, and about half a dozen wriggles, we both spent at the same moment.

I believe, had her husband come in at the instant, we could not possibly have disengaged ourselves from each other's arms, for we lay there in a transport of bliss, and I could not help pluming myself on the admirable *savoir faire* I had manifested in my management of the whole business.

'What on earth made you do this, Mr. Clinton?' said Mrs. Leveson, still holding me and keeping me in her, with her legs entwined around my backside, but blushing all the while.

'My darling,' said I, 'the moment I saw you I felt that if I had to commit a rape I should be obliged to enjoy you, though it cost me liberty, or, indeed, for the matter of that, life.'

A slight movement outside the door here attracted our attention, and hiding me under the sheet, Mrs. Leveson enquired 'who was there', to this there was no response, and we breathed freely again.

'My darling,' said Mrs. Leveson, looking at me with beaming eyes, 'I am so delighted, that although I know we have both committed a great sin, I feel as if the pleasure had not been too dearly bought, but for fear of discovery, hurry back to your own room,' and kissing me affectionately, both on mouth and prick, I took my leave of her for the time.

I had no sooner got outside the room and pulled the door to after me than I was suddenly struck dumb with surprise and fear, for I found my own chamber door open, and, I felt certain, that I had not been such a ninny as to leave it so. I entered the room on tip toe, in fear and trembling, and found De Vaux standing by the window, looking white and thoughtful.

'Hallo,' said I, 'what, in the Devil's name, brings you here?'

'I came back,' replied he, to fetch some large shot which I had in my other shooting pouch.'

'Well, you've lost your bet,' said I, triumphantly.

'I know it,' he gloomily made answer, 'and what worries me is I cannot understand it. You are not a better looking man than I am. Except in the matter of a few thousands a year and a larger tool, nature, luck, and birth, have not favoured you more that me, yet you absolutely mount a woman you have only known forty-eight hours, while I have for three long years tried in the same direction, and utterly failed. I will let you have the pin to-morrow.'

'But you only saw me coming from her room, how do you know that I absolutely won the trick?'

'How do I know, why I opened your door quietly to see if you were asleep, and finding you absent I looked round, and saw Mrs. Leveson's door open. I also heard you both hard at it, and could not forbear from peeping in. Oh, what a sight it was; there was she, lovely thing that she is, rising to every stroke, and I could see your long prick actually coming clean out of her, *reculer pour mieux sauter,* and then dashing in again till the sight nearly made a lunatic of me. How in the name of God did you work it, for it seems to me little short of miraculous?'

I didn't satisfy his curiosity, but left him to ponder over it, while I wrapped myself up, for the morning was getting chilly, and fell asleep.

De Vaux proceeded to the *battue,* but if his shooting was not superior to his spirits, the birds must have had a distinctly fine time of it, for if ever there was a man at a country luncheon table possessed by the megrims, De Vaux was that individual, when I met him a few hours later.

DE VAUX'S CHAGRIN – A PROPOSITION

During the afternoon, as good luck would have it, a wire from Hull (Oatlands Hall was thirty miles from that town) came for Mr. Leveson, desiring him to repair there to meet an old college chum, who was passing through the seaport en route for Norway. So about five o'clock we had an early dinner, and wished him good bye until the following day.

Mrs. Leveson had a splendid voice, and as two other musical friends dropped in later on, we had a most harmonious evening.

Towards ten o'clock, while I was turning over Mrs. Leveson's music for her, I seized an opportunity to whisper, 'Shall I come in to you, or will you visit a poor benighted bachelor to-night?'

'The latter,' she replied, and blushed up to the roots of her hair. She had not yet learnt how to deaden the qualms of conscience, but she was woman enough to intimate, very *sotto voce,* 'That we should be observed if we whispered any more.'

'Mr. De Vaux, would you mind turning over for me, Mr. Clinton is so very awkward.'

This was the cut direct, before three others, too, but I grinned and bore it.

'She did not find you so awkward this morning, Clinton,' whispered he, as he leisurely took his stand by the piano, and I passed into the adjoining apartment, where there was a 'cut-and-come-again supper,' to which I did ample justice.

About eleven o'clock, the guests having gone, Mrs. Leveson bade us both good-night in a stately, formal, way, and retired, and De Vaux and I proceeded to the billiard room.

'I have a proposition to make to you,' said he, as he was chalking his cue for a game.

I couldn't think what De Vaux's rather serious manner imported. At first I imagined he was sore at losing his pin, and as my intrigue had been so delicious, I told him I knew what he was about to say, and that he might keep the heirloom (for I always believed it was an heirloom), I didn't really want it, and pointed out that he could salve his conscience in not paying the bet, as I had won it under circumstances which savoured of unfairness, but De Vaux stopped me.

'Let us sit down,' he said, 'I hardly feel in the humour for the green cloth to-night. Listen to me a few minutes.'

I sat down, feeling curious to know what was coming next.

'The pin is yours, Clinton,' said he, 'and I have even forgotten that I ever possessed such a thing, but I wish to speak to you upon another matter.'

'My dear, De Vaux,' said I, 'wait until I have lighted another cigar. Now, fire away.'

'You are, as you justly call yourself, a Cunt Philosopher; lately I have gone in for arse castigation a good deal, and the passion that I once had for the more genuine article I foolishly imagined had died out.'

'What the devil does all this prelude mean, old man?'

'Simply this. Three years ago I was seriously, nay madly, in love with Mrs. Leveson. I would have given my finger tips to possess her, and when I made advances which were spurned, and eventually proceeded to extremes, which resulted in my being politely told to make myself scarce, I was cut up more than I have ever been in my life, either before or since.'

'What damned nonsense you are talking, De Vaux.'

'I'm speaking the sober truth, Clinton. I accepted Leveson's invite down here thinking I had got over my foolish passion, but before I had been in her company ten minutes I had all the old feeling come back again with renewed force, and knowing how hopeless was the endeavour to become possessor of her charms, I made up my mind to cut short my visit.'

'What noble, lofty sentiment is this, my worthy friend; I'll be shot if I can understand it.'

'When I came in and discovered you this morning, the first feeling that predominated was rampant jealousy, and I really believe that had I not governed myself by walking hastily away from the scene, I should have shot both of you.'

'Damn it, man, the bet was of your own making.'

'I know it, and I cursed myself as a blasted idiot for having made it, and then calmer thoughts prevailed. Now, as you have enjoyed one of the divinest women that was ever cast in beauty's mould, I want you to do me a good turn. I have, I think, without wishing to remind you of obligations rendered, done you one or two services in the fucking line.'

I remembered Lucy, and at once acquiesced.

'Tonight, knowing what I did, I watched you and Mrs. Leveson, and, although I heard no words spoken, am quite sure that at the piano you arranged an assignation.'

'I did.'

'In your bedroom, or hers?'

'In my own.'

'Clinton, be a d — d good friend,' said De Vaux, earnestly, 'let me take your place.'

'She will find you out,' said I, not altogether falling in with his view, for although I had guessed what he was leading up to, I didn't quite relish the situation.

'What if she does, it will not matter once I am well in her; she won't cry out, that I can bargain for.'

'Well,' said I, 'how do you propose to work it?'

'Simply in this way, I take your bed, you take mine.'

'Right you are,' said I, and I really meant to oblige poor De Vaux at the time, but I was always a practical joker, and as I knew Hannah, the dread of her master being removed, would be sure to run up within an hour of my retiring, I looked forward to some fun.

RINGING THE CHANGES

We wished each other good-night, exchanging rooms as agreed, and acting upon my advice, De Vaux extinguished his candle, for fear of Mrs. Leveson coming in too soon. I waited to hear him piddle, and get into bed, and then undressing myself, hastily crossed over to my darling.

She was lying, propped up by the pillows, reading 'Ovid's Art of Love', a book I had seen in the library, and during the evening had recommended to her notice.

'Dear Mr. Clinton, I thought I was to come into you.'

'No, my precious,' said I, 'the bed is too narrow, and De Vaux sleeps so lightly he might hear us.'

As I said this I lifted the bed clothes lightly off her, and found that with natural bashfulness she had gone to bed in her drawers.

'Off with those appendages, my love,' said I.

'Oh, Mr. Clinton, don't be indecent; my modesty forbids.'

'Julia,' for I had ascertained her name, 'take off those stupid hindrances to love's free play, or, stay, let me take them off for you,' and you would have laughed to have seen me executing this feat, for I lingered so long round her cunt every time I approached it, that it took me a good five minutes.

All this time Julia was fairly on heat, for the sight of my huge prick, as upright as a recruiting serjeant, would have excited Minerva herself.

'Now, my darling,' said I, 'let us have a little eccentricity. I understand both you and your husband want a youngster; now just tell me does he ever have connection with you except in the old-fashioned way – belly to belly?'

'Never, Mr. Clinton. How can there be any other method.'

'Good God,' said I, 'what venal innocence. Look here, my pet, kneel down as if you were praying for a family.' She did so.

'Now, clutch the iron rail at the foot of the bed, and put the top of your head hard down on this pillow, as if you were going to try to stand on it.'

'My dear, Mr. Clinton, why all these preliminaries; I'm dying for it.'

'You shan't have long to wait, my pretty one,' for as she had minutely obeyed my instructions, her fair, round arse towered high in the bed, and I could just see the little seam of her vagina peeping at me from underneath.

Drawing back my foreskin until my best friend's topnut stood out like a glistening globe, quivering with excitement, I cautiously approached her, for I would have it understood, gentle reader, that tyros in cohabitation should always be cool when engaged in this particular style of sport.

'Straddle your knees slightly, my sweet one,' I whispered.

'For God's sake hasten, Mr. Clinton, this delay is killing me.'

Drawing back once more to allow the candlelight to play on the spot, so that I could not miss my mark, I bulged forward, and got the tip well placed for the final rush, but Julia anticipated me by suddenly squatting backwards, and for the moment I thought bollocks and all had gone in.

Then commenced one of the most memorable fucks in my life's long record, and certainly one of the most pleasurable.

Every time I felt the inclination to spend I purposely stayed myself on the threshold of bliss in order to prolong it.

At last, after Julia had saturated me three times, and was beginning to get pumped out, I brought all my forces to the charge, and giving several decisive lunges, which meant mischief, I fairly bathed her womb in boiling sperm, and the way that solid queenlike cunt closed on my prick, and held it as though we twain were one flesh, convinced me that the estate of Oatlands would in less than a year be *en fête*, and the joybells of the old village steeple would ring out to tell of a birth at the Manor House.

'In the meantime what had been going on in my own bedroom?'

It had fallen out precisely as I had predicted.

Hannah had sneaked upstairs, and had slid into my bed, and De Vaux, without speaking, had fucked her with the dash and genuine passion born of a three years' forlorn hope.

Nor did he discover himself even after it was all over, but having in his ecstasy shagged her twice in ten minutes, he allowed her to escape, merely whispering in her ear, that he hoped she had enjoyed it.

Hannah, on the contrary, had found out the imposture the moment she got De Vaux's prick in her. She had never felt but two, the coachman's and mine, and De Vaux's, although long and sinewy, was no match for either of ours in point of build, still it was better than not being fucked at all, and as De Vaux's ardent imagination was riding Mrs. Leveson, the servant got all the benefit, and not only prudently preserved her incognito, but lifted her brawny arse in such rare style that De Vaux was more than satisfied.

In the morning I went in to see him before proceeding downstairs; he shook hands with me cordially.

'Did she disappoint you?' asked I, with feigned innocence.

'My dear Clinton, she's a perfect angel, and you're a trump.'

Leveson came back the next day, and I never got another chance of landing Mrs. Leveson, who had fallen *enceinte* by me, and presented her husband with a son and heir nine months to the day.

De Vaux fondly imagines the kid must be his, and I am quite willing he should continue to think so, but every time Leveson compares dates he thinks of his night's stay at Hull, shakes his head, and mutters that 'it's damned extraordinary,' yet he wouldn't consider it at all extraordinary, if he knew as much as we do, reader. 'What do you think?'

ON GAMAHUCHING;
OR THE MAGIC INFLUENCE OF THE TONGUE

The 'gamahuching,' process should only be employed as a preliminary and never should be permitted to go to the extent of more than starting the tap. No woman living is able to stand a moist and well-trained tongue. Even those in whom desire has long been dead have been known to shriek for the relief which only an erect penis can afford.

Jack Wilton, the greatest essayist on cunt in an analytical form who ever lived, goes further, and even says – 'a judicious tongue can galvanize into life a female corpse.'

This, of course, I do not admit, but there is a well authenticated instance of a Somersetshire farmer's wife, who had fallen into a trance, and was believed by all her neighbours to be dead, but who was recalled to life simply through the husband giving her fanny one last loving lick.

It is astonishing how prevalent the habit has become in England of gamahuching, and I would, while touching on it, maintain that there is nothing unnatural in it.

A tongue, soft and fleshy, fits in the vagina as though made for it, and though it can only titillate the clitoris, it serves the useful office of *avant courier* to the prick. The proof, if proof were wanting, that there is a distinct physical sympathy between the latter and the tongue, is that in the case of syphilis the tongue is affected almost as soon as the penis shows signs of having made a mistake. The proof again of its being natural to animal life is the fact that if one carefully observes the collection in the Zoo, it will be seen that when the beasts are in dalliance with one another the male invairably licks over the vagina of the female before proceeding to business.

This is my own observation, and if my readers doubt the statement, a run up to Regent's Park, and a few hours in front of the cages will generally corroborate it.

I think to watch a man 'gamahuching' a woman is more exciting than to see her being absolutely poked.

I remember staying on one occasion at an hotel in Paddington where a very pretty chambermaid showed me my room. I had not extinguished my candle more than five minutes before I heard a woman's voice in the next room, 'Are you going to sit up reading all night?'

I couldn't for the life of me understand this, and thought the wall must be very thin, but it arose from the fact that some distance up the oaken partition there was a hole, caused through a good-sized knot in the wood falling out, and although this hole had a coat hanging in front of it, I very speedily discovered it. It did not take me very long to remove the coat, and I saw the welcome light gleam through. Then, standing on a chair, I applied my eye to the hole, and saw a man leisurely undressing, and a ladylike-looking woman, about thirty, with a splendid head of hair, lying quietly in bed awaiting him.

Now, thought I, there is going to be some fun, when a slight knock at my own door caused me to get down and open it.

'A telegram came for you two hours ago, sir, and they forgot to give it to you at the bar.'

'One moment, my girl,' said I, hastily slipping on my trousers, and then opening the door, I lighted my candle. The chambermaid was on the point of bolting.

'Don't go, my girl, said I, hastily, 'there may be an answer to this, wait until I read it, and listen' – then, lowering my voice to a significant whisper, 'if you want to see a sight that will interest and amuse you, get on that chair and peep through the hole.'

'I daren't, sir, I should lose my situation if anyone were to know I was in a gentleman's bedroom.'

'I'll swear I won't harm you,' said I, and I really didn't intend to, for although the girl was a perfect little beauty, only sixteen and a half, I had done a long railway journey that day, and felt knocked up.

The girl hesitated for a moment, but as sincerity was prominent in the tones of my voice, and she was burning with curiosity to see what was going on, she quietly stepped into the room, and I helped her on to the chair.

'Stay,' whispered I, 'the candle must be extinguished, or they may see you, if they have put their's out.'

So saying I placed the room in darkness, and then the light streaming through the hole, Mary, for such the *soubrette* called herself, immediately peeped.

For at least ten seconds she never stirred, then, getting another chair, and in the darkness nearly falling over the po, I placed it by the side of Mary's, and stood on it, with one arm round her waist.

What was going on in the next room I could only guess by the palpitation of Mary's heart. At last I said, 'May I peep, my dear?'

'Oh, sir, wait a moment, I never saw such a thing in my life, do wait a moment.'

'Certainly, my angel, if you wish it,' said I, then taking her hand, which was trembling all over, I gently allowed it to rest on my prick, over which by this time I had lost complete control.

She clutched it wildly, and passed her hand all round the balls, then pulled the skin back, and so proved to me in less than three seconds that her exclamation just now might be a little bit qualified.

'Oh, sir,' said she at length, as I passed my hands up her petticoats and found her quim quite damp with excitement, I shall be missed downstairs. I must be going, but I should like to see the end of this.'

'You shall feel the end of this,' said I, 'and that's much more to the purpose.'

So, helping her down, I lifted her neatly on my bed, and planted it with such force that she cried out with the pain.

But, whenever I have a new thing in cunts, I am always perfectly reckless of consequences, and so I gave no heed to her ejaculations, but fucked her to the bitter end.

Yet, although I enjoyed it thoroughly, I question very much whether she did, as the next morning she came to see me in a most disconsolate manner, and said she was afraid she would have to go to the hospital, as I had completely split her up, but a 'tenner' soon squared that, and I would remark here that I have introduced this incident merely to show that the sight of a woman being 'gamahuched' is far more exciting than witnessing an ordinary fuck.

Had it been the latter that Mary had glanced at when she mounted the chair, she might have felt a passing interest, but it would have been no novelty. She would probably have called me a dirty beast, fled the apartment, and had a jolly good laugh over the adventure with the cook, but being a new sensation she was glued to the aperture, got excited, and had the implement put in her hand to quiet her.

It is true that she was a bad judge of size, or she might have hung back, but a split-up cunt is no great misfortune, since once the soreness has passed away it enables a woman to enter upon any amorous encounter without the fear of meeting a foe too big for a fair fight.

AN ADVENTURE AT FOLKESTONE:
THE YOUNG WIFE AND HER STEP-DAUGHTER

Generally I have not been considered a very plucky man, but an event that occurred about this time almost caused me to believe in my own courageous qualities. I have since, however, in reviewing the past, come to the conclusion that it was sheer devilry, and the mad obliviousness of consequences which supervenes when an excited prick will not listen to the calmer instincts of reason.

I had run down to Folkestone for a brief holiday, and was staying at a large house on the Lees. I had taken the drawing-room floor, which consisted of the drawing room itself, facing the sea, a large bedroom and a smaller one, which I used as a bath and dressing room.

An old General, who had recently come from India, and who in the days gone by had been accustomed to put up with Mrs. Jordan, the landlady, applied for apartments, but as there were only two rooms to let, and he had a young wife and a grown-up daughter, it was quite impossible to accommodate him. I learnt this accidentally through the landlady's daughter, with whom I was cultivating an intimacy that I hoped would develop into something sultry eventually, and immediately offered to give up my bedroom and sleep in the dressing room.

The General was apprised of this, and was naturally enough charmed with my good nature.

A friendship was struck up over a weed, and the old nabob, in the course of a few days, settled down with his family, to whom he introduced me.

I did not know which to admire most. The wife, Mrs. Martinet, was a petite blonde, with those lovely violet eyes which change to a grey in the sunlight, just the sort of large reflective orbs historians ascribe to that darling Scottish Queen, who was fonder of a fuck than any woman born since the days of Bathsheba.

The daughter, Miss Zoe Martinet, was tall and queenlike, dark with the suns of Hindostan, but with a splendid cast of countenance, which seemed to indicate that her Aryan mother had been one of the high caste women of India, who had lapsed with the gay English General when he was plain Colonel Martinet, twenty years before, and while the Grand Cordon and Star of India were unknown to his breast.

The General was a confiding old fellow, but at sixty-eight one should not trust a wife of twenty-three with a stranger, especially when that stranger boasts a prick which, fully extended and in form, will touch the tape at eight inches.

Every day we went for long walks, General Martinet was very fond of going over to the officers' quarters at Shorncliffe, but although Eva and I were frequently left alone, her society and conversation were so intellectual and refined, that I was in a dilemma how to open the ball.

One day, however, as she sat on the beach sewing, the opportunity occurred.

'What a lovely child,' said she, as a little girl of some three summers toddled by with a handful of flowers for some waiting mamma.

'Yes, lovely, indeed,' said I, 'some day or another I hope to have the pleasure of seeing one with your face and eyes, and if it should be a boy I should take a delight in him for the sake of his mother. You are very fond of children, are you not?'

'Passionately,' she murmured.

'I thought so,' I observed, 'I have often remarked the absorbing interest you appear to take in babies with their nurses on the beach. How long have you been married?'

'Three years' – this with a sigh.

'Three years, good gracious! what time you have been wasting.'

She looked down at her embroidery, and became very interested in a wrong stitch.

'It is too bad of the General,' continued I, 'much too bad, I don't think I should have allowed you to wait all this time.'

'Mr. Clinton, what do you mean?'

'Do not feel angry, Eva, for you will forgive my calling you that dear name once in a way, what I mean is this, that you are a woman fond of children, and, therefore, formed to be a mother, and in not obeying the voice of nature, and becoming one, you are offending against the Divine law, which teaches one to procreate.'

'I have tried, Mr. Clinton' – this in a whisper, with a deep blush – 'and have failed.'

'Say, rather,' said I, now thoroughly excited, 'the General has, and it is not your fault; but, my dear girl, every man is not verging on threescore and ten, and we have not all, thank God, been desiccated on the scorching plains of Hindostan.'

'Mr. Clinton, do not tempt me?'

'Eva, it is your duty. If the old General were to have a son, your future would be secured. On the other hand what security have you that at the end of a few years he may not die, leaving all his fortune to this half-bred, lady-like daughter, Zoe.'

'That is very true,' said she, 'but still I don't think I could deceive him.'

Our conversation was prolonged for another half-hour, and when I retired to rest that night I had lovely visions, in which the landlady's daughter, Zoe, and Eva were all mixed up higgledy-piggledy, but I had an indistinct idea when I awoke that I had not been idle during the night, for I seemed to remember performing on two of them, and it was only the cold sea-water bath that brought me to my senses, and made me lose that great lump of muscle at the bottom of my belly, till I began to believe that I should have had to pick it out with a pin – periwinkle fashion.

WHERE IGNORANCE IS BLISS;
OR BLISS IN AN ARM CHAIR

The General was a great gourmand, was fond of sitting over his dinner a long time. The following day, after the conversation related in the last chapter, he invited me to share the repast with him, and after the meal regaled me with long stories of his conflict with the Sepoys and other natives of India.

'Why, sir,' said he to me, pointing to a pair of highly chased revolvers on the mantlepiece, 'Zoe's mother once fell into the hands of three vagabonds, and I shot them all, and rescued her with those very weapons, that was how we became acquainted, and I would do as much today, old as I am, to any blackguard who dared insult her daughter.'

I cordially agreed with him that such would be only a just retribution, but I inwardly added that Zoe's cunt would be worth running the risk for.

After this we re-joined the ladies in the drawing room, as I had insisted on their using that apartment. After sitting here and chaffing for about half an hour the General dozed off into a heavy sleep, and Zoe asked her step-mother to come out for a little while.

This Mrs. Martinet declined to do, on the ground that it was slightly chilly, so Zoe, who was a wilful specimen of womanhood, wished us *au revoir* and sallied forth.

I then poured out a glass of port, for Eva rather liked that wine, and unobserved by her, dropped out of my waistcoat phial enough Pinero Balsam to have stimulated an anchorite.

'Do have half a glass, I intreat you, it will put life in you, I have remarked that you seemed languid to-day.'

'Well, I will just take a wee drop,' said Eva, and she half emptied the glass as she spoke.

'Your husband sleeps soundly, Eva.'

'Hs'sh; don't call me that here. Yes, he always sleeps so after dinner for a good half-hour.'

I was sitting in the arm chair during this colloquy; Eva was standing by the window, and I could just reach her skirt by leaning forward. I did so, and with both hands gently, but with adroit force, pulled her backwards, until she sat upon my lap.

'For God's sake,' whispered she, in an agony of dread, 'let me go; if he were to wake he would kill us both.'

'But he won't wake. You told me yourself he would be sure to sleep for half an hour, and there is ample time for what we want to do in that space. Come into my bedroom for five minutes my darling.'

'Mr. Clinton, I dare not; think of the exposure.'

'I can think of nothing but this, my sweet, Eva,' and suiting the action to the word, I clapped my hand upon her lovely rosebud of a snatchbox before she had the slightest idea that I was anywhere near it.

She proved a game girl; she didn't cry out, for that would have meant death and damnation, but she appealed to my good sense.

'Not now,' she said, imploringly, 'be counselled by me; not now, some other time.'

'My darling,' said I, 'stand up for one moment.' She did so, and I instantly lifted all her clothes, having in the meantime brought out my stiff straight cock, which I was mortally afraid would discharge its contents before it was properly positioned.

'Now sit down, dear.'

She obeyed me, and as she did so, I opened with the thumb and finger of my left hand the delicate sprouting lips of her seraphic orifice, the backward pressure of her arse did the rest, and I went in with a rush that made my very marrow twitter with pleasure.

'Oh, God,' burst from Eva's lips, 'this is heavenly.'

The old man turned uneasily on the couch; the back of the arm chair was turned to him, so that all he could see was the top of Eva's head.

'Is that you, Eva,' said the General.

'Yes, dear,' replied his wife.

'What are you doing, my love?'

'Still embroidering your new smoking cap, dear.'

'Where's Clinton?'

'He's gone out for a smoke,' said the trembling girl.

'All right, call me in half an hour,' and in less than three minutes the dear old soldier was once more in the land of Nod, but during that three minutes we seemed to have lived an age. I would have gladly got out of her and sneaked away, for I could not help thinking of the revolvers, but she had never tasted the exquisite bliss a young man's prick can convey, and was, to use a 'servantgalism', rampageous for it. She had never had a fuck before in such a position, but women are quick to learn a lesson when sperm is to be the prize, and in less than a minute she had wriggled out of me more genital juice than had ever rushed up her seminal ducts before. When she found she could draw no more, she quietly rose and walked to the window, leaving me to button up, and vanish on tiptoe out of the drawing room, and I did not meet her any more that night.

THE MYSTERIOUS NOTE AND FRENCH LETTER SEQUEL

The reader knows my character by this time sufficiently well to be fully aware that I did not permit a single opportunity to escape of performing on Eva, till I think that young lady grew to look for it as regularly as a cat watches for the advent of the horse-flesh purveyor.

One morning, however, I did not keep my appointment with her as usual, for we generally went out about mid-day, as I had found a quiet cowshed in a field on the Dover-road, behind which the grass grew thick and long, and there we were free from interruption.

There, too, if there be any truth in the general belief that semen is a great fructifier of the soil, the grass should grow thicker than ever by this time, for I am sure that Eva and I bathed it with the best essence we possessed many a time and oft.

This particular morning, however, I received a note in a handwriting I did not know, the letter ran thus:

Sir,
Your *liaison* with Mrs. M — is known, and it depends upon you whether it will be divulged to her husband. Meet me near the spot you *generally* meet her, at two p.m to-day.
                    Yours,
          'ONE WHO HAS SEEN ALL.'

It was a woman's hand, and I was puzzled. I dropped a few lines to Eva, saying I could not keep my appointment with her, and proceeded to the rendezvous to find my fair anonyma.

I arrived at the back of the cowshed and turned the corner, when to my intense surprise Zoe stood there, in her hands a bunch of fresh wild flowers, and as she was expecting me, whereas I never dreamed that she had sent the note she had me at a decided disadvantage.

'Well, sir,' said she, 'you received my communication?'

'I did,' replied I, for I felt that I must put a bold face upon it, 'and I'm sorry to think "you have seen all", for I was hoping to some day afford you the novelty of examining it.'

'Mr. Clinton, kow could you have been so wicked, my poor old father is not far from the grave, you might have waited until Eva had been left a widow.'

If you look at me another moment with those flashing eyes I shall do you over in the same way, my pet, thought I.

'Let us sit down, and reason, Miss Martinet; you have chosen a strange place for a serious conversation, but it will be infinitely better for you to sit down and then the tall grass will conceal you from view, whereas standing up every country yokel who passes by sees us both, puts his own construction on it, and your reputation is irretrievably ruined.'

'You are perfectly right,' said Zoe, 'I will sit down, especially as I note some uniforms on the road yonder, and they might be officer friends of my father's.'

Zoe sat down, and put up her parasol, but the two gentlemen she had remarked came round the bend of the road at the same time. They were two lieutenants of the – th, at Dover, and I had been to a ball where I had knocked up against them some little time before.

'Hallo! Clinton, what the devil are you – Oh, I say – a petticoat. Well, I'm damned – *alfresco*, eh? under the azure dome of heaven. Well, good luck, my boy; but give me a pair of nice clean sheets and native nakedness,' and down the road went the pair, humming a godless tune they had picked up in the camp before Sebastopol a few years before.

I turned to Zoe.

'What a fortunate thing you were out of sight, my dear,' said I, sitting down beside her.

'Yes, it was, indeed,' said she, trying with her short skirt to conceal a shapely ankle, which, in a pair of elegant scarlet stockings, looked simply delicious.

I know it was very rude and ungentlemanly of me, but I could not help remarking aloud what an exquisite *tournure* the stocking gave to her leg, and enquired whether she thought the colour had anything to do with it.

'Mr. Clinton, I think we had better go,' was all the answer she gave me.

'But, my dear Zoe, I thought you had brought me here to read me a prim lecture on morality?'

'Alas!' said she, sighing, 'I could not tell of poor dear mamma, she is so artless, and – '

'And I am so artful, you would say; but, my dear young lady, I admit having made a great mistake in intriguing with the General's wife, I can see it now.'

'And I hope,' said she, making a pretty bow, 'that you are contrite?'

'Yes,' I said, 'I am, but shall I explain to you the error I committed?'

'If it will not take too long in the telling.'

'Well, my mistake was in going for the wife, and not the daughter.'

'Mr. Clinton, how can you say such a thing?'

'Zoe, from the moment I first saw your matchless face your eyes burnt into my bosom's core like fire, and now, by heaven, that we are here alone, with none but bright Phoebus as our witness, I must – ' here commenced a struggle in the grass, but it was of short duration.

She threatened to scream, but I hurriedly pointed out that if she accused me of rape I could bring the two young officers as witnesses that I had a lady with me who was sitting on the grass apparently only waiting for it, and besides – but all my entreaties were of no avail, until at length growing desperate, and with a prick on me like a bull's pizzle, I forced her legs apart, and would have ravished her by sheer strength, when she whispered in my ear, 'For God's sake use a French letter, I'm so afraid of falling in the family way.'

Now I never stir from home without a letter, but I hate using them when I know the cunt is fresh, and untainted with a *soupcon* of an afterthought, so that although the request coming from one I had supposed a virgin rather astounded me. I was fully equal to the occasion.

Taking one from my waistcoat pocket, and beginning to fit it on, I said, 'Then you've had the root before, Zoe.'

'Yes,' said she, 'once, with a young captain in Pa's regiment at Allahabad, but this was when I was seventeen. He always used them for fear of the consequences.'

By this time I had fitted it, and Zoe showed her perfect readiness to wait patiently for the operation.

'Let me have one peep, darling,' said I.

She laughingly lay back flat on her back, and showed me a large forest of hair, as glossy as a raven's back and as black, while beneath it I saw as neat a little quimbo as one could wish for.

Reader, do you blame me, if, after seeing such a sight I surreptitiously pulled off the letter and let my John Thomas approach his lair *au naturel*. I should have been more than mortal to have refrained, flesh is one hundred per cent better than a nasty gutta percha cover, and although Zoe was unaware of what I had done, she showed herself fully appreciative of my premier thrust, though her action took me completely by surprise.

Whether it was the springiness of the soft green grass on which we lay, I know not, but with all my experience I cannot recall to mind any wench, even one, having her first grind, who showed such arse power as Zoe.

The Hindoo and English cross must be a good fucking breed I thought, but scarcely had the fleeting idea passed through my brain than one more vigorous push brought on the crisis of delight.

Zoe, at this point, was working her bottom with what the Yankees would call an all-hell-fire motion, when she suddenly seemed transported with delight, and kissing my neck, bit me in a frenzy till she actually brought the blood.

Much as I had enjoyed myself, this was a style of emotion I was not enamoured of, and I screamed out with the pain.

I got up, leaving Zoe still lying exhausted on the ground, when to my horror I heard a step behind me, and before I could button up found myself confronted by Eva.

I do not know why it should have been so, but although the meteorological record for that year does not return the weather in May as being particularly warm, I found it at least 212 Fahrenheit on that eventful day, in spite of the sea breeze, so not liking tropical heat, I returned to town, and I have met Zoe in society since, but poor Eva, after tasting forbidden fruit, and finding it so much sweeter than the withered-up stuff obtainable from the husband's orchard, went wrong again and again, and was finally bowled in the very act, but, luckily for the gay Lothario, the General had left those chased revolvers at home.

A DISAGREEABLE MISTAKE

Not always have I had the happiness of being fortunate in my amours. It is true that I have managed to escape the dread fate of those poor unfortunate devils whose tools are living witnesses to the powers of caustic and the lethal weapons of the surgery, but I have on occasions been singularly unfortunate, and as the warning voice of my publisher tells me I have little more time or space at my disposal, I will devote the present chapter of this work to detailing a most unpleasant incident, which all people are more or less liable to who go in for promiscuous intercourse to any large extent.

My only sister, Sophy, came up to London with her husband shortly after my return from Folkestone, and although he was a perfect brute of a fellow, and a man I disliked very much, I made myself as agreeable as I could, and took a furnished house for them during their stay, near the Regent's Park.

Frank Vaughan, a young architect, and a rising man, was one I introduced them to, as my sister had brought a friend, Miss Polly White, with her, who lived near our old home in the country, and being anxious to see London, her parents had placed her under my sister's guardian wing to do the 'lions' of the metropolis.

Polly was an only daughter, so knowing the old people had a good nest egg, I thought it would be a capital opportunity to throw Frank in her way.

I told him precisely how matters stood, and advised him to make a match of it.

'The old people are rich,' said I, 'but if they object to you on the score of money, fuck her, my boy, and that will bring them to reason.'

'Is she perfectly pure now,' said Frank, 'for to tell you the truth I haven't come across a genuine maid since I landed a stripling of thirteen, nearly ten years ago. Are you sure *you* haven't.'

'I'll swear it, if you like,' returned I, laughing at the soft impeachment, 'but take my advice, Frank, and win her. She'll be worth at least £40,000 when the old folks snuff it.'

'I'm on the job,' said Frank; and it was easy to see from the immaculate shirt front, the brilliant conversation, and the great attention he paid her, that he meant business.

One night, however, I was puzzled, for I thought Frank was far more assiduous in his manner to my sister than he should have been, considering that the 'nugget', for so we had christened Polly, was present.

I could not understand it at all, and determined to watch the development of the situation.

There was, I must tell you an underplot to all this, for several times I had noted that Polly's regard for me was a trifle too warm, and once or twice in the theatre, and in the brougham, coming home particularly, I had felt the soft pressure of her knees, and returned it with interest – but, to my story.

Frank proposed going to Madame Tussaud's, and as Polly had never been, and my sister knew every model in the show by heart, Frank suggested that he should take the 'nugget', 'unless you would like to go with us,' said he to me.

'Not I, indeed,' was my reply, 'besides, sissey here will be alone, as her beautiful husband has been out all day, and will, I suppose, turn up beastly drunk about midnight. No, you go together, and enjoy your little selves.' So off they went.

When Polly passed me in the hall, she gave me a peculiar look, which I utterly failed to comprehend, and asked me to fasten her glove. As I did so she passed a slip of paper into my hand, and when she had gone I read on it these words: Be in the study about nine o'clock.

What can the little minx mean, was my first thought. She surely wouldn't go about an intrigue in this barefaced fashion; she has been brought up in a demure way, yet what on earth can she mean. At any rate I will do her bidding.

Making an excuse to my sister about eight o'clock, for I was as curious as possible to know what it could all portend, and saying I was going out for a couple of hours, I slammed the hall door behind me, and then quietly crept upstairs to the study.

I found it in perfect darkness, but knowing where the couch was situated, at the far end of the room, I made for it, and I must confess the solitude, the darkness, and a good dinner, all combined, made me forget curiosity, Polly, the warning note, and everything else, and in less than five minutes I was fast asleep.

I was awakened by a scented hand I knew was a woman's touching my face, and a low voice whispering in my ear, 'You are here then; I never heard you come in.'

Damn it, thought I, it's an intrigue after all; but she's too tall for Polly. Oh, I see it all, she's our prim landlady (who retained one room in the house, and was, I knew, desperate nuts upon my brother-in-law). Polly found out about it, and set me on the track, so without saying a word I laid her unresistingly on the couch, and in a few seconds was busy.

I could not help thinking while wiring in that she displayed much vigour for one of her years, since I judged the lady to be at least forty-five, but her ardour only made me the more fervent, and at the end of a long series of skirmishing the real hot short work began.

It would be impossible to express my horror at this moment

when my hand came in contact with a cross she was wearing round her neck, and I found that it was my own sister I was rogering.

I had, unluckily got to that point where no man or woman could cease firing, but the worst part of the damned unfortunate affair was that I burst out with an ejaculation of dismay, and she, too, recognized my voice. The situation was terrible.

'Good God!' said I, 'Sophy, how on earth has this come about?'

Then, sobbingly, she told me that her husband had abstained from her more than two years because he had contracted a chronic gonorrhoeic disorder, and that Vaughan had won her over to make this *rendezvous,* and had intended letting Polly be shown through Tussaud's by a friend he had arranged to meet there.

'But,' added she, 'how was it I found you here?'

This I dare not tell her, as it was now evident that Polly was aware of the assignation, and to let my sister know – that would have been death.

Poor girl, she was sufficiently punished for her frailty, and Polly, who had caught a few words of the appointment, was sufficiently revenged.

Polly never forgave my friend Frank for what she always considered his base desertion.

As for Sophy, I got her a divorce from her husband shortly afterwards. I give her an allowance myself, and I believe in my heart, that as women go, she is a very good one. I know that she has never ceased to pray for what she calls her great sin, but which I term my damned misfortune.

Polly married a brewer down in Devonshire, and as I have had several opportunities of testing her quality, I can assure my readers that the brewer has no cause to complain of his draw in the matrimonial lottery.

REFLECTIONS ON AULD LANG SYNE, HAPPY MEETINGS, AND CONCLUSION

Fifteen years have now elapsed since I scribbled the former part of my experiences. Times are sadly altered with my best friend now, and I am rapidly approaching the time when all may prove 'Vanity and vexation of spirit', for although I still carry a most formidable outward and visible sign, the inward and spiritual grace so necessary to please the ladies is now almost dormant in my fucked-out nature.

Just now I have been reading a fine little book on re-juvenescence, called 'Abishag', by David II., which I think gives an excellent remedy for such cases as mine. George the Fourth must have thoroughly understood the theory advocated by the writer, for although in earlier life his motto was 'fat, fair, and forty', he afterwards was found frequently engaged in seducing by any means, fair or foul, the youngest and most innocent girls he could find.

The more I study the character of the first gentleman in Europe, as he was called, the more thorough a voluptarian he seems to have been; his youthful vigour at first delighting in the charms of thoroughly developed and sensual women, and gradually in his latter years turning to the worship of Molech, sacrificing to his lustful God the unfledged virginities his numerous myrmidons placed in his way.

Years ago I remember how I looked with something like contempt upon the art and science of flagellation as dilated upon by Monsignor Peter, of the Oratory, now I am quite converted to his theory.

A most fortunate rencontre has been the means of this conversation; lately sauntering down Regent-street, thinking of the time when I used to do three or four pretty demi-mondés in the day, 'Ah, Gerty, do you know him, too?' in an ever to be remembered voice, caused me to suddenly turn and confront the speaker, who proved to be none other than Mrs. Leveson, looking almost as lovely as ever, and incomprehensibly in the company of my old flame Gerty, of the Temple.

This was a delightful renewal of old acquaintanceships, and a very few explanations let me thoroughly into the situation.

Leveson had been dead several years, leaving his wife sole guardian of their son (my son, she assured me, in a loving whisper, 'he is now eighteen – never can I forget the night you made him for me').

Gerty had been persuaded by Mrs. Leveson to give up her dressmaking business, and live with her as a kind of companion housekeeper, the former's Sapphic tastes having attached her to the voluptuous Mrs. L, who discovered it from Gerty's remarks on the women of the day in Paris, who prefer their own sex as lovers, and care very little for the attentions of men.

'My son is abroad with his tutor; will you, Mr. Clinton, come home to dinner, and spend the evening at our quiet little town house. James is such a rake – just like his father – I don't mean Mr. Leveson, poor dear, he was rather too good, and never made a baby for me or anyone else. Gerty knows all about it, but your name was never mentioned, and now I suppose you are the Temple student who seduced her with finery, and took advantage of her young inexperience, although she never mentioned you?'

'Really this is most charming, but, my dear ladies, I can only accept your hospitality if you promise we shall be a happy family – free from jealousy.'

'Make yourself easy, dear Mr. Clinton, as to that, everything is common between us in thought, word, and deed, in fact, with our dearest friend, Lady Twisser, we are three loving communists, each one's secrets as sacred as if our own.'

'Lady Fanny Twisser, who was separated from her husband because he couldn't believe his dildoe was the father of her boy!' I exclaimed.

'Good God, Mr. Clinton, there you are again; you must be a universal father, now I'm sure it's you did that service for dear Fanny, and we'll wire to her at once to come and join our dinner party.'

Highly elated they conducted me to their carriage, which was waiting outside Lewis and Allenby's, and soon reached Mrs. Leveson's house, in Cromwell-road, South Kensington.

Gerty showed me to a room to prepare for dinner, and it was arranged we should have a real love séance after the servants had gone to bed.

At dinner I saw Lady Fanny, who met me with a most fervent embrace, assuring me, with tears in her eyes, that I was the source of the only happiness she had ever had in her life (her son, now at college at Oxford).

All dinner time, and the long while we sat over dessert talking over old times. I felt as proud as a barn-door cock, with three favourite hens, all glowing with love and anxious for his attentions, the ardent glances of lovely Mrs. Leveson told too plainly the force of her luscious recollections, whilst Lady Fanny, who sat by my side every now and then, caressed my prick under the table, as he slightly throbbed in response to her touches.

At length coffee was brought in, and the servants told to go to bed.

'At last!' sighed our magnificent hostess, springing up and throwing her arms round my neck, 'I have a chance to kiss the father of my boy; what terrible restraint I have had to put on myself before the servants. Dear James, you belong to us all, we all want the consolation of that grand pracititioner of yours; have which you please first, there's no jealousy!'

'But, darling loves, how can I do you all? I'm not the man I was some years ago!'

'Trust to Gerty's science for that, she let us into the 'Pinero Balsam' secret, and we have a little of it in the house for occasions when it might be wanted. It's very curious how you ruined the morals of both Fanny and myself, two such paragons of virtue as we were; we could never forget the lessons of love you taught us, and, now we are both widows, with dear Gerty here, we do enjoy ourselves on the quiet. Fanny's boy has me, and thinks it is an awfully delicious and secret liasion; my James returns the kindness to my love's mother; whilst dear abandoned Gerty is only satisified sometimes by having both with her at once, yet neither of them ever divulges their amour with Fanny and myself. And now, how is the dear jewel, you surely don't require the balsam to start with,' she said, taking out my staff of life, and kissing it rapturously.

Lady Fanny did the same, and was followed by Gerty, whose ravishing manner of gamahuching me recalled so vividly my first seduction of her in the Temple.

She would have racked me off, but I restrained myself, and requested them to peel to the buff, setting them the example, my cock never for a moment losing his fine erection.

Having placed an eider down quilt and some pillows on the hearth rug, they ranged themselves in front of me in all their naked glories, like the goddesses before Paris disputing for the apple.

'Catch which you can,' they exclaimed, laughing, and began capering around me.

I dashed towards Mrs. Leveson, but tumbled over one of the pillows, getting my bottom most unmercifully slapped before I could recover myself. My blood tingled from head to foot, I was mad to be into one of those luscious loving women, and in a moment or two caught and pulled down Fanny on the top of me, the other two at once settled her, à la St. George, and held my prick till she was fairly impaled on it. They then stretched themselves at full length on either side, kissing me ardently, whilst their busy fingers played with prick and balls, as the darling Fanny got quickly into her stride, and rode me with the same fire and dash, which characterized her first performance on her brother's bed in the Temple.

My hands were well employed frigging the creamy cunts of Mrs. Leveson and Gerty – what a fuck, how my prick swelled in his agony of delight, as I shot the hot boiling sperm right up to Fanny's heart, and she deluged me in return with the essence of her life as she fell forward with a scream of delight. Her tightly nipping cunt held me enraptured by its loving contractions, but at the suggestion of Gerty, she gently rolled herself aside, and allowed me to mount the darling Leveson before I lost my stiffness.

What a deep-drawn sigh of delight, my fresh fuckstress gave, as she heaved up her buttocks and felt my charger rush up to the very extremity of her burning sheath.

'Let me have the very uttermost bit of it! Keep him up to his work, Gerty, darling,' she exclaimed, excitedly, then glueing her lips to mine she seemed as if she would suck my very life away.

A smart, tingling, swish – swish on my rump now aroused me to the fact that both Fanny and Gerty had taken in hand the flagellation, and gradually putting more force in their cuts, raised such a storm of lustful heat, that I fucked dear Mrs. Leveson, till after some minutes I spent in such an ecstatic agony of bliss, that both of us lost our consciousness for a time, and when we recovered ourselves, declared that no such exquisite sensations had ever before so completely overwhelmed either of us.

Such was the power of the rod to invigorate me, that Gerty soon had her cunt as well-stuffed as the others had been by my grand prick, as it seemed to be bigger and stiffer than ever.

This loving séance was kept up to the small hours of the morning before I could think of tearing myself from their seductive delights; but I now often join this community of love in the Cromwell-road, and no pen can by any possibility adequately describe the delights we manage to enjoy under the influence of the birch.

THE
FARMER'S DAUGHTER

My father was a gentleman farmer on a large scale, and took in gentlemen to teach farming. My mother was always very busy about the house and dairy, and I was but a girl. My cousin Johnny had been living with us for many years, and was my dearest friend, he was about a year older than I. We used to play about in the barns, woods and fields, with no one to look after us, and great was my grief when Johnny was sent to school and a governess kept for me.

Johnny returned for his summer holidays, and we had a high old time of it, he had grown as I thought, quite a man, and was so clever, but all the time was not a bit above playing and wandering over the farm with me, and my governess did not mind where I went as long as we were together.

One wet Sunday we took ourselves to the barn and lay on the straw, telling each other stories, and often kissing each other as of old, but soon Johnny began pulling up my frock, which rather frightened me, but he made me feel so funny with his fingers that I began to like it, and very soon he taught me to play with him, and once begun we rarely missed a day without doing it.

I did miss him so when he went back to school, but in a year or two it was arranged that he was not to live any more at our house, and I lost sight of him, but my blood was now fired, and longed for something I did not know what, and used to lay awake at night wishing for Johnny's hand.

Now Johnny's room used to be next to me, and there was an old ventilator between them, each side of which would take out, and we used to stand on a chair and talk through this, and often by taking my side out have I watched Johnny dressing when he did not know it.

Now about this time my father began to take in a farm pupil, his first being a Mr. Howard, and when I found he was to have Johnny's room when he arrived, I was most impatient for his arrival. At last he arrived. He was not bad looking, rather delicate, and very dark hair and skin.

I got up very quietly and early the next morning, and watched him through all his tubbing and dressing. How different he was to Johnny, I saw a man's weapon for the first time, true it was lying limp as he took his bath, but what a length, and covered with hair, whereas Johnny had none, I was mad with excitement and felt quite sick.

This went on for some mornings, but one warm morning he had been reading in bed as he usually did before getting up, when he suddenly threw the clothes off and pulled his night shirt up, and there behold was the weapon at its full stretch. He looked down on it from his high pillows, and pulling the weapon forward with his fingers let it spring back against his belly, which it did with a smack, and he did this several times with evident pride and pleasure; then he pulled the skin off the top, displaying a charming red top, and this he did slowly for a time, then I noticed a glassy look in his eyes. He took the whole of his weapon in his right hand, and with his left played with his large appendages, and this rubbing and playing evidently excited him, for he wriggled his legs about and sometimes rolled half on his side. At last he began to rub very quickly, his legs stretched out to the full length, and with a deep sigh, quite a quantity of white liquid shot all over the bed, and then he lay quiet for some time till it was time to dress.

I was fired to such a pitch that all the time I was rubbing my thighs together, and when all was over lay down on my bed quite faint, and at breakfast my mother noticed how poorly I looked. My governess had now been sent away, and I was to have another when one could be got.

After a time I got more accustomed to these manly sights, and Charles, as we called him, was liked by all of us, but he only treated me as a little girl.

One day my father and mother had started early after breakfast to the market, and I had gone up to my room for something,
and Bessy I heard was making Mr. H's bed, when I heard Mr. H
go up to his room, and soon after Bessy saying in a severe tone,
'Leave off, Mr. Howard, I will tell master. Leave off do. Get along
with you. Oh! don't, I will tell the Master, Mr. Howard, what are
you doing?'

I jumped up to the ventilator, and saw the fat Bessy being
dragged by the waist to the bed, and though she struggled it did
not seem she was very keen to get away. Still she continued, 'Oh!
do leave off. I will tell on you, Oh! you wretch. Oh! do leave
off.' By that time Mr. H's hand was up her clothes, and she on
her back on the bed. 'Oh! don't, Oh! get up. Oh! you are crushing me. Oh! don't, I really will tell. Oh! don't, Oh! don't, Oh!' He
had produced his weapon and was lying between her fat thighs,
and at the last Oh, her legs clung round Mr. H's, but still she went
on, 'Oh! don't, please, please don't Mr. H. Oh! Mr. Charles don't,
don't, Oh! oh! don't Mr. Charles. Oh! dear, Mr. Charles don't. Oh!
oh! oh! Charles, Oh! oh! oh! Charles darling, Oh . . . '

All this time she was wriggling her body in the most fetching
manner, her fat strong arms pressing dear Charles closer to her.
Her eyes half shut, and her face very red, and at the last few Oh's
her legs shot out their full length, at times her thighs opened
wider, and 'Charles darling' worked quicker and harder, till at last
a shudder went through both.

Bessy recovered herself first, saying, 'Now give over and go
downstairs at once, you have behaved shameful.'

I could not sleep for nights after this, and used to go over every
detail, but what puzzled me most was why Bessy should have so
much hair about her pussy and I none, and also how she could
bear such a weapon in her, for I was sure I couldn't.

I was lucky enough to witness two more combats like this, but
in each case Bessy gave up without a struggle, and even seemed
to assist in pulling up her own clothes, and directing the weapon.

But now I found, for I watched them carefully, that when it
was Bessy's Sunday out, she slipped into the old barn, and was
quickly followed by Charles, and there they spent their after-
noons.

So knowing there was a loft over the old stable where I kept
my rabbits, and which was only separated from the barn by a
wooden boarding, I soon had arranged a capital spy-hole, and

found that these lovers, having the whole afternoon before them, used to commence with a deal of light-fingered play, a game Bessy used to make no secret of enjoying, and her contortions and sighs were enough to awaken the owls when Charlie's fingers were at work, and when he got on her he used to go on until I thought he would never stop.

Sometimes she would entreat him to stop, but before then her fat legs had several times signalled the critical moment, and by their wild beating of the air, and by the note of her Oh's, I could count each throb of her warm little corner, and knew when the last mighty throb came, that brought down the shower, and made dear Charles's weapon bound again, and the head swell inside her, 'as big as a bullock's heart,' as she once graphically described it in my hearing.

All this did me no good. I longed for Charles to do the same to me, and pined for Johnny to share in the little game, but I dare not suggest anything, and Charles and Bessy always treated me as a child, though I was now growing up fast, and few could have known more or seen more for my age.

At last Mr. Charles left us for good, and poor Bessy was for a long time inconsolable, but quite by chance I heard a noise in the barn, sneaked up to my peep hole, and spied Miss Bessy preparing for action with Jack, the carter.

But what a different proceeding! Mr. Jack first ogled at Bessy, then produced his machine, a fearfully broad-backed, bullet-headed engine, and rather short, he rubbed it up a little, then spit on the top, I suppose to make it work easier.

Bessy all the time seated on the straw looking on, and then contented with his arrangements, Jack rolled on her, she lifting her clothes and opening wide her thighs, giving me a good view of her pouting parts.

Jack was not long getting into her, but he evidently hurt her, and was very rough, for she really cried out in pain at first, and did not seem to relish her first encounter, and after it was over, Jack sat beside her, put her hand on his weapon, and made her prepare it for the next, which she soon succeeded in doing; but the next encounter was a prolonged one, and I could see she thoroughly enjoyed it, poor Jack making fearful noises between his final short thrusts, and groaning out, 'Eh! lass, eh! lass,' and I never saw a more foolish countenance than his when all was over.

These clumsy performances often went on, but at last the old story, a child appeared, and Jack married her, and I suppose now performs in bed, for I can never find them in the barn.

I had now no one in the next room, and nobody to excite me, but I was very restless and slept very badly, and when I did get to sleep it was only to have the most vivid dreams of some unrecognizable man doing to me at last what I longed for, and just as the happy moment arrived I would awake, only to find that I had come, alas without a partner.

At last I began to look so ill that I was sent to my aunt's house near the sea, for a change, and there I remained for nearly six months, and regained my health.

During my absence from home my mother had become a great invalid, and could rarely leave her bed, and a nurse had to be kept for her.

Susan, the nurse, who was about five and twenty, and a very pretty, jolly looking girl, was more a lady help than a sick nurse, and used to assist me in the farm and house work, and very great friends did we become, but I never confided to her the secrets of my bedroom ventilator, or the old barn, and glad I was that I had not, for a Mr. Robson turned up one day to learn farming, a strong healthy looking man, standing about six foot in his socks, and was put into the next room to mine.

He was about thirty, and I needn't say I watched his movements in his bedroom most carefully, and with interest, and was rather surprised and disappointed never to see him play with himself like Mr. Charles, yet when he jumped out of bed and into his cold bath his staff was always stiff and erect, or on the lob, in a sort of 'half cock', but the cold water soon reduced it to its uninteresting condition.

Henry, for that was Mr. Robson's Christian name, never got down to breakfast till nine, and as Susan did the morning work I used to get down about the same time, my father always leaving the house punctually at five during these summer months.

Well, matters went on most virtuously for a month or two, except perhaps that I once or twice caught Susan and Henry having what looked like a harmless flirtation, until one morning just after my father had gone out and slammed the door after him, I heard a whispering in the next room, and looking through the ventilator, there was my Susan in a dressing gown, seated on Henry's bed, and he pulling her head towards him and kissing her wildly.

He then got up, pulled off her dressing gown, and there she was in a pretty night-dress. He kissed her on her mouth till I thought he meant eating her, then he undid her night-dress at the collar, and pulling it down left her shoulders and breasts bare, and even I was obliged to admit their beauty. He covered them with kisses, and when he seized her nipple between his lips, Susan's eyes sparkled, and I could see she meant going the 'whole hog'.

He then lay her on her back as she was sitting on the side of the bed, putting a pillow under her head, and kneeling on the floor with one of her white thighs on each of his shoulders, he, to my surprise, began kissing her pussy.

Susan at first struggled faintly against this operation, and tried to keep her thighs closed, but he began tickling her thighs with his tongue just above her knee, and at last forcing his way to the flat of her thigh, her muscles seemed to lose their power, and he slowly kissed his way to the soft point.

Her little 'don'ts' got fainter, her eyes shut, and her hands, which had been feebly pushing Henry's head from her, now seemed to be involuntarily pressing it to her body.

What a sigh she gave to be sure when at last H had reached the point, her eyes half opened, a flush came over her pretty face, and her thighs slowly opened and closed.

Then how she heaved her body up and down, how she struggled, and her breathing came short and heavily, and the final struggle and sighs surpassed anything I had ever yet seen.

After it she seemed to lay back in a faint, and H putting her feet on a chair, left her a few moments, and then returning he slipped off his night-dress, exposing his grand machine in all its pride, and then standing between her thighs he placed one of her feet on each of his shoulders, and while she lay on her back on the bed, he standing on the floor, he began his entry, not a difficult one after the late encounter, which had well prepared Miss Susan for the next.

He drove it in slowly but surely, and I could see that at last it was buried to the roots, and their hairs were touching.

How he did poke her to be sure, she came again very soon, I could tell by her struggles and sighs, and he stopped for a time, I suppose to prolong his pleasure, then he began again, and after a time the encounter got warm.

His strokes became shorter, their breathing deeper, she tried to get her legs free in her struggles, and at last they came, he falling forward on her, and kissing her almost lifeless little face. Then they put on their gowns, and off tripped Susan, appearing at breakfast with a pretty flush, and all the better for her exercise, which is more than I did.

Susan now became a constant morning visitor, and many were the gambols and positions they went through.

They were very fond of the old family way, which is described as – 'She on her back layeth. He on her belly falleth,' – but to a spectator this was not so answering as a Saint George, and how well I recollect did she ride Master Henry one morning.

They had been larking about the bed, when just as he had his head towards me, and lay on his back, she jumped on him, and he, nothing loth, lay still. Then slipping off her night-dress and pulling his up to his neck, she got hold of his machine with her hand, drew the lips slowly back, and directed the red head to her warm spot. It was soon buried, and then slowly sitting down as it were, it disappeared until nothing but the hilt was to be seen.

She was now sitting on him in a kneeling position, one knee on each side, and leaning forward a little, supported herself with her outstretched arms, and between her bonny breasts I had full view of what was taking place, as her face being towards me, I could watch her change of feature.

Having driven it well home, she let it remain quiet for a few moments, then slowly raising herself she exposed his majesty once more, and he looked as if he had swollen to twice the size, then moving herself up and down, as Henry lay quiet with his legs at full stretch, she was mistress of the position, and now it was up to the hilt, and then she was playing with the head just between the lips of that soft spot, but she could not control herself, and her rubs became most energetic, and at last she fell on Henry's breast with a sigh, and there lay.

At length he got from under her, and I was surprised to see that he had not yet come, and having laid her on her back, he paid Miss Susan off in her own coin for the audacity of getting on him, and she was late coming downstairs that morning.

I only once caught them in the barn, and that was one Sunday when we three had been out, and it came on to rain, we took shelter there, and I left them saying I would look after my rabbits till tea-time, when I would come back to them.

I at once went to my spy-hole, and saw Henry closing the door, and then after a short whispering to each other, he made her lean forward on some trusses of hay, and he lifted her clothes up from behind, and entered her that way, at the same time putting his hands round her soft belly, and in that way, while his machine was driven home, he could tickle her with his fingers, the result being apparently most satisfactory.

Poor Susan moved her legs and sighed deeper and oftener than I had ever known before, and her face, when she turned it round to implore Henry to finish which she frequently did, was very flushed. It seemed as if this double attack on her tender part had the effect of giving her acute pleasure the whole time, and that she was spending at very short intervals. At last she fell forward, apparently from sheer exhaustion, and Henry had then enough to do to hold her on her legs, while her body lay heavily on the truss. Then working with a will he too came, and fell forward on her, and both appeared to have fainted.

A quarter of an hour afterwards, I went to them, Susan was then sitting on a truss, looking very weary, though her eyes sparkled, and she could hardly walk to the house.

When she arrived she went to her room, saying she did not feel well, so I took her her tea, and I thought she looked prettier than ever as she lay back in her chair, but she always did look prettier after a bout I noticed, and have noticed that all women do.

Six months later Susan left us, owing to a death in her family, and a few months after, I don't know how it came about, Henry slipped into my room one night and into my bed.

I often think I should not have allowed him to get his own way so easily, but at the time I was thirsting for it, and could not help myself.

We soon had gone through every posture I had seen, and how he laughed when I confessed how I watched Susan and him. He left before I met my husband, and now I shall not tell you any more, being of opinion that what passes in the privacy of the conjugal chamber should not be revealed to the world, whereas the youthful escapades here narrated fall under quite another category, and serve to amuse an idle half-hour.

Extract from

FLOSSIE:
A VENUS OF FIFTEEN*

'MY LOVE, SHE'S BUT A LASSIE YET'

TOWARDS THE END of a bright sunny afternoon in June, I was
walking in one of the quieter streets off Piccadilly, when my eye
was caught by two figures coming in my direction. One was that
of a tall, finely made woman about 27, who would, under other
circumstances, have received something more than an approving
glance. But it was her companion that riveted my gaze of almost
breathless admiration. This was a young girl of fifteen, of such
astounding beauty of face and figure as I had never seen or
dreamt of. Masses of bright, wavy, brown hair fell to her waist.
Deep violet eyes looked out from under long curling lashes, and
seemed to laugh in unison with the humorous curves of the full
red lips. These and a thousand other charms I was to know by
heart later on, but what struck me most at this first view, was
the extraordinary size and beauty of the girl's bust, shown to all
possible advantage by her dress which, in the true artistic French
style, crept in between her breasts, outlining their full and perfect
form with loving fidelity. Tall and lithe, she moved like a young
goddess, her short skirt showing the action of a pair of exquisitely

---

*The full title of this publication was, *Flossie: A Venus of Fifteen by One Who
Knew this Charming Goddess and Worshipped at Her Shrine*. When first
published this book had a print run of 500 copies, all of which would have been
for private circulation.

moulded legs, to which the tan-coloured openwork silk stockings were plainly designed to invite attention. Unable to take my eyes from this enchanting vision I was approaching the pair, when to my astonishment the elder lady suddenly spoke my name.

'You do not remember me, Captain Archer.' For a moment I was at a loss, but the voice gave me the clue.

'But I do,' I answered, 'you are Miss Letchford, who used to teach my sisters.'

'Quite right. But I have given up teaching, for which fortunately there is no longer any necessity. I am living in a flat with my dear little friend here. Let me introduce you, – Flossie Eversley – Captain Archer.'

The violet eyes laughed up at me, and the red lips parted in a merry smile. A dimple appeared at the corner of the mouth. I was done for! Yes; at thirty-five years of age, with more than my share of experiences in every phase of love, I went down before this lovely girl with her childish face smiling at me above the budding womanhood of her rounded breasts, and confessed myself defeated!

A moment or two later I had passed from them with the address of the flat in my pocket, and under promise to go down to tea on the next day.

At midday I received the following letter:

Dear Captain Archer,

'I am sorry to be obliged to be out when you come; and yet not altogether sorry, because I should like you to know Flossie very well. She is an orphan, without a relation in the world. She is just back from a Paris school. In years she is of course a child, but in tact and knowledge she is a woman; also in figure, as you can see for yourself! She is of an exceedingly warm and passionate nature, and a look that you gave her yesterday was not lost upon her. In fact, to be quite frank, she has fallen in love with you! You will find her a delightful companion. Use her *very* tenderly, and she will do anything in the world for you. Speak to her about her life in the French school: she loves to talk of it. I want her to be happy, and I think you can help. Remember she is only just fifteen.

'Yours sincerely,
'EVA LETCHFORD.'

I must decline any attempt to describe my feelings on receiving this remarkable communication. My first impulse was to give up the promised call at the flat. But the flower-like face, the soft red lips and the laughing eyes passed before my mind's eye, followed by an instant vision of the marvellous breasts and the delicate shapely legs in their brown silk stockings, and I knew that fate was too strong for me. For it was of course impossible to misunderstand the meaning of Eva Letchford's letter, and indeed when I reached the flat she herself opened the door to me, whispering as she passed out, 'Flossie is in there, waiting for you. You two can have the place to yourselves. One last word. You have been much in Paris, have you not? So has Flossie. She is *very* young – *and there are ways* – Goodbye.'

I passed into the next room. Flossie was curled up in a long chair, reading. Twisting her legs from under her petticoats with a sudden movement that brought into full view her delicately embroidered drawers she rose and came towards me, a rosy flush upon her cheeks, her eyes shining, her whole bearing instinct with an enchanting mixture of girlish coyness and anticipated pleasure. Her short white skirt swayed as she moved across the room, her breasts stood out firm and round under the close-fitting woven silk jersey; what man of mortal flesh and blood could withstand such allurements as these! Not I, for one! In a moment she was folded in my arms. I rained kisses on her hair, her forehead, her eyes, her cheeks, and then grasping her body closer and always closer to me, I glued my lips upon the scarlet mouth and revelled in a long and maddeningly delicious kiss – a kiss to be ever remembered – so well remembered now, indeed, that I must make some attempt to describe it. My hands were behind Flossie's head, buried in her long brown hair. Her arms were round my body, locked and clinging. At the first impact her lips were closed, but a moment later they parted, and slowly, gently, almost as if in the performance of some solemn duty, the rosy tongue crept into my mouth, and bringing with it a flood of the scented juices from her throat, curled amorously round my own, whilst her hands dropped to my buttocks, and standing on tiptoe she drew me to her with such extraordinary force and vigour that our lower parts seemed to be already in conjunction. Not a word was spoken on either side – indeed under the circumstances speech was impossible, for our tongues had twined together in a caress of unspeakable sweetness, which neither would be the first to forego. At last the blood was coursing through my veins at a pace that became unbearable and I was compelled to unglue my mouth from hers. Still silent, but with love and longing in her eyes, she pressed me into a low chair, and seating herself on the arm passed her hand behind my head, and looking full into my eyes whispered my flame in accents that were like the sound of a running stream. I kissed her open mouth again and again, and then feeling that the time had come for some little explanation:

'How long will it be before your friend Eva comes back?' I asked.

'She has gone down into the country, and won't be here till late this evening.'

'Then I may stay with you, may I?'

'Yes, do, do, *do*, Jack. Do you know, I have got seats for an Ibsen play to-night. I was wondering . . . if . . . you would . . . take me!'

'Take *you* – to an Ibsen play – with your short frocks, and all that hair down your back! Why, I don't believe they'd let us in?'

'Oh, if *that's* all, wait a minute.'

She skipped out of the room with a whisk of her petticoats and a free display of brown silk legs. Almost before I had time to wonder what she was up to, she was back again. She had put on a long skirt of Eva's, her hair was coiled on the top of her head, she wore my 'billycock' hat and a pair of blue pince-nez, and carrying a crutchhandled stick, she advanced upon me with a defiant air, and glaring down over the top of her glasses she said in a deep masculine voice: 'Now, sir, if, you're ready for Ibsen, *I* am. Or if your tastes are so *low* that you can't care about a play, I'll give you a skirt-dance.'

As she said this she tore off the long dress, threw my hat on to a sofa, let down her hair with a turn of the wrist, and motioning me to the piano picked up her skirts and began to dance.

Enchanted as I was by the humour of her quick change to the 'Ibsen woman', words are vain to describe my feelings as I feebly tinkled a few bars on the piano and watched the dancer.

Every motion was the perfection of grace and yet no Indian Nautch-girl could have more skilfully expressed the idea of sexual allurement. Gazing at her in speechless admiration, I saw the violet eyes glow with passion, the full red lips part, the filmy petticoats were lifted higher and higher; the loose frilled drawers gleamed white. At last breathless and panting, she fell back upon a chair, her eyes closed, her legs parted, her breasts heaving. A mingled perfume came to my nostrils – half *'odor di foemina'*, half the scent of white rose from her hair and clothes.

I flung myself upon her. 'Tell me, Flossie darling, what shall I do *first*?

The answer came, quick and short. 'Kiss me – *between my legs!*'

In an instant I was kneeling before her. Her legs fell widely apart. Sinking to a sitting posture, I plunged my head between her thighs. The petticoats incommoded me a little, but I soon managed to arrive at the desired spot. Somewhat to my surprise instead of finding the lips closed and barricaded as is usual in the case of young girls, they were ripe, red and pouting, and as my mouth closed eagerly upon the delicious orifice and my tongue found and pressed upon the trembling clitoris I knew that my qualms of conscience had been vain. My utmost powers were now called into play and I sought by every means I possessed to let Flossie know that I was no halfbaked lover. Passing my arms behind her I extended my tongue to its utmost length and with rapid agile movements penetrated the scented recesses. Her hands locked themselves under my head, soft gasps of pleasure came from her lips, and as I delivered a last and effective attack upon the erect clitoris, her fingers clutched my neck, and with a sob of delight she crossed her legs over my back, and pressing my head towards her held me with a convulsive grasp, whilst the aromatic essence of her being flowed softly into my enchanted mouth.

As I rose to my feet she covered her face with her hands and I saw a blue eye twinkle out between the fingers with an indescribable mixture of bashfulness and fun. Then as if suddenly remembering herself she sat up, dropped her petticoats over her knees, and looking up at me from under the curling lashes, said in a tone of profound melancholy.

'Jack, am I not a *disgraceful* child! All the same I wouldn't have missed *that* for a million pounds.'

'Nor would I, little sweetheart; and whenever you would like to have it again – '

'No, no, it is your turn now.'

'What! Flossie; you don't mean to say – '

'But I *do* mean to say it, and to *do* it, too. Lie down on that sofa at once, sir.'

'But, Flossie, I really – '

Without another word she leapt at me, threw her arms round my neck and fairly bore me down on to the divan. Falling on the top of me she twined her silken legs round mine and gently pushing the whole of her tongue between my lips, began to work her body up and down with a wonderful sinuous motion which soon brought me to a state of excitement bordering on frenzy. Then shaking a warning finger at me to keep still she slowly slipped to her knees on the floor.

In another moment I felt the delicate fingers round my straining yard. Carrying it to her mouth she touched it ever so softly with her tongue; then slowly parting her lips she pushed it gradually between them, keeping a grasp of the lower end with her hand which she moved gently up and down. Soon the tongue began to quicken its motion, and the brown head to work rapidly in a perpendicular direction. I buried my hands under the lovely hair, and clutched the white neck towards me, plunging the nut further and further into the delicious mouth until I seemed almost to touch the uvula. Her lips, tongue and hands now worked with redoubled ardour, and my sensations became momentarily more acute, until with a cry I besought her to let me withdraw. Shaking her head with great emphasis, she held my yard in a firmer grasp, and passing her disengaged hand behind me, drew me towards her face, and with an unspeakable clinging action of her mouth carried out the delightful act of love to its logical conclusion, declining to remove her lips until some minutes after the last remaining evidences of the late crisis had completely disappeared.

Then and not till then, she stood up, and bending over me as I lay kissed me on the forehead, whispering: 'Then! Jack, now I love you twenty times more than ever.'*

I gazed into the lovely face in speechless adoration.

'Why don't you say something?' she cried. 'Is there anything else you want me to do?'

'Yes,' I answered, 'there *is*.'

'Out with it, then.'

'I am simply dying to see your breasts, naked.'

*'This is a fact, as every girl knows who has ever gamahuched and been gamahuched by the man or boy she loves. As a *link*, it beats f ... ing out of the field. I've tried both and I *know*.'

Flossie.

'Why, you darling, of course you shall! Stay there a minute.'
Off she whisked again, and almost before I could realize she
had gone I looked up and she was before me. She had taken off
everything but her chemise and stockings, the former lowered
well beneath her breasts.

Any attempt to describe the beauties thus laid bare to my ador-
ing gaze must necessarily fall absurdly short of the reality. Her
neck, throat and arms were full and exquisitely rounded, bearing
no trace of juvenile immaturity.

Her breasts, however, were of course the objects of my special
and immediate attention.

For size, perfection of form and colour I had never seen their
equals, nor could the mind of man conceive anything so alluring
as the coral nipples, which stood out firm and erect, craving
kisses. A wide space intervened between the two snowy hillocks,
which heaved a little with the haste of her late exertions. I gazed
a moment in breathless delight and admiration, then rushing
towards her I buried my face in the enchanting valley, passed my
burning lips over each of the neighbouring slopes and finally
seized upon one after the other of the rosy nipples, which I
sucked, mouthed and tongued with a frenzy of delight.

The darling little girl lent herself eagerly to my every action,
pushing her nipples into my mouth and eyes, pressing her breasts
against my face, and clinging to my neck with her lovely naked
arms.

Whilst we were thus amorously employed my little lady had
contrived dexterously to slip out of her chemise, and now stood
before me naked but for her brown silk stockings and little shoes.

'There, Mr. Jack, now you can see my breasts, and everything
else that you like of mine. In future this will be my full-dress
costume for making love to you in. Stop, though; it wants just
one touch,' and darting out of the room she came back with a
beautiful chain of pearls round her neck, finishing with a pendant
of rubies which hung just low enough to nestle in the Valley of
Delight, between the wonderful breasts.

'I am now,' she said, 'the White Queen of the Gama Huchi
Islands. My kingdom is bounded on this side by the piano, and
on the other by the furthest edge of the bed in the next room.
Any male person found wearing a *stitch* of clothing within those
boundaries will be sentenced to lose his p . . . . But soft! who
comes here?'

Shading her eyes with her hand she gazed in my direction: 'Aha! a stranger; and, unless these royal eyes deceive us, a man! He shall see what it is to defy our laws! What ho! within there! Take this person and remove his p....'

'Great Queen!; I said, in a voice of deep humility, 'if you will but grant me two minutes, I will make haste to comply with your laws.'

'And we, good fellow, will help you.' (*Aside*).

'Methinks he is somewhat comely.'* (*Aloud*). But first let us away with these leg garments, which are more than aught else a violation of our Gama Huchian Rules. Good! now the shirt. And what, pray, is *this*? We thank you, sir, but we are not requiring any *tent-poles* just now.'

'Then if your Majesty will deign to remove your royal fingers I will do my humble best to cause the offending pole to disappear. At present, with your Majesty's hand upon it – '

'Silence, sir! Your time is nearly up, and if the last garment be not removed in twenty seconds . . . So! you obey. 'Tis well! You shall see how we reward a faithful subject of our laws.'

And thrusting my yard between her lips the Great White Queen of the Gama Huchi Islands sucked in the whole column to the very root, and by dint of working her royal mouth up and down, and applying her royal fingers to the neighbouring appendages, soon drew into her throat a tribute to her greatness, which from its volume and the time it took in the act of payment, plainly caused her Majesty the most exquisite enjoyment. Of my own pleasure I will only say that it was delirious, whilst in this as in all other love sports in which we indulged an added zest was given by the humour and fancy with which this adorable child-woman designed and carried out our amusements. In the present case the personating of the Great White Queen appeared to afford her especial delight, and going on with the performance, she took a long branch of pampas-grass from its place and waving it over my head, she said: 'The next ceremony to be performed by a visitor to these realms will, we fear, prove somewhat irksome, but it must be gone through. We shall now place our royal person on this lofty throne. You, sir, will sit upon this footstool before us. We

---

(*) *Don't believe I ever said anything of the sort, but if I did, 'methinks' I'd better take this opportunity of withdrawing the statement.*

Flossie.

shall then wave our sceptre three times. At the third wave our knees will part and our guest will see before him the royal spot of love. This he will proceed to salute with a kiss which shall last until we are pleased to signify that we have had enough. Now, most noble guest, open your mouth, *don't* shut your eyes, and prepare! One, two, *three*.'

The pampas-grass waved, the legs parted, and nestling between the ivory thighs I saw the scarlet lips open to show the erected clitoris peeping forth from its nest below the slight brown tuft which adorned the base of the adorable belly. I gazed and gazed in mute rapture, until a sharp strident voice above me said: 'Now then, there, move on, please; can't have you blocking up the road all day!' Then changing suddenly to her own voice: 'Jack, if you don't kiss me at once I shall *die*'.

I pressed towards the delicious spot and taking the whole cunt into my mouth passed my tongue upwards along the perfumed lips until it met the clitoris, which thrust itself amorously between my lips, imploring kisses. These I rained upon it with all the ardour I could command, clutching the rounded bottom with feverish fingers and drawing the naked belly closer and ever closer to my burning face, whilst my tongue plunged deep within the scented cunt and revelled in its divine odours and the contraction of its beloved lips.

The Great White Queen seemed to relish this particular form of homage, for it was many minutes before the satin thighs closed, and with the little hands under my chin she raised my face and looking into my eyes with inexpressible love and sweetness shining from her own, she said simply: 'Thank you, Jack. You're a darling!'

By way of answer I covered her with kisses, omitting no single portion of the lovely naked body, the various beauties of which lent themselves with charming zest to my amorous doings. Upon the round and swelling breasts I lavished renewed devotion, sucking the rosy nipples with a fury of delight, and relishing to the full the quick movements of rapture with which the lithe clinging form was constantly shaken, no less than the divine aroma passing to my nostrils as the soft thighs opened and met again, the rounded arms rose and fell, and with this the faintly perfumed hair brushing my face and shoulders mingled its odour of tea-rose.

All this was fast exciting my senses to the point of madness, and there were moments when I felt that to postpone much longer the consummation of our amour would be impossible.

I looked at the throbbing breasts, remembered the fragrant lips below that had pouted ripely to meet my kisses, the developed clitoris that told of joys long indulged in. And then ... And then ... the sweet girlish face looked up into mine, the violet eyes seemed to take on a pleading expression, and as if reading my thoughts Flossie pushed me gently into a chair, seated herself on my knee, slipped an arm round my neck, and pressing her cheek to mine, whispered: 'Poor, *poor* old thing! I know what it wants; and *I* want it too – badly, oh! so badly. But, Jack, you can't guess what a friend Eva has been to me, and I've promised her *not to*! You see I'm only just fifteen, and ... *the consequences*! There! don't let us talk about it. Tell me all about yourself, and then I'll tell you all about *myself,* and when you're tired of hearing me talk you shall stop my mouth with – well, whatever you like. Now sir, begin!'

I gave her a short narrative of my career from boyhood upwards, dry and dull enough in all conscience!

'Yes, yes, that's all very nice and prim and proper,' she cried. 'But you haven't told me the principal thing of all, – when you first began to be – naughty, and with whom?'

I invented some harmless fiction which I saw the quickwitted little girl did not believe, and begged her to tell me her own story which she at once proceeded to do. I shall endeavour to transcribe it, though it is impossible to convey any idea of the humour with which it was delivered, still less of the irrepressible fun which flashed from her eyes at the recollection of her schoolgirl pranks and amourettes. There were, of course, many interruptions*, for most of which I was probably responsible; but, on the whole, in the following chapter will be found a fairly faithful transcript of Flossie's early experiences. Some at least of these I am sanguine will be thought to have been of a sufficiently appetizing character.

---

*The first of these is a really serious one, but for this the impartial reader will see that the responsibility was divided.

'HOW FLOSSIE ACQUIRED THE FRENCH TONGUE'

'Before I begin, Jack, I should like to hold something nice and
solid in my hand, to sort of give me confidence as I go on. Have
you got anything about you that would do?'
I presented what seemed to me the most suitable article 'in
stock' at the moment.
'Aha!' said Flossie in an affected voice, 'the very thing! How
very fortunate that you should happen to have it ready!'
'Well, madam, you see it is an article we are constantly being
asked for by our lady-customers. It is rather an expensive thing
– seven pound ten – '
'Yes, it's rather stiff. Still, if you can assure me that it will always
keep in its present condition, I shouldn't mind spending a good
deal upon it.'
'You will find, madam, that anything you may spend upon it
will be amply returned to you. Our ladies have always expressed
the greatest satisfaction with it.'
'Do you mean that you find they come more than once? If so,
I'll take it now.'
'Perhaps you would allow me to bring it myself – ?'
'Thanks, but I think I can hold it quite well in my hand. It won't
go off suddenly, will it?'
'Not if it is kept in a cool place, madam.'
'And it mustn't be shaken, I suppose, like *that*, for instance?'
(*shaking it*).
'For goodness gracious sake, take your hand away, Flossie, or
there'll be a catastrophe.'
'That is a good word, Jack! But do you suppose that if I saw a
'catastrophe' coming I shouldn't know what to do with it?'
'*What* should you do?'
'Why, what *can* you do with a catastrophe of that sort but
swallow it?'
The effect of this little interlude upon us both was magnetic.
Instead of going on with her story Flossie commanded me to lie
upon my back on the divan, and having placed a couple of
pillows under my neck, knelt astride of me with her face towards
my feet. With one or two caressing movements of her bottom she
arranged herself so that the scarlet vulva rested just above my
face. Then gently sinking down she brought her delicious cunt
full upon my mouth from which my tongue instantly darted to

penetrate the adorable recess. At the same moment I felt the brown hair fall upon my thighs, my straining prick plunged between her lips, and was engulfed in her velvet mouth to the very root, whilst her hands played with feverish energy amongst the surrounding parts, and the nipples of her breasts rubbed softly against my belly.

In a very few moments I had received into my mouth her first tribute of love and was working with might and main to procure a second, whilst she in her turn, wild with pleasure my wandering tongue was causing her, grasped my yard tightly between her lips, passing them rapidly up and down its whole length, curling her tongue round the nut, and maintaining all the time an ineffable sucking action which very soon produced its natural result. As I poured a torrent into her eager mouth I felt the soft lips which I was kissing contract for a moment upon my tongue and then part again to set free the aromatic flood to which the intensity of her sensations imparted additional volume and sweetness.

The pleasure we were both experiencing from this the most entrancing of all the reciprocal acts of love was too keen to be abandoned after one effort. Stretching my hands upwards to mould and press the swelling breasts and erected nipples, I seized the rosy clitoris anew between my lips, whilst Flossie resumed her charming operations upon my instrument which she gamahuched with ever increasing zest and delight, and with a skill and variety of action which would have been marvellous in a woman of double her age and experience. Once again the fragrant dew was distilled upon my enchanted tongue, and once again the velvet mouth closed upon my yard to receive the results of its divinely pleasurable ministrations.

Raising herself slowly and almost reluctantly from her position Flossie laid her naked body at full length upon mine and after many kisses upon my mouth, eyes and cheeks said, 'Now you may go and refresh yourself with a bath while I dress for dinner.'

'But where are we going to dine?' I asked.

'You'll see presently. *Go* along, there's a good boy!'

I did as I was ordered and soon came back from the bathroom, much refreshed by my welcome ablutions.

Five minutes later Flossie joined me, looking lovelier than ever, in a short-sleeved pale blue muslin frock, cut excessively low in front, black openwork silk stockings and little embroidered shoes.

'Dinner is on the table,' she said, taking my arm and leading me into an adjoining room where an exquisite little cold meal was laid out, to which full justice was speedily done, followed by coffee made by my hostess, who produced some Benedictine and a box of excellent cigars.

'There, Jack, if you're quite comfy I'll go on with my story. Shall I stay here, or come and sit on your knee?'

'Well, as far as getting on with the story goes, I think you are better in that chair, Flossie – '

'But I told you I must have something to hold.'

'Yes, you *did*, and the result was that we didn't get very far with the story, if you remember – '

'Remember! As if I was likely to forget. But look at this,' holding up a rounded arm bare to the shoulder. 'Am I to understand that you'd rather not have this round your neck?'

Needless to say she was to understand nothing of the sort, and a moment later she was perched upon my knee and having with deft penetrating fingers found her way to the support she required, 'solid' enough under her magic touch, began her narrative.

'I don't think there will be much to tell you until my school life at Paris begins. My father and mother both died when I was quite small; I had no brothers or sisters, and I don't believe I've got a relation in the world. You mustn't think I want to swagger, Jack, but I am rather rich. One of my two guardians died three years ago and the other is in India and doesn't care a scrap about me. Now and then he writes and asks how I am getting on, and when he heard I was going to live with Eva (whom he knows quite well) he seemed perfectly satisfied. Two years ago he arranged for me to go to school in Paris.

'Now I must take great care not to shock you, but there's nothing for it but to tell you that about this time I began to have the most wonderful feelings all over me – a sort of desperate longing for something, – I didn't know what – which used to become almost unbearable when I danced or played any game in which a boy or man was near me. At the Paris school was a very pretty girl, named Ylette de Vespertin, who, for some reason I never could understand, took a fancy to me. She was two years older than I, had several brothers and boy cousins at home, and being up to every sort of lark and mischief, was just the girl I wanted as a confidante. Of course she had no difficulty in explaining the whole thing to me, and in the course of a day or two I knew

everything there was to know. On the third day of our talks Ylette
slipped a note into my hand as I was going up to bed. Now, Jack,
you must really go and look out of the window while I tell you
what it said:

"*Chérie*,
"*Si tu veux te faire sucer la langue, les seins et le con, viens
dans mon lit toute nue ce soir. C'est moi qui te ferai voir les
anges.*
"*Viens de suite à ton*
"YLETTE.""

'I have rather a good memory, and even if I hadn't, I don't think
I could ever forget the words of that note, for it was the
beginning of a most delicious time for me.

'I suppose if I had been a well-regulated young person, I
should have taken no notice of the invitation. As it was I stripped
myself naked in a brace of shakes, and flew to Ylette's bedroom
which was next door to the one I occupied. I had not realized
before what a beautifully made girl she was. Her last garment
was just slipping from her as I came in, and I stared in blank
admiration at her naked figure which was like a statue in the
perfection of its lines. A furious longing to touch it seized me and
springing upon her I passed my hands feverishly up and down
her naked body, until grasping me round the waist she half
dragged half carried me to the bed, laid me on the edge of it,
and kneeling upon the soft rug plunged her head between my
legs, and bringing her lips to bear full upon the *other* lips before
her, parted them with a peculiar action of the mouth and inserted
her tongue with a sudden stroke which sent perfect waves of
delight through my whole body, followed by still greater ecstasy
when she went for the particular spot *you* know of, Jack – the
one near the top, I mean – and twisting her tongue over it, under
it, round it and across it soon brought about the result she
wanted, and in her own expressive phrase '*me faisait voir les
anges.*'

'Of course I had had no experience, but I did my best to repay
her for the pleasure she had given me, and as I happen to
possess an extremely long and pointed tongue, and Ylette's cunt
– oh Jack, *I've said it at last!* Go and look out of the window
again; or better still, come and stop my naughty mouth with –

I *meant* your tongue, but this will do better still. The wicked monster, what a size he is! Now put both your hands behind my head, and push him in till he touches my throat. Imagine he is *somewhere else*, work like a demon and for your life don't stop until the very end of all things. Ah! the dear, darling, delicious thing! How he throbs with excitement! I believe he can *see* my mouth waiting for him. Come, Jack, my darling, my beloved, let me gamahuche you. I want to feel this heavenly prick of yours between my lips and against my tongue so that I may suck it and drain every drop that comes from it into my mouth. Now, Jack now . . . '

The red lips closed hungrily upon the object of their desire, the rosy tongue stretched itself amorously along the palpitating yard, and twice the tide of love poured freely forth to be received with every sign of delight into the velvet mouth.

Nothing in my experience had ever approached the pleasure which I derived from the intoxicating contact of this young girl's lips and tongue upon my most sensitive parts, enhanced as it was by my love for her, which grew apace, and by her own intense delight in the adorable pastime. So keen indeed were the sensations she procured me that I was almost able to forget the deprivation laid upon me by Flossie's promise to her friend. Indeed, when I reflected upon her youth, and the unmatched beauty of her girlish shape with its slender waist, smooth satin belly and firm rounded breasts, the whole seemed too perfect a work of nature to be marred – at least as yet – by the probable consequences of an act of coition carried to its logical conclusion by a pair of ardent lovers.

So I bent my head once more to its resting-place between the snowy thighs, and again drew from my darling little mistress the fragrant treasures of love's sacred storehouse, lavished upon my clinging lips with gasps and sighs and all possible tokens of enjoyment in the giving.

After this it was time to part, and at Flossie's suggestion I undressed her, brushed out her silky hair and put her into bed. Lying on her white pillow she looked so fair and like a child that I was for saying goodnight with just a single kiss upon her cheek. But this was not in accordance with her views on the subject. She sat up in bed, flung her arms round my neck, nestled her face against mine and whispered in my ear: 'I'll never give a promise again as long as I live.'

It was an awful moment and my resolution all but went down under the strain. But I just managed to resist, and after one prolonged embrace, during which Flossie's tongue went twining and twisting round my own with an indescribably lascivious motion, I planted a farewell kiss full upon the nipple of her left breast, sucked it for an instant and fled from the room.

On reaching my own quarters I lit a cigar and sat down to think over the extraordinary good fortune by which I had chanced upon this unique liaison. It was plain to me that in Flossie I had encountered probably the only specimen of her class. A girl of fifteen with all the fresh charm of that beautiful age united to the fascination of a passionate and amorous woman. Add to these a finely strung temperament, a keen sense of humour, and the true artist's striving after thoroughness in all she did, and it will be admitted that all these qualities meeting in a person of quite faultless beauty were enough to justify the self-congratulations with which I contemplated my present luck, and the rosy visions of pleasure to come which hung about my waking and sleeping senses till the morning.

About midday I called at the flat. The door was opened to me by Eva Letchford.

'I am so glad to see you,' she said. 'Flossie is out on her bicycle, and I can say what I want to.'

As she moved to the window to draw up the blind a little, I had a better opportunity of noticing into what a really splendid woman she had developed. Observing my glances of frank admiration she sat down in a low easy chair opposite to me, crossed her shapely legs, and looking over at me with a bright pleasant smile, said, 'Now, Jack – I may call you Jack, of course, because we are all three going to be great friends – you had my letter the other day. No doubt you thought it a strange document, but when we know one another better you will easily understand how I came to write it.'

'My dear girl, I understand it already. You forget I have had several hours with Flossie. It was her happiness you wanted to secure, and I hope she will tell you your plan was successful!'

'Flossie and I have no secrets. She has told me everything that passed between you. She has also told me what did *not* pass between you, and how you did not even try to make her break her promise to me.'

'I should have been a brute if I had – '

'Then I am afraid nineteen men out of twenty are brutes – but that's neither here nor there. What I want you to know is that I appreciate your nice feeling, and that some day soon I shall with Flossie's consent take an opportunity of showing that appreciation in a practical way.' Here she crossed her right foot high over the left knee and very leisurely removed an imaginary speck of dust from the shotsilk stocking.

'Now I must go and change my dress. You'll stay and lunch with us in the coffee-room won't you? – that's right. This is my bedroom. I'll leave the door open so that we can talk till Flossie comes. She promised to be in by one o'clock.'

We chatted away on indifferent subjects whilst I watched with much satisfaction the operations of the toilette in the next room.

Presently a little cry of dismay reached me: 'Oh dear, oh dear! do come here a minute, Jack. I have pinched one of my breasts with my stays and made a little red mark. Look! *Do* you think it will show in evening dress?'

I examined the injury with all possible care and deliberation.

'My professional opinion is, madam, that as the mark is only an inch above the nipple we may fairly hope – '

'*Above* the nipple! then I'm afraid it will be a near thing,' said Eva with a merry laugh.

'Perhaps a little judicious stroking by an experienced hand might – '

'Naow then there, Naow then!' suddenly came from the door in a hoarse cockney accent. 'You jest let the lydy be, or oi'll give yer somethink to tyke 'ome to yer dinner, see if oi don't!'

'Who is this person?' I asked of Eva, placing my hands upon her two breasts as if to shield them from the intruder's eye.

'Person yerself!' said the voice, 'Fust thing *you've* a-got ter do is ter leave old of my donah's breasties and then oi'll *tork* to yer!'

'But the lady has hurt herself, sir, and was consulting me professionally.'

There was a moment's pause, during which I had time to examine my opponent whom I found to be wearing a red Tam-o'-Shanter cap, a close-fitting knitted silk blouse, a short white flannel skirt, and scarlet stockings. This charming figure suddenly threw itself upon me open-armed and open-mouthed and kissed me with delightful abandon.

After a hearty laugh over the success of Flossie's latest 'impersonation', Eva pushed us both out of the room, saying, 'Take her away, Jack, and see if *she* has got any marks. Those bicycle saddles arc rather trying sometimes. We will lunch in a quarter of an hour.'

I bore my darling little mistress away to her room, and having helped her to strip off her clothes, I inspected on my knees the region where the saddle might have been expected to gall her, but found nothing but a fair expanse of firm white bottom which I saluted with many lustful kisses upon every spot within reach of my tongue. Then I took her naked to the bath-room, and sponged her from neck to ankles, dried her thoroughly, just plunged my tongue once deep into her cunt, carried her back to her room, dressed her and presented her to Eva within twenty minutes of our leaving the latter's bedroom.

Below in the coffee-room a capitally served luncheon awaited us. The table was laid in a sort of little annexe to the principal room, and I was glad of the retirement, since we were able to enjoy to the full the constant flow of fun and mimicry with which Flossie brought tears of laughter to our eyes throughout the meal. Eva, too, was gifted with a fine sense of the ridiculous, and as I myself was at least an appreciative audience, the ball was kept rolling with plenty of spirit.

After lunch Eva announced her intention of going to a concert in Piccadilly, and a few minutes later Flossie and I were once more alone.

'Jack,' she said, 'I feel thoroughly and hopelessly naughty this afternoon. If you like I will go on with my story while you lie on the sofa and smoke a cigar.'

This exactly suited my views and I said so.

'Very well, then. First give me a great big kiss with all the tongue you've got about you ... Ah! that was good! Now I'm going to sit on this footstool beside you, and I *think* one or two of these buttons might be unfastened, so that I can feel whether the story is producing any effect upon you. Good gracious! why, it's hard and stiff as a poker already. I really *must* frig it a little – '

'Quite gently and slowly then, *please* Flossie, or —'

'Yes, quite, *quite* gently and slowly, so – Is that nice, Jack?'

'Nice is not the word, darling!'

'Talking of words, Jack, I am afraid I shall hardly be able to finish my adventures without occasionally using a word or two which you don't hear at a Sunday School class. Do you mind, very much? Of course you can always go and look out of the window, can't you!'

'My dearest little sweetheart, when we are alone together like this, and both feeling extremely naughty, as we do now, any and every word that comes from your dear lips sounds sweet and utterly void of offence to me.'

'Very well, then; that makes it ever so much easier to tell my story, and if I *should* become too shocking – well, you know how I *love* you to stop my mouth, don't you Jack!'

A responsive throb from my imprisoned member gave her all the answer she required.

'Let me see,' she began, 'where was I? Oh, I remember, in Ylette's bed.'

'Yes, she had gamahuched you, and you were just performing the same friendly office for her.'

'Of course: I was telling you how the length of my tongue made up for the shortness of my experience, or so Ylette was kind enough to say. I think she meant it too: at any rate she spent several times before I gave up my position between her legs. After this we tried the double gamahuche, which proved a great success because, although she was, as I have told you, two years older than I, we were almost exactly of a height, so that as she knelt over me her cunt came quite naturally upon my mouth, and her mouth upon my cunt, and in this position we were able to give each other an enormous amount of pleasure.'

At this point I was obliged to beg Flossie to remove her right hand from the situation it was occupying.

'What I cannot understand about it,' she went on, 'is that there are any number of girls in France, and a good many in England too, who after they have once been gamahuched by another girl don't care about anything else. Perhaps it means that they have never been really in love with a man, because to *me* one touch of your lips in that particular neighbourhood is worth ten thousand kisses from anybody else, male or female and when I have got your dear, darling, delicious prick in my mouth. I want nothing else in the whole wide world except to give you the greatest possible amount of pleasure and to make you spend down my throat in the quickest possible time – '

'If you really want to beat the record, Flossie, I think there's a good chance now – '

Almost before the words had passed my lips the member in

question was between *hers*, where it soon throbbed to the crisis in response to the indescribable sucking action of mouth and tongue of which she possessed the secret.

On my telling her how exquisite were the sensations she procured me by this means she replied: 'Oh, you have to thank Ylette for that! Just before we became friends she had gone for the long holidays to a country house belonging to a young couple who were great friends of hers. There was a very handsome boy of eighteen or so staying in the house. He fell desperately in love with Ylette and she with him, and he taught her exactly how to gamahuche him so as to produce the utmost amount of pleasure. As she told me afterwards, 'Every day, every night, almost every hour, he would bury his prick in my mouth, frig it against my tongue, and fill my throat with a divine flood. With a charming amiability he worked incessantly to show me every kind of gamahuching, all the possible ways of sucking a man's prick. Nothing, said he, should be left to the imagination, which, he explained, can never produce such good results as a few practical lessons given in detail upon a real standing prick, plunged to the very root in the mouth of the girl pupil, to whom one can thus describe on the spot the various suckings, hard, soft, slow or quick, of which it is essential she should know the precise effect in order to obtain the quickest and most copious flow of the perfumed liquor which she desires to draw from her lover.'

'I suppose,' Ylette went on, 'that one invariably likes what one can do well. Anyhow, my greatest pleasure in life is to suck a good-looking boy's prick. If he likes to slip his tongue into my cunt at the same time, *tant mieux.*'

'Unfortunately this delightful boy could only stay a fortnight, but as there were several other young men of the party, and as her lover was wise enough to know that after his recent lessons in the art of love Ylette could not be expected to be an abstainer, he begged her to enjoy herself in his absence, with the result, as she said that *'au bout d'une semaine il n'y avait pas un vit dans la maison qui ne m'avait tripoté la luette, *ni une langue qui n'était l'amie intime de mon con.'*

'Every one of these instructions Ylette passed on to me, with practical illustrations upon my second finger standing as substitute

*Uvula

for the real thing, which, of course, was not to be had in the school – at least not just then.

'She must have been an excellent teacher for I have never had any other lessons than hers, and yours is the first and only staff of love that I have ever had the honour of gamahuching. However, I mean to make up now for lost time, for I would have you to know, my darling, that I am madly in love with every bit of your body and that most of all do I adore your angel prick with its coral head that I so love to suck and plunge into my mouth. Come, Jack. Come! let us have one more double gamahuche. One moment! There! now I am naked. I am going to kneel over your face with my legs wide apart and my cunt kissing your mouth. Drive the whole of your tongue into it, won't you, Jack, and make it curl round my clitoris. Yes! that's it – just like that. Lovely! Now I can't talk any more, because I am going to fill my mouth with the whole of your darling prick; push it down my throat, Jack, and when the time comes spend your very longest and most. I'm going to frig you a little first and rub you under your balls. Goodness! how the dear thing is standing. In he goes now . . . . m . . . . m . . . . m.m.m.m . . . . '

A few inarticulate gasps and groans of pleasure were the only sounds audible for some minutes during which each strove to render the sensations of the other as acute as possible. I can answer for it that Flossie's success was complete, and by the convulsive movements of her bottom and the difficulty I experienced in keeping the position of my tongue upon her palpitating clitoris, I gathered that my operations had not altogether failed of their object. In this I was confirmed by the copious and protracted discharge which the beloved cunt delivered into my throat at the same instant as the incomparable mouth received my yard to the very root, and a perfect torrent rewarded her delicious efforts for my enjoyment.

'Ah, Jack! that was just heavenly,' she sighed, as she rose from her charming position. '*How* you did spend, that time, you darling old boy, and so did I, eh, Jack?'

'My little angel, I thought you would never have finished,' I replied.

'Do you know, Jack, I believe you really did get a little way down my throat, then! At any rate you managed the '*tripotage de luette*' that Ylette's friend recommended so strongly!'

'And I don't think I ever got quite so far into your cunt, Flossie.'

'That's quite true; I felt your tongue touch a spot it had never reached before. And just wasn't it lovely when you got there! It almost makes me spend again to think of it! But I am not going to be naughty any more. And to show you how truly virtuous I am feeling I'll continue my story if you like. I want to get on with it, because I know you must be wondering all the time how a person of my age can have come to be so . . . what shall we say, Jack?'

'Larky,' I suggested.

'Yes, 'larky' will do. Of course I have always been 'older than my age' as the saying goes, and my friendship with Ylette and all the lovely things she used to do to me made me 'come on' much faster than most girls. I ought to tell you that I got to be rather a favourite at school, and after it came to be known that Ylette and I were on gamahuching terms, I used to get little notes from almost every girl in the school over twelve, imploring me to sleep with her. One dear little thing even went so far as to give me the measurements of her tongue, which she had taken with a piece of string.'

'Oh, I say, Flossie, *come now* – I can swallow a good deal but — '

'You can indeed, Jack, as I have good reason to know! But all the same, it's absolutely true. You can't have any conception what French school-girls of fourteen or fifteen are. There is nothing they won't do to get themselves gamahuched, and if a girl is pretty or fascinating or has particularly good legs, or specially large breasts, she may, if she likes, have a fresh admirer's head under her petticoats every day in the week. Of course it's all very wrong and dreadful, I know, but what else can you expect? In France gamahuching between grown-up men and women is a recognized thing – '

'Not only in France, *nowadays*,' I put in.

'So I have heard. But at any rate in France everybody does it. Girls at school naturally know this, as they know most things. At that time of life – at *my* time of life, if you like – a girl thinks and dreams of nothing else. She cannot, except by some extra-ordinary luck, find herself alone with a boy or man. One day her girl chum at school pops her head under her petticoats and gamahuches her deliciously. How can you wonder if from that moment she is ready to go through fire and water to obtain the same pleasure?'

'Go on, Flossie. You are simply delicious to-day!'

'Don't laugh, Jack. I am very serious about it. I don't care how much a girl of (say) my age longs for a boy to be naughty with – it's perfectly right and natural. What I think is bad is that she should *begin* by having a liking for a girl's tongue inculcated into her. I should like to see boys and girls turned loose upon one another once a week or so at authorized gamahuching parties, which should be attended by masters and governesses (who would have to see that the *other* thing was not indulged in, of course). Then the girls would grow up with a good healthy taste for the other sex, and even if they did do a little gamahuching amongst themselves between whiles, it would only be to keep themselves going till the next 'party'. By my plan a boy's prick would be the central object of their desires, as it ought to be. Now *I* think that's a very fine scheme, Jack, and as soon as I am a little older, I shall go to Paris and put it before the Minister of Education!'

'But why wait, Flossie? Why not go now?'

'Well, you see, if the old gentleman (I suppose he *is* old, isn't he, or he wouldn't be a minister?) – if he saw a girl in short frocks, he would think she had got some private object to serve in regard to the gamahuching parties. Whereas a grown-up person who had plainly left school might be supposed to be doing it unselfishly for the good of the rising generation.'

'Yes, I understand that. But when you *do* go, Flossie, please take me or some other respectable person with you, because I don't altogether trust that Minister of Education, and whatever the length of your frocks might happen to be at the time, I feel certain that, old or young, the moment you had explained your noble scheme, he would be wanting some practical illustrations on the office armchair!'

'How dare you suggest such a thing, Jack! You are to understand, sir, that from henceforth my mouth is reserved for three purposes, to eat with, to talk with, and to kiss you with on whatever part of your person I may happen to fancy at the moment. By the way you won't mind my making just one exception in favour of Eva, will you? She loves me to make her nipples stand with my tongue; occasionally too, we perform the "*soixante-neuf.*"'

'When the next performance takes place, may I be there to see?' I ejaculated fervently.

'Oh, Jack, how shocking!'

'Does it shock you, Flossie? Very well then I withdraw it, and apologize.'

'You cannot withdraw it now. You have distinctly stated that you would like to be there when Eva and I have our next gamahuche.'

'Well, I suppose I *did* say.'

'Silence, sir,' said Flossie in a voice of thunder, and shaking her brown head at me with inexpressible ferocity. 'You have made a proposal of the most indecent character, and the sentence of the Court is that at the first possible opportunity you shall be *held to that proposal.* Meanwhile the Court condemns you to receive 250 kisses on various parts of your body, which it will at once proceed to administer. Now, sir, off with your clothes!'

'Mayn't I keep my — '

'No, sir, you may *not!*'

The sentence of the Court was accordingly carried out to the letter, somewhere about three-fourths of the kisses being applied upon one and the same part of the prisoner to which the Court attached its mouth with extraordinary gusto.